SOMEONE
Beside Me

THE PASSION SERIES
BOOK ONE

Someone Beside Me © Copyright, N. Slater 2023

All rights reserved. Published by OffBeat Publishing, LLC.
No part of this publication may be reproduced, distributed, or transmitted in any form or by any means, including photocopying, recording, or other electronic or mechanical methods, without the prior written permission of the publisher, except in the case of brief quotations embodied in critical reviews and certain other noncommercial uses permitted by copyright law.
For Information regarding permissions, write to: OffBeatReads@pm.me

This publication includes works of fiction. Any resemblance to actual events or persons, living or dead, is entirely coincidental, a product of the author's imagination, or used fictitiously.

ISBN (Print): 978-1-950464-37-1
ISBN (eBook): 978-1-950464-38-8

SOMEONE
Beside Me

THE PASSION SERIES
BOOK ONE

A SLATERESQUE INFINITIES ORIGINAL

N. SLATER

*To Manney, my inspiration across the sea –
without you, this book wouldn't exist.
Continue to be strong.
I love you.*

But the past few weeks had taught her a lot about herself. Sure, she was hurt. She was heartbroken. But she wasn't stupid. A relationship with Anders would have never worked; she was too headstrong. "I'm sorry if my drab attire offended you. Have fun at your wedding. It was nice. *Really*. But I have work to attend to." Mia meant every word. It was the wedding she had spent nearly a year preparing. It was a gorgeous ceremony.

"You always worked so much. It really put a strain on the relationship."

Mia squinted at him, wrapping her arms around her chest when she caught his gaze dipping below her neckline. *Seriously?* Anders was off on business trips half the year, but her stable job in Bryxton was too much on the relationship. Right. She decided not to dignify the statement with an answer, bristling when one of the bridesmaids shuffled in to drag Anders back to reception.

"Step off, girl. You had your chance."

Mia turned on her heel and crossed the street, swinging open the door to her office with an anger she hadn't known she was holding in. The moment the door latched, she released her frustration in a scream that she hoped the wedding guests hadn't heard. *Much better.*

She flipped on the lights, let out a deep sigh, and then glanced around the silent lab and at the metal boxes aligned on opposite walls. "Sorry, guys. It was the worst wedding. Anders really married that bimbo but still expects me to feel for him." It was too bad she didn't have the confidence to say those words to the one man who truly needed to hear them.

Her jaw clenched as she stepped farther into the room, shuffling around her tools. There was no reason for her to be here, the entire town having closed down for Anders' wedding, but it was the one place Mia could escape to without anyone following her.

"Who are you talking to?" *Well, almost anyone.*

down the aisle, parading off the richness of the ceremony. *My ceremony.* She had been appalled when Anders hadn't changed much when he switched partners, going so far as to ask for her wedding book to finish planning the event.

Anders had known how much Bryxton's park meant to her. It had been one of her favorite places as a child. She would fly kites with her father or picnic with her mother as her father watched from the coroner's office across the street. And yet, none of that had mattered when Anders substituted just one thing in the wedding she had created. *Her.*

The moment the couple made it to the reception area, Mia dashed toward her office across the street. There was no point in staying for the festivities to fake nice with people who should have been celebrating her. It wasn't lost on her that everyone still thought she had done something to ruin the relationship rather than the other way around.

Wiry fingers wrapped around her wrist, and Mia yanked herself away from the touch and rubbed at the point of contact as if she had been stung. *Him.*

His pine scent stung her nose as she shuffled a step away from him. "What do you want?" Albeit a little harsh, he deserved it.

"Is that how you speak to me?"

Mia fought the urge to recoil and apologize from his thundering tone, realizing how emotionally abusive her ex had always been. *How did I not notice that?* "Anders, I'm no longer your little pet. You made that pretty obvious when you married someone else. Go to *her.*" She rubbed at the section of her wrist that Anders had touched.

"That could have been you, you know. But you never dressed nice, and you're always so … dreary." Anders leaned back a bit, his dark eyes flashing with amusement as if he were waiting for Mia to apologize, to fall at his feet, to *give in,* just like she always had.

newest relationship all around the small town of Bryxton, silently pointing out all the things that his new woman did that Mia didn't.

Dress better.

Smile more.

Play dumb.

Roll over.

Be a good little pet.

Fuck that. Mia shifted her dress, pulling it down over her knees as she kept her attention locked on the loving couple. She had studied too hard to play the airhead. Being her town's coroner hadn't been her lifelong dream; it had fallen in her lap after her father passed away. With nothing else lined up, Mia had taken on the responsibility without complaint. Unfortunately, it also dimmed the number of respectable prospects because, to everyone in town, Mia was the girl who played with dead bodies.

Mia absolutely did *not* play with them, but she felt a little less lonely when she stepped into her office surrounded by those metal cases along the walls. As her father had always told her, the dead didn't judge.

Anders shared his vows, eyes locked with Mia's instead of his new wife's, waiting for a reaction. But Mia wouldn't give him one. She was there out of obligation to her town, not out of courtesy, and definitely not out of any lingering feelings for the man who had twisted her future.

That spot beside him had been hers, but telling herself that she shouldn't want it was harder than she imagined. A small part of her still wished this nightmare was just that, a *nightmare*. Mia would wake up and Anders would sweep her off her feet with those kisses that used to make her squirm with pleasure. *No, he's not worth it.*

The same damn thing she had been telling herself since she had been so rudely discarded.

Mia bowed her head, unable to stomach much more of the unnecessary romance the new couple put forth as they strolled

ONE

MIA

Dressed in a pale peach dress garnered with lace, Mia crossed her ankles as she leaned forward in her white folding chair. The warm summer breeze ruffled her curls, the ones she had desperately tried to tame minutes before attending the wedding. And now she was watching the man of her dreams passionately kiss another woman. A woman he had met on what was supposed to be *just* a business trip.

A business trip Mia hadn't even known about until he sauntered back into town, glowing in a way she hadn't ever seen him before.

Three weeks later, Anders had discarded her for his new piece, whirlwind wedding and all. Mia bit back a scowl as she watched the blonde preen for Mia's ex-fiancé in a dress that was supposed to have been *hers*.

Mia knew she had dodged a bullet, but it still hurt that she wasn't good enough or shiny enough. Anders had paraded his

Mia paled, whipping around to match the rich baritone voice to a human figure. Speaking with the dead was only as comfortable as it was because they were dead. Two solidly built individuals in dark suits pushed into her lab a moment later. She took in their strangely powerful presence, noticing the way their muscles bulged beneath the thin cloth.

Their suits were absent ties, the top button undone to reveal chiseled collarbones. Mia continued her gaze upward, her neck at an awkward angle to meet their fiery gazes. One sea green and the other one almost black as they stared back at her. The sea-green one's hair was a mess of blond curls, shaved on the sides, giving him a strange boyish look despite his wide stature. The dark-eyed one's midnight hair was pulled tight into a ponytail, but not the kind of repulsive rat tail that women balked at. The kind of ponytail that rivaled a perfect man bun.

That's when she realized she was still dressed in peach lace, her hair done up with butterfly clips and snow-white heels that should have never been within five feet of her lab.

"Them," Mia finally answered, pointing to the metal boxes along the walls.

The green-eyed one chuckled, his entire chest moving with the sound. "They're dead. They can't hear you." His eyes flashed with amusement, but he wasn't laughing at her.

She managed a small shrug, tempted to follow through with her ritual of chucking the heels and unloading the day's events to the bodies in her lab. Unfortunately, she had these mysterious visitors. "Their souls linger, and that can be lonely. Not the point. Can I help you?" She angled her chin up a little more and then stepped back. *Fuck, they're tall.*

The dark-eyed one smiled and nodded. "Yeah, most of the shops are closed, and we just needed to get to the town hall."

"Oh, yeah. There's a wedding. Town hall is about half a mile in the other direction." *What do they need there?* Mia could see the confusion in their expressions that the entire town had shut down for a wedding. She felt no need to explain. She just wanted them to leave so she could destress.

"If there's a wedding, why are you here?" the green-eyed one asked as he shoved his hands into his pockets, leaning forward.

Her breath caught in her throat as she noticed the gentle beauty of his features. "I was at the wedding. It's over now."

"Looks like the festivities just started."

She bit her lip, trying to understand why this conversation was both easy and difficult at the same time. She didn't know these men and didn't know why they were here. "Not a fan of the people, all right? Is there something else you needed?" Mia wasn't usually this short with people, but Anders' last grab for her attention had put her on edge.

"What time will the festivities be over? We were supposed to check in today."

"Check … in?" Mia took in their attire again, wondering how she hadn't made the connection before. "You're the new detectives they hired." It was the only plausible explanation.

"One and the same." The green-eyed one shot Mia a wide smile. "I'm Kenn. This robot is Jan." *Kenn, really? He's a full-on muscle Barbie. That's just not fair.* Mia stared at Kenn before turning her attention to the dark-eyed one.

Jan's tough exterior wasn't hard to look at either, both of the men sending her thoughts into wild fantasies. These men were going to be working here with the sheriff and other officers, which meant that she was going to have to deal with them, too.

"Mia," she offered. "What's so urgent though? It's a Sunday."

Kenn raised an eyebrow and smiled again. "This fucker just gets antsy with nothing to do. We'll be out of your hair. Thanks for the directions. I'm sure we'll be seeing you around."

Mia watched them leave the way they came, that powerful aura dissipating when their presence left the building. More personnel at the sheriff's office meant that trouble was on its way. Or was already here.

TWO

MIA

Monday morning meant more of the same – another godawful day of sorting through the bodies that had come through during the weekend. Mia masked her yawn behind weary hands. She hadn't even gone home last night, deciding that doing so would induce more questions than she had answers for. Her mother was always so nosy and demeaning, especially when it came to Anders.

Why aren't you at the wedding?

Wasn't it such a pretty ceremony?

Oh, they looked so in love!

It was as if her relationship with Anders had never existed, as if the bimbo on his arm was all that mattered. But that bimbo hadn't grown up in Bryxton, didn't know it like the back of her hand, hadn't played with the school kids. …

Mia could go on and on about all the things that Anders' new wife didn't know, but the fact was, that woman was here to stay. For a while anyway.

She stifled another yawn as she slid off one of the metal slabs that bodies were reserved for, glad she had changed into her scrubs at some point last night. She had never understood why, but the silence amongst the metal cases gave her a sense of inner peace that the chaotic world around her couldn't.

Mia wasn't crazy enough to sleep *inside* one of the metal drawers, but she was tempted to try it. Maybe when the surrounding boxes were empty.

Maybe.

She trudged outside for her daily dose of sunshine before she got down to work, stretching and relishing the way her back cracked. That's when her eyes landed on the empty storefront two blocks over that wasn't quite ... empty anymore. *That's weird. Could have sworn that Gran sold that place a few months ago.*

Gran was one of the oldest women in town. She was everyone's grandmother, the sweetest old lady that ever lived, but in her old age, she had been unable to keep open her candy shop. The average age of their town wasn't getting any younger, which had been a sore point for decades, but there was nothing to do when they were smack dab in the middle of a long dusty road miles away from the rest of civilization.

Most of the excitement they received was from out-of-towners looking for rest or a bit of fun. Granted Bryxton was pretty small, boasting a population of only 150, but it had dwindled over the years, and the young ones kept leaving and not coming back.

Mia lingered for a moment longer by her office's front door before deciding to visit the shop, the smell of fresh coffee beans hitting her like a freight truck as she crossed the street. *A new coffee shop?* Her heart swelled at the thought. They hadn't had a fresh coffee shop other than Tanner's Deli and the rundown diner toward the edge of town. Sure, there were a host of chain restaurants in the city about twenty miles north, but no one offered *freshly ground* coffee. And yes, it made a difference.

She continued to sniff, delighting in the mingled scents of hazelnut and chocolate as she pushed open the door. What had been an out-of-service shop front had transformed into a cozy cafe. The walls were bare, just like Gran had it, but there was now a counter in the small place, blocking off the back room from the rest.

Rich mahogany and marble spread across the floor and onto the counters and tables.

How did I miss this?

The shock of how much she had probably missed by trying to avoid Anders and his bimbo was unnerving. She probably hadn't been anywhere other than Town Hall, the sheriff's station, and her office in weeks. The door wiggled close behind her, reminding her that this still held the heart of Gran's essence. Chimes signaled her entrance as she continued to take in the transformation, tears welling up in her eyes. *I've missed so much. I'm so stupid because of one man … ruining my life. …*

"Um, miss? We're not quite ready yet. But I'm brewing a fresh batch of coffee. It'll be just a minute."

Mia blinked a few times, the Southern drawl bringing her back to the present. A young man, not much older than her twenty-seven years of age, was leaning over the counter. The dim lights highlighted the vibrant amethyst in his eyes. Her breath caught in her throat as his smile widened, dimples popping up in his cheeks.

He straightened up, his hands pressed against the counter. Her eyes continued to roam, taking in the way wisps of intricate black designs wrapped around his arms and splayed out onto his neck. A scar darkened the left side of his collarbone, disappearing down the front of his shirt, which was at odds with his cheery aura.

Whoever he was, he didn't belong in this town.

"Miss?"

Mia jerked forward and smiled awkwardly. "Yes. I'll wait."

"That's wonderful. You'll be my first. Just a few minutes."

A voice called out from beside her, "Your first? You can't just go off telling girls that, Matty boy! They'll get the wrong idea."

Mia froze, recognizing the voice as chuckles filtered into her ear. She slowly turned to see the two detectives from yesterday sitting beside Kingsley Sanders, the sheriff-in-training, all three dressed in that pale green throw-up color of a uniform. She blamed her sleepiness for having missed not one but three men settled around one of the tables.

Jan was ramrod straight, fingers tightened around his coffee mug like someone was threatening him. Mia wondered if that uptight demeanor was a cover for something else or if he really was just that put together. It had to be tiring.

Where Jan had this seriousness about him, Kenn was more of a *no fucks given* type of look. He had slouched in his chair, arm thrown over one side, legs splayed as if inviting trouble. He sent Mia a wink, at which she blushed furiously.

Kingsley Sanders shifted uncomfortably in his chair. He was the bane of Mia's existence and the sole reason she hated her job. His father was a wonderful man who had given her the opportunity to prove herself when most of the town thought she was a waste of time. Their partnership grew and Kingsley's father listened to her input. But Kingsley wasn't half the man his father was.

Mia and Kingsley had grown up together, thick as thieves at one point until Kingsley decided that he was better than her and everyone else in town. He was smart, Mia would give him that. But he was stubborn and didn't listen to anyone unless he was forced to. The only reason he was in line for sheriff was because of his father *and* no one else wanted the job. Being sheriff out here was boring as shit. Mia undoubtedly had more work than he did.

There were few deaths other than the older Bryxton population, however, just outside of town, it seemed like this place attracted people who wanted to end it all. The number of bodies found along the roads and some of the ravines was ridiculous. Mia's job was to prep them and send out identifying information to the surrounding police departments in order to get a positive ID. Some bodies were never claimed, and they were buried in the makeshift burial ground behind her office.

"Miss? Do you like cream and sugar?"

"Huh?" Mia glanced back at the man behind the counter and then nodded, biting back her embarrassment. She couldn't help but smile, though, at his cheery demeanor. He prepared the coffee and handed it to her in a paper cup with a lid. "How much?" she asked.

"Oh, no. On the house. Have to give people a reason to come back." The man winked and Mia blushed again.

Kenn sauntered up to the counter and slid his mug over to the guy. "Stop doing that. Women get the wrong idea, Matty."

The man grumbled, "It's *Matthias.*" He grabbed the cup and disappeared into the back to refill it.

Kenn called after him, "*Matty*, you look like a child. You're never getting rid of that name."

"Did you guys come in together?" Mia said. She realized how ambiguous her question was as soon as she asked it, but wasn't able to clear it up in time.

Kenn pointed to Matthias and then chuckled. "Fuck no, sweetheart. He's basically Jan's little brother, kind of. You'd think he was, anyways."

"You guys all came here at the same time, though. Why?" Mia clutched her coffee and realized she hadn't even taken a sip yet. She put the spout to her lips and closed her eyes as she sipped. Rich beans coated in hazelnut and what reminded her of churros coated her tongue, a little moan slipping from her lips.

Kenn raised an eyebrow but didn't address it otherwise. "Jan and I had work to do, so ... we all just kind of moved here."

"Bryxton is in the middle of nowhere."

He shrugged. "It's nice."

Matthias returned with another coffee, but it looked nothing like the one she had. Kenn's monstrosity was coated in whip cream, chocolate chips, and was that ... cinnamon? She eyed him strangely and Kenn took a big swig, a dollop of cream settling on the tip of his nose. He kept her gaze as his tongue reached up to lick it off.

Mia fought the urge to show Kenn just how much she enjoyed that show as she took another sip of her coffee and nodded. "Thanks, really. I have to get to work."

"Glad you like it, miss. Come back tomorrow and I'll have bagels."

Mia giggled. "The way to every woman's heart."

Kenn sighed dramatically, the playful look in his eyes telling Mia all sorts of things she wasn't sure she was ready for. "Matty *always* gets the girls!"

Mia started for the door when Kingsley's voice stopped her. "You can take the day off, Mialopolus. No need to work so hard. There's not even enough shit to do around here."

She glared back at him. "I have like five bodies that have to be prepped for transport, Sanders."

"That's *Sheriff* Sanders to you," Kingsley stated, standing up to his full height of five-eight, which was taller than her but paled in comparison to the other men in the cafe. Mia's eyes drifted to the sheriff's badge on his chest and she gasped. He nodded. "Yep. Dad passed it off this morning. Told me it was time."

Mia knew that was a load of shit; there was supposed to be a ceremony, one that she was required to be present for as part of the sheriff's department. Instead of creating a scene, Mia threw him a tight smile and said, "That's wonderful, *Sheriff* Sanders. And

I'm thankful for the day off, really. When the transport arrives, I'll make sure to fuck off into my own little corner. Will that do?"

Her hands gripped her coffee tighter, unable to hide her anger at the disrespect Kingsley was showing her. Because he was sheriff now, she knew that he was going to be a bigger pain in the ass than usual.

"Watch it, Mialopolus."

"*Make me.*"

Mia stormed out of the cafe and back to her office, slamming the door behind her.

THREE

MATTHIAS

Matthias stared after the spitfire of a woman who had just blazed through his shop at 5:30 in the morning. Her mess of brown hair - tussled nicely with a stray butterfly clip hanging by her ear - made him smile, but her doe eyes and the way her scrubs were wrinkled filled him with an entirely different desire. He loved his women strong, fierce, and smart. She was all of those things.

What he couldn't understand was the pain in her eyes.

He was curious but knew he couldn't just ask her about it. He and his brothers were new in town, and that brought attention, attention that he didn't want on her. *Didn't even ask her for her name.*

Kenn clapped his back, startling him out of his daydream. "Quite a looker, eh?"

Matthias couldn't hide the smile that spread across his lips, "Don't be crass. Who is she?"

Kenn nodded in the direction she had sauntered off to. "That's the coroner. I think. Or maybe the tech?"

Kenn's boss rudely slammed down his empty mug on the counter and shifted his sheriff's badge like he was worth something. Matthias knew a fake when he saw one, having been deployed overseas a handful of times. The man before him was definitely a fake, and goddamn self-righteous, if his conversations over the last twenty minutes were anything to go by.

"She's the coroner, took over for her father. She's weird, so don't worry about her. Besides, we probably won't need her in a few months. She's on borrowed time."

Matthias frowned. He had left the service years ago, but he still understood the ins and outs of the criminal system. His brothers came to him all the time with questions, even if he was the youngest at thirty. A coroner was a damn important piece to the puzzle, especially in a town as remote as this. He also understood that Kingsley had disrespected the woman before she had walked out, and he wanted to strangle the man for it.

He kept his clenched fists beneath the counter, jaw tense to keep himself in check. Everyone thought that Jan was the one with anger issues, which was true. But Matthias, when he blew his lid, it was *explosive*.

A heavy hand plopped onto his shoulder, the following yawn alerting him that their final brother had surfaced from the depths of the storage room. "What'd I miss?" The ex-military man stretched and then popped one eye open, scowling at the light filtering in through the front door. "How long was I out?"

Matthias smiled, the anger seeping out of him. "Nichlas, it's only like six a.m. Go back to sleep." In reality, the fucker had slept for over sixteen hours. None of them truly knew what Nichlas did after he was honorably discharged from the Marines, but they didn't question it. His help had been invaluable to some of

Kenn and Jan's investigations, so they simply turned a blind eye to whatever three-letter agency he worked for.

Still … *sixteen* hours?

Kenn lightly punched Matthias in the arm, dangling his coffee cup for more. Matthias sighed. "You're a goddamn addict, and I hate that you can still sleep all eight hours at night."

Kenn laughed. "It's the genes, baby."

"Fuck your genes," said Jan, who approached the counter and handed his empty mug to Matthias; the jesting smile on his face told them he wasn't bothered by the comment.

Matthias prepared another coffee, this time in a to-go cup, for Kenn and a mug for Nichlas, who was obviously not going back to sleep. In between the four men, the fifth – Kingsley – seemed like the nerdy kid that people like the others used to bully in school. *Sheriff, my ass.*

He wasn't sure why the previous sheriff had asked for extra hands or why Kenn and Jan's boss had readily agreed. Kenn and Jan weren't run-of-the-mill detectives who transferred because they had nothing else to do. They were top tier, called in because no one else could do it.

Which meant something in this town was wrong. Something that needed attention. Something that that beautiful coroner might have more insight on than the fake-ass sheriff standing before him.

Kenn and Jan waved their goodbyes, following behind Kingsley like two ridiculously out-of-place bodyguards, and Matthias couldn't help but wonder what they would uncover.

"Looked like you were going to swing at that officer earlier," Nichlas mumbled behind a sip of coffee. He was by far the quietest of the four when it came to observing and cataloging information, but it was no secret that Matthias wore his emotions on his sleeve.

"I was. And he's not an officer. That was the sheriff."

Nichlas sputtered, placing his mug on the counter and wrangling Matthias until they were standing face to face. "Matty, that's *worse.*"

"He disrespected a lady in her craft." Matthias neglected to mention anything about how interested he was in the coroner. Nevertheless, he would have done the same thing even if it was a man.

Nichlas clicked his tongue, his expression hardening as he donned a serious tone. "So ... defending her honor? That's real noble. But we can't go punching people even if they're dickheads."

"I'm going in the back to knead dough," Matthias responded, deciding that avoidance was the best tactic. Nichlas didn't push it, just nodded and mumbled something about going back to sleep.

"For what?" Matthias said. "What were you even doing yesterday?"

Nichlas chuckled and then gulped the rest of his caffeine. "None of your beeswax, sir." He gave Matthias a terribly formed salute, and Matthias grunted in return. "Best coffee yet, Matty."

"I can't fucking stand you." But even as the words came out of his mouth, Matthias smiled, his dimples returning to his cheeks.

"Copy that, Sergeant. Can't fucking stand you either."

They broke out into laughter as Matthias followed Nichlas into the back. He pulled out the dough and began preparing what he needed to make tomorrow's bagels as Nichlas shifted back onto his cot and closed his eyes.

Matthias couldn't help but wonder what would happen when the dick showed up again when his brothers weren't around.

FOUR

MIA

Mia idly poked at the brain sitting in the weigh barrel, a deep sigh falling from her lips. She didn't even have the motivation to finish the last autopsy before she took the rest of the day off. Kingsley had told her she wasn't needed, but she knew what he meant. He was trying to push her out of her craft, out of town. He hated that his father leaned on her. Kingsley believed he didn't need anyone other than himself, but Mia was pretty sure that he was going to have a hard fucking time wrangling in those new detectives.

They didn't look like they took shit from anyone.

She sighed again and pushed away from the body, ripping off her gloves and walking to the sink to wash her face. She wasn't sure why she was so restless. A week ago, she would have still been wallowing in bed. Now she was trying to bury herself in work that didn't exist.

She had mentioned to Sheriff Sanders – the real one – that there was an odd similarity with the last couple of bodies she had autopsied. He had given her the OK to look into it and report back to him her findings. Unfortunately, she had found fuck all, and now that he was no longer sheriff, Mia was pretty sure her research would be shut down before it even took off.

Transport wasn't coming for another few hours, but those bodies had been prepped for weeks. The one autopsy that was critical to an investigation was currently splayed out on the table she had slept on last night.

But something was off.

"What's going on?" Her tech, Quinn, asked her. She stared at him, having forgotten the kid was there. He was in training, using this valuable time as an internship before he entered medical school. She used to babysit him way back when, reading him medical books to put him to sleep until he chose medical school as his one-way ticket out of this town. *Oh, the irony.* His parents had died a year ago, leaving him with a house, some money, and only his grandmother for guidance, although he seemed to be faring well.

"Nothing."

"Really? You've sighed like fifteen times in the past hour. Was the coffee not strong enough?"

"No, that was fine." She thought of those gorgeous dimples and the purple eyes smiling at her. She brushed away the image before she started blushing again. "It's just–"

"They made Dickwad your boss and now you have to answer to someone who doesn't know the first thing about your job?"

Fucking kid was always so observant. "Yes, I suppose that's part of it."

"Come on. Spill. There's no one else here to talk to." Mia raised an eyebrow and Quinn added, "That can talk back."

"Well, it's–" The door flung open, and the last person in the world she wanted to see stormed through. "That. *That's* my problem," Mia hissed. She shrugged off her coat and exited the lab to keep Anders from pushing through into what was supposed to be the equivalent of a cleanroom.

"If you take him back, I'll shoot you," Quinn mouthed from behind her. Mia shook her head, smiling. Quinn was the little brother she had never had. And he knew it, too, throwing around judgment like he owned the place. She would be devastated when he left for college next year.

"Anders."

He thrust her against the wall, grabbing her left wrist and snarling in her face. Mia shriveled in his presence, unsure of what he was going to do. Quinn had the desk phone halfway to his ear when she shook her head frantically. Calling the sheriff meant that Kingsley would find out.

No, she'd have to deal with this one on her own.

"What do you think you're doing?" Anders said.

"What?" Mia exclaimed, trying unsuccessfully to rip herself from him.

"You little *whore*. You couldn't have me, so you throw yourself at every new man there is? I was going to give you a second chance. But Mia, you disappoint me." He thrust her backward again, her back slamming against the wall and shocking her system. She whimpered as she nursed her wrist and willed herself not to cry.

Quinn came to her rescue, stepping in between them. "What are you talking about? She was here all night and this morning."

Anders' expression flashed with rage, but he stepped back now that his access to Mia was hindered. "Who are they? Who did you decide to jump into bed with the moment I turned away?"

Mia frowned. "I still don't understand–"

Anders punched the wall by her head, and she grabbed Quinn around the waist, pulling the kid toward her chest as they side shuffled, her eyes falling on the new hole in her wall. Anders had never been physically violent, but something had really rattled his cage. "The men. Two of them last night. Another one this morning. You were all smiles."

"You mean the detectives? And I went for coffee this morning. I–"

"It's a nice cover, Mia. Really. But I'm not buying it."

Mia cowered in the corner, stuffing Quinn behind her. She'd been conditioned to bow away from danger than face it but if the choice was between her or Quinn getting hurt, it was going to be her.

His words began to unravel as she finally wrapped her mind around everything he had said. "You're married," Mia breathed. What chance was he hoping to give her? And how did he even know that the detectives had visited last night? In such a small town, word traveled fast, as did rumors, but ... "Why the fuck were you watching me during your wedding?" *Wrong words, Mia. Wrong words!*

Anders blew out a deep breath. "Mia, you're lucky I still love you. Tell me about the men and no one gets hurt."

"There are no men! And it wouldn't matter if there were. You're *married*. You left me. Left me for her! Why are you doing this?" Tears began to fall down her cheeks as she stared at him.

"Because I love you, sweetheart. I always have. Marrying her was a mistake, maybe it was a test. I don't know. But I don't love her."

Mia knew a toxic relationship when she saw one, except when it was hers. Her heart leaped at the idea that the man in front of her hadn't dumped her for the bimbo but instead had made a lapse in judgment. Fortunately, she came to her senses quickly.

He inched closer, his hands moving to cup her cheeks. She squirmed away from him, rushing toward her lab. The exit was behind Anders, and she'd never make it, but desperate times called for desperate measures.

She whipped out one of her scalpels, Quinn holding onto her scrubs from behind for protection. "Is he on something?" the kid whispered.

Mia didn't answer, pure adrenaline rushing through her as she pointed the scalpel at Anders, inching her way toward the front door. If she moved within arm's reach of Anders, the game would end. He'd be able to strangle her into a position that she couldn't wrangle out of. But at this distance, they could dance around until her back was against the door and they could rush outside. Not that anyone would believe that Anders had demanded they get back together. After all, she was the girl who played with dead bodies. Anders would *never*. Not to mention that he was in thick with Kingsley.

Mia continued to inch around, watching Anders stay far enough away, hands up as he watched her. "Just a few more steps, Q," she said quietly back at the kid.

"What the fuck is going on here?"

Mia straightened up but didn't drop the scalpel, eyes drifting to the entrance to meet heated purple eyes. Purple eyes that were currently trained on her. Purple eyes that weren't the same glowing warm shade of hazy warmth she had met in the coffee shop. They were two globes of deep, threatening violence, flashing with an anger Mia couldn't understand but somehow seemed safer than Anders. The smell of cinnamon raisin bagels filled her nose, and she had an idea.

She tried to mask her terror with a smile, dropping her hand and mustering up an uneasy laugh. "Just playing around. We like to do that sometimes. Did you bring bagels?" Her voice wavered as her gaze dropped to the bag.

Matthias glared at Anders, who responded by shrugging and walking out the door. "We'll catch up later, Mia. It was fun."

Mia shuddered but nodded anyway, trying to keep up pretenses.

Matthias set the bag on the counter, that hardened stare falling on her once again. Unfortunately, Quinn wasn't as great of an actor.

"Fuck, I think I peed myself a little. Are those really BAGELS?" He snatched the bag and ripped it open, moaning excessively as he stuffed one into his face. "Did you make these? My god, it's heaven in my mouth. Like, rich and …"

He trailed off, and Mia knew that it was nerves speaking. Had Matthias not arrived or had Mia not picked up any of the self-defense training she had learned from her father, the situation could have been much worse.

Matthias was tense, his entire body vibrating, eyes flashing a deep purple. The darkness that radiated from him was terrifying, but it wasn't directed at her. Not completely. "What happened?" he said.

Mia grabbed one of the bagels and bit into it. *God, this man really checks all the boxes, huh?*

"Just a misunderstanding."

"I know a standoff when I see one."

"And I told you we were playing a game."

"Too real to be a game."

Matthias had lost his dimples. Mia wasn't sure about this side of the man, but something about the mysterious darkness still called out to her.

"Please just leave it. I know you're trying to be nice and helpful, but you just got here and you don't understand—"

Matthias reached for the scalpel. "No, I don't understand why a trained medical professional would *want* to injure another person. Can you explain that to me? Can you explain why you looked like you would have stabbed him had I not shown up?"

Mia didn't answer that question, biting into her bagel and swallowing. "Thank you for the bagels. They're delicious." She glanced back at Quinn and said, "Get some water before you choke, you idiot!"

Matthias' eyes swept the place again, landing on the new hole in the wall. His eyes darkened again before his expression smoothed out and his dimples returned. It was a little unnerving to watch how fast he hid his emotions. "I'm just across the street, okay? You need anything, just holler."

"Of course." Mia held up the bag and jiggled it. "Thanks again."

Matthias walked out the door, a little too slow for her liking. They narrowly avoided a confrontation, one that she wouldn't be able to explain away.

She turned to find Quinn stuffing his face, hiccups between every bite, his cheeks stained with tears.

"Q, I'm so fucking sorry."

"I thought he was really going to do something."

"And you little shit stepped in front of me! I should kill you right now!" A little chuckle came from her as she pulled him into a tight hug, rocking him until his tremors ceased. It brought her a little comfort that Matthias was across the street, but it wouldn't do any good. She wouldn't call him. She wouldn't run to him. She couldn't make something out of what had just happened. Then everyone would know. And that just couldn't fucking happen.

FIVE

JAN

Jan flipped through the stacks of files on his desk. He had known that this job was going to be a pain in the ass, but he didn't know he was going to be working for one as well. Kingsley Sanders had been handed the badge hours after they had met his father. His father was a respectable man, one who Jan had no problem following.

Despite not having served like Matthias or Nichlas had, Jan still had an appreciation for the men who had. But Kinglsey? The little shit didn't know his right from his left. Sure, he was a walking encyclopedia when it came to laws and regulations, but how to apply them? How to interact with the general population? How to ensure that his town was safe from whatever evils plagued the surrounding area? *Clueless.*

Jan still wasn't sure why their chief had agreed to partner with this town to send them out here; he hadn't questioned it at the time. He should have. Nichlas and Matthias had been itching to do something different and had jumped at the opportunity to come with. The fact that Matthias had opened an entire bakery in a week was impressive, not to mention Nichlas' uncanny ability to disappear and then return for an abnormal amount of sleep.

Kenn kicked him from under the desk, Jan grunting in response. Their desks were across from each other on the other side of the office from two officers who had been strangled into their positions. They seemed a lot more relaxed and sheepish, signaling they were nothing more than Kingsley's lackeys.

Kenn geared up for another kick until Jan sent him a glare that froze him in place. Kenn shot Jan a sheepish smile before asking, "What the fuck are we doing here?"

Jan sighed, leaning forward and resisting the urge to run his hands through his hair, instead opting to rest his forearms on the desk. "No fucking clue. But maybe a little more professionalism couldn't hurt. Kingsley looked like he was going to strangle you for stepping out of line." Kenn was one of the best detectives around, but he had a knack for pissing off all the wrong people. Unfortunately, Kingsley was easy to pick on, easily distressed, and way too quick to anger.

Kenn cracked a lopsided smile, "That's *Sheriff* Sanders to you." He cackled quietly. It was Jan's turn to kick him in the shin.

"Just ... read through a file or something."

Kingsley had given them no direction on how to proceed with their job, and at first, Jan thought that meant there wasn't any work to be done. But when they returned to town hall and Kingsley had deposited them at their desks, Jan quickly realized that the kid just didn't know how to do his job. There were caseloads of folders resting on the edges of their new workstations that hadn't been touched in a month.

The other two officers were throwing wads of paper back and forth, chuckling about something funny that had nothing to do with an investigation.

Jan trained his eyes on yet another file, skimming the contents. Each one referred to some case just outside the grounds, a coroner's report fully detailed with each one. The name *Mia Andreasen* populated each report, her delicate signature at the bottom of each page. A second name, *Quinn Collins*, appeared occasionally just under Mia's.

And with each report he pulled, a coroner's report was attached. It was the *only* detail in most of them, telling Jan that the real hero of this office was Mia, not Kingsley.

Jan had been aware that Kingsley's father had handed off most of the duties to his son months before the kid received the real promotion, but he had hoped the office was in better shape than it was.

Kenn faked a yawn, plopping back into his seat. "Seriously, what the fuck are we supposed to be doing here?" Jan hadn't noticed he'd gotten up.

"You've been a detective for like seven years. Figure it out. Do some detecting." *There's a lot of fucking bodies just outside of town.* Jan skimmed the details of the reports, trying to read between the lines. This town wasn't on a map and it wasn't a destination. So why was it the end for so many unlucky travelers?

"Har, har, Jan, real funny. I'm serious. I didn't come out here to do nothing." Kenn waved his hands and let his head fall to the desk with a loud thud. The other two officers didn't even break concentration from their game.

"And you know that's not why Chief agreed to this little one-month stint. Something is going on, and we're supposed to figure it out."

"Like *what*, Jan?" Kenn said. He took a folder from the stack, stared at the one lone page, and then tossed it onto the other side of his desk with an agitated sigh. "What could *possibly* be going wrong in this place? It's so sweet, and there's all these flourishing shops and shit. Not to mention that delicious little coroner that's got Matty's panties already in a twist."

Jan didn't acknowledge that last part of the statement because that was an additional problem. Anyone who caught Matty's eye meant trouble – damsel in distress kind of trouble. He tossed a folder at Kenn, the detective sitting up straight with a scowl on his face. "Maybe for starters, we figure out why all these cases aren't finished. There's maybe thirty open cases just sitting here." Kenn raised an eyebrow as Jan continued. "You first." Kenn had that annoyed expression tucked into his eyes again, meaning that he had happened on information when he disappeared.

"Kingsley is a piece of shit."

Jan resisted the urge to whack the guy across from him. "Figured that. Anything else?"

"The other detectives are just glorified security when needed. They get a paycheck based on donations from surrounding counties."

Donations?

"Apparently, donations come from solved cases and stuff," Kenn said.

That seemed ... odd. Especially since the only details in any of these cases was from the coroner's report. Jan shuffled to find a particularly interesting case that involved two dead bodies with similar markings. "Kingsley mentioned that these piles were the ones that needed to be sent out for closure. But the only thing in them is this." He pulled out the coroner's report and handed it to Kenn. Kenn stared at it, his brows furrowing with confusion. "Just the coroner's autopsy or final comments. That's it. Oh, and this." Jan handed Kenn a small picture of the deceased, which was most likely used for identification purposes.

"Wait. These cases are what bring in the donations?" Kenn's expression darkened as he realized the truth behind the sheriff's office. The fact that Kingsley wanted to make Mia's position redundant meant that he had *no* idea how the office was paid. "She's doing all the goddamn work to fund this place."

Jan nodded, pushing away from his desk as he grabbed the file. "I think we know who we have to go talk to."

SIX

MIA

Despite how much he protested, Mia had sent Quinn home to sleep.. The kid was still shaking and wasn't going to be of much help with any of the remaining tasks. Mia told herself that she was just going to finish up after the transport and then go home as well. She'd ignore the massive number of questions from her mother while trying to regain her equilibrium after Anders' intrusion.

But it wouldn't be that easy.

As she reached over the body to finish sewing it up, her hand trembled. It had been doing that all afternoon. Drinking water hadn't helped. Taking deep breaths hadn't helped. She had even popped a Xanax, and that had done fuck all for her nerves. She knew she was staving off shock, and when she eventually did end up panicking, she hoped she was far from civilization.

No one needed to know how much Anders bothered her.

A knock on her lab window made her look up in terror. When she recognized the two forms behind the glass, she mustered up a smile and discarded her gloves as she forced herself out of the lab to greet them.

Kenn waved at her with a boyish grin, but Jan's frown told her that he was seeing everything that was wrong. He gestured to the back wall. "What happened?"

Mia tensed and then relaxed her shoulders, stuffing her hands into her lab pockets to hide the tremble. "Just a mishap. What's up?" *Deep breaths, Mia. It's fine. Anders is gone.*

Both men eyed her for a minute before Kenn broke the ice, choosing to move on from the strange ambiance in her office. "Just a few questions about the last couple of cases you closed."

"Kingsley doesn't know you're here." Mia hadn't meant to be so abrupt, but it was true. She bowed her head and scuffed her heel against the floor. "He'd never send you here about questions regarding closed cases." Mia never saw the cases after she turned in her reports. There was never any pushback, no questions, no need for clarification, *nothing*. She still received a check every week, so she hadn't really ever thought about it.

But now Mia saw the obvious disconnect between the way she was treated and the way her father had been. Her nose crinkled as she started thinking of all the ways she could fuck Kingsley over. Professionally, of course.

Kenn brushed off the comments, waving two yellow folders at her. "Have you seen these cases after you gave the sheriff your reports?"

"No need. My only job is to do the autopsy. Those are my folders, though. Where's the rest of the case folders?" Mia knew what a case folder looked like. Her father had brought enough of them back to the office over the years. His folder had always gone *inside*, but they were holding her reports as if that was all there was.

Jan let out a deep sigh, stepping a little closer. "Do you know what the rest of the investigation entails?" Before Anders, Mia would have enjoyed his musky smell, the scent of fresh-cut wood and pine, but right now, it was a little too close for comfort. She shifted back a step and then thought better of it, rounding her desk so that there were at least six inches of space between them. Her limbs were beginning to feel like lead, terror building in her chest. She was about to go into shock. Now. In front of them. Timing really sucked.

"No-o." Her voice wavered.

Jan's look hardened, but Kenn kept talking. "Sweetheart, the *only* thing in here is your report."

Mia stared at the open folder in Kenn's hands as he slid it across the desk. She reached for it weakly, her fingers brushing his, and a whimper escaped her throat.

The men froze, Kenn's hands hovering over her desk. His expression soured, his gaze flashing with concern. "Sweetheart?"

Mia glanced up at them, trying to understand what was going on as her brain dissolved into a muddled mess. The panic and terror had finally settled in, and her entire body trembled at the thought of what could have happened. Her stomach revolted against her, and she lost her lunch behind her desk. Kenn rounded the surface, rubbing his hands down her back. "Breathe, sweetheart. *Breathe.* That's good, let's sit down."

She felt a chair being pushed toward her as sobs wracked her chest, her hands limply reaching out to grab something, *anything.* Two firm hands grabbed hers, giving her the ability to steady herself.

Fuck, this isn't good.

"Kenn, I don't think this is because of the report."

"And I don't have fucking training for this."

Through the haze, Mia could hear a phone being dialed and a voice on the other line. "Yeah?"

"Matty, get over here. She's in shock. I don't know. What the fuck? Get your ass over here. Sweetheart, you're doing so well. Just keep breathing, with me. With me."

Mia did as she was told, the two men holding her steady as she tried to regain her composure. It had been awhile since her last panic attack, but a few moments with Anders had brought all that terror back. All the memories she had tried to block out. All the times she told herself that she loved that man and wanted to spend the rest of her life with him despite the fear he wielded over her.

Her breath caught in her throat as she tried to breathe, and fell into a coughing fit that not even the two arms wrapped around her tightly could stave off. *God, this is so embarrassing.*

SEVEN

MATTHIAS

Matthias had worked through all the dough. He'd ground a fresh batch of coffee beans. Many customers had stopped for a coffee, word going around quickly about the quality and aroma of his drink. He relished the distraction from Mia and that terrified boy.

Something had happened in that office, something that could have been a lot worse if the way Mia had been shaking had anything to do with it. He was pretty sure he had seen that man somewhere else the day before. … *The groom!*

He wouldn't have known had he not been asked to help with the baked goods at the wedding for a last-minute touch-up. Why the groom had been at Mia's office and why he seemed like he had been the issue was beyond Matthias' comprehension.

Mia seemed to attract trouble. *A lot* of it.

He tried to keep from thinking of anything but the coffee beans, passing the day as best he could. Since leaving the service and following his heart into baking, he had found peace within himself. There was no fighting, no wars, no reason to constantly be on alert.

Except where women were concerned. And he always seemed to find the ones who needed the most help but would never ask for it.

He knew for a fact that Mia wouldn't come to his bakery in search of help, which worried him. He had debated for at least an hour whether to take her a fresh batch of bagels, but his desire to see her again had won out.

It was a good thing it had.

A hand squeezed his shoulder and Matthias donned his smile again, staring up at Nichlas. "What?"

"That's the third coffee you've overpoured."

"And?" Matthias quickly set down the pot and grabbed a rag. It was actually the seventh one he'd overpoured, but who was counting?

Nichlas' brows furrowed with concern. "You're distracted."

"So?"

"You're *never* distracted. You told me baking was your true love or some shit. What's got your panties in a twist?" The man snickered at the terrible use of words.

Matthias turned up his nose but let out a sigh anyway. "Mia."

"The girl who came in here?"

"I took some bagels over to her this morning."

"Aren't you just the gentleman?" Another snicker.

"She was armed with a knife, kid at her back, and there was the groom from the wedding yesterday across the room."

Nichlas' expression darkened as the same fight Matthias was resisting breached the surface. "Excuse me?"

Matthias hated having to resist the urge to rip the groom apart for scaring the woman. He returned the pot of coffee to its rightful place and dumped the cup's contents into the sink. He hadn't even been pouring the coffee for any good reason. It had just been something to do. "She said they were just playing around, but I've been in enough places to know true terror. And there was a hole in the wall that I'm pretty sure was from a fist."

"Fuck. Did you report it?"

"To who? The dickwad of a sheriff that doesn't like her?"

Silence fell between them as Nichlas leaned against the wall post, staring at Matthias for a response to a situation he usually cracked from. Matthias was the least stable of the four, finding ways to calm his natural response to anger way more important in the grand scheme of things.

"I tried to ask her what was going on, but she didn't want to talk about it," Matthias began, avoiding Nichlas' gaze. "I don't think it's because she's scared of him, though, more of what everyone in town will do about it. Or won't."

"That's brutal. You at least leave your number?"

Matthias shook his head. "No. I told her she's always welcome in here, but I don't think it will help."

Nichlas donned a wild grin. "Are you asking for my help?"

"Can you just figure out what's going on? I … I can't–"

Nichlas clapped his back, cutting him off so that he didn't have to relive one of the instances he had lost someone. "Don't worry. That won't happen. I'll check things out and report back to you." He threw him another terrible salute and disappeared into the back for his jacket before heading outside.

Years ago, Matthias had lost someone to negligence. His officers hadn't routinely checked on each other to make sure everyone was okay. Someone ended up dying as a result. Matthias couldn't stomach that again. But Nichlas would dig and find out what that guy had been doing in there and hopefully make sure it didn't happen again.

Unfortunately, Matthias wasn't going to be able to focus on his baked goods without knowing Mia was safe. His gaze fell on her office down the way, surprised to find Jan and Kenn waltzing in that direction. Matthias waited for something. Anything. Anything that would require his help. Whatever was happening in this town – for whatever reason Kenn and Jan had been called in – he was pretty sure it involved Mia.

He grabbed his cellphone, silencing the vibration seconds after it began to ring.

"Matty, she's in shock." Kenn's voice filtered through the speaker.

Matthias' jaw clenched at the memory of the man leaving Mia's office and her pleading with him to leave the situation alone. "Not surprising. She should be."

"I don't know. What the fuck? Get your ass over here. Sweetheart, you're doing so well. Just keep breathing, with me. With me."

The fact that she hadn't broken down in that moment, in front of the kid, was a testament to her sheer willpower. Her ragged breathing could be heard echoing through the speaker as Matthias tried to calm his own with the counting exercises a therapist had told him about a few years ago.

It wasn't working.

And now Matthias wished he hadn't been waiting for that *something* to require his help. A woman in need was his greatest weakness, and Mia was one of the strongest contenders he had met in a while.

EIGHT

NICHLAS

Nichlas waited for Matthias to get off the phone before saying anything. The youngest's fists were clenched, the phone clattering to the floor as he grit his teeth to keep from punching the nearest appliance. Nichlas wiped the sleep from his eyes, swallowing the chuckle when he realized that this situation wasn't a joke.

"Matty, what's going on?"

"Jan just called. They – someone – she's in shock."

Nichlas nodded, approaching Matty slowly and in his line of sight, hands and fingers outstretched. He had approached the kid once from behind when Matthias was in one of these moods, and it hadn't been pretty.

Nichlas knew the signs of when Matty went rogue. Three main criteria set the youngest of the four off. Disrespect. Dismissal. Assault. But when all three happened? Someone was going to end up seriously broken. Or dead. They couldn't afford a body right now, regardless of what the reason was.

Nichlas had only been privy to some of the conversation, but he knew enough. The coroner had been attacked in her office and was now going into shock – Jan and Kenn over there trying to keep her from falling apart. The problem was – shockingly enough – that Matthias was the only one versed in enough psychology to do anything about it.

They should send for a doctor, but somehow the three other guys had taken to this woman over the one day they had been in town. Nichlas wasn't about to stand in the middle of that.

That lame excuse for a sheriff had no idea who he had set off by disrespecting the coroner and dismissing her craft. And now someone had tried to assault her in her own office. If Matty found the person responsible, they were as good as dead.

Nichlas grabbed Matty, the man seething, radiating pure anger as he growled in the middle of their small cafe. It was a good thing there weren't any customers – none of them would return if they saw their friendly neighborhood barista wilding out like this.

He dragged a hand down the back of the kid's neck, Matthias's head dropping as he took in deep breaths. No words were exchanged between them, but Nichlas knew that this woman was either going to be the death of them or bring them closer.

Matthias sighed, his shoulders relaxing. "I'm good now."

Nichlas snorted, "Yeah, okay. You won't be okay for a while. Just keep doing that deep breathing shit and don't kill anyone. Let's go."

Matthias stared at him, his eyes black with anger and worry. The baker with the dimples and excellent taste in coffee was gone. This man was all military, running scenarios through his brain. "No one's going to die." He grinned. "Today."

Nichlas followed after the kid, grumbling.

They entered the coroner's office and Matthias made a beeline for the withered woman being rocked in Kenn's arms. Kenn immediately released her into Matthias' care, the kid kneeling before her and grabbing her arms to get her attention.

She was hiccupping, eyes frantically searching Matthias' face. Nichlas watched the kid's expression change from that hardened, terrifying glare to the softest, warmest expression full of dimples, but one, he knew, tinged with a silent promise to destroy whatever had ruined her day.

Her chest rose and fell a little slower as she took in a ragged breath, calming as their gazes remained locked.

Nichlas turned his attention to Kenn, who seemed worried, and then Jan, who was wearing a blank expression, arms folded, attention focused on the opposite wall. Nichlas followed his gaze, landing on what seemed like a fresh hole. "What happened?"

Kenn scowled. "Not even sure. I mean I can guess, but she hasn't really said anything."

Watching Matthias calm the girl until her body stopped vibrating was mesmerizing. One of his hands that had been resting on her shoulder had reached up to caress her cheek, Mia leaning into the touch. Matthias slowly slid to the floor, Nichlas recognizing the act of submission that the kid used when he needed to seem less terrifying.

Mia calmed even further as Nichlas gestured for the other two to find seats so they could discuss next steps. It seemed they were all going to take a hand in protecting Mia's wellbeing.

Matthias' expression hardened again. He took Mia's hands in his as he sat forward, his violet eyes flashing with an anger Nichlas hadn't seen in years. "Now tell me what happened here. No lies."

The woman cringed, tears gathering in her eyes as they flicked to the hole in the wall and then rested on him. "I ... *can't*." Her shoulders began shaking again as she cried in Matthias' hold.

"You weren't playing a game with him, Mia. Were you? You were protecting yourself and that kid."

Nichlas tensed as he watched the exchange between Matthias and Mia, piecing together details of a situation gone wrong. His eyes trailed back to the hole, imagining the scenario, and frowned. If what Matthias was signifying had actually happened here, whoever had assaulted Mia in her own office wasn't just dead. There were going to be four trained killers on his ass. That guy would wish he were dead. Just as soon as Mia stopped crying.

NINE

MIA

Through hiccups, snot, and a bucketful of tears as she snuggled into Matthias' shoulder, Mia tried to swallow the horror bubbling up in her throat. Four men surrounded her, two of whom were Kingsley's new lackeys, and the mysterious one who terrified the shit out of her. Matthias' gentle hand was still rubbing up and down the middle of her back, the other wrapped protectively around her waist. She was almost able to forget this morning's events as she took another deep breath to calm her nerves. His woodsy scent surrounded her, building a cocoon of safety that she never wanted to leave.

But she'd have to. Sooner rather than later.

Especially when she remembered that they all had jobs that didn't include nursing her emotional wounds.

Mia pulled away from Matthias, wiping the back of her hands along her cheeks to catch the snot and tears. "You all have jobs, you need to be—"

Matthias shot her a hard look, matching the three other expressions currently trained on her. "We need to be right here. Tell. Me. What. Happened."

There was so much concern in his words, yet no room to argue, as his violet eyes flashed with silent promises to end Anders' career. Maybe also his life. Mia wasn't sure how to feel about that.

Another hiccup escaped as tears threatened their descent again. "I … it was just a disagreement." A flash of Anders' anger ran through her mind, and she flinched instinctively.

"Disagreements don't end up in holes in the walls and you protecting a kid as you wield a knife." Mia heard the three sharp intakes of breath from the others but didn't dare spare them a glance. They couldn't have known, and it seemed that Matthias hadn't told him.

"Sweetheart," Kenn said and rounded the desk and knelt before her, much the same position that Matthias was sporting. Despite their large stature, the fact that they were below her calmed her somewhat. "He's not going to stop asking."

It was a gentle push, but a push nonetheless. "I don't want anything to happen, okay? I just …" *I live here.* Ratting on Anders was akin to a death sentence in a town as small as Bryxton. They had both grown up in the same town, made the same friends, and went to the same parties. The problem was that when Anders broke her heart, it was *her* problem. *She* was the one ruining everything, not the man who cheated.

Matthias took her hands back into his, the roughness of his touch giving her strange ideas that made her belly squirm with unease. "What are you afraid of?"

If they weren't going to leave without the truth, she had to tell them *something*. "I live here, okay? You guys strolled in for god knows what reason, and when you leave?" Terror pulled at her expression as she thought of all the things Anders would try when her newfound protectors fucked off to the next mission or town or whatever the mysterious one did.

Matthias stared at her, his head tilting slightly as if surveying her reactions to the four of them. "I'm not leaving. Tell me."

In that moment, something changed. The air shifted and she felt herself relax, her shoulders dropping and the tension leaving her body. Now she was just tired, so goddamn tired. "My ex ... he's just emotionally abusive, okay? He scared me and I overreacted." Four growls were ripped from the men surrounding her, her body cringing from the vibrations it sent through her.

Jan stood and she met his deep-brown eyes, flashing with intent to kill. Two fists swung by his hips as his jaw clenched. "Who's the hole in the wall from, then?"

Mia didn't want to answer that. She shifted in her chair uncomfortably, all four men rising to their feet as they slowly closed in on her. She should have felt terrified, her heart beating in her chest, the sound of blood pumping in her ears. Instead, Mia just felt grateful. Grateful that someone cared enough about her well-being to be angry in her stead.

"Mia?" they asked in chorus.

"*Him*," she mumbled out, sinking farther into her chair as exhaustion overwhelmed her. She just wanted the day to be over. Tomorrow would come and she could resume her responsibilities. Now that she knew she was holding the department together, even her job didn't seem as appealing as it had last week. It was no longer a way to escape, was it? Especially not with the information that Kingsley kept telling her to forget, to leave out of the reports altogether.

Matthias leaned forward, teeth bared, when Kenn ripped him back and settled him with a rough jostle to his shoulder. Mia just stared, unable to comprehend the situation. Jan approached. "Has he been violent before?"

"What?" Her attention had moved from Matthias to the mysterious one with his wilting stare. He intrigued her, which meant that he was trouble. They all were, to be honest. He flashed her a tight grin and she squeaked, her cheeks flush with embarrassment. "No. He's ... no. Just *no*. He won't come back here." Additional memories sifted through her head of all the times she almost got hit, times she hid in her room, or locked herself in her office with the music blasting so she didn't have to face her thoughts. All of the times that Anders pleasured himself with her body but left her wanting. All of the times he made her feel like she wasn't good enough. All of the times. ...

The mysterious one ripped her from her thoughts with a firm grip on her jaw. Something about the power they wielded calmed her. She didn't want to think about it. "He will come back. That's what men like them do. They need control. We'll have additional security installed for you. We'll put in a panic button, too, wire it to the sheriff's station so—"

"No!" Mia screamed. Four pairs of eyes again trained on her. Kenn still had his hand on Matthias' chest, the man she knew as the dimpled barista switched out for some feral version with terrifying purple eyes. Jan wasn't much better, but he wasn't actively growling, and the mysterious one just seemed alarmed at her outburst.

Mia nibbled on her lip, wringing her hands together as she surveyed the room, somehow softening as her gaze fell on Matthias. He stilled beneath her stare. *I'm crazy. I have to be.* "Him. Make it call him."

The mysterious one let out a nervous chuckle and nodded, dragging Jan outside as the tension dispersed. Kenn's hand left Matthias' chest and he whispered to him until Matthias' eyes turned back to the beautiful amethyst she had first seen. He nodded a few times before approaching her, promptly sitting back on the floor, and pulling her into his lap without a word.

Mia let out a deep sigh, blinking her eyes a few times before curling into his hold, unsure why she found it comforting. She should have pulled away, asked questions, wondered why their dangerous aura comforted rather terrified her. It didn't matter. His scent and the smell of hazelnut lulled her to sleep. He rocked back and forth slowly, arms tensing around her as he stuffed his face into the crook of her neck. When she heard her front door open and close, signifying that Kenn had left, too, Mia didn't understand why she felt so safe.

These men were *strangers* and had bulldozed into her town and her office. They equaled trouble on the horizon, but for the moment, she was going to enjoy the space and peace that Matthias was offering, because if she stopped lying to herself, she'd realize that she had never felt like this with Anders.

Or anyone else.

TEN

KENN

K enn caught up to the other two, pushing into Matthias' coffee shop. "How fast can you–"

Nichlas had already dragged his bag out from the back, rifling through the electronics he had grabbed before they embarked on this adventure. "On it. I've got some shit here. The rest I can pick up tomorrow." The perks of being undercover meant contacts in every state, sometimes every city, or at the very least someone who could meet him nearby.

Jan chuckled as he set himself up at one of the rounded tables meant for customers. The sign had been turned to "Closed" and the door was locked, which meant they could talk freely. "Do I want to ask how you're picking up this shit already?"

"I had a feeling we'd need it," Nichlas ground out. Mia was a wildflower, a very dangerous one, by the looks of it. Matthias had almost lost himself in there, and the fact that Kenn had left him meant that she meant a lot more to that kid than Nichlas had originally thought. "y'all basically fell all over her the moment we saw her."

Kenn sighed, hopping onto the counter and swiping the coffee pot and a mug. "You don't feel anything toward her?"

Feel anything? Nichlas frowned as he stared at the blond-haired guy, wondering how with all of his boyish charms, he still commanded respect. "She's gorgeous and wounded. All of your types." Silence fell between them as Kenn sipped his coffee obnoxiously loud and Jan rocked back and forth in his chair. "What?"

Kenn's smile fractured, his chest rumbling with silent laughter. "She's also headstrong and resilient. *Your* type."

Kenn wasn't wrong, but it would never work. Nichlas threw him the finger as he continued laying out pieces he'd need to set Mia up with security. "And I've got more scars and skeletons in my closet than all three of you combined. She'll fall in love with you guys and she'll be happy. I haven't seen Matthias smile like that in years. She's dangerous, sure, but she'll be good for him."

"Don't rule yourself out so fucking quickly," Jan offered. He had stopped rocking, his chair balanced on the two back legs, the man's arms stretched and folded behind his head. Nichlas had a mind to kick those legs out from under him.

"What good is it if we all like her?"

Kenn slurped his coffee again, his green eyes dancing with amusement. "Shit, man, it's not a foreign concept."

Nichlas stopped fiddling with the tech and glared at him. "A small-town girl like Mia would never fucking go for something like that." Even as the words fell from his lips, he knew that was a load of shit. Years ago, sharing had been their M.O. It had worked. They were all gone so long that they could never hold a relationship down to save their lives. But when a woman agreed to be shared between them? Someone had always been home, had always made sure she was taken care of, and she had been happy.

Until she decided that she wanted the traditional, one-man, white-picket-fence relationship. Aside from Stacey whom they had been engaged to, these women never lasted longer than a couple of months, wounding his heart just a little more until it shattered when Jocelyn cheated on them with twins who promised her riches and publicity for her clothing line. Each of those women had enjoyed the thrill of a relationship, the kink of sharing four, well-trained men, but that's all it was.

A high.

A high that wore off with enough time.

Sharing a woman was just as heartbreaking as having one at all, which is why Nichlas enjoyed remaining in the shadows during their excursions. It hurt less.

Kenn patted the table, grabbing Nichlas' attention again. "How do you know until you've asked?"

"Fuck you. I'm not asking that poor girl to spread her legs for four guys." Again, another load of shit.

Jan stood up and approached the counter, wiggling his fingers for a mug of that velvety goodness Kenn was currently chugging. "Stop being so crude and get your head out of your ass."

Nichlas grunted and returned to fiddling with his tech. Had he been honest with himself, he would have realized that he had already opened his heart to the coroner. He would have never busted out his FBI grade A tech for someone who was just a passing thought, and yet the idea of sharing her terrified him. They couldn't. Not with her. There were too many wounds and nightmares for Mia to bear between the five of them. Someone like Mia who was still fighting her own demons wouldn't stand a chance.

And yet, Nichlas still wanted her.

They were all fucked. That's just how it was – utterly and truly fucked.

Nichlas focused on the reason he had followed his guys to the sleepy town in the middle of nowhere, knowing that he was going to have to confront Mia sooner or later to see if she found anything suspicious. With the sheriff's office being less than forthcoming, he assumed Mia had more information than she let on. Unfortunately, he had seen how she looked at him.

This was going to be a problem.

ELEVEN

MIA

Mia was still cradled in his arms as she raised her head from a nap she didn't know she had taken. There was a bagel in a decorative bag just in front of her, cinnamon raisin by the smell of it. Her eyes surveyed the man holding her, his resting face too sweet to ignore. The man looked like he battled his own demons but was pure when he slept, with his soft features and boyish haircut. Scars and tattoos wound around his neck and slipped beneath his shirt. Mia wondered how far south they traveled.

No, no bad thoughts.

She squirmed, pressing her thighs together as she continued to observe his relaxed figure, his intensity drawing her in until she was pressing her lips to the edge of his. His arms tensed, his breathing slowed and eyes widened, a darkened purple that seemed to see straight through her. Mia went to climb off his lap, utterly horrified before he drew her into another kiss.

His hand slid up to her cheek, caressing the skin as he tasted her, his tongue lightly running along the seam of her lips. Mia shuddered in his hold, butterflies running amuck in her stomach as she kissed him back. When he pulled away, she profusely apologized through the sensual haze. "I'm sorry. I just–"

He smirked, eyes flashing with amusement as the dimples came back into view. "Don't apologize for that. *Never* apologize for that. I wanted it just as much as you did."

She searched his expression for the anger that was sure to surface, but only understanding met her. It didn't make sense. Anders would have been furious if she had taken something that he hadn't been ready to give. Yes, even a kiss. Touch might have been one of her love languages, but Anders only gave when he wanted to. It was the only time he held her and it was usually rough. "I can't. I just got out of a–"

He nipped at her nose with another kiss before releasing her and helping her stand up. "Mia, calm down." Matthias towered over her as he pulled her flush against his chest, his smile widening as he beamed down at her. "It was just a kiss. Whatever comes of it, we'll deal with it then. But it was a very good kiss, and I hope there are more in my future."

Mia couldn't understand how two very different sides resided in the same man. She knew that he wouldn't hurt her as he held her against him, but she knew how dangerous he could be. She had met men like him over the years, being in the coroner business, but she had never felt attracted to them. It was a bad idea to follow her emotions, especially with Anders and the entire town watching her every move.

These four men told her that they would protect her, but there was only so much of the day that they could be beside her.

She blew out a breath through her nose. "I need to get back to work." She mumbled the words, knowing full well she had no strength to do that.

Matthias growled at her, lifting her chin with a tight grip. She whined in his hold, but he just grinned. "You need to sit down, eat something, and then go home. These bodies will still be waiting for you in the morning." She opened her mouth to throw out yet another excuse, and Matthias took that as an invitation to kiss her again. She didn't fight him, falling into the sensation that was Matthias. He kissed her until she was writhing against him, silently begging for a release she knew she couldn't have.

He pulled away all too soon, handing her the bag and placing one last kiss on her lips before he was gone with three simple commands. "Eat. Go home. Go to sleep."

Mia sighed as the fight left her, overwhelmed by the day's events and the lingering taste of Matthias on her lips. Her cheeks pinked as she scrambled for her bag and stuffed the bagel into it so she could begin her trek home. She slid out the front door and wandered along the back to avoid passing Matthias' shop. She wasn't sure how to deal with all of the attention from the four men.

She let her mind wander as her feet took her down the same path she took every day to return home, knowing her mother would be in the kitchen to ask why she was home so early, or at all. It had been on her list to move out, but somehow it had never materialized. Her feet took her on the scenic route, which consisted of a long dirt road that ran along the border of the town, a pitiful stream gliding alongside it, patches of dust upending its journey.

"Wielding a knife at my husband wasn't really the smartest thing you could do, was it?"

Mia halted mid-step, staring ahead at the body attached to the voice. *Anders' wife?* She fought hard for a name but came up empty, so she just stared. It was rude for this woman to block her path anyway.

"You *know* who I am, right? Why aren't you a little more respectful?"

Mia hardened her stare as much as she could, but the day's events had weakened her resolve. She didn't want to deal with any more surprises, and Anders' wife was the very definition of a surprise. Those two were peas in a pod; Anders might have been more violent, but this woman seemed downright crazy.

"I'm Anders' wife, Natalie. You are not. You are no longer his plaything. You missed out on that chance when you decided to be—"

Mia held up her hand and shook her head. "I get it. I don't know what you've heard or seen, but he's all yours."

"Then why was he at your place this morning? The whole fucking town heard about it before I even woke up. It's been *one* day and you're already—"

Mia scowled, her shoulders falling as she tried to remedy the situation with thoughts of that cinnamon raisin bagel in her bag. "He wanted to make a few things clear. He got the message across. There's no reason for him to—"

"Then I must be crazy considering the rumors talking about how much you want him back that you're using the new barista to make him jealous?"

"Wha-at?" Mia glared at the woman, trying to understand the strange connection between Anders' rage and Matthias showing up at her office. It was true that Bryxton liked to gossip, seeing as how this was the biggest scandal in years. Mia was pretty sure that this was just the woman's attempt at a warning, but it was a pretty stupid one.

It did, however, tell her that starting something with Matthias was a recipe for disaster — something she already knew but was hoping wouldn't be the case. She didn't want Matthias anywhere near Anders' crazy.

"You know exactly what I'm talking about, bitch." *Slap.* "Stay the fuck away from my husband." *Slap.* "And stop trying to make him jealous by selling your pussy to the highest bidder." *Slap.*

Mia held her face, tears streaming down her cheeks as she stared at the woman in disbelief. None of the things out of her mouth were true and yet Mia couldn't help but crawl into herself with the self-loathing Anders had formed over the years.

I didn't, she thought but refused to voice. Instead, she nodded, giving the woman the validation of her confrontation. The woman left with a grunt, Mia continuing on her journey home but without the light spirit Matthias had instilled in her.

Mia raced home and mumbled a greeting before scrambling to her room and hiding under the covers, willing for Tuesday to come so she could start over.

TWELVE

JAN

Jan raised his hand to wave at Mia, but the woman seemed determined to reach her destination. He could have sworn he saw dried tears on her cheeks, but Kenn stopped him from charging toward her for answers.

He let out a deep sigh as he turned back to the sandlands – what Kenn had dubbed them – the sparse vegetation just outside the town where bodies continued to be found before being delivered to Mia's lab. They had been out there for no more than an hour or two, but there had been no clues as to *why* this seemed to be a graveyard.

There was one thing Jan had concluded, though: This wasn't the killing site. Bodies were dumped here. He flipped through a few of the reports he had snapped a picture of on his phone, recognizing similar markings on each of the bodies. Mia had to have drawn that conclusion and passed it off to the sheriff – Kingsley's father – but why hadn't anyone mentioned anything?

Was this why they had been called over?

Terrifying quacking sounds ripped him out of his head as his glare landed on Kenn. The man changed to neighing and then an awful rendition of a goat. "Would you quit being annoying and start helping?" Jan hissed. He fucking loved Kenn like a brother, but the guy was downright insufferable sometimes. Unfortunately, his less than kosher tactics always helped in some odd way or another.

Kenn burst out laughing after trying to roar. "Trying to hear the echoes, man. Everything *always* echoes. But there's nothing around here ... so no echoes. That's why people keep dying or getting dropped off – because *there's nothing around here.* Someone knows that." The man kicked at the gravel, running a hand through his blond hair, his gaze distant.

"What are you saying?"

"I'm saying," Kenn grimaced, "that maybe it's time to really sit Mia down and ask her about her reports. I know you've made the same deduction, big guy. I don't think these are accidental deaths. There's no bridges. Nothing to die from. No wild animals. Just sand. The bodies in Mia's morgue and her reports don't tell the story of well-traveled Jane and John Does. It wasn't like they starved to death out here. Someone's behind this."

"I was afraid of that."

Jan shoved his phone in his back pocket and marched back up the little hill to the main path, wiping his dusty hands on his pants. Kingsley hadn't given them much direction on how to do their job, and their boss hadn't mentioned anything about the body count. He wanted to ask but was pretty sure how that conversation would pan out.

"Boss, what the fuck are we out here for?"

"Something weird is going out there. Figure it out."

"Any clues? Like there's—"

"*Don't ask me. Just figure it out. Close up the case and then get your asses back here. I have another assignment.*"

It was the same thing every time. His boss knew more than he let on but refused to give them any hints, letting them reach their own conclusions. However, this trip had been a lot more rushed, and there was a lot less to work off of than previous jobs.

He gritted his teeth as he started toward the apartment they were renting behind Matthias' coffee shop. Kenn quickly caught up with him. "What's on your mind, big man?"

"I have a feeling we're going to be here for a while."

"So? We've had a few jobs that take a few weeks before we move on."

"Yeah, and I think we'll need it. God, even Nichlas has a job here."

"Wait, what?"

"You didn't notice how quick that man pulled out his security equipment for Mia? That man barely says a word in public and he's already bending over backward for her? Something's up. There's more to this case, and I don't think we're going to find the answers so easily like last time."

"Shit."

"She's obviously gone home for the night, but tomorrow we'll catch her at the office."

"Not Matthias' shop?" Kenn snickered and Jan threw him a disappointed glare. "Oh, come on. We both know who she's going to fall for first – the bad boy with tattoos and dimples that makes a mean cup of coffee. I'd kiss him first, too."

Jan stifled a chuckle. If anyone could break down Mia's walls and get to her heart, it'd be Matthias.

THIRTEEN

NICHLAS

Nichlas glanced up and watched Matthias stroll in, a new twinkle in the man's eyes. "You kissed her. Good for you. She'll be good for you." Matthias froze, unsure of whether to smile or accept the comment before continuing to the counter to clean up the mess Kenn and Jan had left.

He rounded the counter and started another pot for Kenn before glancing in Nichlas' direction. "Us."

Nichlas grunted, sitting back in his chair. He was only missing a camera and an electronic lock to outfit Mia's office with enough security equipment to keep away the crazies. The extra electronic lock would be for her home, because someone like Anders wouldn't stay away from there either.

"Not you, too," Nichlas finally responded.

Matthias managed a shrug as the aroma of hazelnut and chocolate filled the air. "Just you wait." A grin pulled at the edge of his lips as he danced his way around his kitchen.

Nichlas stood, knowing that a happy Matthias wasn't always a good thing. "What are you doing?" His face paled when he realized what Matthias' intentions were. "You can't go after that guy. You heard what she said."

Matthias nodded, pulling cups out of the dishwasher and hanging them on the grid. "I heard her tell me that she didn't want any more trouble in this town because she lives here. I wouldn't do that to her. But to let him think he's gotten away with that? He doesn't deserve that kind of peace." His violet eyes flashed with a thousand plans, including torture and death.

Nichlas rounded the counter, grabbing the kid by his arms and shaking him to his senses. "Fuck. No. You're not planning anything."

The barista shot him a smile that radiated all the evil he held beneath the surface. "Me? Of course not. You on the other hand have a certain gift for staying under the radar. Do some reconnaissance. You know … make him hurt." He smiled wider at the last word before pulling out of Nichlas' hold and continuing to clean the kitchen.

Nichlas wasn't sure what to make of it. Matthias was crazy through and through. He was volatile. But this was the first time the kid was handing over the reins, allowing someone else to fight for what he wanted. In so many words, Matthias had just asked for help.

If that wasn't a sign that Mia meant more than whatever this job was worth, Nichlas wasn't sure what was.

FOURTEEN

NICHLAS

Nichlas headed to Mia's office, intent on installing every security gadget he could find. People like Anders dragged similar idiots along with them. It would only be a matter of time before the guy tried to have someone else do his dirty work. Two feet from the front door, he froze. *Fuck.*

He didn't do feelings. They were a waste of time, and people always got hurt. Mainly him. Yet here he was trying to make sure that Mia was safe and protected. To anyone else, it would look like he was doing Matthias' bidding. But he knew better. Mia meant something to him, too, and soon enough he'd start hoping he meant something to her as well.

He brushed off the idea, the shrill ring of his phone pulling him from his thoughts.

"You said you need more equipment? You've been there a *day*."

"A dead body situation," Nichlas muttered, praying that Cross wouldn't ask too many questions. The guy let out a whoop, entirely too excited by the prospect. Granted, it was the only action he got even after being married for five years. "Nothing that serious. Someone's targeting the coroner." *Lies.*

"She's hot, ain't she?" Nichlas heard Cross's chair creaking, and he could imagine the fucker spinning around in his chair, cradling Mia's picture in his hands. Unfortunately for Nichlas, the statement brought back the image of the first time he'd seen Mia. She had on that peach lace dress at the wedding, those gorgeously tortured doe eyes, terror and heartbreak lurking just beneath the surface. Saving her had been the only thing on his mind before he remembered his mission.

"Sure, not the point. Someone smashed her wall in. She needs protection." *More lies.* Nichlas entered the office with the key he'd been given, scouting out the best places for cameras and then scowling when his eyes landed on the hole in the wall. How terrified had Mia been at that moment?

"Goddamn." The creaking sounds stopped. "All right. I'm sending over what I've got on this Anders Lund guy. Pretty filthy dude. And his wife is worse. Stay away from them."

Nichlas chuckled because they both knew why Nichlas had been sent to Bryxton. He felt his phone vibrate, signifying he now had access to more information about Mia's personal life than he probably should.

"Why him?" Cross asked. Nichlas didn't answer, focusing on entering his credentials to access the file. "Nic! Snoop later. Why him?"

"Rubs me the wrong way." *He tried to hurt Mia.* Nichlas wasn't sure how long he was going to be able to continue lying to himself. He began setting up a camera in the farthest corner, unboxing the grade A equipment with ease. Surveillance was his baby, and fuck if anyone was going to try that shit again.

Cross barked out a seedy laugh. "Already attached to your lady friend, huh?"

"Not everyone thinks with their dick, Cross."

"All right, I'll lay off. Don't get attached to that little place in the middle of nowhere. I've heard they're creating a team and you're first in line."

Nichlas grimaced, knowing that meant going dark for who knew how long, and as much as he loved those missions, they were getting a bit old. "Where to?"

"Dunno. I just know it's deep. Enjoy your freedom, man."

Nichlas sighed, hanging up the call and opening the file, his expression souring as he settled into a chair and began skimming the file. Anders wasn't just filthy, his past was downright revolting. The man had a rap sheet that most criminals would blush at – everything from tax evasion to swindling money from business partners.

"How the fuck has no one figured this shit out?" Nichlas mumbled to himself. The guy had been in jail a few times for a few months in the past ten years, but in a small town like this, information like that should have spread like wildfire. Instead, this guy was the golden boy who could do no wrong. Nichlas was ten seconds away from calling Cross back to yell at him why they weren't rounding the guy up when the big reveal showed up a few seconds later with a *Thought you might like this* text from Cross.

What the actual fuck?

Anders was working with the FBI. In exchange for a clean record, he agreed to spy on his business counterparts. Anders was small fry in the big picture of things, but that didn't lighten any of his more recent transgressions.

Nichlas hurriedly dialed Cross back, "You better have a good motherfucking—"

"Calm your tits. There's only one reason you've been sent there. Sure, something fishy is going on over there with all those dead bodies, and the sheriff is less than forthcoming. Figure it out if you like but, Nichlas? That's not why you got dropped over there. Your mission should you choose to accept it, is Anders."

"Cross …"

"Sorry, I've always wanted to say that." He cleared his throat. "Anders has been with the agency for a year, but he hasn't produced any reliable information. We need to know what's going on. Cozy up to him. Figure him out. Be *cordial.*"

Nichlas hung up and chucked the device against the wall, surprised when it didn't break. Be cordial with the one man he wanted to tear to shreds? And how would that work exactly? He couldn't even tell his brothers what was going on. Mia would see it as a betrayal, and he wouldn't even be able to explain. Nichlas could already see the disappointment in her eyes when she caught him with her ex. The fact that it pained him told him that Mia already meant more than just the job to him too.

FIFTEEN

MIA

*C**link.*

Mia's eyes fluttered open, unsure if she was still dreaming. Another clink sounded against her window, drawing her out of bed to find the offending sound. She rubbed her eyes, shoving the glass pane upward only to see Matthias with a wild grin, poised with a handful of pebbles at the ready.

"What are you doing here?" she hissed.

"Check your phone." His grin widened, those purple eyes of his dancing with happiness she couldn't possibly match this early in the morning.

Mia clamored back to her nightstand for her cell, pressing the power button several times. Returning to the window, she shook the black screen in the dim light. "It's dead."

"Apparently a body was found." He was nearly bouncing out of his skin as he spoke, but the only energy she had she was using to stand. "The guys told me and I offered to come wake you up. I brought coffee. Get dressed. The call sounded urgent."

Why Kenn and Jan were sharing details with Matthias was beyond her. She waved him off, shutting her window, and grumbling how she wasn't a medical examiner. At two in the morning, she could have used a few more hours of sleep to avoid thinking about Natalie's threats.

Traveling to the scene wasn't her thing. It hadn't been her father's thing, either, but Kingsley was determined to cut costs any way he could. Without all the proper training as a crime scene tech, the only thing she would be doing is contaminating the crime scene. But if that's what the sheriff wanted, that's what he was going to get.

Mia shoved herself into the closest pair of jeans and a black top that was just a little too tight for her liking. It covered everything but the peach lace bra that showed through at different angles under the moonlight. Peach had been Anders' favorite color. She had filled her entire wardrobe with it at one point until the color rubbed off on her and she realized that it suited her skin tone. It still reminded her of him, but she chose to wear it for different reasons.

With no time for makeup or any decent way to cover the growing bruise from Natalie's abuse, she donned a baseball cap and rushed outside to meet Matthias. He shoved a cup in her direction, caramel and cinnamon reaching her nose. "This one's different."

He grinned, those dimples making an appearance again. "I'm experimenting."

She gripped the cup, taking a swig before trying to speak. The flavors melted on her tongue, a moan threatening to release itself into the darkness. "It's delicious, but yesterday … we can't … I'm just not ready." Mia knew those were all lies. She was terrified of what Anders and Natalie would do if she tried to move on.

They had already shown her what they were capable of. She met Matthias' gaze, hoping that he could see the seriousness in her expression.

"No worries." Pain flickered across his face. "I'll just walk you to the scene."

"I mean it. I'm not–"

Matthias grunted, cutting her off. "I refuse to let you walk there knowing Anders is still lurking around, all right? Please. For my sanity. Let me do this." His words trailed off, and an emotion she hadn't seen before settled into his features. This wasn't the first time something like this had happened, and by the way his jaw tensed, it hadn't ended well.

Mia nodded, letting him lead the way as they fell into a silent rhythm. She sipped at her coffee, the flavors warming her from the inside. She could see herself with Matthias, the world he could offer her – but not with the threat of her ex looming around. She tugged her hat lower and avoided Matthias' silent questions as they continued to walk. The scene was less than a mile from her house, just at the edge of town. This was a different spot than usual, which could signify a few things, none of which she wanted to think about this early in the morning.

Kingsley strolled up to her, dressed in his complete uniform, scowling at her coffee cup. "I need that report by today." Mia could feel Matthias tense beside her, one of his hands resting on the small of her back. If it had been any other situation, she would have shied away from his touch, but it seemed like it was the only thing keeping him from raging out.

"Today?" Mia stared at the body a few feet away. It looked dead from here. That was about all she could tell. She wasn't an investigator, so anything sitting at the crime scene meant nothing to her. She knew how to read a body in the silence and comfort of her lab. Out here in the dark, she was just as clueless as the next person. "I don't even know who that is. Or how he died. Things take time."

"Well, you've got all day."

Mia thought about giving in, the way she always did, but she was getting fed up with everyone taking advantage of her. She had already lost her love life. She wasn't going to lose her work life as well. "No."

"No?" He stepped closer till she could feel his hot breath against her cheek. She flinched but stood her ground, the warmth from Matthias' hand giving her the strength she needed. "Look, Mialopolus, we don't need your job. I think you know that. Get it done."

That's it. I've had enough. Mia's father had built the coroner's office into a respectable position, despite what everyone in town thought. She would not be disrespected because a little shit had become the sheriff. "And you know you're full of shit. Those case files are just my reports. I tell you when the report is done, and it won't be today."

Tension built between them as Mia stood her ground. Kingsley huffed and threw his shoulders back before walking off. "First thing tomorrow, Mia."

"I will bring it over when it's finished."

"Use the newbies. *Get it done.*"

Jan and Kenn joined her, glaring after Kingsley before giving her their full attention. Silence dragged on as they stared, Kenn finally slipping off her hat. There was no use in hiding any longer as their expressions darkened. "What happened to your face?" Kenn asked, his fingers running along the outside of her bruise.

"Don't worry about it." She yanked her hat from his grip and set it back on her head. "I have a job to do."

Strong arms kept her from moving, Jan tightening his hold around her waist. Kenn removed her hat again, fingers grazing over the spot once more. She winced involuntarily, unable to meet their eyes. These alpha men were too much for her to handle, and this early in the morning, she just wanted to crawl back into bed and avoid the world.

Matthias stood off to the side, those violent purple eyes glowing with anger again. Kenn glared at her. "I asked you what happened."

"Was it him?" Jan asked from behind her, slowly releasing her when he realized she wasn't going to run.

Mia slapped his hands away, reaching for her hat. She felt the tears begging to let loose, but she couldn't let them see her break down a second time. "No. Can you please—"

"Mia."

She looked at Matthias approaching her, his jaw set. Her bottom lip trembled as she gave in to his piercing stare. "It wasn't him! It wasn't him. I *promise*. I'm not lying. It wasn't him."

Mia navigated her way to the van as she tried to calm her emotions, knowing that they were all going to show up at her office sooner or later. They had looked murderous when she told them Anders had threatened her but hadn't touched her. Mia wasn't sure what would happen if she told them about Natalie. She wasn't planning on finding out.

SIXTEEN

MATTHIAS

Matthias smiled as best he could while Nichlas helped fill orders. They seemed an odd fit for such a small cafe, their large statures out of place in the quiet town. He knew that Nichlas was only sticking around the cafe to keep him out of trouble after he stormed back this morning, grumbling about Mia's bruised face. He needed to bake and brew to avoid doing something he'd regret. Anders had it coming as well as whatever bastard had roughed up that gorgeous face of hers and left her with that haunted expression.

A group of young women covered in too much makeup to be healthy, golds and silvers adorning every wrist and finger available, entered his cafe. Giggles poured into his space as they made their way to the counter, one of the women taking the lead. She swiped her nearly white-blond hair over her shoulder with an exaggerated flip of her fingers, throwing him some version of what she obviously thought was a sultry smile.

It was not.

"Heard the coffee is all the rage. Give us a few cups, will you? We'll be sitting over there." She pointed to a table near the entrance, as if table service was a given. Matthias just nodded, unable to find the effort to fight her.

Nichlas came up behind him. "You don't do table service."

He shrugged, grabbing last week's flavor for their order. They didn't deserve the same delicacy he had offered Mia this morning. "Nope. But they look like a bunch of bitches, so arguing won't do me any good." He prided himself on his self-control as he delivered the mugs to their table a few minutes later. Matthias mentally patted himself on the back that he hadn't even let his smile slip.

They all sipped, giggling again as they cooed over the taste also. Matthias expected it, but that didn't mean he was enjoying the way they were falling all over him. He had other things to attend to, things that didn't involve the annoyance they brought to his shop.

"This is delicious. Sit with us." The main one fluttered her lashes, trying to lure him in, but after a lifetime of fake women and military experience that would make war junkies blush, it just didn't do anything for him. Not to mention that Matthias was currently vying for Mia's attention, and she had a little more … substance to her personality.

"I'm working."

Her hand shot out to graze his, Matthias biting his tongue to keep from lashing out at her. "Surely, you're not too busy to sit, especially when you've got enough time for that skank across the street."

"She's not a skank," Matthias replied hastily.

"She dumped her fiancé and then fell into your lap. She's got guys wrapped around her finger until they figure out who she is. Always ending up single." The other women snickered, slurping at their mugs as they left rings of red and purple lipstick along the top. Matthias wanted to rip them from their seats and dump them outside. Such disrespectful people didn't deserve his delicacies.

He clenched his fists, hiding them behind his back before taking a deep breath and letting out the one sentence that had been swirling around in his head for the past five minutes. "You're married." The look on the head bitch's face was priceless. *We're too old for high school.* And yet, it was the easiest tactic in the book to use.

She sputtered, setting her mug down a little too hard so that the muddy liquid splashed onto the table. "Did you just call me a bitch?"

"*Yes.*"

Enough to offend her and her posse, she shot to her feet, yanking the others to abandon their coffee. "I think I'll find my coffee elsewhere. The service is a bit lackluster. If you know what's good for you, stay away from the coroner."

His brows furrowed as he tried to understand why everyone had it out for the sweet girl across the street. Was there some sinister secret he hadn't come across? Had she killed people? Had she actually been the one to cheat on Anders? Was she the *other woman?* He slowly reeled in his thoughts, diverting his attention from the senseless questions. Mia wasn't like that. She couldn't be. "Is there something wrong with her, or are you just so obsessed that you can't see that you're just a bitch?"

The woman's face scrunched up in childish anger, her mouth propped open to lash out. He knew from experience that his tendency to fight first and ask questions later was going to bring on unwanted trouble, but the more he thought about it, the more everything seemed to fall into place.

"You're that fucker's wife."

A garbled sound fell from her lips. "Anders is my *husband*, a man that the skank across the street lost out on because of who she is. You'd do well to remember that when she tries to climb into your lap for comfort or whatever the fuck a whore does."

Matthias lurched forward, a spiel of hate at the ready when Nichlas placed a firm hand on the back of his neck and dragged him backward. Matthias fell silent as the women laughed, a few of the other patrons scurrying to pack up to avoid any more unpleasantness. He focused on his breathing, enjoying the silence until his gaze fell on the table, the wasted coffee sitting idle in the mugs. *A fucking waste.*

"Who pissed in your cheerios?" Nichlas asked, releasing his hold. Matthias didn't want to answer, stalking back to the other side of the counter. Mia had said she wasn't ready, that it wouldn't work, but the more he saw, he realized it wasn't because of *her*. It was because of everyone else around her and how hard they judged her every move.

He snarled as he thought of the disrespect Anders' wife had shown not just him or his coffee but the woman he was falling for. If he was honest with himself, he had already fallen.

"Anders' wife," Matthias finally spit out, his hands finding dishes to load up the washer. "*That* bitch pissed in my cheerios." Nichlas knew better than to touch him again, but he blocked his exit from the kitchen to keep Matthias from embarking on any deadly adventures. If Anders had something coming before, well, it was much worse now. Matthias didn't hit women. It wasn't going to change now, which meant that Anders was going to take double the pounding.

SEVENTEEN

MIA

Mia watched as a technician rolled the body into her lab, handed her a clipboard to sign, and then left her to the silence that death brought. She stared at the unidentified male on her favorite metal slab, wondering if his body would show the same signs as the others. Another one so soon meant that a lone killer – her theory – was ramping up his kills, or there were multiple killers. And because no one listened to her, there would be more victims before the suspect or suspects were caught.

She slammed her hand down on the slab, the body rocking slightly as the vibrations ran beneath it. "This is fucking bullshit."

"Yes, it is." Mia froze at the familiar voice, turning around to see Jan's hardened expression as he pushed forward. She stepped back to avoid his reach, stopped by Kenn, whose hands landed on her shoulders. *Where the fuck had he come from?*

"What do you want?" she said through her teeth, realizing too late that her hat had been discarded somewhere in her office.

Jan tsked. "The truth, Mia. Who hurt you?" His eyes focused on the tender flesh below her eye, her fingers grazing the skin as she tried not to reveal her emotions.

Her heart swooned at the fact that they *cared*, but they were going to get hurt – case or not. She also didn't feel like fighting them anymore. "It was a slap," she mumbled.

"Go on."

Mia hated this part, laying out past events and the feelings she had experienced. "From Natalie." They looked confused. "Anders' wife. She thinks I still have feelings for him, which is why he was here. The whole town is talking, and I don't usually care what they say, but he humiliated me in front of everyone I know. It hurts." She didn't mention the fact that she was pretty sure her mother didn't even believe her. Her mother absolutely loved Anders.

"That doesn't seem like everything, sweetheart," Kenn purred in her ear, sending shivers down her back.

Mia knew she needed to step away from these dangerous men, but something about their aura felt safe. If she would stop lying to herself, she would have realized that it wasn't just safety she was drawing from their attention but comfort. A comfort Anders had never once offered her. "She said that I was only hanging around you – Matthias – to make Anders jealous. But that's not it – I didn't – I mean, we kissed – but it's over now – I didn't …" Her words tumbled over each other as she wrung her hands and avoided their gaze.

Jan stepped closer, inches from her as the heat in the room rose several degrees. "Relax, angel. Why's it over?"

"It can't happen. I don't want to drag him into this shit."

"He's a big boy, Mia," Kenn purred again from behind her. They stepped closer, cautiously, pressed against her until she was encased by the two men on either side. Kenn's hands fell to her waist, Jan's cupping her cheeks as he leaned in.

Her breath hitched in her throat as her body tensed, warmth flooding her senses. "What are you doing to me?" she whispered.

They both chuckled, Jan's thumb grazing over her bruise. "You'll have to be more specific, Mia." A wild grin spread across his lips as his head dipped a little lower.

"I – you came in here with all that bravado, trying to save me, those smiles – and you're dangerous. Even the mysterious one." Her cheeks colored with embarrassment, Kenn's chest rumbling with silent laughter at her description of their fourth.

"Nichlas?"

Jan leaned an inch closer till their lips were nearly touching. "Tell me I can kiss you, Mia."

"I – no, Matthias." Mia stared at the man before her, horrified. How could he even think – no she wasn't with Matthias. None of this mattered. In the long run, she couldn't have any of them. They weren't for her. They were only in town for a little while before they would leave her to deal with the mess they had created and the wrath their presence had temporarily staved off.

Kenn nipped at her neck, his fingers slowly squeezing into her hips until she was arching against Jan's chest for more. "We're all grownups, Mia. Besides, if Matthias wanted, all he'd have to do is look at the cameras we installed in here. You were the one that wanted the screens over there." A shiver ran through her as she pressed her thighs together. The thought of him watching them brought a different kind of heat to the situation. "You like that, don't you?"

Jan let out a hearty chuckle. "You like the thought of Matthias watching you as you're with us, as we hold you and kiss you and–"

"We don't know each other."

"Mia – you're stalling."

Mia let out a little moan, nodding frantically as they dove in with kisses and light touches, drawing her in with their sensual mood. She felt their growing arousals pressing against her stomach and back, daring her to try something a little riskier. Jan sucked at her bottom lip, asking for entrance as Kenn took what he wanted, those devilish hands sliding upwards to cup her breasts.

Everything about their touch was foreign, the heat incomparable to anything Anders have ever given her. Passion and desire erupted between them as she kissed Jan back until that pesky little woman bound into her head, reminding her of the terror waiting for her just outside her office.

"You know exactly what I'm talking about, bitch." **Slap**. *"Stay the fuck away from my husband."* **Slap**. *"And stop trying to make him jealous by selling your pussy to the highest bidder."* **Slap**.

Mia jerked away from their touch, shielding her bruise with her hand as she frantically tried to catch her breath and distance herself from them. Startled, they hadn't moved, eyes still full of desire. "God, I can't ... fuck ... I'm not – *no.*" They didn't approach as their hands dropped to their sides, expressions morphing into worry. This was never going to end well. Mia wasn't sure why she had even started.

EIGHTEEN

MIA

After taming the horror in her expression, Mia shoved the detectives onto the street, flaming a bright pink when her gaze met Quinn's. His hand was poised inches from the knob, a sheepish smile plastered on his face as Kenn and Jan tumbled onto the sidewalk, a little flustered and less than pleased with themselves. She didn't address the disheveled state of her shirt or the blush on her cheeks as she hastened her step back into the lab.

"That good, huh?"

"Nothing happened."

Quinn hummed, and Mia stood in front of the newest body, observing a few cuts along the torso. She could feel her intern's curiosity, but he didn't ask any questions, instead flitting around the lab to restock and prepare for work that would show up later in the week.

Her attention zoned in on the neck and wrists of the lifeless form in front of her, a frown tugging at her lips. *Not possible.* She didn't want to believe that there was yet another connection, a growing assumption that all of these "suicides" weren't as cut and dry as they seemed. Quinn peeked over her shoulder, Mia resisting the urge to scream.

"I've seen those before." He rushed over to the metal wall, yanking open one of the casket doors and sliding out a Jane Doe. He held up a wrist, dangling the stiff limb so that she could see it from across the lab. Her shoulders drooped, a heavy sigh permeating the cold lab air. "Document it!" He squealed, rushing back over to her side, and then grunting at her less than excited expression.

Mia headed for her desk, shaking her head. "I can't." She returned with a camera and snapped a few pictures. "Kingsley – the sheriff – will just have me redo the report. You know that." However, Mia wasn't stupid. She had her own files stashed away in a drawer at the back of the lab, documenting all of her findings and connections. At one point it had been spread across the wall until Kingsley's father had stormed in and demanded her to take it down.

She revealed her stash, Quinn gasping at the sheer amount of work she had stored in her hideout. His fingers fumbled through the pictures and returned reports. "No fucking way. What are you going to do? Someone's going around and killing people and they're just ignoring it?" He stomped his foot like a child, bringing a smile to her face.

"There's nothing we *can* do. No one believes me. No one wants to talk about it." Mia managed a small shrug as she closed the drawer and returned to the body, trying to figure out how she would write up some elaborate backstory for this John Doe.

Quinn saddled up beside her, wiggling his eyebrows. "Talk to those fancy-ass detectives."

"I ... don't want to talk to them." Her cheeks heated as she remembered their hands on her body. She shook away the memory and tried to focus.

The kid burst out laughing, "Why? Because they're all alphas that look like they could tame your sass?" Mia threw him an embarrassed look. "What?! It's true." Mia didn't acknowledge it, but Quinn wasn't wrong. All four of them reminded her of the passion she had wanted with Anders, the attention that she craved from a partner, the respect she felt like she deserved.

All four of them could offer that, but she wasn't going to go down that path. She couldn't. Even as attracted as she was to each of them, yes, even Nichlas. Her gaze fell to the body once again, fingers itching toward the one part of the body that would cement her fears. She pinched at the neck, wincing as the small pinprick came into view. *Just like the others. Fuck.*

Quinn shook her out of her thoughts as he headed toward the front door. "I'm going to get some coffee." Mia didn't acknowledge his exit, knowing full well that that kid wasn't going over there *just* to get coffee. But without any reason to tell him not to go, she simply waited until she heard the door click, and then grabbed the remote to her father's ancient boombox and turned it on to the first rock station she could find. And then she turned it to an unbearably loud level, chucked her shoes in the corner, and let her shoulders fall.

No one was coming anyway, and she needed to destress.

Besides, the dead didn't judge.

NINETEEN

KENN

Kenn tried to mask his emotions by inhaling his coffee, but three cups in he realized the only thing he was accomplishing was a caffeine high. His leg bounced erratically under the table as he pored through the files they had removed from the office. The only reason they had free reign to work from Matthias' shop was the fact that Kingsley hated everything they represented.

They were outside help called in by higher authorities and didn't answer to his command. And they stood behind Mia rather than the lackluster sheriff's office.

Running through yet another report, he could tell details were missing. With the two bodies he had seen, Kenn knew that Mia was holding out on the reports. He just needed to figure out why.

Jan shuffled into the seat next to him, pushing another cup at him. Kenn raised an eyebrow, unsure why the "all brawn, no brain" was serving him. His dark eyes flashed with annoyance. "Matthias said he tried a new mixture of flavors. Asked me to try it, but I'm shit with this stuff, so it's on you," Jan said and then added: "I'll regret all that caffeine you're pouring down your throat later. Right now, I just need you to appease Matthias."

Kenn glanced back at their resident little brother, on whose face a dark expression lurked, those gorgeous dimples reappearing with every customer and then disappearing almost as fast. "What's up with his moody ass?" Without even asking though, Kenn knew. Mia had gotten to all of them and seeing that bruise under her eye this morning had set them off, Matthias more than anyone.

Matthias prided himself on the protection he offered, the love he freely gave, and the fear he could instill. But when it wasn't enough? They got the crazed version of a man whose nightmares made horror movies look like child's play. The little piece Mia had seen was nothing compared to the monster Matthias was constantly trying to hold back.

"These reports are shit. We have to go back and ask—"

Jan shook his head. "Not now, we can't. Not after … that."

A long, exasperated sigh fell from Kenn's lips. "Goddamnit. I can tell she wants it, you know? That she wants to give in and yet … it's like she's been groomed to think she owes everyone else her image."

"We're still not going to go over there and ask her. Give it some time."

Kenn winced at the memory of the horror on her face as she pushed them away. It was like Anders' will controlling her from afar, he thought. He sipped at his new coffee, nose scrunching up at the odd taste. *Orange?* He sipped again, rolling the flavors on his tongue as a mixture of nutty orange and vanilla swished around his mouth.

"So?" Matthias stood beside them, that usual inquisitive smile gone.

"It's … different? To be honest, it's a lot. I'm sure someone will enjoy it but …" He sipped again. "It's growing on me."

Matthias sported a dark smile. "Leftovers from two different pots. I'll have to put it out sometime." Kenn scowled and Jan snorted. A young kid walked in, Matthias' look sobering immediately and melting into recognition. "How is she?"

TWENTY

MATTHIAS

Matthias could see the confusion in his brothers' faces. "He works with her," he said and gestured for the kid to come closer, trying to let go of the anger coursing through him. "How is she?" Matthias asked again.

Quinn shuddered, a timid expression settling on his face. "Not great? I think she's just a little overwhelmed. I've never seen her this shaken before, but with everything and then the murders and then … shit." He bit his lip, his gaze traveling between the three of them before dipping his head. "I just came in for some coffee." Matthias could see through the bullshit excuse, but in his current state, coherent sentences were a lot harder to form than he had hoped.

Jan and Kenn pushed to their feet, sounds of scraping wood deafening in the tense silence. "What murders?" Kenn asked, leaning forward. His green eyes flashed with a deadly intrigue

Matthias hadn't seen in months. With their combined bulk, Quinn seemed so much smaller, trapped by their semi-circle.

Quinn took a step back, wide-eyed, hands thrown up in defeat. "I ... I can't say anything," he stuttered. "I ... Mia told me we can't make conclusions. That's for the investigators." He let out a little squeal when Jan grunted, Kenn taking up the reins.

"And we're investigating," Jan said and nodded toward Quinn, gesturing for him to spill the rest of whatever the hell Mia had figured out.

The kid wrung his hands together, eyes flitting between the three of them before words began tumbling out of his mouth. They drank in everything: the endless Jane and John Does, the reports, the pushback from the sheriff's office and the constant verbal abuse Mia suffered from Anders.

Matthias felt the anger simmering in his chest, begging to be let out, his expression darkening with every word Quinn said. Kenn placed a gentle hand on Matthias' shoulder, squeezing ever so slightly to bring him back to the present. "Kid says he came for a coffee. Matty, you're up."

He managed a small smile before stalking back to the counter to procure two cups, the second one for Mia. After everything Quinn had said, god knows the woman could use it, and for selfish reasons, Matthias wondered if she'd think of him while she drank it. Quinn opened his mouth to protest when Matthias refused his money, shaking his head. Kenn came to the rescue with a full sentence as they sent him back across the street. "You're bringing us information. The least we can do is give you coffee."

The kid's face turned the color of a tomato as he rushed back to Mia's office, a steaming cup of coffee in each hand. Matthias glared at his brothers, wondering what they were going to do with the information. Scratch that, how *fast* they were going to do something with the information. He wasn't sure how much longer he could play the reformed Army man who just made coffee every morning.

TWENTY-ONE

NICHLAS

Nichlas gritted his teeth as he answered Cross' call, knowing exactly which words were going to come out of that man's mouth.

"Your coroner *is* hot. Go for it."

"And you know why I won't." Between the nightmares, the missions he was constantly on, and the baggage he was dragging behind him, Nichlas would never subject a woman as sweet as Mia to his shit. Let alone the fact that she was dealing with her own demons, which reminded him of the one task that he was dreading.

Cross' crass voice filtered through the speaker again. "Yeah, yeah, keep protecting that fragile heart of yours while you saddle her up with all this high-grade tech." Nichlas tuned him out as he made his way to Mia's office, knowing full well that every excuse he was throwing out was bullshit. He liked the woman well enough, but this sharing thing that his brothers had set their mind to wouldn't work.

It just couldn't.

Mostly because he was always the one who ended up with the broken heart or the short end of the stick. The women never fancied his dark aura, his brooding stares, and his rough way of love. He couldn't be as lighthearted as Kenn, as put together as Jan, or pull off the boyish charm that Matthias embodied.

His love was intense, and there were no two ways about it. Mia didn't need that in her life. It wouldn't work.

Just keep telling yourself that.

He wondered why he hadn't just called her when Nichlas pushed into Mia's office, and found her twirling around in her lab. Her hair slapped against her shoulders and face, that pained expression he had first seen at the wedding back, her delicate feet bare as they glided across the tiles. A tight smile adorned her lips as she fell into the music, her hips swaying in a way that made his blood travel south.

He fought the urge to adjust himself, Mia's phone clattering to the ground when her eyes landed on him lurking just inside the door. The music was silenced, an unsettling tension growing as they stared at each other. But while she seemed mortified, Nichlas couldn't help but crack a smile as she scampered into the office area.

"You always dance with the dead?" he jested.

"They don't judge," she spit back, nose scrunching up in a way that made his nerves soften. Goddamn, this woman wasn't going to make it easy on him, was she?

He was tempted to call Cross and tell him that he was aborting the mission, that he couldn't possibly see the woman in front of him look at him with the same expression she reserved for her ex. But Nichlas had told himself that he wasn't going to hand over his heart, so it wouldn't matter.

And yet, somehow, it still felt like he was betraying her.

TWENTY-TWO

MIA

Mia tried to calm her emotions as Nichlas began explaining the tech he had installed in her office and lab. The shivers running down her back weren't just from his threatening aura, even if it was more protective than murderous. Her gaze drifted more than once to his hands, the pure strength as the veins shifted and moved beneath the skin heating her from the inside out.

He stepped back after explaining the door lock, eyeing her with an amused expression as if he had caught onto the fact that she wasn't as focused on the tech as she was supposed to be. "Any of this doesn't work, ask Matthias."

She frowned, staring at the door and then at the mysterious fourth man who had arrived in her town a few days ago. "Why not you? You installed it." His eyes flashed again, the way they had been doing since he had walked into her office. Amusement? Interest? Annoyance? Mia couldn't place it, but every time it happened, her heart skipped a beat.

"You're terrified of me," he said. He wasn't wrong, but he wasn't right either. She was terrified of what he was capable of doing. But Mia was pretty sure he'd never hurt her.

She shrugged, heading back to her desk. "You're all dangerous. You all scare me. That doesn't mean I'm stupid. You installed it, so you'd know it works."

Nichlas gave her a nod. "Great. That's settled. Now why—"

A shriek left her as Jan and Kenn slipped through the door. Her eyes flitted between the new arrivals and Nichlas, waiting for an answer until Quinn pushed around them with a cup of coffee in his hands.

The kid shoved it into hers and Mia immediately hid behind her desk when Kenn and Jan's eyes fell to her bare feet, something she had forgotten about. "You're just a little too comfortable around the de—"

Quinn grunted, "They don't judge! Sorry for shouting." Mia dared herself to sip from the drink, swallowing down the moan threatening to emerge. They were all on edge after yesterday, which was understandable, but the constant gatherings in her office were starting to ramp up her anxiety.

Kenn took a seat, gesturing for the others to do the same. "We have a few questions about the case." Mia gripped her cup a little tighter, bracing herself for whatever judgment they were going to bestow upon her. Kingsley's father was usually dismissive. Kingsley shouted. They … well, Mia wasn't sure what they were going to do.

Nichlas leaned forward from his perch on the edge of her desk. "I'm curious, too." When Kenn seemed confused, Nichlas clarified. "I know you figured out why I'm here." Mia tried to decipher the reaction between the men, not understanding the meaning behind the words but realizing that Nichlas was telling a half-truth. Something about his cryptic sentence was off.

With these three men in her small space, she couldn't stop feeling the pressure of her job beating down on her. Sitting before her were two men she had kissed just an hour ago and another man she had thought about in ways that weren't appropriate. Heat bloomed in her core, even as she tried to fight it. Their attention was more than she had had in years. She trembled and they tensed, unsure of how to proceed.

Quinn slapped the table, stealing their attention. "She's overwhelmed. Back up, you alpha-holes!" Mia bit her lip, failing at reining in a giggle as the three men settled in their chairs. For a nineteen-year-old, he was pretty good at reading the room. It helped that he was essentially the overprotective little brother she had never had.

"Kingsley won't let me put it in the report." Mia refrained from talking about the man's father, as it wouldn't do any good now. She had put a complaint in with the main office in the city and they had told her they were looking into it. But that had been over six months ago and nothing had changed. "The last dozen or so bodies, there's been glaring similarities. And some of them have like this pinprick on the neck."

"Mia, in your professional opinion, what's going on?"

She didn't answer. She had been told so many times to just write up the report, paint a story, and make sure that no one would return to ask questions.

"Mia?"

"The murders are connected," she mumbled. Nichlas raised an eyebrow. "There's only one killer."

"And how did you get to that conclusion?"

"There's nowhere to die out here." Her shoulders sagged as she headed for the front door, Quinn begging the men not to follow her.

TWENTY-THREE

MIA

A sigh tumbled from her as she walked smack dab into a chiseled chest she had memorized from being tucked into it once. *I really need to get my act together.* Two strong hands caught her by the waist, jolting her from her chaotic thoughts. She pushed against Matthias' chest, not sure if she wanted him to let go or pull her closer.

"Would you all just leave me alone?" *I don't mean that.* He didn't let go immediately, Mia shimmying from his grasp on her own. "Don't touch me. Then I'll …" Her face heated as her words trailed off.

Matthias smirked, those devilish purple eyes heating with her unspoken desires. "Then you'll *what?*" *Then I'll want you.* She didn't have to say anything. He already knew. "Is that so bad, Mia?" A few fingers caressed her cheek, lightly brushing over her bruise. She refused to meet his eyes, not wanting to see the pain and anger from something he could do nothing about. Mia had asked that these four men do nothing about the assault, but she could see revenge brimming just beneath the surface. Her words were merely an obstacle holding back the beasts within. It was only a matter of time before things fell apart.

"*Please*," Mia whispered. She trembled as his fingers moved to her jaw and then under her chin, pulling her gaze to his. Her lips fell open at the gesture, her back arching into the touch against her will. She wanted to give in so fucking bad.

"I'm not here to push you, baby girl." Her stomach flipped at the pet name, but she didn't react.

"You're all hovering like vultures, waiting for me to give in. But I can't. This is my livelihood and you're just here for—"

Those damn fingers began moving again, his entire hand settling at the base of her neck while his fingers lightly gripped it. A flash of desire moved through his expression, and she willed herself not to react to his movements. Mia bit back the whine sitting at the edge of her tongue. Goddamn, her panties were *soaked*.

"I'm not going to let you get pushed around, Mia. I can't do that."

There was no lie in his words as much as she wanted them to be. She was desperately trying to find a reason that would tell her brain she couldn't pursue these men, but she kept failing. They kept telling her they'd protect her and she kept telling herself it wouldn't be enough.

She opened her mouth to respond, but Matthias just shook his head. "Don't belittle yourself like that, Mia. I don't like it." A command, not a suggestion. This man knew what he wanted. "I understand this isn't the opportune time. I won't push you. But *that*." His hand moved from her neck and brushed against her bruise. "If that happens again, I'll have to do something about it."

"What?" Mia hissed at him, stepping back into her office when she caught one of the other shop owners shooting her a dirty look. No doubt Matthias' close proximity would be spread all over town in the next few hours. The other three men were still huddled in her office, Quinn in the lab working on one of the cases. "What are you all still doing here? No, that doesn't matter. What are you going to do with the information I gave you?"

They all tensed, as if her words had any power, their full attention falling on her again and then her feet. Mia knew she was just a little too comfortable in her own space, but these men made her flustered. She almost took off down the street without shoes. *That* would have been the talk of the town.

"We're going to figure out what's going on," Jan responded.

"Kingsley is going to have my ass," Mia whined, thinking of all the ridiculous names Kingsley would call her before reprimanding her and then trying to get her to go out to dinner with him. She hadn't mentioned that part of their relationship to these four, not that it was any of their business. Kingsley was the embodiment of every little boy who thought tugging on a girl's pigtails would have them falling over their feet to confess. As an adult, his go-tos were name-calling, degrading, and trapping her into metaphorical corners until she gave in.

The advances had waned when she found Anders, but the fact that he was calling her Mialopolus again? Not a great sign.

Kenn playfully nudged her arm, bringing her back again. The fact that they noticed when she crawled into her head was embarrassing. "Tough cookies, kitten. We work for him. Makes sense we'd find out." *Another pet name?* She couldn't hide the heat rising to her cheeks as she wrung her hands together. She *really* fucking liked it, too. Sensual images ran through her head which she quickly fought to shove down deep in her conscience. *Why the fuck am I thinking about this?*

Because you haven't been satisfied for years. No, no, Anders doesn't fucking count.

And he didn't. He never cared about her pleasure and within the last two days, these men had made her feel like she was the center of their universe. It was insane how little it took to make her feel special and it made her hate herself a little more that she had settled for *so much less.*

Mia let herself be drawn back into the moment, eyeing each of the three men standing before her. She could feel the heat of Matthias' presence at her back, a heat she wanted to step into but didn't. "You guys were sent here for the case." Nichlas' jaw tensed, which meant there was something else. "I'm not stupid. The men here don't look anything like you." Kenn raised an eyebrow in amusement, drawing a smile to her lips. "None of them have been in the Army or military or whatever. You came in, looked like you meant business. I just figured there was something wrong, but I wasn't sure what it was."

No one answered her, but she knew she was right. Her words were cemented when Nichlas shot her a dark look and then told everyone he needed to call it in before slipping outside, phone pressed to his ear.

"Who does he work for? Why isn't he with Kingsley?"

Matthias laid two hands on her shoulders, giving a light squeeze before backing away with a chuckle. Kenn shook his head, those blond strands cupping his face in a way that made her want to run her fingers through them. "That dumbass? Nichlas would shred that kid nine ways to hell. As for who Nichlas works for, who doesn't he work for would be easier. Just know that you're taken care of in this town while we're here."

Jan patted her shoulder when he passed her, Kenn placing a kiss on her forehead before they slipped outside. Embarrassment flooded her system with the public displays of affection. Kenn had kissed her *in front of* Matthias. Sure, it was on the head but *still.*

The worst part wasn't the lack of incidents when they were all showing interest in her. The worst part was the fact that there would be a time when all four of them left.

TWENTY-FOUR

MIA

With the chaos and rumors swirling around town, Mia had cooped herself up in her office, burying herself in old records to pass the time. She had sent Quinn home at some point, despite his protests that she at least come over for a bite to eat. The kid was the best thing that could have happened to her in this small town.

After her father's death, her mother wanted nothing more than for Mia to succeed. Unfortunately, that included being married and producing grandbabies. Her mother *adored* Anders. Still did. Even more than she loved her own kid. Every time Mia had brought home her issues with Anders, her mother insisted that she had done something wrong.

Anders was an angel in her eyes.

Still was.

In fact, everyone except for Quinn and his grandmother thought that Mia was the devil incarnate, working with dead bodies and driving all romance out the window with her lackluster appearance and personality. It pained her a little to know that her mother hadn't stood by her side. The fact that it wasn't anything out of the ordinary made it a little easier.

Mia sifted through a few more files, eyes drifting to the body on the slab. She had sent a flurry of calls to the surrounding districts to delay pickup for some of the older cases, in an attempt to research a little more. She wasn't ecstatic that Jan and Kenn were here to figure out what was going on – she was going to be in so much trouble tomorrow – but if she could determine anything to help them, she would do it.

"There's a pattern. I'm sure of it." She chuckled to herself as she plopped on the floor amid the mess she had created. Her shoes had disappeared again, as well as her lab coat. A pale green sundress hugged her body, the cool tile pressing against the back of her legs. "Mia, you're certifiably crazy talking to yourself. But you're right, there must be a pattern."

She flipped through one of last year's cases, frowning at the details she had made on a post-it note – *It's him!*

"Well, fuck. I didn't remember it going back that far." Mia opened another file, pulling out her phone to research the name that had been assigned to John Doe #35 when a loud crash in her office startled her. She wasn't sure how she swallowed the shriek that had been her go-to reaction, scrambling for one of the tables at the edge of the lab. Nerves on edge, she refused to check out the disturbance.

Mia shoved her phone into her bra to get rid of the light, terror running through her limbs as she slapped a hand over her mouth to keep her breathing under control. Tears gathered at the edge of her eyes as she scrunched into a ball, watching a dark figure walk into her lab and slowly approach the dead body on the slab.

His hand caressed the body's cheek, fingers dragging down along the torso and grazing the limp appendage between the corpse's legs. A sob left the man's lips as he drew the body against him, cradling him with such passion and sorrow that Mia almost said aloud, *What the actual fuck?*

"I'll take care of you," the figure mumbled before gathering the body into his arms and walking back out the way he came.

Time froze as Mia tried to reconcile what just happened. Someone had stolen a body from her lab. But it wasn't just *someone*. It was the killer. It *had* to be. The shock of the situation set in, adrenaline hurling her toward Matthias' bakery. She knew about the apartment just above the shop, praying that someone was awake to hear her furiously banging on the door. Homes weren't generally built in the heart of the town, her only saving grace that everyone wouldn't be clamoring into the street to find the source of the ruckus.

The door swung open, the momentum throwing her into Kenn's arms, the other three in different states of exhaustion and murderous intent. "Kitten, what's going on?"

Mia felt the tears running down her cheeks but couldn't stop them as sobs racked her chest. Broken words filtered through her lips, speech she didn't even recognize, as Kenn handed her off to Matthias. She tensed, hearing the rumbling growl in his chest before settling against him. Her thoughts began to calm as she sank into his musky scent, enjoying the way he cradled her in his arms.

He moved to sit down, drawing her into his lap as the others pulled up chairs around her, creating a barrier to the outside world. She had never felt more safe and protected in her entire life. As she came back to her senses, eyes fluttering open to meet the gazes focused on her, she realized they were in different states of what could be considered pajamas, *all* of them shirtless. Rippling muscles and tattoos fed her fantasies, scars heightening the images rather than detracting from them. Kenn was leaner than the other two but no less breathtakingly beautiful. Jan had a certain control beneath his demeanor that she wanted to explore. And Nichlas' hands. His fucking *hands*.

She squirmed in Matthias' lap, willing herself to focus on the fact that some fucker just *stole a body from her office,* but it was hard to concentrate. Matthias stilled her movements, a growing interest bulging between her cheeks that had her freezing against him. He didn't acknowledge it but he didn't apologize either. "I—"

Nichlas stood, cocking his gun back with a hooded look in his eyes as he slipped out the door.

"What's he going to do?"

Kenn ran his hands through his hair and settled back in his chair, those eyes focusing on her with a concern she hadn't seen before. "Check out the security system. See if it caught anything. You had the door locked, right?" Mia nodded timidly. "It should have set off your system. The fact that it didn't—"

Jan kicked him, but Mia knew what he was going to say. The fact the system hadn't gone off meant that the dark figure knew what he was doing. He wasn't just some amateur.

Kenn stood up, tugging her from Matthias' lap and wrapping her up in the warmth that he possessed. It was different than Matthias' and yet just as desirable. She clung to him as another set of terror passed through her, Kenn graciously waiting for her to calm down with sweet words pressed against her ears. She felt another presence at her back, the gentle touch of lips against her neck. *Matthias.* None of this made any sense and yet … she wanted whatever they were offering.

"It's late, kitten. You can sleep upstairs, all right?"

Mia leaned against Kenn, shaking her head furiously. Town chatter was a given, but staying here? With these four men? She'd never get any sleep. She already needed to run home and burn off some steam with the toy in her nightstand drawer. "No, I'll just go home. I wasn't supposed to be at work anyway." She tried to step away, but Matthias threaded his arms around her waist and pulled her in, Kenn stepping back.

Matthias kissed her neck again, a kiss she didn't shy away from. Whether it be nerves or just giving in, she was kind of done fighting it – especially with the way that Kenn stared at her while she was in his friend's arms. The adoration, the heat, the lust that bloomed in his gaze was too hard to ignore. But there was one emotion she was surprised was absent – jealousy.

"Kenn's going to make you something to calm the nerves and then we're going to go upstairs to sleep, baby girl."

Another one of those statements that didn't leave room for questioning. She could have, of course, but she didn't really want to.

TWENTY-FIVE

KENN

Kenn grabbed the ingredients for his famous hot chocolate, including the homemade whip cream that Matthias made daily. He was pretty sure the main ingredient was crack – something he had joked about more than once – but now, it was going to a woman who had captured his heart and had been dealt the worst hand.

His jaw tensed as he waited for the milk to heat, fists tightening beneath the counter to keep Mia none the wiser. He knew she had caught onto their dark personas, that they carried a lot more heat and baggage than they let on. It didn't scare her the way he thought it would and yet, he also knew they were pushing her too fast.

Sure, she said otherwise. But there were a lot of barriers to break through before that woman would even entertain what they were offering. His eyes drifted to the frail form in Matthias' arms, that green sundress doing nothing to hide the vast advance of bare leg, Kenn unsuccessfully trying to steer his thoughts to her *wellbeing* rather than the beautiful woman sitting a few paces away. Her head pressed against Matthias' shoulder as he held her like a precious treasure in the booth seat a few inches from the counter.

Matthias was the worst of them all, a man with a darkness that rivaled most people's nightmares. The fact that Mia was able to ignite that fire and calm him at the same time? She was meant for him. *For us.*

Matthias' hands shifted, one falling to her waist as he gripped it softly, the other slipping around her neck. Her eyes flung open to meet his, body tense at the silent question behind those deep purple orbs. Kenn could see his brother's expression, full of hope and desire and need, wondering if Mia would succumb to the charm that was Matthias.

She laid a hand, almost timidly, against his chest and then pressed into him as their lips met in a gentle embrace.

Well fuck me sideways, that's hot.

Jan clapped Kenn on the back, startling him from the passion unfolding before him. "You drugging women now?"

Kenn frowned and stared at the ingredients on the counter before scowling. "Ha ha, not funny." The "crack cocaine" of whip cream was an added pleasure, a running joke, but it felt sour in the moment. He poured the milk into the cup and mixed in the cocoa with a dash of cayenne pepper. "I just want to make sure we're not pushing her."

"Says the guy who started calling her kitten."

"Seems hypocritical." Jan had been seconds from giving her a pet name during that heated moment in her office before he caught himself. Kenn wondered what it was, but now seemed like the wrong time to ask. His eyes drifted to Matthias and Mia again, a wild smile spreading across his lips as he watched Matthias dole out little kisses along her cheek and jaw until she was giggling and squirming in his lap. "How could someone be after that girl? That doesn't make any fucking sense."

The shrill ring of his phone interrupted Kenn's opportunity to answer. Nichlas' voice filtered over the speaker. "The wire to the entire system is cut. Not even sure how they knew where to look. And the body from earlier on the table is gone." Nonchalant Nichlas had disappeared, the gruff voice that met his ears remnant of the lethal persona Nichlas hid all too well.

"What the fuck?" Kenn made his way around the counter with the hot chocolate, Nichlas still on the phone. Mia sat up slowly, taking the delicacy in her hands, still cradled in Matthias' arms. "Kitten." Her eyes lit up at the name, lips pressed thin as she stared at him. "Was there a body on the slab?"

"He took it." Her voice was barely above a whisper, that gentle shake of her body starting up again as she relived the moment. "Yes, he even … god, it was like he cared about him. I just …" Kenn patted her knee as Matthias tucked her back into his chest and moved back to the counter next to Jan. "You heard that?"

"Fucking hell," Nichlas said, fumbling with something on the other line. The man could pick up details that most men didn't notice. "You're not gonna like this, but somehow I think the killer knows she's on to him. Be careful with her."

Nichlas ended the call, Kenn homing in on his last sentence. Mia really had gotten under all their skins. That man didn't care about anyone other than himself and his brothers. The few times they had tried a group relationship, someone got hurt. Usually, Nichlas or Matthias. Or both. The fact that he wanted them to tread carefully with the coroner meant that he was on the same wavelength they all were.

Unfortunately, this incident was going to set them back a bit.

Not just because of Mia's fragile mental state, but because Matthias wasn't going to keep standing on the sidelines, watching his girl take the shit that kept being thrown at her.

They were all loose cannons, but when Matthias snapped? God help whoever his attention was set on.

TWENTY-SIX

MIA

Mia didn't want to rely on the warmth and strength that these men gave her, but she was falling apart at the seams. Her mind was a jumbled mess of nightmarish chaos, and she couldn't calm the terror racketing through her body, regardless of how many sips she took of Kenn's hot chocolate. She was still cradled in Matthias' arms, those lethal violet eyes flashing every so often with the desire to do more than hold her.

She snuggled in farther, trying to calm his unrest while failing to do so for herself.

"Baby girl." His voice was deeper than usual, a rasp at the edge of his words as he leaned down to kiss her. His tongue dragged across her upper lip, sucking the runaway cream from her drink. It had been like this for the past few hours, the dreamy kisses and playful touching that she never wanted to stop.

Tomorrow would be a different ordeal, but tonight, she was going to drink up every bit of attention she was given. Twenty-four hours ago, her life had started spiraling, things only getting worse. Tonight she would bask in the adoration, and then tomorrow she would face the music.

"I really need to go," Mia whispered in between kisses. Her hot chocolate was cold, and no doubt the sun was peeking over the horizon. If she didn't leave now, she'd never make it home before the whispers started.

"You don't need to do anything," A squeak left her as she remembered both Kenn and Jan were still in the cafe, both men still shirtless and way too fucking gorgeous for having rolled out of bed a few hours ago. "Matthias is taking you up to bed."

Her breath caught in her throat as Matthias maneuvered her to her feet, intertwining his fingers with hers and then leading her up the stairs to the apartment. Fear latched onto her wild emotions, Mia unsure if she was supposed to continue fighting their offer or just give in. She wanted to give in. God, she was tired and worn out but the rumor mill ... and her mother ... and–

"You're thinking too much." Matthias gave her a panty-dropping smile clouded by the sleepiness in his expression. It was almost cute. "Mia, rest. We'll figure this out in the morning."

He opened a door to a drab room, a full bed pressed against the wall with gray sheets. She couldn't imagine the turmoil that would lead to *wanting* a room without any décor or touches of light. There wasn't even a window in here, and for some reason, Mia knew that had been on purpose.

Matthias placed a gentle kiss on the top of her head, pointing to the closet. "There's extra blankets and pillows in there. I'll grab a towel for you so you can take a shower and then–"

Her emotions clouded her better judgment, words tumbling from her lips before she could stop them. "Don't leave me." He tensed behind her and then relaxed, hands falling to her waist.

"Baby girl, I wouldn't dream of it." Leading her to the bed, he let her crawl in first and then slid onto the bed after her. It was a tight fight with his bulky frame, but she snuggled in against him, his arms wrapping tightly around her waist. "Like this?"

Mia nodded, hoping that sleep would claim her and his presence would shoo away the nightmares. She was being selfish during one of her weakest moments, knowing that she couldn't entertain the thought of a relationship with everything going on, giving Matthias hope without being able to promise anything in return.

TWENTY-SEVEN

MIA

Mia stretched, immediately missing the added warmth of another body in her bed. She had barely slept, constantly reliving the moment with that dark figure in her lab.

Shouting downstairs woke her up even further, and Mia scrambled into the bathroom to fix her hair before finding her way down the stairs. Her gaze immediately tried to find Matthias, but she quickly squashed that thought. It wasn't like she could just cuddle up into his chest again like last night. They weren't dating and she wasn't entertaining anything of the sort so why …

She knew *why*, but she kicked away that pesky detail and focused on the shouting match by the counter. Kingsley and Jan were in a heated discussion about dead bodies and late-night shifts, her look souring when the sheriff stalked toward her. Mia flinched, hopping up a few steps before Kenn intercepted him with a snarl, fingers gripping the back of the sheriff's uniform with a terrifying hold on the collar.

"Lay off it, sheriff." Mia's cheeks warmed as she watched Kingsley's face pale, fear flashing through his expression.

Kingsley wrangled out of the man's grip, but his snarl wasn't even half of Kenn's. "You don't fucking talk to me like that. I am your superior!" Anger flushed through his eyes, his face going from ghostly white to beet red as he faced Mia. "You decided Anders was too good for you, so you decided to shack up with one of these riffraff? Or is it all of them?" Mia stuttered for an explanation, but Kingsley didn't give her a chance to speak. "And then I hear that someone broke in and took the body?" She opened her mouth, but reliving that memory yet again was more painful than she had imagined. What if that figure had seen her? "No, I've had enough of this, Mialopoulos. I've been waiting for this day and now that I have it … god …"

Mia blinked a few times in disbelief. This was too far. His undying need to corner her and make her beg for his protection, his love, his presence by her side … it was too much. If she was helpless, with no way out, she would run to him – at least that's what *he* thought.

"You already hired a new coroner?" What should have been a shock wasn't a surprise. It had been building for a while, the power struggle that made Kingsley think he needed to rule every part of the town with an iron fist. When his father had handed over the reins to the city, it was game over for everyone else.

Kingsley grinned, that sneaky smile brightening as he peered at her from around Kenn. Kenn still had a hand on his chest to keep the sheriff from getting closer, but the damage had already been done. "You fucking betcha. You've always been a useless piece of–" His eyes drifted to the wild animal holding him back, and he thought better of it. "Pack up your things, Mia. You've got the day to clear out. Make sure you leave all the files."

And with that, the sheriff pulled back, straightened his uniform, and waltzed out of the cafe, leaving them in silence. Mia would be forever grateful that early morning patrons hadn't filtered into the shop. Matthias immediately went to her side, Mia trying to shoulder the growing panic brought on by Kingsley's destructive behavior.

    She playfully slapped at Matthias' hands, heading back up the stairs to wash up, but she was failing at keeping herself together. She knew none of them would believe her nonchalant façade, but if it got her out the door without crying, she'd continue to hide behind it.

TWENTY-EIGHT

NICHLAS

Kenn had run after Mia when she left to pack up her office, while Nichlas stormed back into the cafe and upstairs to their makeshift gym with murder on the brain. There were a few people on his list now, namely Anders and whatever motherfucker had messed with their woman. He was startled at the change in mindset regarding Mia. *Our? When did she become ours?*

His eyes snagged Matthias' dark form, his thoughts lost to the war within. The kid was seconds from snapping as his fists hit a punching bag located at the edge of the room. The leather bounced back, each swing sending it farther in momentum than the swing before it. Without an outlet, Matthias was going to unleash serious damage on a town that didn't need any more evil.

As pissed off as he was, Nichlas knew the best step was *inaction*. His insides churned at the idea that someone had their sights on Mia, no idea what their plan was or when they'd strike next.

After another powerful punch, Matthias' rumbling growl following it, Nichlas knew he had to step in.

"Don't fucking do anything, Matty!" Nichlas yelled across the room. He knew better than to approach the guy when his eyes were the darkest shade of purple known to man. Still, without a few words, Matthias would have Anders on his ass in five different pieces before the day was up.

Matthias gritted his teeth together, fists still clenched, blood smattered along his knuckles. *The kid hadn't even put on gloves?* "Can't promise that."

When Matthias lost it, he lost *everything*. The ability to feel. To reason. To wait. Tunnel vision was his best friend, and his target had better hope and pray that Matthias never found him. The fact that he was punching the leather bag without gloves meant he was already a step too far.

"The whole fucking town is against her," Matthias whisper-yelled, throwing another punch at the bag. "And for what?" He punched again; eyes still unfocused on the bag. His shoulders tensed for a moment and then relaxed into a ready position. When he turned to track down whatever target he had picked in his head, Nichlas knew he only had a matter of seconds before that charging bull left the protection of the cafe.

Fucking hell.

Nichlas whipped out his gun, undid the safety, and shot the floor inches from Matthias' foot, hoping to jolt him out of that murderous mode he was stuck in. He froze, eyes locking on Nichlas, teeth bared like an animal before the fight began to seep from his eyes. The anger was still there, but that animalistic need to murder someone had disappeared.

For now.

"I *said* ... don't do anything."

Matthias didn't respond, staring down at his knuckles and then the bag. For a moment, Nichlas thought the kid was going to acknowledge he needed to cool off and take a shower. No such luck. The kid headed back for the punching bag and continued his assault on the leather, mindless grunts filling the space.

They were working on borrowed time, and not because whoever was leaving bodies was already onto the next one, but because Matthias was about to start adding to that number.

TWENTY-NINE

MIA

Another shiver ran down her spine as she packed items and trinkets from her desk she had collected over the years – a replica of a skull from a conference, her plaque from school, pens from different universities, and her father's ink quill, among other things. Not that it mattered anymore. Nothing did.

Kenn laid a reassuring hand on her back, giving her the strength to keep the tears packed away, but everything just seemed like a chore. Especially when Quinn popped in and started rapidly firing questions in her general direction, which turned into him calling Kingsley a good-for-nothing pig and every other name under the sun.

She didn't have the energy to deal with him as Kenn helped to pick up the papers still strewn across the floor. "Kitten, where do you want these?" Mia tried to reach his gaze but just pointed to her box. They weren't case papers, just notes she had made over the past year. She wasn't going to let the similarities go without a little investigation, even if it meant giving up her father's office to someone who didn't know the first thing about dead bodies.

Sure, Kingsley had found "someone," but knowing him, it was someone who would bend to Kingsley's will, not someone who understood the position.

Kenn intercepted Quinn after a few minutes of shouting and tears, directing the kid to sit down and shut up. He mentioned something about stress and giving her room to breathe, but she was more focused on saying goodbye to the one place she could disappear to without judgment.

"Kitten." Firm hands gripped her arms from behind, Kenn pressed against her back as he pulled her into a hug. Arms wrapping around her waist, he kissed her temple and stood there, a silent wall she could lean against. It became easier to breathe and to think as she silently waved each of her memories goodbye. "You'll be all right. Everything will work out. We'll—"

Her office door swung open, and Mia jumped out of Kenn's arms. She headed for the door without grabbing her box, running into a body she had never seen before. Kingsley was speaking about the office and where everything was – as if he knew – before acknowledging her. "What the fuck are you still doing here?"

You said a day, dickwad. It's barely lunch.

She pulled her lips into a thin smile, nodding to the new guy, who seemed completely out of his element. His unnaturally dark eyes didn't match the innocence surrounding him. "Um, who's this?" he asked, almost curious and maybe a little hopeful about her presence.

"She's just leaving, weren't you?" Mia knew Kingsley wouldn't introduce her to the new coroner. He wanted her to suffer, to crawl back to him. Giving her any sort of title would rid him of that opportunity. His eyes drifted around the office, falling on the hole that Anders had left. "And that'll come out of your salary," he whispered into her ear before pushing the new guy into the lab.

Mia nearly acted on the disrespect she had been given when Kenn grabbed one of her hands and squeezed, out of the sheriff's sight. She didn't fight the hold, heading for the door when she heard Kingsley stop Quinn from following her. "You work here, don't you? Show him where everything is. I hope to hear a good report. And by law, everything that happens in this office stays here. People that are no longer employed by the Bryxton sheriff's office are not privy to any information."

Kenn didn't let her dwell on Kingsley's words as he guided her back to the cafe, Matthias' pained expression from behind the counter softening with her presence. Her feet took her to him of their own accord, her body folding into his without reserve. She was getting a little too comfortable, her resolve to face the music waning with every touch and comfort that these men offered.

"I'm not sure why I'm here," she mumbled into Matthias' chest. "I need to get home." She noticed there still weren't any customers in the cafe, but that seemed like it had been on purpose this time.

A dark chuckle slipped from Kenn as he reached over the counter for the coffee pot. Matthias tsked, but it didn't stop Kenn from pouring himself a healthy cup. "Do you ever take a break?"

She shook her head, pulling away from Matthias. "I never needed to. That was my escape. It's all I had. Kingsley knew that, and he took it from me." Her bottom lip trembled with the emotions bubbling up inside of her. She hadn't dealt with any of them, just stuffed them out of sight for another time.

A hand slid along her jawline, angling her face up to see concern behind two beautiful violet eyes. "You're not going to fight for it, baby girl? Wasn't that your fathers?"

His fucking eyes are dangerous. She shimmied out of his hold, letting out a deep sigh, and shook her head again. "It won't do me any good. I never actually wanted to stay here, but my father passed away, and it all just worked out nicely. Kingsley always wanted this just so he could–" Mia pressed her lips together and bowed her head, but neither male was having.

"Finish that sentence, kitten."

"Um ... he ..."

"Baby girl," Matthias' tone warned her that she had better spill Kingsley's true intentions before he found out on his own.

"He wants me, okay? But he doesn't love me. He just wants to possess me, but it won't work. He's been trying since we were kids. It's dumb ... wait, no! Matthias, *don't*." Her eyes widened, panic thrumming through her veins as she watched Matthias' jaw click and his expression turn lethal. A whine permeated the air around her as she shakingly waved her hands at him to grab his attention. "*Please*."

Silence followed her whispered plea, tension thick and heavy as it settled around them.

"I'm going to go," she mumbled before heading out the front door, vaguely remembering the box she had left at the office. Hopefully, Quinn would know what it was and grab it on his way out.

THIRTY

NICHLAS

With Mia gone, Nichlas had returned to the main level, watching with interest the way Matthias seemed to be entertaining the customers who just walked in with a heightened enthusiasm that didn't match their conversation. Something was off, but without airing their dirty laundry to the entire town, it'd have to wait.

He made his way behind the counter, leaning against it as he eyed the coffee pot and thought better about it. He hadn't slept since Mia had stumbled into the cafe and he wouldn't if he indulged in the morning bean now. Matthias shuffled around the kitchen, that terrifying glint just beneath his expression.

"I think the killer's in this town," Nichlas let out just as the last of Matthias' customers returned to their table. "That's the only thing that makes sense." They had all been thinking it but he had found no explanation otherwise. A person from this town would understand all the ins and outs, the less traveled roads, *and* where

Mia's lab was. And yet ... everyone here seemed so *innocent*. "We're going to need you on this one, Matty."

The kid tensed and then frowned, eyes meeting everything but his. "Absolutely not."

"It's a tall ask, I know that. But Mia needs us. I just ..." Nichlas grunted, yet again realizing that he was thinking of himself as one of Mia's future partners. It couldn't happen. Not with the task he had been given. And asking Matthias for his help was all but ruining the kid's chances with her as well. The last few times Matthias had "helped" out, it had taken a while for them to bring him out of his head. Releasing that animal was a last resort and, well, *not* releasing it would be worse.

Matthias threw him a scowl as the wheels turned in his head, both considering the offer and rejecting it. Three women bounced up to the counter, interrupting their conversation, the middle one someone they both recognized as Ander's wife. Nichlas fought the urge to throw the woman an evil glare, keeping his expression neutral as they ordered cups to go.

"Thought I'd come back. We started off on the wrong foot and your coffee *was* delicious. Thought my husband might like a cup while he works." She giggled as Matthias put on his charm, thinly veiling his desire to rip the woman apart. Nichlas kept his scowl to himself as he saw right through her lie, almost missing the unnatural movement of her hand across her belly.

"How far along?" Nichlas leaned over the counter as Matthias poured the cups, hoping to catch the woman in a lie. He didn't even know her name, but the fact that she was married to Anders made her an enemy. And for what? Because she had been disrespectful to Mia and the relationship their girl had with ... *Our girl? Fuck, I'm doing it again.*

"Three months." She shot him a wide smile, one that probably ensnared a handful of men with weak morals. Matthias cursed under his breath, and Nichlas glanced back to see one of the cups spilled on the floor. She leaned forward, hands propped on the counter, hair crowding around her cheeks. "Such a klutz, aren't you? But you're cute, so I can forgive that."

Matthias didn't respond to that, the girls gossiping about muscles and the color purple in a way that made Nichlas' blood boil. "You flirting when you have a husband?"

"I would *never*," she spit out dramatically. "But you can never have too much eye candy." Nichlas kept his mouth shut as they sauntered out with their full cups, his eyes dragging to that little round belly attached to a woman he despised. Anders was a piece of shit, sure, but Nichlas had had no idea he was *that* kind of excuse of a human.

THIRTY-ONE

MIA

M ia had made it home in one piece, only shedding tears after she stepped into her house and her mother had started shouting every insult in the book. Everything revolved around catering to what Anders wanted and needed. How could she be so stupid as to break Anders' heart? What had she done to make Anders choose someone else? How could she be so promiscuous as to sleep over in a house full of men that she didn't know? How could she disrespect Anders' current wife?

The insults continued to fly long after Mia had hidden in her room and stuffed her face into her pillow. Without her father's business to fall back on, she had nowhere left to hide, to disappear to when life became too much to deal with. Those four gorgeous and highly dangerous men weren't an option. Not in a small town like this.

She couldn't even bring herself to believe that pesky little voice in her head that told her she deserved a little happiness in her life.

Her father would have never wanted to see things spiraling out of control like this. He would have been appalled at her mother's behavior.

But he wasn't here to protect her.

Worn out from her current state of despair, Mia checked her phone, horrified to see that she had spent a day cooped up in her room. Messages littered the screen from Matthias and Kenn, both of them checking in on her. There were a few from Quinn and then a voice message he had sent thirty minutes ago. His voice shot through the speaker, cackles muffling his words.

"Where the fuck did the sheriff find this guy? He sucks ass! Oh, my god, he ... he yelled when I – he touched the gizzards. Fuck, this is so much fun. I miss you, but ha! He's ... he's ..." The message trailed off into gibberish, a small smile settling on her lips. At least Quinn wasn't suffering in her absence, although it was only a matter of time before Kingsley had her right back at the office so that the money would start rolling in again.

Mia scrolled through an onslaught of calls, mostly from the sheriff's station and a few from a number she had deleted but still recognized. Voicemails were attached to each one, but she wanted nothing to do with the man associated with those vile words.

"Mia! Get your ass down here!" She shot up in her bed, staring at her locked door and wondering why in the world her mother was yelling. She scrambled to her bathroom and patted down her hair, washing her face as quickly as she could and shrugging into a clean shirt. The barely there sleep shirts didn't cover much, but fuck if she was going to shrug into something ... well, more. *It'll have to do.* Mia threw her door open and hopped down the stairs, freezing at the sight of Anders seated at her kitchen table. Looking to her mother for answers, the woman smiled, placing an opened beer beside her ex. "He just wants to talk. You owe him that much when you so rudely dumped him. I'll get out of your hair."

And with that, her mother disappeared down the hall, leaving Mia to face the one man she wanted nothing to do with. In her mental state, this was sure to send her over the edge. She stood at the other end of the table, refusing to sit.

Anders leaned forward, his eyes sparkling with an intent she couldn't read. "How are you, baby? I haven't heard from you since they started revolving around you."

Mia frowned, eyes narrowing at the man who all but ruined her life. "Why would you hear from me? You married someone else. And then you almost hit me! Why would I reach out to you?" The man had to be deranged, especially because he knew – as the whole town did – that his wife was after her as well.

"You wielded a knife, baby, and if they knew …"

"Kingsley already fired me," Mia spit out, throwing her arms across her chest when she remembered that she was standing in her kitchen braless. She couldn't hide her legs, but it was a start. Anders' gaze hadn't dipped there yet, but it would, and she really didn't need to know how he felt about her state of undress.

Anders stood, taking a swig of his beer and then smiling down at her. It didn't feel nearly as good as when Matthias did it. Or Kenn. Or Jan. Or even Nichlas. "It's not surprising. Look, just come back to me." Mia tilted her head to the side, trying to understand what was going through Anders' mind. He couldn't possibly be that stupid, could he?

"You're married." When that didn't seem to deter him, she pointed at the fading bruise on her cheek. "Natalie hit me yesterday because she thinks I can't stay away from you, which isn't even remotely true. *You* left me and got married to her. Now you want me back? Why? To torture me? I don't fucking understand!" Emotions raged within, bubbling over the top as tears spilled down her cheeks. This was all too much.

"Language, Mia."

The urge to make Anders truly understand how much he had fucked up was too great to ignore. She needed him to know. No more "nice girl," no more hiding in the shadows as everyone talked about her, no more getting ridiculed for shit that she hadn't done.

"I'm not yours anymore, you bastard!" Fear wracked her body as she realized there was no one out here to protect her. Her mother thought she was a demon, breaking Anders' heart, and Mia already knew that Anders had a violent streak, a man who was currently holding a glass bottle. Still, she wasn't going to back down. Not ever again. "You can't control me!"

"No, you just think you can open your legs—"

"You're fucking disgusting!" Mia shouted. Anders saw her as a tool, as a piece to further his life. She was going to make his white picket fence a reality, but she was never a woman to him. He obsessed over her until the passion was gone, and now that he had Natalie, he realized that Mia was the better option. But that's all she was – an option. Her fingers curled into fists as they dropped from her chest, fury and fear mingling together as she faced Anders.

His brows furrowed and his face reddened, fingers gripping that bottle with a little too much force to be innocent, especially when he raised that hand over his head and chucked the glass right at her face. Mia stood there, defiant, even as the glass shattered against the wall behind her, beer and shards spraying across the kitchen.

Liquid trickled down her right arm, but Mia didn't dare move. She had a point to make. She swallowed her terror, knowing that her usual reaction situations like these only fueled his anger. Anders stalked around the table and grabbed her by the throat, thrusting her against the same wall that was covered in glass and booze. "You don't *ever*—"

Words dripping in venom cut off as the door burst open and Anders released her into a coughing fit, Quinn placing himself in between them. He was wielding a wooden bat, bug-eyed as he dragged Mia away from the wall and toward the stairs. He was trembling like a leaf, hand wrapped around Mia's wrist.

"Goddamn, where the fuck is your mom? I heard Natalie talking about it and I just … come on." Anders hadn't moved from his spot, shocked by Quinn's presence and determination to rescue her. He also knew that touching Quinn was out of the question. Quinn's mother wouldn't just roll over and die like hers apparently had.

Back upstairs in her room, Quinn started emptying her drawers into a duffle bag – wherever the fuck he had found that – huffing and puffing about not being able to trust anyone in town. "I'm … I don't know what you need. We'll get you more. Ma said you could stay with us. Okay?" Another round of tears found their way down her cheeks as she stared at her savior.

"How did you know?" Mia whimpered, feeling like a complete failure.

The question had Quinn turning to her, concern flooding his face when his eyes landed on her arm. "You're bleeding! I'm going to kill him. No, I'm going to sic the terrifying one on him. Nichlas? Yeah him. And then I'll bring popcorn and watch Anders burn alive. Fuck, this is bad." Mia winced as Quinn's fingers grazed her arm, blood dripping from her forearm. There were definitely pieces of glass stuck in there that she was going to have fun digging out.

Mia helped Quinn finish packing, both of them skirting past Anders and her mother without a word. Halfway to Quinn's place, the kid finally spoke again. "Next time he tries that, I'm calling the cops."

"Kingsley?"

"Not *those* cops."

Her face warmed at the thought of her four protectors barging in to find the threat, but it immediately turned ashen when that image became a very real threat. There was darkness in those men, and when they found out that Anders had threatened her — and they would find out — it wouldn't be a laughing matter.

It should have worried her how turned on she was by that.

THIRTY-TWO

MIA

Mia gladly took the warm hug that Ma gave her, Quinn squealing with excitement like he had just gained a big sister. She wriggled her way out of Ma's arms and gave Quinn a pointed look that had his cheeks flaming. "How did you really know that Anders was at my house?"

"Um ... well, Matthias wanted to check on you and I happened to run into him while I was coming home, and we saw Anders go in. He looked like he was going to kill your ex so I had him over here. And–"

She blinked a few times, frowning. "Over here?"

Two strong arms slid around her waist, freaking her out as she twisted around to see two deep purple eyes that were nearly black. A deep growl resounded as he stared down at her, the boyish charm gone, replaced by the devil himself. If Nichlas was terrifying, Matthias was darkness, itself.

"I would have ripped off his head," Matthias spoke, his words raspy and dripping with an edge of venom that far outweighed the terror Anders had caused. Her thighs quivered in response, but she bit back the moan sitting at the edge of her tongue out of respect for Ma and her house.

Quinn whined from his perch at the other side of the kitchen. "He told me I had to get you out if we didn't want another body. And he wasn't talking about yours." Mia heard someone bite into an apple and wondered how the kid could be eating while Matthias was possessively holding onto her like some kind of animal. Even Ma hadn't commented on it, although Mia knew the woman wasn't going to. Unlike her mother, Ma was this carefree woman that believed love came in all forms and refused to cage anyone's dreams.

Ma clicked her tongue, two little feet pattering along the tile. Mia knew the two had left them alone when steps could be heard on the staircase.

She felt Matthias relax slightly against her, but not enough as he inspected her bruise before his gaze dropped to her neck. His jaw tensed, eyes darkening further as he continued to inspect, another growl leaving him when he saw her arm and she winced at his touch.

"Explain."

She had noticed once before when his emotions got the better of him that he had a hard time speaking in full sentences, something she found both incredibly hot and terrifying at the same time. She was going to get whiplash from all these emotions.

"Mia. Did. He. Touch. You?"

"Yes," she rasped, angling her chin up toward him as he gripped it and dragged it toward him, lips brushing her own with silent promises. Her lips parted as he squeezed harder, the pain welcome as she squirmed in his hold.

"Settle." Her body froze beneath his command, heat licking up her spine. Despite the anger flowing through him, he was still in control, a control she wanted him to have in this moment. She wanted nothing less than to let go. "Tell me what happened."

And then the words just spilled out. "I … he was in the kitchen. Mom left me with him, and he was angry that I wasn't giving in anymore. I told him. I told him that I didn't want him. That I wasn't his. He didn't like it, so he threw his bottle and then he grabbed me. Quinn came in then. I'm fine. I'm—"

"I don't quite believe those words, but I won't press it." Matthias released his grip on her face and she fell the few centimeters forward into his chest, breathing in his deep scent and missing his touch already. "You did good, baby girl." She had no warning before his hands dropped to the back of her thighs and yanked her upwards. He closed the distance between the nearest wall and pressed her against it, her chest flush with his, face stuffed so far into her neck she thought he was going to eat her.

It was a much different sensation than the force Anders used, this one full of raw passion and desire. Her back arched in response, nipples pebbling with desire, her fingers digging into his shoulders until she was sure she would draw blood. "Matthias," she breathed, wondering what was going on in that big head of his.

He ground himself against her, his interest undeniable as it pressed against her core. She bit back a cry – knowing that Ma and Quinn were just upstairs – but couldn't help the heat coursing through her veins and pooling between her legs. Matthias pulled back, eyes trained on her lips before he claimed them. She didn't even care about the pain and phantom touch of Anders on her neck as Matthias took what he wanted, thrusting his tongue into her mouth, licking her from the inside out.

This time she couldn't hold back, moaning into his mouth as he rocked against her, driving her up the wall with want and desire. Warnings to push Matthias away went ignored as she let herself experience everything the man had to offer, one hand still firmly gripping her thigh as the other one dove under her shirt and yanked her tit into a rough hold. His fingers tugged and teased the sensitive nub until she was all but dry humping him for release.

She knew she had to stop. She knew she needed to pull away, to tell him that it couldn't happen, that she couldn't promise him anything.

But she didn't want to.

His attention on her breast ceased, two fingers diving straight between her legs without little resistance, around her panties. Her legs were spread wide around his hips, ready for anything he desired. She yelled into his mouth as his fingers curled and stroked inside of her, his thumb pressing into her clit with a fierceness she hadn't felt before.

"God," he said and pulled away, still sucking on her full bottom lip. "You're so goddamn wet." She made some unsexy sound that had him speeding up until she was riding his fingers for completion, the thought of someone walking in only making her hotter. "Come for me baby girl. Squeeze my fingers." Mia wasn't sure if it was the command or the overwhelming sensation that was Matthias but her body shuddered with the power of her release, her head falling forward against Matthias' shoulder as he pumped into her through her orgasm.

She wasn't sure where this left them, Matthias' fingers still firmly seated in her pussy, kisses trailing up and down her neck with a gentleness that didn't match the terrifying aura from a few moments ago. He let her down, giving her a moment to gather herself before kissing her forehead. "Let's get you cleaned up, all right? Then we need to talk."

The bulge between Matthias' legs was very much still prominent, but he didn't address it. He didn't ask her to take care of it, and he didn't ask if she could give him a moment. Instead, he sat her at the table and pulled out a first aid kit without so much as a question before taking her arm and beginning the painstaking task of gently dislodging the glass from her arm.

Sweat clung to her forehead and glistened on his as she wondered what the fuck had just happened. This scene would have never existed in her world with Anders. Anders demanded pleasure, but he rarely returned it. If she did get off, it was always on accident. And the idea that he would be sated with just *her* getting off? Impossible.

With anyone else, she would have thought that Matthias had just been playing on his emotions, ignoring any future discussion about the incident as he was owed her pleasure. But with Matthias, his silence wasn't dismissal or ownership. He was giving her a chance to process, to choose, to make her own her path, and she very much wanted the man in front of her – if she could just squash that stupid voice in her head.

"Shit!"

Matthias glanced up at her apologetically, a pair of bloodied tweezers in his hand with a small shard of glass dangling from them. It shocked her that there was more than just concern and desire in those eyes, that boyish charm returning. Besides the anger and beneath the strength and darkness, there was something else. Love.

An emotion she never thought she'd see directed at her again.

THIRTY-THREE

KENN

By the time the weekend rolled around, emotions were running high, and Matthias had never looked more tense in his life. He had been spending every waking moment not occupied by running his cafe with Mia, but it didn't seem to help cage the beast the way they had all hoped. It probably had more to do with the lurking threat that had yet to be dealt with than Mia's ability to calm him.

Which is why Kenn had advised them to settle on a plan before doing *anything*. Of course, this was going to happen outside of Kingsley's reign and possibly without Nichlas' help, but Matthias needed to know they were working on it.

Kenn took a deep breath as he rumbled through the duffle bag at his feet, glad that Matthias had thought ahead and closed the shop for the night. He unearthed yet another Glock, checking the safety and then the chamber. Guns littered three of the customer tables, polished blacks, grays, and browns shining back at him. They needed to be ready.

For anything.

Including ready for whatever crazy Matthias was about to break out.

"Fucking snap out of it man." Kenn kicked Matthias' chair, the kid's eyes refocusing from the murderous haze he had settled in for the past hour since returning from being with Mia. Nichlas had shared with Kenn that he'd had to shoot his gun to get Matthias to refocus, that using the kid in this situation might do more harm than good. Kenn knew as much, but keeping the kid locked up while their girl was being targeted? That was worse. "She'll be *fine*," Kenn reiterated, but he couldn't promise that.

None of them could.

None of them really knew why Mia was being targeted, although they could guess. And they didn't even know who "they" were. It was all just a shot in the dark at this point.

"Matty, Nichlas will make sure she's safe, all right? Just … don't do anything. Not yet." He nodded, but Kenn wasn't sure the kid was all there. He also wasn't sure what was going on with Nichlas, who was absent from this meeting. Nichlas, as mysterious as he was, had never once lied to them, and yet there had been more lies in the last twenty-four hours than he could count.

Nichlas never told them where he was going or what he was doing when asked. Today? He had told them, but it wasn't true. None of it. And then there was that growing sadness lurking in his expression as if he regretted the choices he was making.

The guy didn't do guilt, or regret. He stuck by his own decisions and paid for his mistakes.

And then there was Jan, the guy who always got the bad rep for being all brawn and no brains. He was in the corner silently polishing his favorite pistol, mind far away from the cafe, calculating a certain person's demise.

The more he thought about it, the more Kenn realized that there was information he didn't know. He hadn't even thought to ask before now. "Matty, did something happen Thursday morning when you went to see Mia?"

The kid's jaw set and his eyes flashed before he stood up and stalked toward the stairs. Kenn used his speed to intercept the kid and dragged him back to the table, Jan leaning forward from his perch in the corner. Kenn didn't have to ask again before Matthias' shoulders sagged for a moment, then the kid was tense again.

"He hurt her."

"I'm gonna need a bit more than that, Matty."

The kid growled as if the memory pained him, hands curling into fists in his laps as he met Kenn's gaze. "He fucking touched her. Her mother fed her to the wolves, and then he fucking threatened her. He threatened our girl."

Kenn had watched Matthias become possessive of exactly three things in life: his family, his brothers, and his team, but never to this extreme. Never to the extreme of *claiming* them. Whoever had been messing with Mia was really in for it – especially this Anders guy.

Horrible images flashed through Kenn's brain as he tried to imagine the terror Mia had felt when facing Anders. He had so many questions, but now wasn't the time. There was only one thing that mattered. He knelt in front of Matthias, making himself seem smaller so as not to set the kid off. "All right, she's safe though?" Matthias nodded. "Good. That's good. Now, I'm going to need you to take a deep breath and get me a refill."

The kid's eyes lightened as he unearthed a small smile and nodded again, swiping Kenn's cup as he made his way to the kitchen. Kenn didn't need any more coffee, but Matthias needed something to do that wasn't thinking up ways to murder Anders. One look at Jan told Kenn that the kid wasn't the only person they should be worrying about.

Mia was *theirs*, and fuck anyone who thought differently.

Finding the killer was their first priority.

But after that? Anders was going to be their bitch. He had messed with the wrong woman, and he would live just long enough to regret it.

THIRTY-FOUR

MIA

Matthias had stayed for lunch and dinner on Thursday before taking her to bed. Waking up to him had been wonderful, especially when he refused to leave and they cuddled for most of the day. Between kisses and cuddles, Mia never wanted to leave the safety and warmth of his embrace.

But reality was a bitch, and she needed to move on. Without a job, Mia had no time to lie around and goof off. Even Quinn was off working at her old office in between sending her voice messages of him wheezing at the new coroner's inability to function as a human being.

By lunch, Mia had kicked Matthias out, nearly changing her mind after he left her with a toe-curling kiss, but Ma's appearance in the kitchen had squashed that. And now … there was just that lingering feeling of despair as she was left with her thoughts in a house that wasn't her own.

"Oh, we're done with the pity party, Mia. I get it. You were dealt a bad hand, a *really* bad one. But it's time we start fighting back." Mia stared at Ma like she had three heads. Fighting back? She had tried that with Anders and he had retaliated. The phantom grip on her neck was still there, and the ache in her arm hadn't fully disappeared yet. "I'm not talking about *physically*, Mia. But if you keep letting people walk all over you, they're never going to find another carpet."

"That's," Mia scrunched up her nose as she slid into one of the kitchen chairs, "a strange analogy."

"And yet one you understand," Ma responded. She moved around the kitchen with grace, producing a sandwich that looked like it had fallen out of a magazine. "Now eat something so you can go through that box and figure out what's going on in this town." Mia's gaze followed Ma's finger to the box she had left at the office, but before she could comment on it, Ma was already onto another speech. "I'm not stupid. I wasn't born yesterday. Besides, Quinn's a big talker when he gets home. He's like a lovesick puppy. It's always Mia this. Mia that. You've always been the big sister he's never had."

Mia wasn't sure what to say to that as she bit into the mystery sandwich, flavors exploding on her tongue. Roast beef and avocado plus some mysterious sauce ran across her taste buds. She had always known Ma was a great cook but this …

Focus, Mia.

"What are you saying, Ma?" Mia asked around another bite of her sandwich.

"I'm saying, I already know the connection you've drawn between all these bodies. I also know that those new men in town have provided you with more comfort than you've had since your father died." Mia blinked a few times, forcing Ma to spell it out. "Sweet child, I'm saying *go for it*. All of it. Do what you need to do, for you."

She swallowed and stared at her plate for a moment, sifting through her thoughts, her desires, her *dreams*. The ones she had long since discarded in hopes that the pitiful life she had set up in her town would suffice. It hadn't. It had left her wanting.

And the more she thought about it, the more she realized that the four men who had bulldozed through town and her heart were the ones who had shown her that she wanted more. That she needed more. That she *deserved* more.

And this would be the first step to getting it.

"I'll try," Mia finally managed, her voice barely above a whisper.

"And that's all I ask."

A loud thump startled Mia back to reality, her box now firmly seated beside her and Ma disappearing around the corner to leave her to her thoughts. She scarfed down the rest of the sandwich and ran the box up to her temporary room, wasting no time spreading the files and papers on the floor to see if she could find any other similarities. Anything she could give to Jan and Kenn that would further the investigation.

"There has to be a clue."

But she wasn't a detective, and the more she poured over the information, the more questions she had. Other than the mode of death, there didn't seem to be any other pattern. She didn't know most of the Jane and John Does that she found. She didn't know where they came from or who they were. The most she ever did was prep them for transport to the city nearly an hour away.

"Holy fuck." Mia whipped around, hands raised, and then lowered them at the sight of Quinn in her doorway. The house had grown dark as she had lost herself in her work. "You really got up to some shit, didn't you?" He threw her a bagel that she instantly knew was from Matthias. "He asked how you were doing, but like, didn't he *just* leave?"

Mia shrugged. "He cares. Sue him."

"Seems like *you* care. Gonna do anything about that?"

"Maybe." She tried to hide her smile, but Quinn caught it, pointing and laughing like he had just discovered gold.

"Yes! I called it. Anyways, what's all this? What did you figure out?"

She recognized the way he deflected away from the obvious question "how was work?" He'd tell her about it if he wanted to.

"I need to go into the city and pull the records on the bodies that were delivered. I need to see if there's a pattern," she said.

"Just tell the guys. Let them do their job."

"I can do this. I *need* to do this."

Quinn grunted and shrugged. "Up to you. Ma wanted to go out to the diner – you coming?" Mia shook her head, panic gripping her from the inside out at the thought of venturing into public. She'd have to do it sooner or later, but she needed just a little while longer to field the comments directed at her. "Figured. No worries. Just text me your order and we'll bring it back. Looks like you're in the middle of something anyway."

He winked and left her to her own devices, Mia staring at the bagged bagel sitting on her lap. Cinnamon and chocolate met her nose, the overwhelming desire to tear into it rushing through her. Instead, she set it aside as a reward for later. She needed to find a clue, a connection. *Anything*. Because there had to be one. Right?

THIRTY-FIVE

NICHLAS

Nichlas was mentally punching himself as he stepped into Bryxton's only bar, set just at the edge of town. It attracted all sorts of unwanted attention from travelers who needed a break from their destinations, and from all the sleazeballs in town who desperately needed a place to hide from their women. Stereotypical as hell and smelled like straight-up piss, liquor, and ass. Girls who couldn't make it in the city dancing for a living seemed to hang around, trying to bum a cigarette, meal, or extra cash from anyone who wanted a little extra pleasure in their life.

He hated places like this.

They skeeved him out, and he wished for all the world he could be *anywhere* other than in the bar, but Cross had told him the mission was important. He was oh so close to saying fuck the mission and returning to Cross for his next assignment, but Anders and his shady ass had to be real high up on the priority list if Nichlas had been assigned to it.

He took a deep breath and marched in, sidestepping when a girl tried to run a hand down his chest as a conversation starter. He wasn't nearly drunk enough for that, and their girl would never forgive him when she found out that he'd been pawed at by some random woman.

She's. Not. Mine, he reminded himself.

His eyes roamed the dimly lit bar for his target, gaze settling on a nearly drunk Anders, who was trying to grab one of the bartenders' attention for another round. The guy didn't need any more alcohol, but Nichlas was determined to get this shit over with before it dragged along any further. He just needed information on what Anders was doing.

His phone pinged with what was most likely a message from the guys wondering what was going on. Kenn had already become suspicious of his mission, and Matthias wasn't far behind. Ignoring it, he moved to slide in beside Anders and took a deep breath before speaking. "Your wife was looking for you." Nichlas wasn't a nice man in any sense of the word, so starting up trouble was the easiest way to access information, especially with a man like Anders, whose ego was his first priority.

Anders growled at him, wavering dangerously in his seat as one of the bartenders finally complied and slid him an entire bottle of whiskey. *Guess he's a regular.* Mia hadn't mentioned anything about Anders' drinking habits, not that she had mentioned much about him at all.

"She can suck a dick. Any one of them that's not mine," Anders mumbled as he struggled to pour himself a glass. Nichlas helped out, pouring himself one as well, because there was no way in hell he was going to be able to stay sober for this shit.

She won't forgive you for this.

Nichlas tightened his jaw and downed the first glass, pouring a healthy second one and downing that one, too. "What crawled up your ass?" Nichlas forced a chuckle to make himself seem less threatening.

Anders was too far gone to care. "She just thinks she's so much better than me." His words slurred together, Nichlas realizing that "she" wasn't his wife. "You all strolled into town, and she thinks she's got it like that."

Anger flared up in his chest, but Nichlas resisted the urge to take Anders to the floor. The way this man thought about women was despicable. Still, Nichlas had a job to do: Find information. He threw back another drink, knowing he was about to start down a dangerous path.

Nichlas mulled through a few different choice words, deciding on defending Mia's honor while also talking shit about her attitude. It hurt, and he fucking hated every word that came out of his mouth, but with every degrading comment, Anders trusted him a little more. Soon they had bonded over their love-hate relationship with the woman who used to be the town's coroner.

A few more drinks in and Nichlas knew he wouldn't be able to play off "it was just a mission" when he returned home. Halfway through a pool game, Anders gave him the in he needed. For someone that dealt with shady information, Anders had opened up just a little too easily in Nichlas' opinion.

Nichlas wobbled a few steps, regretting the last drink he had chugged. "I'm only here because I was following those assholes. I don't even know what to do for work."

Anders perked up, aiming for one of the pool balls and completely missing as he stumbled into one of the tables and then stalked back to his previous position. "Really? You—" Hiccup. "Can come with me." He blew out a deep breath, a burp following it. "Tomorrow. Eight a.m. I'll come get you."

"That's Saturday."

"Work never sleeps."

Nichlas nodded, taking his turn and wishing for the night to end so he could take a shower and wash off the stench. It was too bad that in the midst of his mission, his only thought was on how to explain to Mia what was going on without breaking protocol.

THIRTY-SIX

MATTHIAS

Matthias set the last of the dishes on the drying rack, fighting a smile as he thought about Mia eating the bagel he had thrown at Quinn hours ago. He had been dying to message her or call her or show up at Quinn's place, but he didn't want to smother her. Especially not at midnight, even if it was the weekend.

Truthfully, he didn't want her to have to deal with his demons on top of hers. Her presence quieted the unrest in his head, but she couldn't be his savior, not when he needed to be hers. Kenn and Jan had since cleaned up their metal atrocity adorning his tables, the clicks of guns and clanks of shells nearly triggering him into a more unstable state than he already was.

He knew they needed his expertise, his ability to think on his feet, and his uncanny knack for finding the truth in the smallest details – in short, his profiling skills. But all that put him in a headspace that he had a hard time getting out of. It involved a different side of him, a side he wasn't so sure he wanted Mia to see.

Mia had figured out there was more than met the eye, that they all carried some kind of terrifyingly dark baggage, but she didn't know the half of it. His brothers were lethal. The things each of them could do with a weapon were nothing compared to what they could do with their hands. He was worse, though. His hands weren't the worst weapon. It was his mind, his words, his ability to drag out information from the darkest corners of the earth in exchange for his sanity.

Sanity he kind of wanted now that he had met Mia.

Maybe she'd understand.

She probably wouldn't.

The cafe door opened, and unadulterated rage exploded in Matthias' chest at the sight that met his eyes. Nichlas and Anders fell over the threshold, giggling about something that wasn't funny. Kenn placed a hand on Matthias' chest to keep him from doing something he'd regret.

"*Explain*," Matthias bit out, his eyes narrowing. Anger took a hold of his mind, blocking everything out except the need to rip apart Nichlas.

A snort flew out of Nichlas' mouth as the two helped each other up and he gave Anders a mock salute as the bastard slipped back out into the street.

"Just business."

Matthias growled, wrenching Kenn's hand off his chest and stalking over to Nichlas before throwing him against the wall. He shoved his arm against the man's neck, baring his teeth. Nichlas didn't deserve the elegance of conversation. "Business? What the fuck are you going on about? They're here for the killer. What are you here for?"

Nichlas didn't struggle against the hold, face paling as Matthias leaned in further, cutting off the man's air supply. "You know I can't talk about it."

And he did. Matthias knew better than the other two that even between brothers, some details couldn't be shared. But that wasn't the true problem here. "This could have worked, but it had to be *him*." He bowed his head before pulling away, fighting the other emotions threatening to emerge. "She won't forgive you for this."

Nichlas ran his hands through his hair, sadness lurking behind his eyes. "She would have never gone for me anyway, Matty. The demons I have. ... She likes you. Let's leave it at that." His eyes searched Matthias' and then the other two before his nose scrunched in confusion. "Did I miss something?"

Kenn placed himself in between the two, dragging Matthias closer to the counter and away from another outburst. Matthias was still pissed off, but he wasn't going to kill Nichlas. Not yet. Jan hopped in: "Anders attacked Mia again yesterday, did a little more damage than just scaring her. Whatever your mission is, make it snappy. You might be all right sabotaging your chances with Mia, but she sees you with him and you're going to ruin more than the lies you tell yourself."

Nichlas managed a grunt, eyes unfocused as he stalked up to his room. Matthias tore his attention away from the man with all the secrets, nodding to Kenn that he'd be fine. He knew Nichlas hadn't chosen his mission, and the man looked just as tortured as Matthias felt. He wasn't going to press the matter. He just hoped that Nichlas had figured out some kind of lie to tell Mia when she found out, because she would find out, and that woman did not need more stress.

THIRTY-SEVEN

NICHLAS

He should have never drunk that much.

Nichlas resisted a groan as he lounged in one of three bright yellow chaises littered around Anders' office that seemed just a little too good to be true. Floor-to-ceiling windows, boardrooms the size of the cafe, and lunch menus that were meant for gods. None of it made any sense, and none of it matched Anders' personality, at least the one he carried around town.

Here, in the city, Anders was one of the big guys. His words held meaning and he was ever the charmer, ladies and gents falling all over him like flies on shit. Frankly, it was quite disturbing to watch the attention Anders drew in when Nichlas knew how abusive the bastard was.

The man looked a little worse for wear – Anders having had *way* more alcohol than Nichlas – but he held himself together well, not well enough that his wife wasn't scowling at him across the office every chance he got.

There had been at least three nonverbal fights before ten a.m., each one revealing just *who* the boss truly was. Anders had said jack shit about what he did, who ran the company, and how they pulled in money. Nichlas hadn't been able to understand the office dynamic, everyone in their own little world, almost as if they were placed there rather than worked there.

His eyes tracked Natalie, watching with amusement as she stalked around the office in her gold stilettos and a size-too-small pantsuit that accentuated every curve, each sway of her hips just a bit too exaggerated.

Who the fuck is she performing for?

Because it sure as fuck wasn't for Anders.

"Hey, okay, sorry about all this. We're ready."

Nichlas frowned at the image in front of him before he blinked a few times and Anders came into view. He was usually better the day after a night infused with alcohol; he had clearly overdone it. "What?" *Ready for what?* He tried to soften his expression, an expression that supposedly terrified the shit out of grown men. It wasn't on purpose, just part of the job.

Anders didn't seem to notice. "Look, I know I explained some of this and most of it's cryptic. It's not illegal, but it's … well, it's part of the gray area." Nichlas raised an eyebrow that Anders took to mean interest. It, in fact, did not mean that. *Is this guy THAT stupid?* "Basically we pass information along and we get paid. It's pretty simple."

Definitely not simple and very illegal. It would have been part of that gray area if not for the fact that the information Anders was handling was supposed to be handed to some of the big three-letter agencies Nichlas worked for, not to the highest bidder. And as a condition of Anders' release, he was required to return the info but instead, he was playing two sides of a coin.

Executive-looking individuals filed into one of the board rooms, people who hadn't been on this floor moments ago. The horrible realization that Anders wasn't just breaking the law but risking lives for greed began to set in. The fact that Natalie seemed to be the ring leader made all of this worse. She was no longer the possessive ditz who needed Mia gone from Anders' life. She was so much more.

Nichlas made a split-second decision to ask a question that could ruin everything, but he had to know, and he was pretty sure Anders would be stupid enough to answer it. "Why's your wife really hate Mia?" He knew he was supposed to hate Mia as part of his cover, but he couldn't, not in this moment.

Anders let out a deep sigh, glancing back at Natalie as she greeted the attendees. "Mia's a distraction. I … it really was a business trip and Nat's my business partner but, I'm not perfect. She's pregnant with my child."

"So you just ripped Mia's life from under her?" Nichlas seethed, biting back the urge to express his anger with the situation.

"I was always going to come back but … Natalie threatened to tell Mia what we're doing here. And I–"

"And what are we doing here, Anders?" Nichlas bit his tongue before he asked the follow-up question, *What was so important that it involved breaking Mia's heart?*

Anders grit his teeth together and shook his head, "Look, just know that I love her. I'm trying to get her to understand that." It sure didn't look like it.

"Why am *I* here, Anders?" Nichlas stood up to his full height, glancing down at an angle to meet the man's eyes. Anders demeanor didn't boast violence, but Nichlas wasn't fooled.

"For protection." Nichlas raised an eyebrow again and this time, it was because of curiosity. "I think Nat is trying to kill me," he whispered before walking into the boardroom, Nichlas following on the man's heels silently, confused as to why Anders thought he could do anything about that. Officials, CEOs, high-rollers, and more were present, telling Nichlas that Anders wasn't just dirty, he was in over his head.

THIRTY-EIGHT

MIA

"What do you mean *you can't control him*?" Another one of Ma's famous sandwiches was hanging halfway out of her mouth as she glared at Quinn for stealing the other half. Kenn seemed to be yelling in the background, Jan whispering cryptic words over the phone. Apparently, something was wrong at the cafe, but Mia wasn't sure how she was supposed to help.

"He's not in his right mind. Nichlas came home this morning and–" His words trailed off and he groaned. "It doesn't matter. We need you."

Mia swallowed, still glaring at Quinn for the other half that she had been denied. He giggled and waggled his eyebrows, but Jan's pleading interrupted the comedic moment.

"Look, Matthias is about to rage, and Nichlas is the only one who can calm him."

"Then get Nichlas. I don't understand–"

"We can't reach him. Mia, *please*."

Her heart beat a little faster as his pleas hit her hard. Jan was not a small man by any means, and the look in his eyes could rival Nichlas' terrifying aura. "What can I do?" she asked even as she was shoving her feet into shoes and waving at Quinn before dashing out the door.

It didn't take her long to race down the street and burst into the cafe to see Jan and Kenn in a standoff with a man she didn't recognize. Kenn grabbed her out of the way of a glass cup hurtling toward her head, a scream on the edge of her tongue as she fell into Kenn's chest. He clutched at her, even as he growled at the threat a few feet away. "Matthias, get your shit together!"

Mia trembled in Kenn's hold, unsure what was going on when she twisted around to see two midnight orbs glaring back at her. There was only one thing with eyes like that – death. And it had come for her. She wanted to know what had set him off so bad that it hurt, her feet taking her toward the threat rather than away from it. Kenn scrambled to pull her back, but she slapped his hands away.

I've lost my damn mind.

Terrified as she was, confidence thrummed through her veins as she approached the man lost in his head with her hands raised. She knew the difference between raging violence and a man lost in his head, unable to take

His expression softened slightly when she laid a hand on his arm, his entire body sagging with the weight of the world until he was kneeling on the floor in front of her, arms wrapped around her waist. His head rested against her stomach as he took deep breaths trying to rid himself of nightmares she didn't understand. She knew a panic attack when she saw one, but this ... this was something different. Her hands fell to his head, stroking his hair as she looked to Jan and Kenn for an explanation.

"It's been a while since this happened. He ... doesn't, he has certain triggers. We all do, but his are the worst," Kenn began. It seemed hard to talk about this, but she needed to know. Anders was both physically and emotionally abusive and as much as she kept trying to pull away, she knew that there was something brewing between her and these men, which is why she needed to know. "Certain things set him off and he gets so wrapped up in his head. Nichlas is always around to be his anchor, but he's got his own mission this time so …"

"Why me?"

Jan chuckled and approached the counter, running a few fingers along Mia's cheek and then the fading bruise on her neck. "Because he likes you. We all do."

"That doesn't explain–"

"I would never hurt you, Mia." The muffled sound came from the man pressed against her stomach, still kneeling at her feet. It was an act of total trust and submission, the embrace holding more weight than anything Anders had ever done for her. Why she was still comparing them to that piece of shit was beyond her. "I'm sorry. I wish they hadn't called."

"I'm glad they did." Mia continued to stroke his hair as she met his gaze and then the other two, before returning to look at Matthias. "I need to know. Not everything, but the more important parts. If this is going to work, I have to know."

Silence filtered into the small space as Matthias stared up at her with every ounce of love and devotion in his expression that he could muster. Her heart bloomed until she couldn't hold down the emotion any longer and she leaned down to kiss him, something small but enough to get her point across.

Two pairs of heated stares focused on her back, and Mia knew she had to address them as well. Slowly, she pulled from Matthias' hold, the man standing up to hold her against his chest as she met Jan and Kenn's gaze. "I … I want this. It might make me selfish, but I want to try." The men gave her seconds to react, Kenn stealing her lips first before Jan tore her from Matthias' grasp and delivered the same attention to her lips, if not more.

"Sweet girl, you have no idea how long we've been waiting for you to say that. And it's not selfish to want to be loved. You deserve so much more than we can give you." Mia let out a small giggle, staring into Jan's eyes and seeing the intensity of emotions she had wished she'd seen in every other man she had ever dated. "Just one question. Nichlas?"

Her cheeks flamed, Jan releasing her back into Matthias' hold. No words were exchanged, but they all knew, as new as this was and as weird as it'd get, she wanted all of them. There were just a few things that had to be dealt with first – mainly the connection between the victims. She thought about telling the two men in front of her but brushed it off.

This needed to be her contribution and without a job, she had all the time in the world. Unfortunately, with the way Matthias was holding her, she wasn't sure she'd be able to disappear as easily as she hoped.

THIRTY-NINE

MIA

Saturday had turned into a cuddle fest in the men's apartment, Mia stretching across the three men as they attended to her every desire. She was constantly graced with touches and kisses, heating up her body to the point that she was squirming for release. After she caught them all with permanent smirks on their faces and Kenn trying hard not to snort and failing, she realized they had been doing it on purpose.

So she returned it tenfold, exploring and doling out touches of her own until their heated looks had nearly made her come undone. Mia had barely escaped after the second flick came on, citing a need to cool down and promising to return for bagels in the morning.

She hadn't, though. Between disgustingly cute texts and a few calls, Mia couldn't pull herself to drudge up the same amount of courage to return to the cafe when the rest of the town was out and about. Kingsley had fired her for "losing" a body, and now she was dating three men, possibly four. She hadn't spoken to Nichlas about it – although the other three assured her that's what they all wanted – so she wasn't sure where they stood.

He still terrified her, but she realized that after she was done hating herself, she wanted them. *All* of them.

Still, she had a singular focus that *wasn't* them and needed to be dealt with. Two hours after Quinn had left for work on Monday morning, Mia gathered that Kingsley was still pissed at her that that body had gone missing, but not because of any professional reason. No, it was one less payday for the department. He was also still holding out hope that she'd miraculously fall into his arms when she was done with the new eye candy that had strolled into town.

Yeah, well, fuck him.

She mentally raised two middle fingers to the sky, Ma chuckling at her expression. "You gonna be all right, sweetheart?"

Mia nodded, blushing as she started back in on the cross stitch that Ma had shown her how to do yesterday. While Mia had been hiding away in her lab and dating Anders, she had missed everything about Quinn's homelife, and all the projects Ma was into. Apparently, this spitfire of a woman aside from being the grandmother to one of the smartest kids in town was also a woman of many, many, *many* talents.

Each talent brought in some income, Ma's slogan that she liked to stay busy and have fun. Whenever boredom set in, she'd just find a new hobby. Every few weeks she'd pack up all these hobbies, travel into the city, sell them and then start all over again. According to Quinn, Ma had garnered some kind of fame at her stall, city dwellers rushing to her table for her one-of-a-kind creations.

Mia tried to focus on the task at hand, but it was hard knowing that her life was going to change amidst the craziness that was this killer. She knew her men thought that the killer was after her, but from what she had seen that night? She wasn't convinced, which spurred her on to figure out the connections even more.

"Hello?" Ma mouthed *sheriff* as she picked up the house phone, a stern look on her face. Mia sat up straight, freeing her hands as she leaned forward to hear what the sheriff had to say through the speaker.

"Where's Mialopolus?"

Mia cringed at the name but was surprised by the tenacity Ma answered with. "Not sure, as I don't know anyone by that name."

"Put Mia on the goddamn phone."

Mia couldn't help it, barking out a laugh as she wiggled her fingers for the phone, Ma handing it over with her own knowing smile. "Don't go easy on him," she whispered. Mia nodded and pressed the phone to her ear. "What do you want, Kingsley?"

"It's sheriff to you."

That pesky confidence was building again. Unsure where she drew it from, she used it anyway. "Yeah, okay. What do you need?" She was about to say that she had a cross stitch to finish, but her confidence didn't reach that far.

"I need you back at the coroner's office. Chad needs help."

She fought the urge to laugh as she leaned back in her chair, imagining Kingsley pulling out his hair as he realized that he had made a grave mistake. "I was fired."

"You're unfired," he threw back almost immediately.

"That's unfortunate, I don't want the job." As much as Mia was playing, she wanted her father's office back. The nice thing was, she knew Kingsley would have never let her go for long, but the pain of being humiliated still hurt and she wasn't going to make it easy on him.

"Get your ass back over there. There was another body over the weekend."

Mia's expression soured as she straightened up, gripping the phone a little tighter. "I fail to see how that's my problem." The

Batman joke fell flat as a bitter taste sat at the back of her throat. The killer's schedule was ramping up. Over the past year, there had been a couple dozen bodies. In the past week, there had been three … maybe four. Mia couldn't keep track anymore.

Kingsley didn't wait to let her sift through her thoughts. "Mia, *please.*"

He's using my name? It had to be serious if Kingsley had stopped playing games. Still, she wasn't going to bow down to the guy and take his shit, not after she had found out that her work was paying the sheriff department's bills. "Fine." Mia took a glance at Ma. "My rate is double what I was getting paid." She swallowed and laid the phone down on the table, putting it on speaker.

"What the—"

Mia cut him off. "Not a chance. *Double.* If you hang up, the next time you call I'll demand triple."

A bout of silence filtered into the kitchen as Mia waited. If Kingsley really needed her, he'd accept the deal. If not, he'd hang up.

"Fine. Double."

Mia took a minute to gather herself. The situation had to be fucked up if Kingsley was asking for help, and she knew she was a little bit twisted to be excited about the prospect of going back. "Good. Ma's here and she heard all that. I expect to see a check at the end of my shift." Mia didn't need the money, but she was going to collect on the mere principle that Kingsley was no longer going to fuck her over.

Besides, there was another clue she had dredged up over the weekend and needed access to the bodies before making her own conclusion.

Mia stared at the unfinished stitches and sighed. "Sorry, Ma. Looks like I've been called into work."

Ma snorted. "You're hardly broken up about it. Go and rescue my grandson from that new coroner." Mia giggled as she sped upstairs to throw on something a little more professional. After all, she needed to make an impression as the highest-paid coroner in the history of Bryxton. Another giggle left her as she thought of the horrified expression plastered on Kingsley's face when she arrived in her well-dressed attire. She was going to ride this wave of confidence into the ground.

FORTY

MIA

Strutting into the office in her favorite sundress, a pale purple one that brought out the little flecks of color in her eyes, she realized just how terrible of a situation she was walking into. Quinn was stuffed in the corner, tears streaming down his face as he tried to explain through giggles and snot about the multiple mishaps around the lab.

The new guy was obviously flustered, flailing at the edge of one of the metal slabs, a body slowly sliding off. "Would you help me?" he cried out. Mia let out a chuckle as she strolled into the area, locked the table, and then shuffled the body back onto the surface.

Flakes of dried blood were everywhere, as well as body fluids, most of which had found their way onto the new guy. She couldn't even remember his name – if he had ever offered it – but she was determined to not use it, to stake dominance in her place of work.

The guy scurried off to the shower in the back, one she had never had to use as she had never been so careless in her life.

Quinn scrambled over with supplies to clean up the mess, still wiping away tears and snot, his cheeks rosy from laughing so hard. "I was really pissed when Kingsley fired you. Like so fucking pissed. But this guy? He's fucking hilarious. I think his name is Charles or something, but he goes by Chad!" Quinn fell into another fit of laughter, Mia strangling him to his feet before he fell into the mess of dead-body piss.

"How many cases have you done?"

The kid took a few deep breaths and shrugged. "Since you left? None, but this body has the ..." Chad reappeared from the shower, looking like a drenched rat. He hadn't bothered to remove his clothes, but even if he had, Mia wasn't sure he'd look any better.

Mia nodded, piecing together what Quinn had been going to say. This body was yet another kill, bringing the total to twenty-six. She needed to tell the guys – as if Jan and Kenn didn't already know – but it would be nearly impossible with Kingsley watching like a hawk. Her eyes traveled the walls of her lab, pleased to see the windows barred with extra security. Her men had taken her safety seriously, warmth spreading through her chest at the thought.

"Just go over there!" Quinn hissed, a wide smile on his face. "I'll help clean up. You, too, Chad!" He let out another snicker as he pushed Mia toward the door, Mia taking the opportunity to cross the street and saunter into the coffee shop.

Had she remembered she hadn't shown up after the kisses and cuddles on Saturday, she might have hesitated walking in with such confidence. The purple-eyed-gorgeousness behind the counter froze at her entrance but quickly finished up with his customer on hand, attention trained on her approach. His smile widened as she leaned over the counter, unable to see anything other than her man.

"Come for sustenance?" he asked, fingers itching on the other side of the counter. She knew what he wanted, what he had wanted all weekend, what *she* had wanted all weekend. The way he held her was different from the others. The others held her with love and passion and devotion – something that should have been premature but didn't feel like it. But Matthias? He held her like she was precious. Like nothing else in the world mattered.

Mia managed a nod, her cheeks flaming as his gaze dipped down to take in her attire. She hadn't planned on seeing him when she left the house – the dress hadn't been for him, just her confidence – but she wasn't mad with the way he ogled her, the way his eyes heated as he drank in her figure.

If only Anders–

She wiped the thought from her mind, stomping on that mangled self-loathing and terrible comparisons she had been doing for the past week. Anders was a terrible human being who had subjected her to emotional and physical abuse. He was no longer an option, no longer worth being in her head. Blinking away any of those pesky thoughts that threatened to upend her happiness, she threw Matthias another smile as he slid her order across the counter.

They stared into each other's eyes, Mia realizing all of this holding back wasn't doing her any good. Rumors running rampant through her little town were causing her to stuff herself back into a shell she no longer needed. She didn't need protection, she needed to be herself. Completely and unapologetically herself.

Which is why she stood on her tiptoes, reached over the counter, and grabbed the front of Matthias' shirt to draw him into a kiss. She planned a small peck on his lips, just to show her ownership over the cute barista behind the counter but hadn't expected Matthias' passion to slip out – she should have known. Matthias gripped her cheeks, taking what he wanted, his tongue dancing with hers until she was wet between the thighs and breathless from the lust wafting from her man. When he released her, Mia tried to resituate herself, knowing that half the town had caught her leaning across the counter and macking on one of four delicious newcomers. If that hadn't proved the rumors, she wasn't sure what would.

She took a deep breath, cheeks heated, and grabbed the cup and bagel from the table. Matthias stood there, smug as he watched he retreat but not before she caught Natalie and her friends crowded around a table, muttering "slut," among other things.

Mia thought about ducking her head and returning to her office. She didn't need to respond, and no one else had heard it. But that's where the problems kept stemming from. She never addressed the problem until everyone thought it was a fact. That little kiss at the counter had told everyone she was done with Anders and had been done for a while.

But to fix her personality, Mia would have to face Natalie.

Her face burned with the memory of Natalie's slap as she turned to face the girls, recognizing them but unable to place them. They hadn't grown up here, but they'd been around. How they had fallen into Natalie's trap was beyond her, but Mia didn't like it.

I am not a slut. I didn't ask for this. Anders cheated on me.

Sentences ran through her mind, but none of them seemed right. Mia knew she was going to regret the words out of her mouth, but at this moment, she needed Natalie to understand she wasn't going to roll over and play bitch. Not anymore. "I think that word is reserved for people who are actually having all the sex, sweetheart." Mia drew on the darkness her men embodied, smiling at Natalie as her and her friends paled. "But what do we call someone who sleeps with a man who's taken?" Mia raised her eyebrows, waiting for the retort, Natalie searching for something to say. The woman hadn't expected Mia to talk back and didn't have something prepared.

But her friend did. "She's three months pregnant, you idiot! Don't say things like that!"

Mia cringed and stalked out the door without another word, too pissed to respond. *Three months pregnant?* Fury exploded from her as she tried to keep from smashing the cup. She knew Anders had been less than faithful to her, that Natalie had hardly been the first and definitely wouldn't be the last. But *pregnant?* Mia didn't know how to react to that, but she knew the next time Anders appeared in front of her, she had a few choice words she was going to say.

FORTY-ONE

MIA

An hour later, Mia had set up shop at her desk again, watching the fake coroner flit around the lab with an expression that mimicked someone being tortured. She took a healthy bite out of her bagel, whimpering as cinnamon and chocolate coated her tongue. She'd have to thank Matthias at some point. She had an image of her on her knees pleasing the man while he thrust forward a little too real.

She pinked, pressing her thighs together as she tried to get rid of that image. *Where the fuck did that come from?* Mia had never wanted to do something like that before, but with Matthias? *Maybe.*

Unsettled, Mia stuffed the rest of her bagel into her mouth, trashing the bag and the cup before Chad stumbled out, hands tugging at the ends of his hair. "You can't leave."

Mia chuckled, watching Chad shift uncomfortably beneath her stare. When Quinn popped up yelling "peek-a-boo," she was pretty sure the guy shit his pants. "Look, Chad, is it? I get paid by the hour. You got the job, not sure how, but you did. Do it."

She waited for the explanation, the explanation would reveal that Chad was a fraud.

"My father's good friends with the old sheriff, thought it'd be a good internship, ya know? But when I got here, Kingsley just told me I was in charge."

That didn't make much sense since the town was in the middle of nowhere and no one willingly came there to work. She'd circle around later, but she needed to hear more about Kingsley pulling strings he had no business messing with. "And then what?"

"I told him I wasn't qualified, but he said I didn't need to know anything. Or do anything. I just had to be here."

Mia cackled, shooing Chad out the door, letting him know that he could leave. Watching him almost retch after Quinn sawed open the man's chest on the metal table was enough to tell her that he wasn't cut out for this. She didn't even bother asking what his major was in as it didn't matter. Surprisingly, Chad didn't fight her, telling her that he'd let Kingsley know he quit before the day was over.

She didn't believe him in the slightest, but it gave her enough time to let her men know the new details she had found and the city trip she had been planning. With one text to their group chat, she knew it would be mere minutes before three bodies stumbled through the door, eager to hear her out.

FORTY-TWO

MIA

Jan and Kenn strolled in, Nichlas following behind them, a man she hadn't expected to see. She stared at the entrance a moment longer, shoulders falling when Matthias didn't appear as well. Had she been thinking, she would have known he was still serving coffee to the rest of the town while warding off all the whispers she just restarted.

The horror of what people were saying now that they had *seen* her kiss Matthias was going to haunt her on her way home. The men present in the room, however, seemed to be oblivious to her inner turmoil, immediately focusing on the spread she had recreated from her room, minus the pictures.

She had studied the cases for so long and so meticulously that the details had been embedded in her head. Quinn helped her paste the connections along the wall as they wrote a list of all the things that might aid in finding the killer.

"Kitten," Kenn approached her with lidded eyes, exuding affection and desire as he pulled her into his arms and placed a gentle kiss on her lips. She squirmed in his hold, peeking around to see Jan and Nichlas with various states of heated expressions. Mia raised an eyebrow, confused that they were just jumping into this relationship thing feet first. "Heard all about you trashing Anders' wife. Made me so happy to hear you standing your ground."

Mia swallowed carefully, trying to understand Kenn's reaction. She could count on three fingers who had ever told her to stand up for herself – her father, Ma, and Quinn. But a partner? No one had ever been *happy* she had finally shoved all that shit hurled at her where it belonged. Kenn wasn't just happy, he was ecstatic. His eyes were dancing and he was doling out kisses like candy to a child.

Her heart bloomed further for this man and the ones behind him at how much they cared. She had been so far in her head about kissing Matthias in public, that she hadn't even started freaking out about lashing out at Natalie. And now she didn't need to because these men would stand right beside her, behind her, or wherever she needed them.

She shimmied out of his arms after placing a small kiss on his cheek, bracing for whatever the other two had in store. Jan cracked a smile as did Nichlas, both of them shaking their heads. Seeming to know how overwhelmed she was with all of these new dynamics, they didn't push. She would be eternally grateful for their restraint as she began to explain what she had found.

Before she knew it, each of her men – including Nichlas – had taken up some spot in her office, raising the temperature a thousand degrees, or at least what felt like it. Quinn was in the lab chuckling to himself about fantasies and dreams come true, but one glare from her shut him up, and he continued to clean and organize.

Jan was leaning against the wall, staring at her so intently, her entire body thrummed with energy. His arms were pulled tight across his chest, ankles crossed as he listened to her explain what she had found so far.

Kenn had been the one asking questions, logging all the information away as he poured through the details. He was constantly pointing at her board and questioning her thoughts, not in a demeaning way but in a way to get her to expand on her conclusions. For most of the discussion, he stood behind her, dangerously close to her backside until one of his arms was wrapped around her waist and his chin was propped up on her head.

Her cheeks heated as she met Jan's eyes and then Nichlas', wondering what they thought of the possessive stance. She expected to see jealousy not desire. Maybe all their promises that this would work between them weren't just promises.

Nichlas had taken residence in her chair, his feet propped on her desk like a terrifying force of seductive allure. She scrunched her nose as her mind went wild with possibilities, fists clenching to hide the expression threatening to unearth itself. If they knew how turned on she was, now that she had let herself accept their attentions?

God, she would never live it down.

Mia threw another glare at Quinn, knowing the kid was watching her fall apart during this discussion before laying out the one fact she had been holding back. The killer was most definitely male, strong, and local. That much they could all agree on. She had even told them about the pinprick on the neck.

"Angel–"

Mia focused on the man in front of her who was several inches closer than he had been moments ago. His voice left no room to stall any longer, demanding the words she had been struggling to say for nearly an hour. "I … um, there's …" Her bottom lip trembled with the weight of her findings, unsure how each of these alpha men would take it. "I thought it was poison, you know, with the pinprick and all. It made *sense*. I wanted to believe that. I really did."

Jan stole her from the comfort of Kenn's embrace, Jan's aura threatening to undo her as he gripped her chin and angled it upward so that she couldn't shy away from his gaze. "Spit it out, angel."

She arched against him, desperately trying not to react to the way "angel" fell from his lips. God, these men and the names they had for her. She wondered what Nichlas' would be if he'd have one at all or if his intense stare would just melt her into a pile of goop.

"Um, there was dirt underneath their fingernails." None of the men spoke. "And scratches. I just thought that's because of where they were dumped. But you – Kenn – told me that there was nothing around where the bodies were found. Nothing that could produce those kinds of wounds."

Jan's expression darkened. "I need to hear you say it, angel."

"They fought back. All of them. They tried so hard not to die and he didn't care. I don't know what it all means, but they didn't go quietly." It didn't make any sense, not with the way that man had caressed the dead body on the night it was stolen, but it was the only plausible explanation. A sob racked her body as she thought about the horrors the victims had been put through. "I have to go."

"What—"

She slunk away from Jan and Kenn, holding her hands up. "No, not like that. I have to go see the bodies that were transported. I didn't write down everything and I just … I need to do this." All three of them sported wicked smiles before they broke out into laughter. Well, Nichlas was just doing one of those dark chuckle things that made her thighs clench together. That wasn't the reaction she had been expecting.

Nichlas rose to his feet, her first instinct to shrink back as he approached but even through the darkness, she could see the feelings he had for her and just hadn't voiced. "I like this newfound confidence, Mia, and I'm all for you piecing together details. However, it's dangerous." Mia stuck out her bottom lip, pouting. God help her if they forbid her. "I can't tell you where to go and not go, but could you please take one of us with you?"

Melting.

That's all she could describe it as – her entire heart and body and mind melting into the floor. Full-on *swoon*. How could anyone be so thoughtful and caring and passionate? Between these four men, she would want for nothing.

Mia nodded quickly after she realized she was staring, releasing a smile to let him know that she was fully on board with that plan. She had expected one of them to tell her to stay put and they would go in her place – but this, this was the best option.

"What the fuck is he doing here?" Quinn's strained voice reached her ears a moment too late, Anders stepping inside the building with a pained expression.

His gaze landed on her, but not before taking in the other occupants of the office. If anything, Anders looked like he was about to have a heart attack with her men's lethal stares trained on him. Words tumbled around her brain as she stared at the man trembling like a leaf, debating whether or not she wanted to release the hate she had for him. With her men standing around her, Mia took a deep breath, hardened her stare, and went in.

"I already said I didn't want to talk to you, but now that you're here? Did you really think I wasn't going to find out that your wife is *three months pregnant?*" Anders gulped, taking a step back when her men let out three satisfyingly dark growls. "You told me the business trip was a mistake, but did you ever think about what people were going to say? You're this ... this god to the whole town with your crazy lies about how I'm nothing more than a girl who works with dead people."

Concern crept into her men's expressions, Anders shocked at the way words were flying off her tongue, but she couldn't help it. Not anymore. She had been willing to look the other way, to move past it. But Natalie had pushed her over the edge – the slut comment she would have ignored. But the fact that Natalie was three months pregnant? That changed things. That changed *everything*.

"But this? You met her on what, a business trip, and then got her pregnant? At what point did marriage come up? How long had you been fucking that woman before you decided you wanted her instead of me?" Tears started their way down her cheeks as her blood heated, anger boiling it to the point of no return. Everything around her disappeared as she focused on the man's face, wanting to push it into the ground. "Actually, I don't want to know. I don't want to understand why I wasn't enough for you because you're wrong. I *am* enough. I was always enough. You were the one who wasn't enough!"

Her chest heaved with those words, clarity following them as she accepted the hangups she had had for so long. Anders had told her that she was plain, so she believed it. He told her that she was boring or didn't dress right or wasn't at his beck and call. She had believed it until she didn't. And now she was seeing how far it had set her back emotionally. Everything he had done had been to cage her in a little box that was perfect for him but stripped her of her freedom.

Anders' face scrunched, his expression unreadable, but the air had shifted. She was pretty sure he hadn't come into her office to start shit, but she wasn't so sure now. Her ex started toward her, hand raised, but she needn't have worried, Nichlas grabbing her and pulling her into his chest.

Mia let out a terrified squeak, trying to reconcile that it was *Nichlas* manhandling her and not Anders. Her ex stopped his approach, but the words still came. "You don't understand. There's things I haven't told you. I need you to–"

She kept her face stuffed in Nichlas' chest, focusing on breathing. "Fuck no! You hit me! You choked me! You don't get to explain. Not anymore." Her heart pounded in her ears as Nichlas held her tighter through the start of another panic attack. She had finally broke, her emotions flooding out onto the floor. Anders knew where he stood now. However, she wasn't all that stronger for it.

She felt drained. She wanted to let go, something Nichlas was offering with the way he shielded her from the entrance. Doors opened and closed, Quinn muttering a goodbye before the place became dead silent. She wasn't sure how much time had passed, the panic subsiding as she pulled away and looked around to see that they were the only two still present in her office.

"What–"

"Mia, are you ready to go home?"

She stared up at him, wondering why he wasn't going to address what happened. She wasn't even sure what *had* happened after she screamed at Anders, but now she was curious.

"Jan and Kenn escorted him out, told him to avoid any direct contact with you or they'd file with law enforcement."

Mia whined, "That's not–"

"Not *your* law enforcement. *Theirs*." Her body shuddered at the thought that Jan and Kenn were going to go over Kingsley's head for her safety. She nodded slowly, Nichlas releasing her. "Now, are you ready to go home, Mia? I think you've handled enough for one day." Once again, a statement that left no room for argument. It sounded like a suggestion, but it truly wasn't. It should have worried her that her men were dominant alphas insistent on protecting her, no matter the cost. It didn't.

FORTY-THREE

MIA

She walked beside him in silence, drinking in his aura. The uncertainty of her future seemed to disappear beside him, a feat that didn't happen with the others. They each provided her with a different peace, Nichlas' darkness was a safe haven all on its own. Before she knew it, she was standing in front of Quinn's house, Nichlas drawing her out of her head one last time.

"Will you be okay, Mia?"

Mia raised her head to meet his gaze, losing herself in his dark eyes, swimming around in those pools of mystery. Unlike the others, Nichlas was still very much guarded with secrets *and* lies. She could tell there was something he was hiding, more so than just whatever reason he had been sent here. Figuring out the link between the bodies could have been part of it, but that wasn't all.

She might have been timid from years of emotional abuse, but she wasn't stupid.

"Mia."

"Yes, *yes*. I'll be fine." His gaze darkened as it ran over her bruises, jaw tightening the longer he stared. Her body warmed beneath his attentions against her will, Mia wondering how twisted she had to be to enjoy the lethal stare Nichlas held.

Mia told herself through the awkwardness that she needed to hop up the steps and disappear into the house. She told herself repeatedly that staring at Nichlas was going to land her in trouble, but she couldn't help herself.

Which was why she was in her current predicament, Nichlas' gorgeous hands cupping her cheeks and tilting her head upward to meet him.

His lips grazed hers, Mia chasing the touch, but his hold was firm, releasing her just as soon as he had grabbed her. "Take care of yourself, all right? Call Matthias if you need anything."

Mia scurried into the house, one hand over her chest to calm her racing heart. Ma's snicker echoed through the kitchen, but Mia didn't wait to have that conversation as she ran up the stairs like a girl who had just been kissed after prom.

The kiss meant so much more than *just a kiss*.

She ran her fingers over her lips, remembering Nichlas pressed against her, those elegant fingers wrapped around her neck as he leaned in. God, she wished she had gotten more than that little whispered taste, that promise of something more.

A promise that Nichlas didn't intend to keep.

Doubt crept in as she settled on her bed, sifting through Nichlas' cryptic words.

Take care of yourself, all right?

Call Matthias if you need anything.

They were similar words he had muttered when he had set up her security system, almost as if he was preparing to not be around. As if he was preparing for her to *not want him around.*

That thought didn't sit well with her.

FORTY-FOUR

ANDERS

"Would you stop antagonizing her?"

Natalie shot Anders a death glare, fluffing at her blonde tresses as she stared in the mirror perfecting her makeup. The woman had been in the mirror for the past hour, hacking up her guts – an event that she made sure Anders was not present for – and then began putting on another layer of magic as if the previous one had disappeared.

After trying to catch Mia alone – his mistake – he had tried to reason with her, to tell her the truth. The *entire* truth, but those bastard detectives had been present and she had just made him so mad.

He realized his mistake *after* it happened and after Mia had started voicing those pesky thoughts in her head. He didn't like it when she talked back to him, but those were words he needed to hear. He had hurt her. He hadn't shown her all the love he could have and he needed to rectify that, as soon as Natalie stopped egging her on.

Mia had been his first love, his forever love, but mistakes along the way had pulled them apart until Anders found himself on the wrong side of the tracks and in jail. While everyone thought he had been at school earning degrees, he had been wasting away in a cell, trying to figure out where his life had gone wrong. He wished he could have said that he was just hanging with the wrong crowd, but *he* had been the wrong crowd.

When the FBI approached him with a deal, Anders jumped on it, knowing that it was the only way to return to Mia. In return for information on his counterparts, he'd be free to roam – with some limitations. Mia had been ecstatic when he returned, falling into his arms and rekindling the relationship from where they had left off.

They would have been married and the life ahead of them would have been full of possibilities if not for Natalie. Anders wasn't even sure where the bitch had shown up, but she had – and with receipts. She knew everything about him, all about his jail time, his deal, and his undying love for Mia. Once again, Anders wished he could say he had fallen in with the wrong crowd but he had been just as much a part of the operation as Natalie.

When the opportunity to sell the information he had gathered had come to pass, earning him hundreds of thousands of dollars instead of the measly hundred given by the government, Anders took a chance on Natalie and her designed operation. What started as a quick cash grab turned into a dark hole he hadn't been able to climb out of. Natalie ensnared him with her sexy wiles and Anders fell for it, hook, line, and sinker. There was no way out anymore.

He let out a small sigh as he leaned against the archway of the bathroom, watching his woman apply a shade of purple lipstick that didn't match the rest of the night's events, but he knew better than to ask. "Look, Mia's old news. Just move on and choose a new bitch to fry, all right?"

The words felt like ash on his tongue, but he needed Natalie to focus on something else.

His woman threw her head back, cackling at the ridiculousness of his suggestion. "Babe, you know I'm not going to do that. You've got your head so far up your ass you think you're still in love with her. It's ridiculous. Like, *seriously*. You beat the poor woman and you think she's coming back for your dick? Fat chance." Natalie leaned forward to apply a second coat of lipstick.

Anders wasn't convinced. "Just back off."

"Give me one good reason why." Natalie capped the lipstick and turned around, smacking her lips together before folding her arms against her chest. Her belly showed the slight curve that had grown over the past three months. It was one of the only reasons he had agreed to marry her, to take care of his child. But as time passed and Natalie became more secretive in her agenda, Anders wasn't so sure that the child was his. When she caught him staring, she moved to caress her belly, shooting him a small, robotic smile. "Growing, isn't it? Now, Anders, give me a reason why I should leave that little whore alone."

He thought for a good reason while staring at the strange way her hands moved over her stomach. It wasn't the movement of a mother-to-be, one who wanted kids, a woman with a mother's instinct. It was forced, a motion that had been trained. Anders wasn't sure what to make of that.

"I'm not backing off, Anders. You keep getting distracted and just because those men are in town, circling her like vultures is no good reason to give up my pastime."

That's what he was afraid of – that Mia had caught Natalie's attention.

With all of the shady shit they were into, the last thing he wanted on Natalie's radar was Mia. He'd reach out to Nichlas to see if there was something the guy could do to make sure Mia was safe, and then after that, get him the hell away from Natalie.

Curiosity finally hit him as he asked the question he had been fighting the urge to. "Where are you going, Nat?"

"Don't question me, big boy." Natalie stalked past him, patting his chest with a tight smile, and leaving a small kiss on his cheek. "You know not to do that." She slipped on a pair of stilettos – way too high for a pregnant woman, he thought – and slipped out the front door without another word, leaving him in the dimly lit apartment with a purple brand on his cheek.

FORTY-FIVE

KENN

He relaxed in his office chair, propping his feet up on the desk as he tried to reason with the direct order Kingsley had shoved in their face when they arrived this morning. After several cups of coffee, Kenn had tasked himself with questioning random Bryxton citizens regarding anything they had seen over the past few weeks, anything out of the ordinary.

Apparently, that was *not* what they should have been doing, because Kingsley ripped them a new one.

"What the fuck were you thinking?" Kingsley screamed, his face redder than a tomato as Kenn leaned back against the couch in the man's office. Two seconds after stepping inside, Kingsley had signaled that they all needed to have a private meeting. Now Jan and Kenn were stuffed into a couch across from Kingsley's desk, the know-it-all sheriff berating at them. "You can't just go around bothering people like that."

Kenn wanted to rage, to yell at the man that this was what detectives did, but he didn't want to clean up a body right now. If he gave in to his emotions,

Jan wouldn't be far behind. Kingsley was a dickwad, but he didn't deserve the kind of death they would deal out, so Kenn settled farther into the couch and just nodded.

"And for god's sake, use the coroner I hired. Mia doesn't work there anymore, and I don't appreciate finding out that she was throwing her weight around—"

A growl accidentally slipped from Jan's lips but he decided to own it. "No, that's not fair. The little shit you hired couldn't even handle body fluids. I don't know where you found him but—"

Kingsley grabbed the closest thing to him – an abstract-shaped golden paperweight – and chucked it at Jan's head. Jan had the reflexes to dodge it, his gaze darkening with the desire to rip the man to shreds. Kenn laid a comforting hand on Jan's shoulder and waited for Kingsley to explain himself.

"You will not question me in my department. Since day one you have followed your own rules. I've been lenient since another department sent you, but no more. I am the law here and you will abide by what I say. No more approaching the locals. Forget Mia, she's my problem to deal with. And for god's sake, stop trying to stir up new cases. I know you probably think you're important. You're not. Now get out."

In any other situation, Kenn would have let Kingsley have a piece of his mind, but here? It wasn't worth it. Which is why they were both settled back at their desks, Kenn sifting through all the information they had pulled together with Mia yesterday and the few bits he had managed to drag out of the townsfolk. His cheeks warmed just thinking of her, the way she responded in his arms as he held her in front of the others until the memory of Anders burst into his head.

Now, he was angry.

A wet wad of paper hit his cheek, startling him out of his head. He hissed in Jan's direction, knowing that the cheap trick was Jan's way of calming him down – weird, but effective.

"Stop thinking so hard. I've got a plan."

"What kind of plan? Does it involve killing Kingsley?" Kenn sat up, dropping his feet to the floor and leaning forward. "Because I really want to rip his head off."

"You and me both, but no. Better." Kenn raised an eyebrow. Something better than offing the sheriff? Bring it. "I spoke with his father."

"When?"

Jan chuckled. "When you were so far in your head raging over whatever the fuck was going on."

"I didn't even know you left," Kenn muttered, feeling a little hurt that Jan had gone off without him.

Jan didn't seem to care as he gestured for them to walk outside. Kingsley was on their ass about staying near the office, but standing just outside seemed acceptable for the time being. "Look," Jan started once they were far enough from anyone who could listen in. "The man's being blackmailed to keep his mouth shut. Apparently, he had an affair last year and doesn't want Kingsley's mother to know."

"Fuck, is that how Kingsley became sheriff?"

Jan nodded. "It makes sense."

"Really? All this shit over a little infidelity?"

"It's a small town, not that that explains things, but it's what I've got."

Kenn sighed, shoulders falling as he ran his hands through his hair. "This shit is messy. I don't like messy. I haven't even figured out why some fucker would steal a body from the morgue, especially not the way Mia described it. That's some really fucked-up shit, and to think that whoever's doing it is *in town*? Let's find whatever we can here and then go find our girl. I'm feeling lonely."

At that, Jan cracked a smile, shaking his head. "You're hilarious. Just text her like a normal person."

"And where would the fun be in that?"

FORTY-SIX

NICHLAS

He would have rather been anywhere but where he was, once again resting in Anders' lounge, waiting for an assignment. He would even rather be back in that awkward moment from last night when he had all but said goodbye to Mia. From the faintest touch of her lips, Nichlas had nearly given up everything to draw her into his arms and take her against the brick of the house with little regard to who passed by. But he was at the very least a gentleman, and he refused to draw her into issues that she couldn't possibly foresee.

Mia would never forgive him once she found out that he was hanging with her abusive ex, so it was only right that he end things before they truly started. Unfortunately, seeing that desire directed at him, Nichlas couldn't help but wonder what could have been had he not sabotaged his chances.

Forget her. You can't have her. Just move on.

Nichlas took a deep breath and focused on the mission at hand. From what he had gathered, the bastard didn't need help at work. He really did want protection, for both himself and Mia. When Nichlas tried to pry, Anders sputtered around the truth, saying something about how Natalie was dangerous.

While that might have been true, Anders was just as dangerous, selling information to the highest bidder. He was selling out innocent people for money, turning crime into a business venture that should have been over had he handed it to the FBI.

Nichlas had called Cross a dozen times since last night, wondering when they could turn the little sleazeball in for his crimes. He had evidence, so he wasn't sure why he was still waiting in the shadows. Cross had explained that this was mainly a recon mission and that for as long as he was told, he was supposed to gather facts.

Which meant that he had to spend *more* time with the man who had made Mia's life a living hell.

He continued to observe from his perch, intrigued that Natalie didn't seem to mind his added presence or the fact that Anders kept running back to him every chance he got.

An hour into sitting and doing nothing more than twiddling his thumbs, Anders made his biggest mistake, a mistake that Nichlas hoped would get him out of this fact-finding shit of a mission for good.

"Hey, Nich." Nichlas bristled at the nickname. He hated people shortening his name unless he trusted them. "Need you to go through these documents and sort by type. Overdue, Current, Finished." A stack of papers was shoved at him as Anders ran to his desk. "I've got another meeting and then we can fuck off for the rest of the day. Nat's said she's got the rest."

Nichlas didn't ask what any of that meant as he stared at the papers, due dates along the top and signature lines pasted at the bottom. The text didn't make much sense at first until he realized that they were contracts, contracts with each "bidder" and the general information they were receiving. Directly in front of him was gold.

As soon as Anders disappeared from the office, Nichlas whipped out his phone and dialed Cross. "This little shit is the most careless fuck I've ever seen." He shot off a round of pictures, Cross dying of laughter on the other end.

"Are you fucking kidding me? Wow. Yeah, that shit's good."

"So, I'm done?" He flipped through a few more pages, wondering at the amount of information Anders had access to. Nichlas believed some of the intel was from Natalie, but *still*. This shit was ruining lives while Anders was making a pretty penny.

"Probably but not until the higher-ups say so. I've got to get this cleared. I'll do it ASAP, I promise."

"*Please.*"

"What's got your panties in a twist?"

Nichlas grumbled out a response as his gaze snagged on Natalie approaching Anders' office. The need to make another bad decision scratched at the edge of his brain, Nichlas ending the call and walking out to meet the woman. "Hey," he began, changing his expression from disbelief to earnest. "Thank you so much for giving me a job to do."

Her smile warmed as she stared at him. "Always. My husband can be very caring, such a good Samaritan that way. It's why he has such a big heart for Mia, but I keep trying to tell him that she's a lost cause."

Nichlas' expression faltered, but he regained his composure just as fast, knowing that Natalie was baiting him for a reaction. He wouldn't give her one. "That's too bad. She needs help, but he's a taken man. A lucky one at that."

She bit her lip seductively, reaching out to grab his shoulder and then squeezed. "As are you. A lucky man that is." Nichlas raised an eyebrow, unsure where the conversation was headed.

"You get to work here. There's so much to do and learn. Really, you've stumbled upon an opportunity." The way her voice dropped, a sultry edge added to her words, Nichlas recognized the double entendre.

He opened his mouth to shut that shit down when an employee raced past them, nearly knocking Natalie on her ass. Natalie shouted a few curses down the hall, brushing herself off and checking her outfit for blemishes before glancing at Nichlas with a scowl.

"Nobody takes their time. Always rushing."

Nichlas tried to understand the feeling in his gut, the acid building up at the back of his throat as he observed Natalie's methodic movements. It didn't make sense. This pregnant woman had just been knocked over, and her first reaction was to check her dress and shoes.

"How's the baby?" he asked.

She frowned, and then recognition spread through her features. "Oh, the baby?" Her hands flew to her stomach, a tight smile on her lips. "Good. Growing. Like three months or something."

Nichlas couldn't understand. He had so many goddamn questions but knew that he couldn't voice his suspicions here. The way she was cradling her stomach was akin to the way someone would hold their belly if they had a stomach ache, not a growing human being.

And the fact that she seemed unsure of how far along she was?

And the one fact that he couldn't possibly ignore among all the others – the way she seemed almost confused when he asked about the baby, as if there wasn't one at all?

Nichlas had already come to a conclusion, one he was pretty sure was correct; but he needed evidence. Evidence he wouldn't find here at the company. He excused himself, saying that he had an emergency to tend to and that he'd reach out to Anders for lunch later.

There was only one thought swirling around in his head as he high-tailed it out of the building.

She's not pregnant.

FORTY-SEVEN

MIA

With yet another day off – apparently, Chad tried to quit but Kingsley rejected his resignation *and* told her not to show up – she decided spending time with one of her men was the best way to while away the time.

For the first time since Matthias' cafe had opened, table service was officially offered, Mia bouncing around the place with a bright smile on her face as she served pastries and coffee to townsfolk who whispered about her behind her back. They seemed cordial enough today as she let the nasty comments slip off her like they didn't hurt, the general mood lightening as the day continued.

She remained in high spirits even as the morning rush died out and the little jabs continued. With each order, she met Matthias at the counter, grinning like an idiot as those amethyst eyes drank her in. Their fingers grazed as he passed off the order, her body heating up with every touch until she was thoroughly aroused with no outlet.

Scanning the cafe for any additional mess as the afternoon sun signaled the café's closing hour, Mia made her way behind the counter to set the last of the dishes in the sink, letting out a yelp when two arms wrapped around her waist and a hard chest pressed her against the counter. Kisses rained down her neck and bare shoulder as she arched against Matthias, her head falling forward from the contact.

God, the *attention* …

Mia pushed back, just enough that she could turn around, giggling as his hands settled on her waist and he met her halfway, lips crashing with hers. Her hands moved up to rest on his chest as he caressed her lips with his tongue, running along the seam, and then dipping inside to taste her. She moaned into the kiss, giving in further as his hands dropped to the back of her bare thighs beneath her dress and lifted her onto the counter.

Oh. My. God.

Anyone could walk in and see the passion unfolding, but for once, Mia didn't care. For once, she was going to satisfy herself. She was going to focus on what *she* wanted. She felt she deserved that much. *Just once.*

Mia's fingers curled into his shirt, grasping for purchase as her thighs tightened around his waist, dragging him closer until she felt his cock thickening between her legs. He swallowed another one of her moans as she gave an experimental rock of her hips, grinning through the kiss when he melted against her.

The movement built her confidence as she continued the rhythm, pleasure shooting through her limbs as his cock stroked her through the fabric of her panties until a groan was ripped from his throat and he tore his mouth away from hers, pleading her to stop. "Baby girl," His words tumbled out in a breathy tone that had her fingers curling tighter. "We can't. Not here. God, I want you so fucking bad." He nipped at her lips, the darkness in his hooded eyes warming her from the inside out.

"I want—"

He chuckled, fixing her dress, and setting her feet back on the floor. "I *know* what you want, baby girl. But I'm not going to do that here. Not for our first time."

Swoon.

She was a puddle of goop all over again at the care in his words. Matthias was far from perfect – that dangerous aura still lurking around him – but god, if she didn't just want to wrap him up and keep him forever.

Forever.

It wasn't a thought she had had since Anders, and if she was honest with herself, she had never truly thought of Anders and herself as *forever* material.

Matthias cradled her against his chest, pressing one last lingering kiss on her forehead before releasing her altogether to return to the neglected dishes. Mia let him be, moving off to the side to watch, biting back a giggle when she realized he was fully hard, his cock straining against his zipper. Fantasies flitted through her mind, an image of herself dropping to her knees and wrangling Matthias into position before pulling his cock out so that she could swallow it whole. Her cheeks reddened the longer she stared, and when she was finally able to rip herself away from the glorious sight, Mia ran to the other side of the counter to grab a glass of water. In a parallel universe, that moment would have never ended. The more she thought about it, Mia decided that next time she wouldn't let it end.

Time seemed to stop when the front door banged open, Mia scrambling to pull her dress down even further although she was no longer indecent. Chad busted in, his expression pained with Quinn in tow. The kid was one second away from falling apart into fits of laughter.

"I can't work with the kid! He's insufferable."

Quinn lost it, his laughter bouncing along the walls, making Mia approach the both of them with a concerned look. He waved his hand at her, sputtering an explanation through tears. "He can't do *anything*. Had to sew one of the bodies up and he—" Peals of laughter fell from his lips as he continued to wave his hands, unable to finish his sentence.

Chad huffed, thrusting his finger forward to reveal the issue. A small needle was stuck just below the skin, threaded through several times where the only way to dislodge it would be to slowly cut it out. Mia frowned, wondering why Quinn hadn't taken care of this at the office and how the hell the thread had gone through *several times*. "What is going on? Why are you over here? There's a first aid kit on my desk." She couldn't help but grin at Quinn's goofy excitement, but he was overdoing it.

"This little shit wouldn't stop laughing," Chad pointed at Quinn. "And … I don't do blood."

Quinn fell silent. "The fuck? What are you even majoring in?"

"Medical technology."

Mia let out a deep sigh.

Before she could direct Chad into a seat, the man was already sitting, Quinn propped up beside him with an open first aid kit, gently working on his hand as his shoulders continued to shake from chuckles he was trying to hide.

She blinked a few times, unsure of what she was seeing, the silent exchange of guilty looks and flushed cheeks reminding her of high school crushes and letters passed in secret. Beneath all the teasing, there was more, wasn't there?

Quinn carefully undid the thread, expertly slipping out the needle and cleaning the wound without a joke or jest in between. Mia stole a glance at Matthias, his eyes dancing with amusement at the scene unfolding in front of them. Trying not to disturb the two, she crept back around the counter, leaning into Matthias. "You see it, too, right?"

He nodded, discreetly sliding a hand around her waist until she was tucked into his side. It felt comfortable there, and she didn't want to leave as she melted against his chest, drinking in his scent. She would have stayed there forever if her day hadn't been cursed from the beginning, two others crossing the threshold. Well, *cursed* wasn't the right word.

She noticed Jan with a tight smile, someone stealing her from Matthias' hold before she could process that Jan *and* Kenn had entered the shop. Kenn rained kisses all over her face and down her neck until she was squirming for him to release her.

"Kitten, I *missed* you."

"The fucker couldn't text you like a *normal* boyfriend." Jan spat, a deep chuckle accompanying his words.

Mia rolled the word "boyfriend" over her tongue a few times before nodding to herself. She liked it. "I quite like the greeting," she purred, patting on Kenn's arms to release her so she could greet Jan. He leaned over the counter and placed a soft kiss on her forehead, smiling as he did so.

"Noted, angel."

Someone clearing their throat brought her back to the present, Mia glancing around Jan to see Quinn and Chad staring at them. A wild smirk was plastered on Quinn's face, but Chad just looked confused, eyes darting between the four of them, widening when Kenn pulled her against his chest again and stuffed his face in her neck.

"Um–"

Quinn saved her, as per usual. "Don't ask questions, Chad. Let's go back now that you're all cleaned up. Don't worry. I won't make you do any more *sewing*." His giggles started back up again as Chad's face turned beet red, the two of them heading back across the street, leaving the others in silence.

FORTY-EIGHT

MIA

With the door locked, she could finally relax. She curled up in Kenn's lap, without worrying that half the town was going to stumble upon her abnormal relationship. She had been at a loss of where to sit or how to address her men as they set up information along one of the tables, but Kenn buried those thoughts when he grabbed her and promptly told her that the relationship was about what *she* wanted and what *she* was comfortable with.

It was a nice thought in theory, but it felt weird *choosing*. Mia decided to address that later as Jan and Matthias sat on opposite sides of the table. The aura in the cafe had darkened, despite the way Kenn was tracing small circles on her hip. Even Matthias' usually lighthearted demeanor had been swapped for that mysterious lethal energy that both terrified her and turned her on.

"Angel, we need to know who'd meet this criterion."

Jan slid a paper toward her, Kenn grabbing it and handing it to her. She tried to squirm off his lap, but as he had mentioned before, he quite liked being useful.

She made a mental list as she went through the checklist of height, general weight, and availability, souring at the thought as one name popped up in her head. "A few people ... and Anders." Matthias let out a little growl, her eyes darting over to meet his.

Kenn gripped her hips to bring her back to the moment. "Where does Anders work?"

"Just outside the city at some accounting office or something," Mia said. She tried to think back to the conversations about Anders' job but realized that he had never explicitly told her what he did. She thought he did something with numbers or information but couldn't clearly pinpoint anything more than accounting.

But Anders in accounting? That had to be a fucking lie.

"Why, what is this about?" Mia questioned, leaning forward so she could twist around to meet Kenn's eyes and then Jan's.

Kenn hung his head, pulling her back into his lap and kissing her shoulder. "Mia, our profiler said this is suspect. That these characteristics ... fuck, we need to talk to Anders."

Mia froze in Kenn's lap, unsure where to look when Matthias' expression darkened further. "What–"

Jan let out a deep sigh, nodding to Kenn to release her. "Matthias here is our profiler. He's been through a lot, so he usually stays out of it, but we were having some trouble." Mia crawled out of Kenn's lap and placed a timid hand on Matthias' shoulder, similar to the time she brought him back before. His expression softened. "He draws from a pretty dark place, which is why–"

"Which is why I initially said I wouldn't do it but then he went after you. Baby girl, if anything happened to you ..." His words trailed off as his hands caught the back of her thighs and he dragged her onto his lap, her thighs straddling her hips. Mia's hands fell to his chest as she tried to read his expression, the man gripping her just a little harder as he arched up to kiss her. Her body moved of its own accord as her hands found themselves in his hair and she leaned into the kiss, pressing herself flush against him.

Two pained groans erupted behind her, Mia ripping her lips away from Matthias to glance at the two men staring at her with heated expressions. Her face flushed at the range of possibilities, the million and one ways this situation could unfold. All those chastity lessons stuffed down her throat told her that she was living through every sin imaginable, that she would be judged at the gates of hell for merely letting Matthias touch her.

And yet, Mia decided to stuff those pesky little thoughts in a corner. For so long, she had succumbed to what everyone else thought she should be – the good little girl, the obedient little girl, the quiet little girl. Mia was done being that girl. She was ready to be herself, the girl who lived for herself, who took what she wanted, and didn't give a fuck what anyone else said about it.

Granted, the last part would take some getting used to, but Mia was determined.

Matthias' grip slid upwards a few inches and pulled her down until her pussy was resting against his crotch in a way that had her moaning for more. "Baby girl, you're running this show, but I have an idea. Do you trust me?" Mia nodded slowly, knowing that whatever this idea entailed, it would include the two sitting behind her. "Good girl," he said and placed a soft kiss on her lips. "Now, I need you to turn around and straddle me, so they can see you."

She blinked a few times, unsure what he was planning. Still, she complied, slowly. Mia slid off his lap and turned around, Matthias catching her at the waist before she sat back down.

"Baby girl, do you need me to grab a condom before we start?" Mia shook her head, knowing for a fact that she wanted to feel him completely for the first time. Fuck, she wanted them *all* like that. Having not wanted children with Anders meant that her birth control was up to date. "If you want to play, Mia, I need you to slide those pretty little panties off for us."

With two heated stares trained on her, Mia felt her nipples harden against her bra, straining to be released. Her thighs quivered with desire as she complied again with Matthias' command. She slowly slid them down, giving Matthias a nice view of her bare ass beneath her dress. His hands cupped those cheeks, massaging gently as she stood back up, waiting for her next command. It was equally calming and terrifying giving up control to someone she couldn't see. But fuck if she didn't love it.

Jan and Kenn had their legs spread, unapologetically stroking themselves through their pants as they stared. Mia tried to understand what was happening, the way everything was driving her up a wall when they hadn't even started. She heard the sound of a zipper and peeked back to see Matthias' stiff cock slapping against his stomach, the man's dark purple eyes back in action. Unconsciously, she licked her lips, wondering what he tasted like.

"*Later*," he chuckled before grabbing her waist and guiding her to straddle him while facing the others. Slowly, she sunk down on his cock, gasping as it slipped in, filling her to the brim. When she was fully seated, they both let out a satisfied moan, Mia stringing an arm around his neck and drawing him into a kiss. "Baby girl," he said as he slowly released her lips. "Your men want to be a part of this. They want to see you fall apart, but they always want you to see what you do to them."

Mia knew what that meant, knew what they wanted from her. She nodded enthusiastically, eyes trained on their thickening bulges, her pussy clenching at the thought that *she* was the cause of it. Matthias thrust upward, unable to hold back, drawing a yelp of surprise from Mia.

"Fuck, I need to move. *Mia*, baby girl, they need to hear it."

"Yes!" Mia squeaked, holding onto the armrests of the chair as Matthias began thrusting upward. Her eyes rolled back into her head as one of his hands dove to find her clit, pinching at it to bring forth her pleasure.

She tried to focus forward, two large cocks being stroked across from her, pulsating between large fingers as pre cum beaded at the tips. Confidence thrummed through her as she blindly reached out a hand, rewarded with the sound of a scraping chair and a cock in her hand.

Mia screamed again as Matthias hit a sensitive spot, her eyes widening as she realized Kenn's cock was in her petite hands, Kenn waiting for her to do something. The man looked wrecked as he stood before her, Mia leaning forward just enough to lick the tip. He groaned, hands falling to her hair and grabbing hard.

She startled, unsure about the force but then realized she liked it. Licking the tip again, Kenn involuntarily pushed forward into her mouth, Mia enjoying the weight on her tongue.

"Fucking hell, kitten. Shit, you're gonna make me blow my load, and we just started." Mia dragged her tongue down his length until he was near the back of her throat before sliding him out and then back in. She had never thought about doing this with anyone else, but watching Kenn fall apart because of her tongue?

"Fuck, that's hot," Jan muttered from his seat, still stroking himself with a blissed-out expression.

Matthias was pounding her from below, little nips and kisses littered along her shoulder, one hand diving into the shoulder of her dress to cup her breast as the other one remained on her clit. Mia arched against the sensation, Matthias driving deeper inside of her as she screamed around Kenn's cock.

It was too much and not enough all at once.

Her body spasmed as an orgasm overtook her, a deep moan vibrating through her as her pussy squeezed Matthias' length. The men's encouragement worked her up toward another orgasm as Matthias continued his assault, his thrusts becoming sloppy as he neared his release.

"She's so fucking beautiful when comes," Jan mumbled, his voice deep and raspy.

"You squeeze me so beautifully, baby girl. Fuck, come one more time for me." Mia tried to focus on sucking off Kenn, Matthias and Kenn's grips tightening around her waist and in her hair. The renewed attention on her clit had her bucking wildly against Matthias' fingers, Kenn grabbing the base of his cock with a silent question.

She didn't even have to think about it. She'd been dreaming about this for *days* as she grabbed at his thighs, lapping up his cum as he spurted it down her throat. He groaned as he pumped in and out of her mouth, fingers tangled in her hair, Matthias thrusting upward one last time before he spilled his seed as well.

Mia screamed through her next orgasm, pleasure shooting through her body as Matthias filled her, spurt after spurt coating her womb. Her eyes trailed over to Jan, cum covering the palm of his hand, and eyes lidded with an undeniable heat directed at her. Her confidence waned a little, embarrassment replacing it as the high wore off but her men weren't going to let her focus on anything but the pleasant, sensual memory of what just happened.

Matthias slipped her off his lap, their combined release slipping down her the inside of her thighs. It felt strange as she pressed them together, cheeks flushing red as she realized what state of undress she was in but before she could comment on it, Kenn had stuffed himself back into his pants and gathered her up on the way to the bathroom. Barely a thought ran through her head before her men were cleaning her up, post-coital kisses and caresses given in between caring looks.

Mia had never felt so cared for in her life and despite the severity of the situation outside of the cafe, she was sure of one thing.

She wanted these men, and nothing was going to take them from her.

FORTY-NINE

MIA

Post-coital bliss was a real thing, Mia could attest to it, as the rest of the day and evening unfolded with constant attention and another round in the shower with Jan and *another* in Kenn's bed while the other two were focused on drawing up a profile for the man leaving dead bodies just outside of town. A week ago, Mia would have cowered in the corner and hidden behind the years of self-loathing she had perfected.

Now? She wanted nothing more than to explore this new side of herself amidst the chaos unfolding around her.

"Mia, *Mia*," Jan chuckled against her lips as she pressed into him, clothed in nothing but his shirt. She had woken up to an empty bed but traveling down the stairs had given her the unbelievably beautiful image of three shirtless men in their makeshift pajamas, sharing cups of hot coffee. Smiles nearly melted her into the ground as she made grabby hands for a mug, falling into Matthias' hold first and then Kenn's before Jan stole her for a round of kisses, cinnamon and sweetness on his lips. "*Mia*, I have to go."

She grumbled, enjoying his hands on her waist just a little too much, those pesky fingers slowly traveling down to cup her bare ass, Matthias cutting in before anything became a little too risqué for the public area.

"As much as I'd *love* to see where this is going …" – he tugged Mia toward his chest and away from Jan, placing a soft kiss on the curve of her neck – "… there's a town hall meeting and *some people* still have to prepare for this morning because last night we were a little busy."

Mia blushed, her cheeks reddening with embarrassment as her confidence waned again. These men wanted her, like *really* wanted her. But why?

Kenn frowned, catching her expression. "Nope, sweetheart, we're not doing that. We're not going to feel guilty. We all want this, to be here, with you."

Mia nodded, trying to get past her self-doubts as she focused on Matthias' words, twisting around to see his face. "I was wondering why the shop wasn't open–"

Jan chuckled. "You were 'wondering,' yet you walked down in that?"

Mia's gaze dropped to the shirt covering everything and nothing at the same time. Her nipples – hard as diamonds – could be seen through the thin fabric, and if she just slightly bent over, her ass would be on full display. "That's – that's not the point," Mia stuttered. "What's the town hall for?"

A smile spread across Kenn's face as he leaned back against the counter. "Jan here cornered Kingsley until he agreed to call a town hall meeting."

"When?" She tried to wrack her brain when there would have been enough time for one of them to slip out between all of the hanky panky last night. A round of chuckles erupted in the kitchen as Matthias pushed her toward the stairs to change. "What for?"

The chuckles ceased almost as fast as they had begun, her men's expressions darkening in return. Jan let out a deep sigh, shaking his head. "The people here need to know what's going on. That it's not safe here."

Mia nodded again, refusing to address the seriousness of the situation as she headed up the stairs. The beauty of last night and this moment began to fade as the threat loomed over her. Just because some things had become easier, it didn't mean everything had.

FIFTY

MIA

Mia had been invited several times by her men, but she declined the invite to the town hall, citing the need to clean up her office. In reality, her office was spotless and there was no lingering work that couldn't wait until later. However, Mia wasn't about to sit through a meeting detailing the horrors she had seen pass through her office over the past year.

Chad wandered in, sheepish but willing to assist in any way he could. "I'm sorry about all this," he waved his hands to gesture to the job. "Kingsley's a really hard person to say no to."

"I know. I'm not mad at you. It was just a bit of a shock." She let out a heavy sigh while pointing to the file cabinet. "Can you grab the top one? I need to check something." The kid sauntered over, eyes snagging on the lab before he froze, shock flooding his features.

"Isn't that–"

Mia frowned, rising to her feet, and approaching the glass window of her lab. To her horror, a body lay on the metal slab in the middle, the very body that had been stolen from her last week. The body was in rough condition, and she wondered how the lab hadn't been the first thing to check when she arrived a few minutes ago.

She swung open the door, the putrid smell of rotting flesh slapping her in the face. *How did I miss this?* She frantically looked around for a culprit, but whoever had returned the body was long gone. Freaked, she hurriedly dialed Kenn's number, praying that he'd pick up. The town hall was just a block or two away but–

"You weren't expecting this to be here, were you?" Chad backed up a little, face draining of color as he pressed himself against the filing cabinets. "He was here. The killer. Fuck, like really?" His words trailed off into nonsensical mumbling, the kid slowly falling apart as Mia prayed for help.

The dial tone droned on, Mia cursing as she hung up and dialed Jan. No luck. She didn't want to worry Matthias, but he was the only one left. Her hands were trembling now, her entire body slick with sweat from the horror of the situation falling apart in front of her. *Fuck. Shit. Damn it all.*

Her front door banged open, Kenn and Jan hastily hauling her out of her lab as Kingsley stomped past with a low growl. She yelped as Kenn crushed her against his chest, rocking her back and forth to soothe her. She didn't miss the way Quinn rushed in a few seconds later and gathered Chad up in his arms to put him back together.

She'd have commented on it if she wasn't just as terrified. "How did you–"

"The cameras, remember? Matthias called after reviewing some of the tapes."

Mia didn't understand how the killer kept slipping in without any warning. The security system was supposed to have kept everyone out, and the only one who knew his way around it was supposed to be one of the men protecting her. It just didn't make any sense.

Kingsley stalked back out of the lab, hands perched on his hips, nose wrinkling from the smell of death. The man was *pissed*. "Mia, I need you to explain what the fuck just happened because I'm this close to—"

Jan slapped a hand on the man's chest and pushed him back, effectively shielding her from Kingsley's anger. "No, we *just* had a town hall meeting about this shit. You're not going to put all this on her. You're also not going to threaten her job."

Mia couldn't stop the tremble running down her spine, Kenn bending down until they were eye to eye. His expression was warm but tight as he asked her to explain what had happened. Tears gathered in the corner of her eyes, panic bubbling up in her chest. "I … we just got here. I have no idea how he got in or why it's there. I just … he *put it back*."

From her amateur sleuthing days, Mia knew there were several reasons for that body to have been returned. The killer could have been done with it, but that didn't match the way he had initially caressed the body before taking it.

More than likely, this was all just part of some sick game to honor or worship his victims, which meant that whoever in town was picking people off, it wasn't just to fill a hole but to fulfill some longing that demanded people's lives.

"Hey, hey, *Mia*, we'll figure it out." Kenn gathered her back up into his arms, tucking her head into his chest, hiding her from the world. For a moment, it was just them, Mia breathing in his scent to calm her nerves. "Until we figure out what's going on, though, I don't think you should be in here alone."

"That's a waste of tax dollars—" Kingsley began but was cut off by a fist to the stomach. "I'll have your job for this!" he wheezed.

Quinn's snickers could be heard in the background, Jan managing a grunt before explaining himself. "You keep forgetting that we don't answer to you. We've been nice, entertaining your holier than thou attitude, but not anymore. There's a killer on the loose, and we're determined to find him before he kills more people. Now, you can either get on board with the plan or you can watch us save your sorry ass town. Your choice."

Mia didn't hear Kingsley's mumbled response but knew that Jan's threatening aura had cowed him into submission. Knowing that one of her men would be beside her at all times assuaged her fears, all except for one. The killer had flown under the radar for so long, grabbing people when they least expected it. Her men were all preparing for the big moments – while she was at work, while she was sleeping, but what about all the other moments?

Because while her men weren't watching, the killer was.

FIFTY-ONE

JAN

Leaving Mia with Kenn had been one of the hardest things he had ever done – not because Kenn was incapable of protecting her, but because the alternative was dealing with Kingsley. The fucker had had it coming for a while, but Jan really just wanted her to curl up in his lap so he could protect her from the world. Seeing her huddled in his brother's arms, fear in her eyes had broken him a little.

He wasn't sure how much more he was going to be able to handle before he exploded; he was still wondering how Matthias hadn't tried some shit yet.

"Now, explain this shit that's going on, Kingsley."

The sheriff just stared from the seat across from him. They had wandered back to the office, Jan hoping that Kingsley's father would be lurking around. He wasn't, and he still wasn't answering his phone, although Kingsley told him that was normal. *Doubt it.*

Jan didn't like it, but that was the least of his problems right now. "Kingsley, you little fucker. You *know* something. People are dying and you're what … trying to save face?" He swore he could see a flash of terror in the man's eyes, which prompted him to push harder. "What could be so much worse than y'all not digging into these murders?" Kingsley growled at him and stomped off, Jan resisting the urge to follow him.

He needed answers, not another dead body.

Unfortunately, when his eyes snagged on one of the lame officers propped up at their desk, Jan knew he had another trove of information. He roughly grabbed the man from his seat, shaking him out of a slumber he shouldn't have been having, and thrust his head down against the table. Jan knew he should have used less force but he was pissed off.

The officer let out a surprised yelp, scrabbling for purchase to wriggle free, but years of training had given Jan the upper hand, not to mention that he was holding down a mere child. The kid couldn't have been older than twenty-one or twenty-two.

"Your boss over there is going to get people killed. Tell me what I want to know and no one gets hurt." At any other time, Jan would have looked over to Kenn to pride himself in such corny words, but he didn't have time for that. He shook the kid again, eliciting a squeal from him.

"Have you ever heard of friendly fire?" the kid choked out, now trying to claw at Jan's hands.

Jan grinned, leaning down until his lips were inches from the kid's ear. "Yes, but we're not friends."

"I'll tell you what you want! Just let me go!" Jan released him and parked his ass on the edge of the kid's desk as he watched the kid sit up and straighten his uniform, eyes dropping to his nametag.

Barney threw his hands up in a stretch, smacking his lips together before answering. "So, what's with all the violence?"

Jan ignored the question. "How did Kingsley get his spot? I've heard that his father wasn't ready to give up the position."

Barney barked out a laugh, but it came out more as a giggle. "Not even time for small talk, got it. You know about the scandal, right? He was trying to hide it and—"

"Smells like bullshit in here."

"Damn." Barney took a moment to think, staving off a yawn before speaking again. "Kingsley never threatened his dad. The guy just handed it over. He was getting weird over the past few weeks, hiding shit, not telling Kingsley what was going on."

Jan mulled that over for a moment, but that didn't add up. "Kid, did it even matter what was going on? I don't think I've *ever* seen you guys in Bryxton. Do you even leave your desks?"

Barney sat up a little straighter, fixing his clothing, eyes scanning the room as he leaned forward. "I shouldn't even be fucking talking. Dude, we're not here for a job. We never have been. We just need this shit on our resume."

"*Explain.*"

Jan was moments away from wringing the kid's neck and was sure Barney knew it as he squirmed in his seat. "Fucking hell, you two are terrifying. You really gonna shake things up and not in a good way. Look, we're kind of in the middle of nowhere, if you haven't noticed. We don't have much in the way of prospects or shit, so working here gives us an in with the ROTC program at some of the colleges in the city."

No. Fucking. Way. The sheriff's office was a front for college and the Army? Jan tried to remember the specifics of the case his boss had shoved at them before they left. Barney hadn't been one of the two officers in the file shown to them before they arrived.

How the fuck had he not picked up on that?

"We get a free ride out of town and in exchange, we don't ask questions. But like, things have been off lately."

"Which would explain all the fucking around. Got anything to say about the coroner?"

The kid's face turned beet red. "Not really. They weren't supposed to pry either but ... the girl, she asks questions. Kingsley's father never liked that, but Kingsley could always get her not to do things."

"And?" Jan growled at the kid, Barney holding his hands up in defeat.

"No more violence, okay? I just – Kingsley will have my ass – we just keep our heads down. Feel free to look through old case files and shit but leave me and my brother out of it." Barney gestured to the empty seat across from him, presumably for the current officer of the week.

Jan's boss was going to have a field day with this shit – after they found the killer of course. Jan patted the kid's shoulder and slipped off the desk, making a beeline for the makeshift archives sitting on the bookshelf at the back of the office, which was just piles upon piles of unorganized shit. Rolling up his sleeves, Jan dove in, not exactly sure what he was looking for. A few hours in, he realized that this case went way deeper than he or Kenn had planned. For one thing, these murders went back much further than just a year or two. Like a full decade. Kingsley and his father had been running this corrupt ship for nearly *five* years, which meant the suspect wasn't an amateur.

FIFTY-TWO

NICHLAS-

Nichlas tried to keep his reactions to a minimum, constantly trying to shrink into the darkness after every encounter with Natalie. Now that he knew how much bullshit she was spewing every time her mouth opened, and the fact that she had more than a little crush on him, Nichlas wanted to be fifty feet from her at all times.

Not to mention that Anders was cowering behind him like a goddamn child half the day.

He had, however, made it inside the boardroom with the big boys, which gave him access to a whole lot more information that he just *wasn't supposed to have*. The reports had been a game changer, but his superiors had told him to hold out a little longer.

He didn't want to hold out anymore.

He wanted to return to his brothers and Mia, the woman who had fallen into their arms. Apparently, they were falling together nicely if the phone calls detailing everything that happened with

Mia were anything to go by, but Mia and his relationship was more transactional. Sure, they had shared a moment, but they had never sat down and shared more than a few words.

And yet, he still wanted her with every fiber of his being – if she would have him after she caught him with Anders.

The last half of the day, Nichlas had been stuck in meetings in the boardroom with Natalie, the woman doling out information like candy. The price was money, assets, or promises of payment in other ways. At one point, Nichlas was pretty sure she had just garnered a night of sex from a dominatrix with Anders right beside her.

Anders seemed almost completely lost about what the payments were, as this wasn't his operation but hers. He was only valuable until he wasn't. He had parked his ass a few seats from them, Natalie insisting that Nichlas sit beside her. It looked more believable that way, so she said. He agreed but he didn't appreciate her wandering hands, nor having to remind her multiple times in the last few hours that her husband was just feet away.

"Is this information even remotely true?" a man that suspiciously reminded him of the mayor barked out on the other side of the table as he inspected his contract.

Natalie threw her head back, her shoulders shaking with laughter as she oddly cradled her belly again. "I would never lie to you. You all pay too much to be lied to. Besides, I need to make sure things are going smoothly."

The bitch had just sold out one of the largest sting operations unfolding in California. He was pretty sure half the information Natalie gave out didn't benefit her at all. It was just part of the big picture for her. Nichlas didn't know any of the officers, but it still hurt that she thought information was just a game. And to the mayor no less. Everyone in this room was a piece of shit.

Including me.

She shook the mayor's hand across the table and nodded, the man gathering up his briefcase and exiting the door before a large gentleman entered, an entourage of people adorned with tattoos and low-hanging chains filing in afterward.

Anders looked like he was going to shit the bed from his perch at the far end, while Natalie had never looked more comfortable in her life as she leaned forward, one hand on the table and the other clutching Nichlas' thigh. Her fingers were dangerously close to his package, inching upward. He caught her hand under the table and squeezed it, relishing the way her dainty fingers strained against his hold.

Natalie seemed to enjoy the pain even if her expression remained neutral as she greeted the man. "Welcome, Snake."

The gentleman grunted after offering his hand for a shake and taking the same seat that the mayor had just been in. "I heard you have a job for me?"

Natalie nodded. "There's some chaos in town and it's quite … distracting. I need you to get rid of it." Her smile widened as she slipped him a sealed file. "Quickly."

Snake pried it open, just long enough to stare into it. He grunted again and gave her a pert nod. "Do I need to be discreet?"

"No. Make a show out of it, just the way I like."

Snake nodded again, laying the folder back on the table, but not closing it completely. Nichlas caught a flash of purple, a color he'd recognize anywhere. For a brief moment, he believed Natalie had hired a crew to take out the killer. Instead, she had just hired them to take out Matthias and possibly the other two.

For some reason, she believed that Nichlas wasn't part of that group, and while he had a duty to fulfill his mission, if she thought it was going to be that easy to pick off his men, she had another thing coming.

FIFTY-THREE

MIA

The sun had set by the time she had been able to convince Kenn she was in her right mind enough to return to work. It had taken a lot of pleading, and only when she gave in to Matthias' command that they stick by her side was she released to return to her office. Quinn had texted her a few hours ago to let her know he was safe and so was Chad.

At some point that morning, Kenn had dragged her into the coffee shop and put her weary ass to bed. She was too stubborn for her own good and would have buried herself in work had her men let her. They hadn't, bless their souls.

Which was why she was now armed with a coffee at nearly eleven p.m., preparing to cross the street, Matthias at her right side and the other two behind her when Nichlas popped up on her left. Mia yelped, Matthias scowling at the intrusion as she stared at Nichlas for answers.

He had been MIA for the last day or so. Being around him felt strange, almost dangerous, and she didn't know how she felt anymore. Protected and terrified didn't make sense, but that's what she felt.

"Just giving you an extra set of eyes."

The thought warmed her heart as she smiled up at him, unsure of her rapidly changing emotions. She swore she could see a faint blush on his cheeks as their eyes locked, that wall he hid behind slowly crumbling. "Okay."

Having all four of them surrounding her was a different kind of feeling, a feeling that she kind of loved once she got past all the secrets that they seemed to be hiding. Jan had returned looking a little lost and Nichlas … he just looked haunted. Kenn was still smiling, but it didn't reach his eyes, and Matthias looked like he was one crummy comment from being set off.

It was a dangerous task, taking on all four of them, but she wanted it. She wanted *this*.

Mia let Matthias put in the code as she shuffled to the left, her arm grazing Nichlas'. The touch sent heat through her limbs, but she refused to address it as she sipped at her coffee, flavors of orange and chocolate meeting her tongue. "Matthias – what – what is in this?"

Nichlas chuckled from beside her, not giving Matthias a chance to answer. "He tried a bit of an experiment on Kenn the other day. Do you like it?" Her purple-eyed boyfriend bit his lip, that darkness in his eyes softening as he seemed almost embarrassed with his creation. Kenn mumbled something about how it wasn't fair as Jan punched him in the shoulder.

"Yes. Just wasn't expecting it. It tastes like those candy oranges." Mia sipped at it again, doing a little jig as an involuntary moan slipped from her lips, the taste coating her tongue with deliciousness.

Kenn's hands dropped to her waist from behind, halting her movements. "Nope, you can't be moving like that and making sounds like those, girl. Now, let's go inside and get what you need, all right?"

Mia nodded, intrigued that her micro-movements were setting off her men. Shaking her ass like that or making sounds like that had never garnered attention like that from Anders. He would have just as soon asked her to go somewhere else because she was distracting.

Nope, not thinking about him.

Pushing inside, she wiped her mind of her ex and focused on the stack of files she had been preparing to take home. Unfortunately, the files were scattered along the floor and a rather large unidentified male was rumbling through her desk's contests. It wasn't the same man from before, but just as threatening – if not more. Her coffee slipped from her hands and the man realized he was no longer alone. The intruder launched toward them, Mia in the direct line of attack.

Nichlas pulled her into his chest a moment too late, her scream echoing through her office as she watched her favorite barista drop the intruder with lethal accuracy.

She wasn't even entirely sure what had happened until the body flopped on the ground, blood pooling around his head. The longer she stared, shock controlling her emotions, the more she realized why there was so much of that crimson liquid. The head wasn't completely *attached* anymore. Jan swooped to the other side, blocking her view of the intruder, but the damage had been done, even in the dimly lit area.

Matthias' shoulders were shaking, Mia hastily searching for a weapon that would explain what was looking at. Her gaze snagged on the sheen of a metal piece buried in Matthias' hand, her mind running a mile a minute with all of the possibilities. She tried to rationalize it, the fact they had been in a kill-or-be-killed situation, but that didn't get rid of the terror settling in her chest. When she turned to meet Nichlas' gaze, she caught a flicker of recognition that didn't make sense. "You know him," she whispered, Nichlas tensing against her.

Matthias heard those words, turning to face them. Mia didn't move, unable to face the man who had just killed someone. She wasn't sure how to feel, but acceptance wasn't one of those emotions.

"Who the fuck is this, Nichlas?" Each word was laced with venom and accusations, but Mia felt that they were warranted.

"Fuck. I … shit. I'm going to be breaking a lot of codes here."

"I don't give a shit."

Mia could feel Matthias' need to hold her, but not after that. She couldn't. She wanted time to herself, but she also didn't want yet *another* person coming after her. Wriggling out of his hold and accepting Kenn's embrace, she buried her face into his chest calm her nerves. These men were too goddamn patient to be real.

Then again, she had just watched one of her boyfriends kill another man.

Nichlas let out a deep breath, "So … long story short, I'm not on the same case you guys are. I'm here for … Natalie." Mia frowned, knowing that something was off with that confession, but she was too shaken to press it. "She thinks you are a threat to what she's doing, so she hired a crew to take you three out."

The tension in the room grew thick and heavy in the silence, Mia wondering what the fuck was truly going on. They had a killer running around and now a crew? Not to mention that Nichlas still wasn't telling the whole truth.

Her lungs constricted as her fingers curled into Kenn's shirt, her breath coming out in pants, and her vision beginning to tunnel. If she kept panicking, her men were sure to drop her. She wasn't worth all the effort. Kenn caught onto her destructive thoughts, hands smoothing down her hair as he pressed his lips to her forehead.

"Shh, baby, I got you. Need to get you laying down again. Let's go, kitten." Mia felt herself hoisted up into Kenn's arms, her mind fracturing as she tried to breathe through the shock, but it was no use as darkness claimed her, Matthias mumbling "I'm sorry," the last thing she heard.

FIFTY-FOUR

JAN

Jan pried Matthias off of Nichlas, the barista fuming at the mouth, his expression darker than it had been in a while. "Cut it out, Matty!"

Matthias' expression softened, if only a little bit, but the kid was still growling. They all wanted to know what the fuck had just happened, especially since Matthias had just *killed someone*. Jan had known something was coming, that the kid was going to blow a gasket, but this …

He had never seen Matthias in action, just heard stories from Nichlas, but this was an entirely new level, and not one he was sure they could come back from.

The horror in Mia's eyes …

Jan refused to think about that when he was actively trying to keep Nichlas alive, besides Kenn had her wrapped up in a protective cocoon in his bedroom. "All right, you better start talking because while I'm keeping Matthias away now, I might just let him go."

Nichlas shifted uncomfortably against the wall of the cafe, a dark bruise forming under his left eye, blood dripping down his lip. Matthias didn't look any better, blood splattered along his clothing, dark splotches sticking to his skin through the cloth. He looked like the serial killer everyone was searching for, and yet Jan knew the kid was just a trove of anger and nightmares waiting to be released into the world.

Unfortunately with everything going on, the dead fucker they had scrapped off Mia's floor had been the last straw. If Matthias hadn't done something, the rest of them would have.

God, and hearing her scream like that?

Nope, can't focus on that.

"Nichlas—"

He let out a deep sigh, shoulders sagging. "I'm not here for Natalie."

"I figured," Jan spat, Matthias offering an unhelpful grunt as he shoved himself in a chair.

"Shit. Anders was brought in on some serious charges a while back."

"No need to sugarcoat it, man."

Nichlas bared his teeth and then settled his expression. "It's not about that. The less you guys know, the better. Anders made a deal. He'd give information for a lesser sentence. He's not doing that. He's selling it to the highest bidder." Jan watched the man's usually non-expressive face flood with emotions. He had been warring with this for a while. "Natalie seems to be running the show, though. Prices are high, but the information they're giving … people are going to die."

Looking back at Matthias, Jan watched the kid's expression sober, a hint of understanding seeping through. Not much, but enough. "How the fuck do you know him?"

It didn't look good for Nichlas as he smoothed his hair back again, clearly uncomfortable with breaking his code. "Natalie paid someone to have you guys gone."

"Just us?"

"She's under the impression I'm not with you. Not the point. Look, there are two different pieces to this. I think. The killer and then Natalie."

A bitter laugh slipped Jan's lips as he shook his head. "I don't believe in coincidences and that many forces of evil. Natalie most definitely has some connection with the killer, especially with the way that guy was shuffling through Mia's desk. A separate threat wouldn't do that. Nichlas, you have to start *talking*. I know you can't share a lot of things but you've been so fucking distant–"

"It's my job!"

Nichlas was thrown against the wall, Matthias' arm pressing against his throat. Nichlas didn't fight, but Matthias also wasn't letting go. "Don't fucking care. You don't lie to us. You can say that you can't tell us, but you can't fucking lie to us. I thought we meant more than that."

A mixture of fear and sadness swept through Matthias' face, Jan realizing that it was the lies on top of everything else that had set him off. Nichlas had always been Matthias' anchor, and with the man's secret mission, he hadn't been around to tether Matthias. Even with Mia's help, it had been a bit hectic over the past week.

Nichlas shoved Matthias off, granting them a small nod. "I don't have much more information. Playing chummy with Natalie is pissing me off. My superiors think there's more to whatever's going on and I'm just supposed to lay low. I don't like it, but I can't exactly tell them that."

Jan drank in the pain and hurt in Nichlas' face, recognizing it for what it was. "You're finally willing to try. With Mia. And you think this is going to ruin it." He didn't need Nichlas to answer, he already knew the truth. It made sense, though. Nichlas had the most baggage, the most secrets. Matthias could be a loose cannon, but Nichlas couldn't speak about the things he did or had done over the years.

"Just don't hurt her," Matthias commanded before stalking off to his bedroom to hopefully take a shower. Mia wouldn't be ready to see him tonight, but hopefully, she'd understand the darkness unfolding in the kid. Worse still, they'd have to report that shit in the morning, but with no one in town they could trust, Jan would have to report it to his boss. And where that would lead them, was anyone's best guess.

None of them were going to sleep tonight, but Jan needed just a little more before he'd be able to retire to his room. Nichlas caught on, moving to the counter before grabbing a bottle of water to chug. "I don't know anything more than you all do."

"Keep lying like that and you'll lose more than Mia."

"Natalie's not pregnant."

Jan blinked a few times, unsure of what he had just heard. "What the fuck? How the fuck did you even find that out?"

"Just trivial details. Pregnant women hold themselves a certain way. There's too many things that don't add up."

"And when did you figure this out?" By Nichlas' non-answer, it was clear that he had found out before yesterday. "What does this mean?"

Nichlas shrugged, sadness coating his expression again. "Not much I can do other than report. It's just a fact-finding mission. I'm not supposed to engage. I can't confront her. Not yet, anyway." He left on those words, but not upstairs. Jan couldn't blame him. Everyone needed to take a step back for the sake of the case, their future in the town, and their relationship with Mia.

Jan just hoped that tonight's events hadn't ruined it. *All* of it.

FIFTY-FIVE

MIA

Spattered crimson liquid mixed with a high-pitched scream tore at her nerves until she realized the sound was coming from herself. Pure horror erupted in her chest as she realized that her favorite, purple-eyed barista had transformed into a lethal killing machine in a matter of seconds. The intruder's head lay a few inches from its lifeless body, an overwhelming sinking feeling taking hold.

Mia shot up in bed screaming and fighting the covers, flashes of the previous night's incident still swarming through her head. Strong arms pulled her into an open lap, wrapping her in a protective cocoon. Her breath settled as Kenn smothered her against his chest, hands rubbing her back in small circles to soothe her panic.

"Sweetheart, *breathe*. That's good. That's great. Just take your time. Deep breaths." She trembled in his hold, fingers curling in her lap as she fought the urge to panic.

How could he? How could Matthias have—

"Nope, you're not going to get lost in your head again. Mia, look at me." She stayed cuddled against his chest, still trying to clear her mind, but Kenn wasn't waiting for her to figure things out on her own. He tilted her head up, pressing a soft kiss to her lips, the intensity of his gaze on her strange after she had just roused him from his sleep. "Mia, there is a lot of history between us four, history you've not been a part of. I can't even begin to think what's going on in that head of yours right now, and I'm not going to apologize for Matthias. It's not my place."

"Why?" she begged, hands wringing in her lap, frantically searching for answers in his expression. She wouldn't find it. Her eyes widened at the implication of a murder in her office. "We didn't even report it. We—"

"Sweetheart, deep breaths. We will, but not to Kingsley. There's more at stake here. We're going above his head because we have to, but right now, I need you to take a deep breath and lay back down. There's nothing we can do tonight."

Mia wasn't so sure about that. Across the street, there was a dead body on the floor of her office, one that anyone could walk into if they got past the security. A tremble ran down her spine, Kenn tightening his hold on her.

Her eyes drifted to the nightstand beside the bed, a mixture of emotions swelling in her chest when she saw a bagel resting on the edge. Matthias had been here, and in some weird way, was apologizing for what happened. But she needed answers. Answers that she wouldn't get cuddled up in Kenn's bed, under his protection.

He seemed to understand that, as his arms dropped to his sides. "You need to see him." It wasn't a question, just an observation. Mia nodded timidly, slowly crawling off his lap and planting two feet on the floor.

The bitter cold of the wood shocked her system, but she needed to see him, to know. She'd never be able to relax unless she confronted the issue head on. The alarm clock on the nightstand told her that it was just past three in the morning, but it was now or never. Kenn stood beside her, guiding her into the hallway until they came to the room at the end, a makeshift gym of sorts.

Mia peered inside, the dimly lit area showcasing a rather pissed-off Matthias attacking a bag while Nichlas kept whisper-yelling a one-sided argument. Her heart cracked a little, watching her tortured barista beat up the leather like it would release the boiling emotions inside. As she continued to watch, arms wrapped around her chest to give her the comfort she needed, she realized Nichlas wasn't arguing.

He was apologizing. Profusely.

They had started this whole relationship thing without much thought, acting on emotions and passion without taking into account the mass amount of baggage they were each bringing into the equation, hers included.

She took an experimental step forward, the creak of a floorboard sounding her arrival and causing the two men to halt their movements. Stares locked on her form, Mia trembling beneath the emotions swirling around the room. Nichlas' shoulders sagged as he stepped backward, Matthias unsure of whether to approach or stay put, so she decided for them.

She approached until she was inches from Matthias, her heart beating erratically. This man had murdered someone with lethal precision. There hadn't been a second thought in his head before he acted. Sure, there had been a threat on her life before and the intruder looked like he was going to complete that threat, but …

The man before her was drained, terrified, and freaked, none of the emotions she would have expected from a killer. But he wasn't just a killer, was he? He was more than that. He was a barista. He was warm and talented. He was caring and passionate. And she loved him.

Mia froze, unable to tell where that thought had come from. *I ... love him?* It had been just over a week since she had met these men, and yet there was a special place in her heart for them. For all of them. Despite their flaws, their baggage, and their darkness.

"I would never hurt you," he whispered, even as he stepped backward. She reached for him, but he shied away again, putting a frown on her lips. "I can't ... I see the fear in your eyes. Baby girl, I–"

This was unfamiliar territory, uncharted waters. Coming from a mentally abusive relationship and living in a town that basically hated her, confidence wasn't her strong suit. Going after what she wanted was foreign to her. And speaking her mind? That might as well have been a pipe dream, but in a relationship like this, Mia knew that communication was key to keeping them all sane, and Matthias seemed to thrive on words.

Words that Mia had trouble expressing.

She took a deep breath to settle her thoughts before speaking. If she didn't say this now, they would never be able to get past this. "Did you really think I wouldn't be scared of you after that?" He shivered, dread filling his features. "You killed a man right in front of me. I *know* if you hadn't, something bad would have happened, but at that moment? I didn't see you. I saw that monster you've been trying so hard to hide from me." Mia wasn't even sure why she was still standing here, thinking of a future with these men after that incident, yet some twisted part of her was falling in love just a little more knowing that she was safe with these men. It didn't make sense, but she wasn't sure it needed to.

Silence filtered around them, everyone's hackles up, but Mia needed them to hear this. She wished Jan was present, but this would have to do.

"*Matthias*, this can't work, not if you all are going to hide from me." Yet another set of words Mia hadn't expected to come from her mouth, but she meant them. Anders had always hidden a side of himself, a side she was fine avoiding until it was too late. It would have saved her so much heartbreak if she had known upfront who he was. She needed to see these men in their raw form, not *everything*, but enough, enough to love them fully as they were, let herself fall for these wonderful people who had decided she was theirs. "I need to see who I'm falling in love with."

Fuck, didn't mean to say that.

The silence was so loud between them, a pin drop could be heard. Embracing the moment, she reached out to Matthias again, grateful he didn't shy away this time. When her hand rested on his arm, she leaned up on her tiptoes to press a kiss to his lips, to *show* him what she wanted. She wanted *him* and everything that came with it.

She didn't have to wait long until Matthias gave in, hands dropping down to cup her ass and hoist her up until her legs were wrapping around his waist. Mia moaned into his mouth as he took what he wanted, one arm propping her up and the other one digging into her tousled hair. They drank from each other for what seemed like an eternity until he pulled away, leaving her breathless and aroused.

"*Thank you*," he whispered against her lips, "*for giving me a chance to love you.*"

The words warmed her from within as he released her back to her feet, pressing another kiss to her forehead. Nichlas stood off to the side, but those words had been for all of them, not just for Matthias, and feeling a little more confident, she marched over to him and poked a finger at his chest. She needed him to know it was all or nothing.

"I know you can't tell me everything, but don't lie to me," she said. "I was so fucking scared when I saw that you knew that guy. You have no idea what I thought."

"You moved away from me." He seemed rattled, a thought she hadn't considered. She could see in his eyes that the demons he fought were every bit as dark and lethal as Matthias'. Moving away from him had crushed his soul a little, but he had to understand that she was playing in the dark. She didn't know what he did or where he went or what missions he was on, not that she believed she was entitled to that information.

But she couldn't stand any more lies and half-truths. Kenn let out a chuckle from behind them. "Sounds familiar. Pretty sure Matthias says that shit to you all the time – 'Just don't lie to me,' " he sing-songed, a wide grin on his face as he pushed off the entrance. "Just kiss and make up already. I'm tired of watching you three beat yourselves up over this shit."

Mia caught herself smiling at Kenn's ability to lighten the situation, the smile disappearing against Nichlas' lips as he shoved his tongue into her mouth. She didn't even have time to react before he dragged her against him, ravaging her lips and sucking on her tongue until she was squirming against him for more than a kiss.

But just as fast as it had started, the kiss ended, Kenn dragging her away from Nichlas with another chuckle. "And that's our cue to leave, baby girl. Don't y'all look at me like that. If I let this go on, none of us is getting any sleep, and *everyone* has somewhere to be tomorrow."

"I don't," Matthias grumbled, amusement dancing in his expression. "I could just close the shop."

"Fine. *I* have somewhere to be tomorrow and hearing y'all go at it like wild dogs means I'm going to be cranky." Mia opened her mouth to protest, but he quickly shut it with a kiss of his own that had her toes curling and leaving her even more turned on than before. "Don't fight me. You're fucking loud – no, you don't get to be embarrassed. I *love* watching you, the way we can make you scream, but not tonight, baby girl. Tonight, we sleep."

Mia giggled as he threw her over his shoulder with a whole new level of playfulness, slapping her ass as he marched back down the hall, Nichlas whispering something that sounded a lot like "cheeky bastard." She could get used to this.

FIFTY-SIX

MIA

Mia was still a little jumpy after the early morning discussion, but brief touches and good mornings from her men settled her despite the nightmares. She had woken up several more times during the night, Kenn rocking her back to sleep every time, not one complaint falling from his lips. He looked a bit worse for wear when she finally managed to pull herself out of bed, the beautiful blond-haired man sprawled out across the mattress as he snored the morning away.

The lying bastard had just stolen her way from her other men for cuddles, hadn't he?

The thought put a smile on her face as she searched for her dress, knowing full well that she didn't want to put it back on and chose one of Kenn's shirts instead. It was going to become a habit, wearing their clothes. With the heated stares she received after descending the stairs, she was pretty sure no one minded.

They were in all different states of dress, Matthias the only one shirtless, as he didn't have anywhere else to be. Jan seemed a little underdressed, what with a plain tee and jeans that seemed a little too sinful with the way they hugged his thighs, and Nichlas was brooding by the sink, a coffee cup pressed to his lips, dressed in all black.

Jan intercepted her before she made her way into the kitchen, whispering how he was on board with the speech they all received last night.

"It wasn't a speech," Mia whispered back, playfully slapping his chest. She wanted to ask about the body, but their relationship was a little bit too raw to bring it up in front of Matthias. He still looked a bit tortured despite her speech.

She felt Jan nuzzle the side of her cheek, teeth grazing her ear before whispering words she didn't know she needed. "Angel, just go to him. If that's what you want. He's still feeling unsure of himself."

The fact that these men could see right through her was a little terrifying, but even more so that they didn't seem to mind how often she got tripped up on things. He nudged her in the direction of Matthias, who was currently focused on kneading dough for bagels that wouldn't make an appearance until this afternoon. She hadn't even touched the one on the nightstand, much happier to have a fresh one.

But now that she was faced with the awkwardness of a morning after that didn't involve sex, she wasn't sure what to do.

Recently, just going for it had seemed to work, so she took a few steps before wrapping her arms around his waist and pressing her face between his shoulder blades. She breathed in his freshly washed scent of mint and juniper, her face warming as the ambiance of the cafe settled. Matthias stilled against her touch, his hands dropping to hers before he turned around in her hold with a tight smile.

The moment their eyes met though, he melted, all that stiffness and awkwardness sliding away as she held onto him. It would take time and a lot of maneuvering, but they would figure this out, wouldn't they? She thought about granting Nichlas the same kind of attention, but they weren't there yet. They would be, she hoped, but it wasn't as easy to open up with him as it had been with the others.

Mia knew she needed to rectify that and fast, but not right now. Right now, she was going to steal one of those wonderful morning kisses from Matthias and then march her ass up the stairs for a much-needed shower. Unfortunately, Matthias wasn't letting go as his head dipped to meet hers, their lips tangling in a lazy duel. She could stay like this forever, tasting his lips and drinking in his scent, her hands pressed against his hard chest. As the kiss deepened, she grew bolder, hands starting to roam until her thumbs grazed over his pecks, the briefest of touches causing his hold to tighten. His cock hardened against her belly, his desire evident as his tongue thrust into her mouth, drawing out one of those "pretty little sounds," as Kenn had dubbed them.

"Well, shit. I guess I missed the morning roll call."

Mia pulled away, her face flushed, to greet a rather tired but joyous Kenn entering the kitchen. He was shirtless as well, clad in less clothing than Matthias, just a pair of midnight boxers that left nothing to the imagination. He let out a rather annoying yawn, chugged an obscene amount of coffee from a cup Mia hadn't known existed, and then dragged her from Matthias' hold, planting a fat kiss on her lips. In doing so, she could feel every hard ridge of his body pressed against hers, including the full length of his aroused cock.

A second later he was climbing the stairs, leaving her confused.

The rest of them shared nervous chuckles, Jan offering his hand to guide her up the stairs for that shower she wanted so much. Mia opened her mouth to ask for clarification – this wasn't the first time Kenn had bulldozed his way through a situation – but Jan gave her a small shake of his head and wiggled his fingers for her to take hold of.

Once in Jan's room, he sat her down on the mattress and pulled a chair from the makeshift desk in the corner. "I can see all those thoughts running around in your head, so I'm hoping to help ease some of that anxiety. This is going to get messy and it won't always work, Mia. I'm not going to lie to you, we haven't done this in a while."

Mia knew what that meant. It meant that they had done this before. It also meant that it hadn't worked out.

He blew out a deep breath as he ran his hands through his hair, trying to calm his nerves. "I heard what you said last night. I didn't want you to stop so I didn't come in, but I heard it. Loud and clear. Secrets and half-truths are going to break us. It's what broke us last time, and there's a few things you need to know."

She tensed, unsure if that was a good or a bad thing. It sounded like a bad thing.

He let out a weary chuckle, pulling himself a little closer until his knees were brushing hers. "Angel, no, nothing bad. It's just where we all fit in, okay? I don't want to talk about exes with you, but in the grand scheme of things, it's better if you know." Mia gave him a silent nod to keep going, placing her hands in his to ground herself. "Matthias has always been the charming one of the group, but that darkness scares people off pretty fast. His anger can be volatile, which, without the right outlet, can be dangerous."

His hands tightened around hers.

"Nichlas finds it hard to connect, but when he does, it's all or nothing. Unfortunately, because he can't share most of what he does, it causes a rift. Our last girlfriend always thought he was cheating. She kept trying to catch him in his lies, going so far as to hire a PI. You can imagine that didn't go well when the PI returned and said he didn't have a high enough clearance. In reality, Nichlas' superiors threatened the PI's job, for good reason."

"She did *that*?"

Jan's grin widened. "It was a bit of a crazy time."

"Why are you telling me all this? I already kind of figured out about Matthias and Nichlas. They need a different kind of attention, different reminders than you two, you and Kenn."

"That's part of it, sweetheart, but not all of it. Kenn and I seem the easiest to navigate, but that's just because we smile more. Our jobs require interpersonal skills. We can't hide behind a persona like Matthias. We aren't shrouded in secrecy like Nichlas, but that doesn't mean there haven't been… hiccups."

"Jan, you're starting to scare me."

"Not my intention. You seem to have noticed Kenn's over-the-top personality and how he seems to be edging himself into situations." Mia groaned, shoulders sagging. *Am I that see-through?* "No, it's okay. This is why I brought it up. Mia, Kenn's used to being ignored."

"How? With that smile? I–"

He tugged on her hands, cutting off her rant. "Listen to me. Matthias and Nichlas are intriguing, mysterious. That darkness is alluring until it isn't, until people figure out that that darkness is lethal. Kenn is the picture-perfect boyfriend, but he loves hard. His emotions are big. And *that* in contrast with the others is a lot for someone to take in. His good intentions are taken for granted until they become expected."

Mia understood what he meant. For years, Mia tried to win Anders through small gestures and actions. Flowers, showing up to events, always being available but when they finally started dating, Anders expected those things. He expected the house to be clean, dinner to be on the table, for her to make herself scarce. She was supposed to be his right hand but also one step behind him at all times. She was a good luck charm that was always supposed to work.

It pained her that her playful detective had been slighted in his intentions over the years.

"And you?" Jan's face twisted as he tried to pull away from her, but she didn't let him. The others had joked about his all-brawn-no-brains persona, but he wasn't that, was he? He was just a big teddy bear under all that personality. "No one sees you, do they? They see big and scary, but you're not just that."

"Mia, I do have … anger issues. I know that. But–"

"But he's got more degrees than all of us. The fucker was a few months away from a Ph.D. before a case called us away. He had the chance to finish it, but he was *bored*." Mia tore her eyes away from Jan and stared at Kenn, staring into those sea-glass orbs that were a bit brighter than before. She had kind of hoped there were bags under his eyes, something to show how terribly they slept, but he was a fucking dream to look at. It was unfair.

Jan bowed his head, trying to pull away again, and this time she let him in lieu of Kenn's explanation.

"Our last girlfriend liked him because of the persona everyone slapped on him, but when this fucker gets comfortable, he tends to talk. Don't get him started on any kind of physics shit. He'll never shut up."

Her eyes widened as she observed the man blushing before her. This was what she was missing, the history, their desires, wants, hobbies – she was missing the parts that made them different, that made them who they were.

Staring at the hulk of man before her, she would have never guessed he had gone to college. He seemed like a damn good detective, but education? It would have never come up. It made her wonder how many other things the others were hiding just beneath the surface.

"*And* there's that look that tells me you're one moment away from asking every question in the book. We can all swap stories later. Let's get you a shower and back to work or Quinn will think we've kidnapped you." Kenn unearthed a pile of towels and a brand-new toothbrush as if he was actually going to let her shower alone. After Jan's little reveal, Mia was pretty sure she'd never shower by herself when she was over here unless she explicitly kicked them all out, not that it'd be a hardship.

Her mind was a chaotic mess of information, but there were still a few things she needed clarified before she could enjoy the mass amount of muscles on display under a steamy waterfall. "I don't want to bring it up but that body. I can't go over there ... you said it – ugh." A somber feeling replaced the elated one she just had, as she continued: "I trust you guys know what you're doing, but there's just so much going on and I don't–"

No one was smiling now, Kenn moving toward the mattress until two men were crowding around her. Jan spoke first. "We've got it handled. I promise, but Kingsley isn't capable of handling something like this. It's why we were called in. You have work to handle and one of us will be with you at all times. Nichlas is going to check the office before you go in."

"What about Quinn? Or Chad?"

Kenn shook his head. "It's the kid's choice. Both of theirs. But we'll be there the whole time."

"And when this ends?"

Jan stared at her intensely as he dragged her off the mattress until she was straddling him on the chair. She clutched at his shoulders, gripping with the uncertainty of the relationship she had started with these men.

"I wasn't aware we were putting expiration dates on things, Mia."

She trembled on his lap, his arms wrapping around her as he held her. "But there *is* one, isn't there? You guys don't live here and I–" Mia almost said her place was here, in this town, but she wasn't as attached to the place as she used to be.

She also needn't have worried because her men seemed to have already discussed this.

Kenn gently turned her face toward him, hands cupping her cheeks in a gentle hold. "Have you been worrying about this? Worrying about when we were going to leave? Sweetheart, we're not leaving. Not without you. We wouldn't have started something if we didn't plan to continue it."

"You're *not* leaving?"

Jan smiled at the worry swirling in her expression. "Not without you."

And just like that, another one of her fears disappeared into the wind as she smashed her lips against Kenn's while Jan held her. She'd worry about the shower later.

FIFTY-SEVEN

NICHLAS

Nichlas threw a jab at Matthias' shoulder, the kid expertly dodging while rolling dough into hand-sized balls. Their playful back and forth had returned after they got everything off their chests last night. Having Mia around to bridge the chasms definitely wasn't a hardship, and watching her gravitate toward both of them had been a lovely surprise.

Kenn had started acting out like he always did, but hopefully, Jan had nipped that in the bud with a discussion that all of them were too embarrassed to have. Nichlas was beginning to see that they couldn't have a relationship with Mia without explaining everything, without giving her the information she needed to make a decision.

They needed to be honest as much as they could, and that meant he'd have to start talking. Talking about what he was doing with Anders and Natalie before Mia found out by herself. It was already Thursday, five days since he had started spending time with two of the most awful people on the planet, waiting for his superiors to release him from the mission.

He had gathered enough information to bring down everyone who had walked through those doors and yet ... they wanted him to stay.

It fucking sucked.

What sucked more was the fact that Anders couldn't see through the ruse Nichlas had set up to drag information from him, which is why the shit wandered into the cafe like he belonged despite the "closed" sign. At least they were all dressed this time.

Anders threw up a hand, giving the warmest smile a demon like him could before gesturing to the pot behind the counter.

"Pour me two cups, will you? The coffee Natalie brought was pretty good." His gaze drifted to Nichlas, almost confused why he was *behind* the counter rather than there as a patron. Nichlas waited for the man to connect the dots, but he was either too stupid or just dumb as shit. "Fancy seeing you here. What are you doing here so early?"

Nichlas knew he had a job to do, that he needed to buddy up to the guy rather than create any doubt in Anders' mind, but he just didn't want to, especially not when Mia was upstairs and they had just fixed things this morning. "I live here," Nichlas spat, waiting once again for the realization.

Anders stared at him and then the stairs before realization flooded his features. "Are you with her, too?" Nichlas didn't even have time to answer as Anders rounded the counter, his real target found. "You're with Nichlas, too? Or are you just throwing your goddamn pussy around to whoever will catch it?"

Mia froze on the last step, stunned at his words, her hair still wet from the shower that by the looks of it, all three of them had taken. She was swimming in Kenn's shirt and a pair of shorts three sizes too big but covering all the bits they would have killed another man for seeing.

Anders was hot and cold, running between apologies and abuse. Nichlas was proud of their woman when she didn't back away or flinch but instead met his eyes and hardened her expression. Jan and Kenn stood behind her, arms folded across their chests as she drew in a deep breath.

"I. Am. Not. Yours."

A fire lit up behind her eyes as she took an experimental step forward, Kenn and Jan following the movement. It was a testament to their promise to her: to protect her, to keep her safe.

"I don't know why you keep coming over here like you care. I bet you think you do, but things won't change. I'm not yours. I won't be. I'm theirs and they're mine. You married Natalie, and you can have her. I'd advise you to stop pushing your way in here and throwing your weight around when the two behind me are detectives and the other two have more lethal power in their hands than you have wielding a gun." Nichlas shared a chuckle with Matthias as he leaned against the counter and watched their women drum up another bout of confidence. Just a few days around them and Mia looked like she was ready to take on the world. "Now, would you *please* take your coffee and leave us alone?"

A bit of fear flickered through her expression – probably having to do with the fact that the rest of the town was going to find out about their less than normal relationship, but she pushed past it as she watched Anders leave without his order, not that Matthias had prepared it.

Nichlas would be eternally grateful that Mia had come down in more clothes than just one of their shirts, the heated stares of his brothers mirroring his own as she sauntered her way into the kitchen, hands snatching a ready-made cup of joe from Matthias' outstretched reach.

Jan and Kenn followed after her, making the space shrink in size with all of them surrounding her, her cheeks beet red. "I just–"

"No need to apologize," Nichlas began. "It's amazing seeing you standing up for yourself, and if he had tried anything, you would have had four protectors at the ready."

Her eyes widened and darted to Matthias, but he was smiling as he drew her against his chest, pressing a kiss to her forehead. "I'm okay, baby. Promise."

Her expression changed on a dime, a smile settling between her cheeks as she sipped at her coffee, thoughts racing a mile a minute. Nichlas leaned forward, catching her gaze as she flushed just a little more. "Mia ..."

"It's nothing! I just ... I need to go into the city. I think. I want to check something." They waited for her to elaborate, a slight tremble to her hands meaning she had spent more than a second thinking about this. "With the bodies. There's something I missed. I *know* it, but I have to see it. I have to be there."

"No." It was out of their mouths before they could stop it, Mia's expression dropping as she looked at all of them, disappointed. Nichlas tugged her toward him, knowing they had the least bit of history between them so it was best coming from him. "Of course you should go, Mia, but take one of us. I think we mentioned this before. For your safety, for our sanity."

That smile returned as she nodded enthusiastically, sipping her coffee again.

FIFTY-EIGHT

JAN

Jan wrinkled his nose as he stepped into Mia's office, Kenn a few steps behind. Spending time with Mia this morning had cleared the air about a few things, and he felt a lot calmer about the relationship ahead of them. They still needed to let Matthias and Nichlas in on the worries running around in Mia's head, but if they continued to communicate, Jan hoped this one would last.

So long as Nichlas sat his ass down and explained what was going on first. With all the secrets relating to his current mission, things were going to fall apart if Mia found out from Natalie or Anders the connection first. And god forbid, if she found out that Natalie *wasn't* pregnant from anyone other than Nichlas …

Jan tried not to dwell on it, instead focusing on the state of Mia's office.

The office had been cleaned up earlier, the body carted off by a "cleaner" they had on retainer for when they had to enact "clean up, ask questions later" Protocols. Not all of their cases were as legal as Jan would have liked. This had been one of those instances, the alternative being Matthias ending up in a holding cell, the absolute worst possible option if the body were to be discovered.

Mia had texted Quinn to come in later or not at all, the boy pleading to be a part of figuring out why that body had shown back up. She gave in rather quickly but told him not to show up before ten, giving them just under thirty minutes to scout out the place and make sure there weren't any nasty surprises hiding in the corners.

That body was still on the slab in the lab, but without further investigation and a deep dive into the security cameras, they'd wouldn't be able to glean any additional information. Jan absentmindedly kicked the edge of Mia's desk, eyes wandering the area and hoping the floors had been scrubbed as well as usual. Mia didn't need any reminders of the incident.

With all four of them, they'd be able to protect her – that is, if Nichlas got his act together and started putting his foot down. Jan knew better than any of them how much loyalty meant in the business, but there had to be a line that wasn't crossed.

He settled into a seat, pulling Kenn down beside him as they dialed their chief, Detective Hanson, his face showing up on the screen a few seconds later.

"Settling in well?" Detective Hanson chuckled, obviously aware of what had taken place early this morning.

"Swimmingly," Kenn said, matching Detective Hanson's grin.

Jan just shook his head. "Look, there's too many things going on here, between the killer, Anders, Natalie, and now people after us? For what?"

Detective Hanson thought for a few seconds, eyes tracking their movements. There were secrets behind those eyes, but as per usual, they wouldn't be privy to them. "I sent you to investigate and figure it out. The bodies showing up at that coroner's office are beginning to be a problem."

"What are you saying?" Jan leaned forward, brows creasing. He had picked up on something that Kenn was still in the dark about. Something was off. "Hanson–"

"That area is a pretty secluded place to die. People venture there when they don't want to be found, but those bodies are being shipped to the adjacent city. Investigations are being opened, and it's garnering a lot of unwanted attention. I need this figured out, pronto."

Detective Hanson ended the call, not giving either of them time to bring up what they were supposed to do with the intruder's body or how they were supposed to address the public, let alone what they were supposed to do with Kingsley and his cowardly ass.

Kenn leaned back in his chair, running his hands through his hair, a low whistle pushing through his lips. "Of course, our boss isn't clean either. The fuck? He's running for election or some shit this year, isn't he?"

Jan didn't know how to respond to the information he had just been walloped with. They hadn't really been sent to close a case but to eliminate a threat to their boss' campaign. It wasn't about saving lives or righting the wrongs done in this town. It was about greed and money and attention. That didn't sit well with him, especially when their side of the case was supposed to be on the up and up. Mostly.

He was beginning to realize that this case was far larger than someone using the outskirts of town as his killing ground. If this was bleeding into law enforcement and politics, protecting Mia was the least of their worries.

"Why do you look like someone killed your cat?" Mia's voice wafted into the office as she approached, all smiles and giggles, radiant from the attention all four of them had been giving her.

Her hair was pulled back in a tight ponytail, a light purple sundress hugging her curves.

Kenn shot out of his chair, the wooden thing toppling to the ground as his back went ramrod straight. If that wasn't obvious they were talking about shady shit, Jan didn't know what was. She raised an eyebrow, silently testing them to break the vow they had made that morning, to be honest with her.

His shoulders drooped as he gave in, faster than he had with their last girlfriend. "We called ... ya know." He waved his hands to the floor, trying to keep from dredging up the nightmare. "We called it in and it seems we're not really here to solve a case. Boss is running for re-election or some position in office and there are too many bodies."

Her gaze drifted to the lab, resting on that body and then returning to Kenn's face. "You mean, he just wants it to go away but he doesn't care how?"

Kenn nodded, Mia closing the distance between them and stringing her arms around his waist. "Thank you for not lying to me. I can't say that makes me feel better, but at least I know. What now?" Jan caught the slight tremble in her slim form, knowing that she wasn't okay with the progression of events. In just over a week, Mia had dealt with more nonsense than most people dealt with in their entire lives.

Jan stood up and pressed himself up against her backside, pressing a light kiss to her neck. "We work together to find out what the fuck is going on and we hope that it's enough. Nichlas is going to accompany you tomorrow to the city and hopefully, you can get your answers." She nodded between them, eyes darting back to the lab.

"I really should start working before Quinn comes." Her voice was quiet, and then she added, "But I really don't want to." Before either of her men could act on those words, she slipped out from between them and dashed into the lab with a wild smile on her face, eyes dancing. It was a rare sight to see Mia like this, but Jan hoped he continued to see this side of her, the side that continued to blossom and shine the more she allowed herself to be unequivocally herself.

FIFTY-NINE

MIA

The day had run its course, Quinn making Chad's life a living hell until Mia sent both of them home, unable to concentrate past the playful bickering and obscene amount of flirting. She was happy for them, but in her current state with everything going on, she couldn't concentrate. Jan and Kenn worked out of her office, sending her heated glares all day until she had to stuff her head into a pair of headphones and keep her head down, focused on the body on her slab.

There weren't any additional marks, and strangely enough, it wasn't more deteriorated than it had been when they found it the first time, which seemed evident of some type of preservation, possibly freezing, but why was the lingering question.

A tap on her shoulder sent her into a frenzy, a yelp tearing from her lungs as she whirled around to see Kenn with his hands up, fear in his expression. She whipped the headphones off, her breathing erratic as he managed a chuckle. "Sorry, I couldn't get your attention. It's *late*. This will all still be here tomorrow. Lock up, we want to go watch a movie."

Mia frowned and peered around Kenn to look at Jan, who shrugged his shoulders. "Angel, it's almost nine. Kenn wants to cuddle, and I'm not about to say no as long as we're not stuck watching some sappy chick flick."

"How are you guys so ... unbothered?" Her gaze flitted between them, each of them taking one of her hands and pressing a spirited kiss on her knuckles.

"Because there's nothing we can do right now other than wait. Why worry *and* wait? That's just stupid," Kenn said, tugging her toward the door. She gave in, pulling away just long enough to pack up the lab and shove a few documents into her desk drawer before tucking herself into Kenn's side.

Her good mood didn't last, as one of Kingsley's officers met her three steps inside the cafe, a tortured, confused expression plastered on his face.

Cuffs dangled from his fingers, his hands shaking with the weight of the statement he was about to make. "Um ... hey, Mia? You're um, under arrest for—"

Her men growled at the lackey, but he wouldn't have finished his words anyway, Natalie storming past him and into the sitting area. "You fucking did it. Finally. Couldn't have him, so no one could? That's real rich, Mia!"

Mia stood there, partially blocked from view by her men, completely confused. "What did I do?" She knew the rumors that had been swirling around town, how she had only been with Matthias to steal Anders' attention back. What with the way Anders kept trying to find her and cause trouble, it wasn't a far-fetched rumor. But other than that, there was no reason for Natalie to be pissed at her, was there? She tugged at Kenn's hand still firmly wrapped around hers, but he seemed just as clueless as her.

Tears streamed down Natalie's face, her face bunched up with a mixture of anger and pain. The emotions almost seemed real – if Mia hadn't known that the woman was just naturally a bitch. "You tried to have him killed. I don't even know who would have listened to your sorry ass but … he's in the hospital and they're not even sure if he'll wake up."

"Excuse me?" Twisted emotions exploded in her chest, her hand massaging at the discomfort. Anxiety and panic began to suffocate her at the thought that someone had attacked Anders, and his wife was standing here, accusing her of carrying out the attack or at the least orchestrating it. Mia didn't even feel bad that Anders had been beaten – the fucker deserved it – but she wasn't about to go down for it.

The lackey took a step forward, dangling the handcuffs. "I … I have to take you in. Then we'll get to the bottom–"

Her men's stares turned lethal, Jan putting a hand on the boy's shoulder with a gesture that told her there was history between them. The boy shivered, pulling back as Jan told him off. "And you know better than to arrest someone without any evidence."

"I have evidence!" he cried out. "A witness."

Jan barked out a laugh. "Mia's been at her office all day. I have *several* witnesses that can corroborate that. Do not mess with me, kid."

The lackey took another step back, unsure of what to do. For sure, Natalie had strolled into the station and grabbed the first person she could find to arrest Mia. Kingsley would have known better, but this kid wasn't smart enough to fight against Natalie's tactics.

Mia tried to think why Natalie would even want her in jail. It didn't add up. There had to be more to it than just her relationship with Anders, otherwise Natalie's disdain for Mia's existence was just overkill. Jan gave the kid a light push toward the door. "I say you two find your way out of here. Kid, if Kingsley gives you the green light, we'll bring Mia ourselves. Until then, don't come back here. Natalie, you and your husband are no longer welcome at this cafe."

Natalie threw the lackey's hands off her, throwing a little temper tantrum at the entrance, drawing Mia's other two men's presence downstairs. "Mia, you can't fucking hide behind them. You'll answer for what you did."

Mia opened her mouth to answer, but Kenn shook his head.

"Besides, they're not even all your men!" Natalie said. "Nichlas has been working for me for a week. He doesn't even *like you*." She spat.

Once again, Mia realized her men weren't giving her the whole truth. Nichlas and her had the hardest time talking to each other, sharing moments that came so easily with the others, but she could see he had been trying.

Unfortunately, if what Natalie said was true, Nichlas had been hanging with her ex for that entire week as well. Were all the words they shared just lies? Were the growing feelings between the most mysterious of the four useless or were they part of a plan to drag her down? Was his plan to rip her heart out and stomp on it?

She didn't want to be *that* woman, knowing full well there was a reason for Nichlas to have been where he was, but it still hurt that she had found out from Natalie, of all people.

Nichlas didn't offer up an explanation, ignoring her confusion as he addressed Natalie instead. "The fact that I'm *here* right now rather than with you should say something."

She huffed out a laugh. "You don't need to hide behind your words, *Nichlas*. You're as dirty as they come, trying to worm your way between me and Anders. You and Mia were made for each other, really."

Mia knew that Natalie was playing the bitch, that she was trying to start a fight in the wake of not being able to get Mia arrested. She resisted the urge to look at Nichlas, the man having stepped closer to the entrance to address Natalie's lies – well, what she hoped were lies.

"It's funny that you say all that, Natalie, especially with what you do over there." Natalie's face blanched, but Nichlas didn't seem content with just a threat. "I've never tried to get between you two. I don't even think you care about him and I'm *still* trying to figure out why you had to marry him, because it wasn't for the baby."

She gasped, hands falling to the curve of her belly, a belly that Mia had forgotten about.

"Just *stop*." Nichlas took another step forward, his arm brushing Mia's in silent solidarity that she found both comforting and patronizing. "Stop with the ruse. It's getting old."

Matthias frowned, interjecting into the conversation. His voice was scratchy from just waking up. "Nichlas, just fucking spit it out."

"She's not pregnant. There's no baby, but I'm fairly sure Anders doesn't know that."

More. Fucking. Lies.

Matthias and Kenn seemed shocked. Jan … he knew, didn't he? She stepped back, throwing up her hands to excuse herself from the conversation. What should have been a quiet night in cuddling with her men was now going to include none of them as she tried to sift through the newly acquired information. She knew when she had started this thing that they wouldn't be able to tell her everything, but she wouldn't have thought it would be so hard to navigate.

Nichlas didn't reach for her, knowing full well he had fucked up, but Matthias did, and slighting him showed her just how much it hurt him, but she couldn't. She just needed a moment. A *lot* of moments.

Natalie was sputtering through an explanation, still awkwardly holding her belly as Mia stomped her way up the stairs and locked herself in the first room available. She didn't recognize the space, realizing she had stepped into Nichlas' room, the thought doing nothing to calm the unrest in her heart and chaos in her head, panic rising in her chest and nowhere to let it out.

Her hands pressed against the sides of her head, whimpers slipping from her lips as she tried to piece everything together.

A killer. Multiple killers? Her abusive ex in the hospital. Natalie wasn't pregnant. Her men had lied to her.

Nichlas had lied to her.

Again.

No, that wasn't right. She wasn't even sure she should have been privy to the information shared down in the cafe. They hadn't lied. Nichlas hadn't lied. It was a part of his job, and she was being selfish to want more than they could give. Finding that happy medium was going to be difficult, but if this relationship was supposed to work, she would need to find it before things blew up.

The door inched open, Nichlas letting himself into a room she had sworn she had locked. This was it, wasn't it? Things were going to come to a head right here, right now. It was too bad that her head was pounding and all she wanted to do was sleep.

SIXTY

NICHLAS

He knew he had fucked up a good thing, Natalie arriving at the absolute worst time when they had *just* had a conversation about being honest. He felt he needed to explain with everything else going on, but continuing to overwhelm Mia wasn't going to help the situation either. Even as he closed the door behind them, he realized that approaching her might have been the worst option.

She had been crying and she looked one step away from a migraine, but he was here now, and he needed to see this through. It was now or never.

Mia was unlike anyone they had been with before, whether it had been for a few nights or a few months. Their last serious girlfriend-turned-fiancé had left some serious damage in her wake, but he had escaped almost unscathed, and it wasn't because he didn't love her. It was because he hadn't allowed himself to love.

Nichlas had learned pretty quickly that the allure of four boyfriends was for the sex, the kink, but not as a stable relationship. Few people believed him and the men downstairs wouldn't get jealous or fight over their shared woman. He was constantly used as the mysterious tall, dark, and handsome boyfriend. They wanted his dominance, his brooding demeanor, but nothing else until they needed everything.

One moment, their woman would tell him she was fine not knowing, and then she'd demand to know *everything*. His job didn't allow anyone other than a spouse to be enlightened about what he did every day. It was a tough way to live, but Nichlas had made his peace with it years ago, and with every girlfriend after that, he had refused to open his heart to them.

He got sex out of it and the others were happy, so Nichlas was content to walk the lonely path until Mia bulldozed her way into their lives and he considered letting down those walls all over again.

But old habits died hard, and the possibility it was too late for second chances.

"Are you here to tell me you 'just need to explain' or some shit? Because I don't want to hear it." Her words were hardened, quiet, but very clear.

"Not here to make excuses, no."

Mia glared at him from her perch on the bed, eyes red as her hands dropped to her lap. "Why do I keep finding information from everyone else? I don't ... do you even like me?"

The accusation hit him hard, Nichlas scrambling for words. This was never his strong suit. He could interrogate a terrorist and drag some of the most difficult confessions out of hardened criminals, but explaining his feelings? Yeah, fuck that.

"Yes, Mia. I like you. I like you a lot."

"Then why won't you talk to me? I need the truth. I can't handle more lies right now."

The fact that she trusted him to give her the truth meant he still had a shot, that they all did. "Mia, I didn't know how to break it to you that I was working with your ex. There's a lot going on, and I knew you wouldn't like it, but I also can't just tell off my superiors."

Mia raised an eyebrow but remained silent.

"He, well, they're *both* into some shady shit. It's bad."

"How long?"

"Just the week–"

She shook her head, eyes watering again. "How long has he been doing this … stuff?"

Oh. Nichlas bit his lip, slightly afraid to let her know that her ex had been doing things long before they had started dating. He didn't have to say anything, his silence answering her question. A cry left her pretty lips, another sob catching her throat as she tried to swallow the overwhelming emotions.

He couldn't help himself as he approached the bed, kneeling in front of her and throwing his arms around her waist. She melted against him, but he could still feel the unchecked rage simmering beneath the surface. "I can't promise you answers for everything, but ask me your questions." Nichlas pulled away slightly, staring up at her, hoping that it would help assuage the unrest in her heart.

"I know you had to play a part, but was she right? Were you wedging yourself between Anders and Natalie?"

Nichlas caught onto the horror beneath the question and shook his head. "Not once. I don't want her, not even if it's pretend."

"Who was the man in my office?"

His chest tightened at the question, unsure if Mia really needed more information she couldn't do anything with, but she asked for honesty. So, she was going to get it. "That shady shit Natalie's into. I think there might be a connection to the dead bodies. She sent a few people after Matthias."

"Why him?" She quickly backtracked. "No, he was going through my desk. That doesn't make sense."

"No, it doesn't."

"You think Natalie's involved."

His shoulder sagged, knowing that he had to draw the line in the conversation. "I can't talk about it." This was the moment their women always demanded more, yelled for an explanation and information they weren't allowed to have. This was the moment they began to distrust and scream about cheating before inevitably finding someone else to spend their days with.

He hadn't been ready for Mia's response, a mere "okay" as the tension seemed to seep from her and she relaxed. "Nichlas, you've told me and so have the others that there are things you can't talk about. I'm trying to get used to it, but it's the only thing that's going to work. Unless I find out that you're lying about not being able to talk about it."

A small smile spread across his lips as he shook his head, arms still loosely around her waist. "I'm trying."

"I know you are, and I appreciate it. I do. There's just a lot going on in my head, and it's hard to process everything. I … I need to try, too." Nichlas nodded, drawing her back into a tight embrace, loving the way she tucked her head into his neck as if it were the safest place in the world.

SIXTY-ONE

MIA

She hated her volatile emotions. She hated the fact that Nichlas was trying so goddamn hard and yet there was still this unexplainable distance between them. She hated the fact that she knew part of the reason why, and it had nothing to do with hanging around men who were constantly working with information that had to remain secret.

For the last couple of days, Mia had noticed that the little touches and kisses from her men made her feel alive. They made her feel loved. With Anders, she had always felt neglected and mistreated. She had been the thing so easily discarded.

Her men, all of them save for Nichlas, made her feel special, and it boiled down to the fact that the bond she shared with the others hadn't been cultivated with Nichlas. She didn't feel connected to him the same way because he didn't dole out attention like the others. She hadn't let him. His mysterious aura had been alluring and intriguing, but the secrets he had to keep had kept her from seeing the man in front of her.

Having him hold her like this showed her that this was yet another thing she was missing from her mysterious fourth man – not just his touch, but his heart. His emotions. *Him*. He'd been hiding behind walls of protection and she had let him, which made sense based on the explanation Jan had given her this morning, but all that hiding was doing was creating more walls.

She pulled away, staring into his eyes to see past the darkness, catching the fear, fear that she'd leave them, that she'd tell them that this wouldn't work, that she wouldn't be able to love him. The last bit tore at her heart.

"You don't think I could love you?" His hold tightened around her waist, shame flooding his features. He didn't speak though, letting his eyes speak for him. Her hands cupped his cheeks, thumbs running over his smooth features, relishing in the complexity of the man kneeling before her. "I could love you," she breathed, leaning in close enough to brush her lips against his. "But, I need to see you. I need to see the man beneath everything else."

Nichlas trembled beneath her touch, a lone tear escaping down his cheek, the last of his walls crumbling down. "It's so fucking hard, Mia."

"Baby steps. I need this. I need *all* of you–"

He nodded, his fingers digging into her waist as their gazes locked on each other. "Anything. *Anything*."

Mia hadn't thought it would be so easy to give him a second chance, but the raw emotion on his face told her everything she needed to know. Nichlas was a broken man, and he'd been failed at every turn, but Mia was determined to give as much as she took. She wanted all of her men equally.

She closed the distance between him, his taste mixing with the saltiness of their tears on her tongue, pure and raw emotion flooding between them. What started as a gentle embrace turned into an unbridled passion, Mia clawing at his chest to get closer to him.

"Let me love you, Mia," Nichlas whispered as he sucked her bottom lip between his teeth, fingers slowly making their way beneath her dress and squeezing her thighs. She arched against him, surprised at his forwardness, mumbling a "yes" before she scooted back to the headboard, Nichlas moving with her.

She felt like prey as he prowled forward, eyes trained on her face until their lips connected again. They fell together as if they had been together for years rather than moments, Nichlas pressing himself against her until every inch of their bodies were touching. Mia squirmed beneath him, heat coursing through her, the desire to be bear with this man growing with every passing moment. "*Please*," she begged.

Nichlas didn't respond to her cries as the kisses moved downward, liquid heat racing to the apex of her thighs. Her dress was pushed upward, bunching around her waist as he dipped his head and kissed her through her soaked panties. Mia cried out at the touch, hips bucking forward from the sensation. Her hands dove into his hair as he yanked her panties to the side and licked a stripe through folds before giving her mound an experimental suck.

Pleasure shot through her, Mia coming hard on his tongue, embarrassed that she had exploded so easily and so fast. She hadn't even known she had been on the edge until he had touched her, the passion between them running hot and heavy. "*More,*" she said and Nichlas complied, crawling back up to capture her lips.

Mia tasted herself on his tongue, the tart sweetness mixing with his musky scent that was wholly him. He rocked his hips against hers, his erection pressed against her belly, the need for him to be inside her gnawing at her until she was grabbing at his clothes all over again, whining for more.

They didn't have time to shed their clothes, Nichlas unbuttoning his pants and unearthing his cock, the veins throbbing, precum beading at the tip. She didn't even have time to react before he reached between them and pulled her panties to the side again and pressed himself against her.

Mia arched as he slid between her folds, every inch stretching her out in the best of ways. He had more girth than Matthias, the fullness just on that side of too much. As he bottomed out, they both let out a sigh of relief, as if this position made everything right with the world. Nichlas leaned down to steal another kiss and another until he was rocking against her while their tongues tangled and danced. She held onto him, each thrust into her sex sending shockwaves of pleasure up her spine until another orgasm barreled through her.

Fucking hell, this man would be the death of her.

He continued moving against her, attacking her lips as if it were a competition, nipping and biting at them in a way that was sure to leave bruises tomorrow, not that she minded. Showing the world that Nichlas had claimed her? That he was hers? *By all means.*

"I won't be able to tell you everything," Nichlas whispered, the words way more sensual than they should have been. She hummed her response, caught in a bubbly haze of orgasmic bliss as he continued. "I can't always tell you where I am." Thrust. "What I'm doing." Thrust. "Or when I'll be home." Thrust. Mia felt a third orgasm bristling beneath the surface, wondering how the fuck it was possible but she was too far gone to give more than a moan as a response.

"But I will not lie to you," Mia whined, fingers curling into his shirt. They were drenched in sweat and fully clothed as he pumped into her, chasing toward a finish line they were going to cross together. "Not anymore." His thrusts became wild and frenzied, Mia throwing her head back as she screamed through her release, Nichlas following shortly after. White hot ropes of cum spurted inside of her, the squelching sounds as he thrust a few more times heightening the dirtiness of it all. Her panties were soaked through, his cum coating her inner thighs as he collapsed, rolling them onto their sides while still inside her.

It was dirty and hot and fucking sexy, something Mia hadn't felt in years. She loved it.

"You're *mine*, Mia. *Ours.*" His lips tugged at the sweet spot at the base of her neck, causing her to gasp as she felt Nichlas' cock start to harden. She wasn't sure she could go another round, but those bundles of nerves between her legs told her otherwise. "And we are *yours.*" Mia's heart swelled that four men wanted her and would cherish her and possibly one day even say that they loved her.

But she didn't have much time to dwell on it before Nichlas had switched their positions again, Mia straddling his waist, allowing her to direct the next "mission." He playfully slapped her ass, Mia moaning at the contact. Nichlas' eyes heated, ideas for future sessions no doubt being stored in his head. "Take it away, firecracker."

And there it was, the fourth and final pet name. Her heart swelled even more until she felt it would burst out of her chest as she began to swirl her hips, moaning at the way his cock hit all the right places. "*With pleasure, sir.*"

Watching his eyes heat, his cock twitching inside of her at the same time, Mia decided to store that title away for future play, a wild smile on her lips as she set the pace until she was screaming out his name, collapsing on his chest after her fourth orgasm of the night.

Whispers of sweet nothings lulled her to sleep, the warmth that Nichlas provided enough to chase the nightmares away.

SIXTY-TWO

MIA

She stumbled to the shower in a haze, unsure what time it was, just that it was late enough to start her trek to the city before she chickened out or one of her men thought it was too dangerous. Mia didn't get very far before she felt a hard body behind her, Nichlas raining kisses down her neck and shoulder. She moaned into his touch as he turned her around and propped her up against the wall, sliding into her pussy like he belonged there.

They rested like that for a minute, their breaths evening out before Nichlas began to move, every thrust driving her higher, the sensual feelings warming her from the inside out. It had been like that for the last several hours, the promise of all that kink lost to the passion and burning need between them. It had gone from fast and dirty to slow and sensual, real quick, the bubbly haze of sweet kisses and gentle caresses alighting her desire to consume Nichlas.

It hadn't even phased her that her other men could hear every last bit of what they were doing. If she was honest with herself, it turned her on a little bit as Nichlas claimed every bit of her body, his lips attaching to his favorite spot on her neck again.

She trembled as she came, holding onto him until the pleasurable shocks passed. No words were shared between them as Nichlas thoroughly washed her body, drawing out yet another orgasm as she stared into those dark eyes of his. When she finally made it down the stairs, albeit on shaky legs, the other three turned to stare at her, silence filling the strangely empty cafe.

If Matthias kept closing the cafe like this, he wasn't going to be very popular with the locals.

Mia glanced down, knowing that she was completely covered in a tee and jeans. Her hair was still wet, crowding her shoulders, but there wasn't anything out of the ordinary or at least she thought. "What now?" she grumbled as one of them stuck a coffee mug in her hands, the sweet aromas of vanilla and raspberry meeting her nose.

"You're glowing," Jan finally told her, pressing a delicate kiss to her forehead. Mia froze, even as Kenn doled out the same gift, both of them making their way to the entrance. "It's not a bad thing, sweetheart. It's a good thing. I'm glad you were able to work it out with Nichlas."

The man in question walked down the stairs, his presence directly behind her as she drummed up the words she had been saving all night while actively ignoring the "glowing" comment. "I wanted to apologize." Her men froze, unsure where she was going with those words but she needed to say this. "I'm ... I don't like all the lies, but it's unfair of me to demand from you what you can't give." Her words had Jan and Kenn scrambling back to the counter but this wasn't a bad thing. "There are things you can't tell me. I know that. It'll be hard to understand that but ... I just need you guys to remind me."

Mia knew venturing into a relationship with four men was completely new territory, worse still, she had started with four men who had more secrets than they could count. They all murmured their agreement, worry coating their words. She hadn't expected that, hadn't expected them to think that she was second-guessing anything, but it was going to be trial and error moving forward, that much she knew.

Jan and Kenn left awkwardly after that, Matthias pressing a kiss to her temple before he returned to his dough.

"You don't have to close the shop every time I'm here, Matthias." His shoulders tensed, but he didn't respond, Nichlas guiding her toward the door. Only until they had made it to the car in back did Nichlas explain.

"Mia, the cafe *is* open but Natalie's been spreading some information around–"

"You were with me all night! How in the hell did you figure that out?"

Nichlas chuckled, pressing a chaste kiss on her lips. "Secrets of the trade. Come on, Mia, your chariot awaits." She grimaced at his words, slipping into the low-riding car that looked like it had come out of a movie. It was sleek and black and completely Nichlas.

MIA FELT LIPS PRESS AGAINST HERS, HER EYES FLUTTERING OPEN AS the kiss deepened. She mewled as her hands reached out to grab Nichlas, the man in question pulling away before she could drink her fill. "We're here, Mia." She hadn't realized she had fallen asleep.

She climbed out of the car, eyes widening at the chaos unfolding before her. Cars zipped up and down the street, angry honks and screeches adding to the fast-paced life of the city. People stalked toward their destination, heads bowed. Savory and not-so-savory smells wafted in from every direction, making her stomach grumble.

"Been a while since you've been in the city, Mia?" Nichlas murmured from behind her, chuckling when she didn't answer. It *had* been a while, years in fact since she had left the safety of Bryxton. After her father passed away and she had returned to her hometown, Mia's entire focus had been keeping up the business and marrying Anders. Her entire life had been consumed with everything everyone else wanted while she neglected her own aspirations and dreams.

And with each passing moment, watching the hectic and frenzied ensemble unfolding before her, Mia realized what she wanted was very different from where she was. Sure, she enjoyed her cozy little office, but in that lab, she was stuck in a moment, in a place where she hadn't been wanted. The people surrounding her couldn't see past her relationship. Her mother couldn't fathom that Mia, her own flesh and blood, was the one to be pitied.

And for *years*, Mia had taken every jab, every joke, every dirty look in stride. But out here, in the city, as much as it terrified her, Mia wanted something different. Something *more*.

Nichlas seemed to understand the faraway look in her eyes, the glaze that had slowly fogged up her somber-colored lenses. He graced her with a small smile, the moment broken by a cat call from a passerby. Mia blushed, tucking herself into Nichlas' chest to which he just chuckled. "You're *beautiful*, Mia. You've just been cooped up in that little town for so long that you seem to have forgotten. But don't worry," He pulled away so that she could see the seriousness in his expression as he cupped her cheek with a rough hand. "We'll make you remember. We'll let you see yourself just as we do. You'll never forget again just how wonderfully gorgeous you are on the inside and out."

He placed a simple kiss on her lips before leading her across the street. Inside she was melting. The mysterious fourth of her men had transformed overnight from someone completely walled off to someone who said such intense things before acting as if those words hadn't been *everything* she needed to hear. Mia kept silent as they approached the medical examiner's building, her heart bursting with love and adoration and every emotion in between. She tugged at his hand, Nichlas halting and turning to her, concern flashing in his dark eyes. His hands settled on her waist as he looked her over, a question pursed on his lips but she took the leap first.

"I love you, Nichlas."

It would have made more sense had she said that to Kenn or Matthias, and it was probably too soon, having known these men for just under two weeks, but they had become her everything. She couldn't imagine life without them and from the many, *many* conversations she had had over the past few days with Jan and Kenn, they weren't leaving. Not without her.

A mixture of shock and giddiness that reminded her of a young child spread through Nichlas' features as his fingers dug into her waist. He seemed unsure of how to act or how to respond or even where the confession had come from.

Was it too soon? Mia shrugged off the thought. It was what she felt, what she *wanted* and she was no longer going to apologize for the things she wanted. Not to herself and damn it hell, not to anyone else either.

She reached up on her toes and drew him into a kiss, light and supple to seal the confession. He responded as he bent her over slightly, his arms wrapping around her waist as if telling her that he'd never let her go. He whispered those sacred three words against her lips as he continued to kiss her, soft and sweet in contrast to the lusting passion from last night.

Mia wouldn't have minded if Nichlas chose not to reciprocate the confession, she could *feel* it, but hearing them cemented just where she belonged – with him, with *them*. And she was going to tell them the moment she got back home. For now, though, there were bodies to be examined and clues to be found. Pushing Nichlas away, though, was more difficult than she had planned.

Maybe she should have waited to say those words until they were back home, because if the rapidly growing bulge pressed against her core meant anything, Nichlas seemed like he was about to undress her on the sidewalk. "Nichlas," she mumbled against his lips playfully before she realized his hands had started to travel. "Nichlas!" Mia slapped at his arms and he released her reluctantly, his eyes half-lidded, a lopsided smirk attached to his lips. He didn't seem to be sorry in the least as he reached down between them and readjusted himself before taking her hand and heading up the stairs.

The goddamn audacity of that man.

SIXTY-THREE

MIA

The building reeked of bleach, bringing not-so-fond memories of her lab after the intruder's demise. She shook them off as she observed the pale marble stones adorning every inch of the inside, echoes from passerby's shoes resonating in her chest. It was eerily cold and she instantly hated being there, but she needed to know.

It had been years since she had stepped into a place like this, security and personnel stationed at every corner, cameras tracking her every move. Walking through the booth, Mia nearly screeched when it beeped, a security officer moving her to the side and explaining that she needed to pat her down. Slowly, she stretched out and let the woman search her for "hidden items" before she was released back to Nichlas' side.

She wanted to grab his hand, to ground herself but seeing as he had shed all contact with her the moment they had entered, Mia figured it was a bad idea – professionalism and all that. She straightened up, trying to mirror Nichlas' stoic demeanor as he flashed his badge and the guard gestured toward the back hall.

Nichlas gave a rough nod and made an abrupt right turn, Mia doing her best to keep up with his long strides. The powerful, no-bullshit aura emanating from him wasn't the reason he was terrifying. It was the ability to change from that loveable cheeky man on the street who had been about to bend her over backward to this frightening, lethal officer of the law.

And yet, her stomach was doing flips and her skin was growing hot at just *how lethal* he truly was. Something was wrong with her for finding her men as hot as they were, but who could blame her, what with the miracle that was Nichlas' hands?

They made it through three more sets of doors before it opened up into the morgue, five covered bodies on metal slabs neatly placed around the room. She hadn't thought all of this would be so easy when she called but Mia quickly realized that her "request" had only been processed with Nichlas' backing. It was the only explanation for why she had been allowed to enter a government building with minimal supervision and even less identification. In fact, she hadn't even shown her I.D., and she still had her phone, while she was pretty sure that was against protocol.

Mia shot a glance at Nichlas and as per usual, he knew what she was thinking. "Having me around can be useful, yes." He purred beside her, kissing the edge of her ear.

"Don't kiss me here. It's disrespectful to the dead."

"And you said the dead don't judge."

Where had this cheeky man come from? He was all act now, ask questions later *two seconds ago*, but in this closed-off room, he was melting her heart with suave smiles and those eyebrows that wouldn't stop wriggling as if he had just said the funniest thing. He hadn't, but he *was* amusing. Mia opened her mouth to throw back a retort when her phone interrupted them.

When she saw that it was Kenn, she didn't hesitate to answer, Nichlas slipping the device from her and putting it on speaker. He held it out in his hand so they could both hear and Mia wasn't sure whether to be worried or excited by the prospect that there didn't seem to be any secrets between the four of them.

"I'm assuming you made it to the city safely."

Nichlas didn't give her time to respond. "I'm more than capable of driving, *Barbie boy*."

"Really? We're going with that stupid nickname again?"

"You died your hair *blond*. Did you really think you were going to get a pass?"

"Whatever. You drive like a maniac. We all know it. I just needed to make sure our girl was still in one piece. Speaking of which, I still haven't heard her voice. You know, *our girlfriend's*?"

Mia stood there in shock, unable to process the childish back-and-forth between her men. Something had changed, overnight as it seemed. They had become comfortable enough around her that she was just one of the boys. Correction, part of the family.

"Mia?"

She startled back to reality, sputtering with a greeting, her cheeks flaming. "Ye-ah. I'm here." All kinds of tingles were doing flip-flops in her belly, a smile slipping onto her lips, unable to contain it any longer. "We're inside the lab now."

"Oh, good. That's good. Uh, Mia?" The quiver in his voice didn't sound great as she stared at Nichlas, silently asking him what it was about. He didn't answer but that cheeky look in his eyes told her he knew and it wasn't bad, per se. She hummed a response as Kenn cleared his throat. "Did you, uh, how was the drive?"

She frowned, unable to understand the double meeting. "I slept most of the way and then we ended up here. Why?" She stared at Nichlas again. "What's going on?"

There was a muffled yelp, Jan's voice filtering into the piece. "Mia, Kenn bet that you wouldn't make it inside without Nichlas bending you over somewhere."

"Oh," Mia whispered and then Jan added: "In public."

The room fell silent as Mia's cheeks heated. She wished the floor would open up and swallow her whole, Nichlas' smile widening to reveal a boyish charm that rivaled Matthias'. She hadn't expected that, nor her reaction as she involuntarily arched toward him, her nipples pebbling through her shirt until she was sure Nichlas could see the pins of steel pressing through the fabric.

Cackles sounded through the speaker, Jan and Kenn unsuccessfully trying to catch their breath before Kenn spoke again. "I'm going to say based on your silence that he *didn't* and Jan owes me ten bucks." Mia still wasn't sure how to respond; none of this made any sense.

For the past week, Mia was sure she had them all worked out. Matthias had the boyish charm and dark edges. Kenn was the fun, loving one. Jan was the strong and silent type hiding massive amounts of intelligence. And Nichlas was the lethal mysterious one with a sensual, passionate way of loving that made her insides melt.

However, in the past fifteen minutes, all of that had been turned on its head. She wondered how much else she still didn't know about these men and she couldn't wait to find out.

"Mia." Kenn's voice softened, but there was still a playfulness to his words. "Meet Nichlas, the *clingy* one."

She blinked a few times and stared at the man standing in front of her. "What?" That didn't compute. Yesterday, they had told her that Kenn was the clingy one. Nichlas was the mysterious one. Now there were two clingy ones?

"I can hear all those thoughts running around, angel," Jan began, "Kenn wants your attention, but Nichlas? Once he's got something in his sights, he'll never let it go. You've been caught,

Mia." His tone took a seductive turn, deepening with a rasp that had her pressing her thighs together. "Be careful where you start something if you're not keen on finishing it, angel."

A little moan left her lips at the mere thought that Nichlas would try something here, in this public area, the man in question shuffling closer, his tongue darting out to coat his lips.

"Listen to me, angel. All he needs is the perfect grip and he'll slide right in, anywhere, any time." It was both a threat and a promise, one that Mia wasn't so sure she wanted to avoid but they had come to the medical examiner's office for a reason. She slapped at Nichlas' hands which had somehow landed on her waist, wriggling out of his hold and hanging up on the laughter that erupted on the other side.

She still wasn't sure what to do with the new information or the tent in Nichlas' pants that she wasn't going to attend to anytime soon. "How long do we have?" When one of his brows raised, his eyes darkening at her words, she clarified before he really did bend her over one of the tables. "The bodies! I know you made some deal. How long do I have to check them out?"

The humor died in his expression as he donned a watered-down version of that stoic demeanor, moving to the door and leaning against it. "Maybe half an hour? Go ahead and find what you're looking for. I'll be here." If she would have paid a little more attention, she would have realized that this "opportunity" was less than sanctioned, and if they were caught, they'd be in more trouble than even Nichlas could talk their way out of.

SIXTY-FOUR

KENN

With Nichlas and Mia out of town, Kenn felt conflicted. He was happy that Mia was slowly becoming aware of their idiosyncrasies and understanding more than what met the eye. Nichlas and Matthias were always the first to draw in their lovers and yet also the reason most of their lovers left, and not for the reasons that Mia probably thought. Sure, their darkness and secrets were a bit much to get around, but the truth of it was Matthias' unmatched, explosive anger and inability to reign in his emotions at times and Nichlas' tendency to crawl into himself and build walls strong enough that the CIA couldn't penetrate.

The fact that Nichlas had attached himself to Mia so soon was incredible, Kenn just hoped it would last because if it didn't, he had a feeling that this, what was left of their hearts, would crash and burn.

"Would you focus?"

Kenn groaned, throwing his hands over his head to stretch as he leaned back in his chair. He had suggested they return to the office, to see if they could glean any additional information from the massive stack of unread files. The other two officers left them alone, officers that were different from yesterday. There had to be more to that than just a boost to these kids' resumes. The speed with which they circled through the station didn't make any sense.

"Kenn!" Jan whisper-yelled, kicking the leg of Kenn's chair from beneath their desk.

Kenn's chair scuttled backward, Kenn grabbing the desk frantically to pull himself upright. "What?" He leaned forward, eyes narrowing at the man who had interrupted his blissful daydream.

"I swear Mia's turned your mind to mush."

He grinned, unable to hide how unapologetically happy he was. "She's turned us all to mush, especially Nichlas." A giggle slipped out, but he owned it before nodding to the file in Jan's hands. "Find anything?"

Jan shook his head. "Not why I was trying to get your attention. There's been another one."

"Another what?" It took a minute for Kenn to screw his head on straight, eyes widening. "What the fuck? When did they find this one?" They had been busy all night, and there had been no talk of bodies showing up at Mia's office. Kingsley would have mentioned it to the others at the very least and Mia would have been more than likely contacted by Quinn or Chad. None of those things had happened, which meant the killer was becoming a little too bold for his liking.

"A few minutes ago. It's in transport to the coroner's office." Kenn waited for the punchline or an explanation, but Jan's words remained cryptic. "Quinn messaged me. Apparently, Kingsley's trying to keep this one quiet."

"But we're his *detectives*."

"And he has his own shady reasons for not saying anything. Let's go before Kingsley finds a reason to bar us from the lab." Kenn didn't need to be told twice as he jumped out of his chair and raced down the street for answers. It took him less than ten minutes to burst into the office, eyes frantically searching for the new body, Chad letting out a little squeal.

Kenn knew what he looked like, wild hair, crazy eyes, and a low growl hovering around him. He also didn't care. Eyes trained on Quinn, he stalked closer, immediately horrified at the scene that met him. It was another John Doe, but this one wasn't intact like the others. This body was battered and broken, lacerations so deep that guts spilled out of the holes, trying to escape.

The face was contorted with fear, the person's last thoughts full of terror and unrest.

If this was the same suspect, the killer had just elevated to a new style. Matthias had believed the killer was trying to right a wrong, trying to "clean up" an evil. But this body didn't match that at all. This body reeked of anger and desperation. It was an attempt to deter them from constructing a profile. It looked deliberate and personal, cementing the idea that the killer was from the townsfolk rather than from a nearby city.

Kenn immediately wished Mia was back home even though he knew she was safe with Nichlas, probably safer with him than anyone else at the moment. Quinn silently pointed to the neck, that same pinprick resting in the curve of the skin just like all the others. It was a stretch, but Kenn was pretty sure all the murders were connected.

It was also a good thing the killer was losing his composure because, unlike the other bodies, this one had held a lot more evidence. Never had Kenn been so glad to see such a battered body in his life, the sinister thought making his lips curl upward, his expression reflecting the absolute hell he was going to rain down on the little shit that thought he could hold this town in fear.

"We're going to catch this son of a bitch."

Quinn quivered by his side, taking a step back from the lethal aura pouring off the detective. "He's ... not going to stay in jail very long, is he?"

Kenn let out a bitter laugh, shaking his head, eyes still trained on the lifeless form. "Not when we get done with him, no." Quinn had no idea what had transpired with the intruder, nor all of the break-ins – although Kenn was sure he was aware of some of it. Quinn took another step back, but Kenn was no longer interested in the body. He had work to do. "Where'd they bring it in from?"

"Same place as the other one."

Kenn gave him a short nod, pushing past Jan, laser-focused on catching the bastard who had them all running in circles. Jan caught up to him rather fast, halting his frenzied movement with a touch grip on his shoulder. "Fucking slow down, man. Get your thoughts together. What is going on with you?"

"He's getting sloppy. This was rushed, hurried. He didn't have time to do whatever the fuck he usually does. Jan, the fact that Kingsley didn't tell anyone about this is to our advantage. The killer probably doesn't even know we've found the body yet."

"Fucking hell."

"There's probably a shitload of evidence left out there if Kingsley followed the usual crime scene protocols and didn't destroy anything." Jan released him, Kenn taking a deep breath before heading for the edge of town.

It was time this guy got what was coming to him.

SIXTY-FIVE

MATTHIAS

Matthias wasn't sure why his chest felt tight. It couldn't possibly be because Mia had ventured into the city without more of them surrounding her, suffocating her with their protection. No, he trusted Nichlas with his life, and yet, not knowing where she was at any given time was putting him on edge. It didn't help that Jan and Kenn were both busy trying to find clues and his cafe hadn't resumed the same level of business as when he had first started.

He ventured outside, letting out a deep groan as he stretched, eyes trained on Mia's office. He knew she wasn't currently in there, but it still gave him peace to lay eyes on the building, reminding him of the first time he truly saw her at the wedding in that peach lace dress while-

"Hey, handsome."

His look soured as he stared at the offending voice, Natalie prancing up to his side with a wide smile on her face. After the big reveal, the one where they all found out she WASN'T pregnant, Matthias thought she would have stayed gone. Unfortunately, news traveled fast, and the fact that Mia was out of town seemed to be of interest to the blond bitch currently trying to saddle up to his side.

Unbeknownst to Natalie, though, he wasn't the nicest of the four.

"What do you need, Natalie?" He spit her name out like poison, hoping that the dark look in his eyes would be a deterrent. It wasn't.

"Just some help. Anders isn't very useful, and I knew you weren't busy."

Matthias bit back the "no thanks to you" comment, knowing full well Natalie was part of the reason his sales had started to slip, not that he needed the money. He knew a trap when he saw one, but walking back into his cafe and shutting her out would draw the wrong kind of attention, just as much as giving into whatever the fuck she needed. Without Nichlas or Mia around to draw him back from an explosive outburst, his best option was to remain impartial to whatever she needed while finding an explanation to disappear.

"Matthias?" A hand rested on his forearm, one with manicured nails and evil intentions. He ripped himself away from her touch, growling at the audacity of the woman. Even if she wasn't such a hateful bitch, she was married to their girlfriend's abusive ex.

His lips curled back as he leaned forward, fingers curled into fists by his side. "Don't you fucking touch me."

Natalie didn't respond by shriveling back the way he thought she would. Instead a devious smile spread across her face, her eyes twinkling with whatever trap she was trying to ensnare him in. "Now, Matthias, we all know you have a temper, but you really shouldn't take it out on a lady." Matthias quirked an eyebrow, features softening at the thinly veiled threat as he tracked her movements. Her right hand moved to unclasp a bracelet on her left wrist revealing a deep black and blue bruise.

It didn't take him long to realize what her plan was when she started screaming. Everything happened too fast as he was slammed to the ground, hands drawn behind his back, and handcuffs locked around his wrists. The feeling of the impact had his mind in a completely different place as he threw off the man at his back, kicking at the air until it collided with skin and bones, rewarding him with a long, drawn-out whine.

He jumped to his feet, raging blindly as a hand landed on his chest, trying to push him backward. Matthias threw his head forward, colliding with a skull, which elicited a high-pitched yell and a loud crack.

A shrouded veil of anger and fear ensnared him as he struggled to free himself, Natalie trying to hide behind her faux terror at the big brute who had just bruised her wrist. Kingsley's appearance halted his outburst, the sheriff's presence signifying that Natalie's plan had been prepared and executed perfectly. Why she wanted him out of the picture was yet to be discovered.

HE GLARED AT THE METAL BARRING HIS FREEDOM, RESISTING THE urge to bare his teeth at the predicament he had found himself in. It wasn't even his fault that he was sitting on the lone bench in the sheriff's holding cell, staring out into the empty office save for Kingsley, who was sitting across from him just outside, a fearful look on his face.

The man was trembling, warring with his own emotions as he clutched the sides of his uniform, debating on whether or not to call an outside agency to take care of this problem.

Matthias hoped that Kenn or Jan found out about his explosive outburst first, rather than Nichlas, or Mia. He *really* hoped Mia would be spared the gritty details of this episode, but with how everyone was already spreading rumors and whispers, it wouldn't be long till the wrong story reached her ears before he could correct it.

Oh, how he had fucked up.

Matthias had to find a way out of this cell, and it was looking like unless he charmed Kingsley, it wouldn't be any time soon.

"I'm trying here, Matthias. I really am. Natalie's been a pain in my side ever since Anders brought her back, but this time ..." Kingsley unearthed pictures of Natalie's bruises that spanned more than just her wrists. Her neck and her side were the same shade of black and blues. "You battered the poor girl. No one fucking deserves that. Not even someone who's threatened your ... well, Mia."

Matthias refused to give Kingsley anything, remaining tight-lipped as he leaned back against the metal.

"Just tell me what happened. I have her story, and it doesn't look good. She said you met up with her last night, that you ... you guys finally acted on the attraction and then you turned on her. Matthias, I just don't understand. I don't even really know what you're doing here. The others, I understand. But you? Give me *something*, Matthias."

His hand hovered over the desk phone, but Matthias knew the moment he opened his mouth it would be one of two things – either he would rage about the fact that everyone had better stay the fuck away from Mia or that Natalie was a lying ass bitch.

Neither one would get him released. The first option would confuse the hell out of Kingsley, and the second would make him look guilty. So he remained silent, closing his eyes as he shifted his position to get comfortable. Despite the calmness of his expression, his thoughts raged and raced through his head.

"Matthias, you're looking at real charges. You broke one of my officer's ribs and broke another one's nose. Matthias!"

His eyes shot open, the lethal stare he had trained for so long locked on Kingsley. He wanted to fight back so fucking bad. He wanted to tell the sheriff that two men had attacked him from behind, that there had been no civilized approach from law enforcement, no reading of his rights. If Kingsley had done his homework, he would have known that approaching Matthias from behind was a death wish.

Matthias had his demons and he owned them, but fuck if he was going to get punished for this shit. Still, he didn't speak. Kingsley let out a deflated sigh, picking up the phone and dialing a number. The dial tone rang a few times, but he didn't get to answer before someone placed a finger on the hook switch, effectively ending the call.

The alarming tone echoed in the emptiness of the office, Kingsley shrinking back as the phone clattered to the floor. "What—"

Kenn's hand wrapped around the sheriff's neck, drawing him in close with those sea-green eyes that had become a torrent of raging waters. "Would you like to tell me what the fuck is going on right now? Why is Matthias behind bars?" The words were spit with such venom that Matthias could feel the room rise a few degrees. Jan was a few steps behind him, leaning against the bars like this was just an everyday occurrence.

Between those two, it probably was. Although they worked for the government, much of their casework was on the shadier side of the law. Matthias had been privy to a few of their exploits, and the outcomes hadn't been pretty.

Jan's attention was trained on the sheriff squirming for air, clawing at the hand wrapped tightly around his neck. Kenn didn't seem to have any intention of letting go, Jan's chilling tone telling Matthias that there was more to the picture than just this hasty arrest.

"Kenn, better let go. We have questions we need to ask him, and you're going to kill him if you hold on any longer."

The sheriff was dropped into a sputtering, blubbering mess as he scratched at his throat, sucking in air. His eyes were bloodshot as he scrambled to his feet, trying to push words out with his hoarse voice. "You – I'm going to–"

Kenn chuckled, but the smile didn't reach his eyes, a terrifying sight for such an upbeat guy. Most days he was the Barbie boy and other days he was an absolute terror. "No, first thing you're going to do is release Matthias, and then the next thing we're going to do is have a nice, long talk about some things."

"You can't!" Kingsley shrieked as Matthias stood up and approached the gate, patiently waiting for the inevitable. "He's a monster! Kicked two of my officers and then–"

"Officers that jumped him from behind. He's a veteran, which I'm sure you knew. You should be happy he didn't do more damage. Now, Kingsley, I won't ask again. Unlock the cage or I have some information that I think our boss would be very disappointed to hear."

Kingsley's face drained of color as he unlocked the gate, Matthias slipping through them only to leer over the sheriff with the pure rage vibrating through every muscle in his body. He knew how he looked in these moments, the way his eyes turned a shade of midnight that mirrored the void in his heart. He wasn't happy to lean on those demons, but Kingsley needed to know who he was dealing with.

They had tried playing Kingsley's way. Now it was time to start playing theirs.

SIXTY-SIX

MIA

Finding the connection had taken nearly the entire thirty minutes, Nichlas shuffling her out just before their time ended. Mia feared there was going to be some big showdown like in the movies, as if she had stolen a piece of evidence and the killer had come to silence her. Even as they exited the building unscathed and they slipped into a booth at a local diner, Mia still worried that someone would be after them.

Nichlas didn't seem worried, pressed against the door, his eyes tracking her every move as he took a call from one of his superiors. She tried to stay focused as she investigated the first body and then the second, but she couldn't help but listen to the whispered conversation across the room.

Years of bullying and unwanted rumors had trained her hearing as she absentmindedly poked at body number three.

"How's the investigation coming along?" the voice on the other side of the phone asked. She envisioned a pudgy man attached to that voice, one of those computer nerds that never got to see the light of day.

"Just fine, as you would know, because you're the one who gets the reports."

"Don't get all testy with me. I'm not the enemy. Anything new?"

"No."

"Glad you didn't lie to me, because I know for a fact you're not with him. What are you doing?"

"Investigating." Mia could tell Nichlas was trying hard to keep his voice low, but the irritation was growing with every word. Whoever was on the other side of that phone was pissing Nichlas off.

"I doubt it. I have a feeling you're looking into the murders, something I think I told you was not to be your focus."

"And the fact-finding mission you have me on is a load of pure bullshit."

"Again, don't come at me. Our boss is a dickwad, we both know that. Once the new mission is all set up, you can split."

Nichlas didn't answer, Mia realizing that his gaze had fallen to her. He knew she was listening, but he also wasn't answering because of the weight of his response. A new mission meant he'd be leaving, and Mia knew that it could be a week or several months till she saw him again.

"About that—"

"Nope. You're the perfect one for the job. Don't put me in an awkward position, Nichlas. I stuck my neck out for you!" The guy sounded almost desperate, Mia tuning out of the conversation as they bickered back and forth and she continued to search for the connecting clues.

"Calm down, Mia. No one's going to come after you, being in there. I might get chewed out for using credentials I wasn't supposed to, but you're safe."

She wanted to relax at those words, but she couldn't, not after what she had found. Not even the promise of greasy food was able to distract her, a fact that Nichlas caught onto rather quickly.

"What'd you find?" Mia bit her lip, her body betraying her as a chill raced down her spine. "Mia?"

"I thought the little pricks in the neck were weird. None of them looked like they were poisoned. The charts didn't say anything about it either. I don't even know why they all have it." She fumbled through an explanation, searching for the right words, but Nichlas didn't push her. "They don't mean anything, I don't think. It's just a deterrent. The dirt under their fingernails will help for DNA, but I have to find a lab that will—"

"I got you covered. Go on."

Mia didn't dwell on the fact that Nichlas just offered to help on a case that the person on the phone had explicitly told him not to. She didn't want him getting in trouble, but she *really* wanted to find out who was behind all these killings. "I never really got time to open them up and look at everything. I cataloged weights of organs and—"

"Mia."

She shuddered at the forceful tone of his voice, a voice that told her to get to the point rather than drabble on about unimportant details. "I found this." Mia knew she probably couldn't remove something from the lab, so she brought it from her own office and compared it with what she had found in the medical examiner's lab. Mia unearthed a small green fragment, the size of a pebble. It resembled the corner of a sponge, but it was dry and rough to the touch, almost like a rock.

"What is that?"

"I didn't know at first, but I kept seeing fibers like these around the bodies. This is by far the biggest piece I've seen." It had come from one of the earlier victim's stomachs, a piece of debris that hadn't meant anything to her at the time until she had accidentally dropped it in the sink.

Mia grabbed her glass of water and poured it onto the evidence, Nichlas watching with wide eyes as it grew to the size of her thumb. These sponges weren't just any kind of sponges, but ones made to grow and expand. They hardened as they dried out, remaining lodged in between wherever they had expanded. "It stays like that."

"Mia, spell it out for me, because I'm really hoping you're not saying–" He left his thought unfinished, as the waiter approached the table with a cheery smile. Nichlas hurriedly ordered two coffees and a Danish, one that would probably be packed away for the ride home. "Continue."

She grabbed the saltshaker next, shaking it over the green substance. It began to break down into smaller pieces before most of it was just fibers and dust. By the shock on Nichlas' face, he hadn't seen that type of sponge before. "The victims fought like hell, but I don't really think it was an attacker they were fighting. I think they were fighting to breathe."

Mia had found similar green pieces, much smaller in size, in the medical examiner's lab. One of the victims still had a piece on her tongue. The others had them cataloged in the "stomach's content" portion of their file.

The idea that someone was suffocating his victims from the inside out began to eat away at her. It was nearly foolproof – slipping a piece of this sponge into someone's food before they washed it down with water. It would expand and harden until the person suffocated. Water would only make it worse. Then all the killer had to do was administer some salt, in pure form or in the form of salt liquid, and the evidence disappeared. Enough of it, anyway.

The only reason Mia hadn't connected the little green substances together was that they weren't available for common use. She'd only used them in the high-tech university labs, and even then, it had only been for demonstration.

Whoever was leaving bodies in their wake was more than just familiar with the area – he was trained and educated with access to technology that most lay people could only dream of.

And there were only four men she knew that had access like that.

Four men that had promised her their hearts.

Four men who had her safety in their hands.

Four men who had been trained to hide their emotions and lie like their life depended on it.

SIXTY-SEVEN

JAN

Without Nichlas or Mia in town, keeping Matthias' demons locked up was going to be difficult, but they absolutely could not have another outburst. Kingsley was already on edge, one step away from calling in the big guns, and they wouldn't be able to stop him.

For one thing, they didn't really have any evidence that what Natalie had said *wasn't* true. They were just scarier than the thugs that had caught Matthias unaware, and they outranked Kingsley in the long run. The problem was getting Kingsley to agree to let Matthias walk out of the office and return home.

"He's not leaving here. He can't. He's under arrest."

"For what?"

"For … for assault." Kingsley cowered back a step beneath Kenn's chilling stare. "Natalie had evidence and—"

Jan laughed bitterly, resting back against the cell, the cool metal calming his nerves. "And we all know that you already had your goons at the ready to take him. The question is why."

Kingsley was silent for a moment, eyes darting between the three of them before he answered. "She ... she's been talking about him for the past week, saying he was dodgy, that he ... he kept threatening to—"

Matthias growled, taking a threatening step forward that Jan easily intercepted. He stood with his back to Matthias' front, cutting off the kid's ascent. God, if the kid took out Kingsley, there would be no explaining their way out of this. As it was, Jan was banking on the fact that Kingsley wouldn't actually call Jan and Kenn's superior. Their superior wanted all this shit to stay quiet so he could run unopposed. That man would do everything in his power for the problem to go away.

Which would mean Matthias would rot in a cell until the elections were over – months away.

"Look, Kingsley. You didn't even read him his rights, not to mention that you didn't even fucking investigate anything she said. Matthias owns a cafe. He also has a girlfriend and three other men who can attest to his whereabouts at any given time."

"But not all of those moments can be accounted for," Kingsley murmured.

Jan had prepared for an answer like that though. "No, you're right. We didn't follow him everywhere. What I can tell you is that Natalie wears a certain rancid perfume." He sniffed at the air. "A perfume that attaches to anything it brushes up against. A smell I think you're quite familiar with."

Kingsley's face blanched as he held his hands up in defeat. "I can explain!"

Jan didn't need him to, though, and neither did the other two. Natalie was a gorgeous woman, a woman who knew what she wanted and refused to take no for an answer. The problem was that she was starting to ruin things she couldn't pay for.

"Kingsley," Kenn began, a tight smile on his lips, that deep blue torrent unleashed in his gaze. "Between this fraternization and the fact that you have been dismissing cases, it's not looking good for you." Jan expected yet another "I can explain," but there wasn't one, just silence. Kingsley was being controlled in some way, but for the life of him, Jan couldn't figure out how. The killer didn't seem capable of that, especially not with the last murder and Natalie's men ... well, possibly.

With a few more threats, Kingsley released Matthias, the three of them now in the safety of their own apartment, Matthias buried in his room, Kenn leaned against Jan's door. "What the fuck are we going to do now? Matthias is going to lose it if he doesn't—"

Jan released a deep sigh, drying off his hair with a spare towel as he exited the bathroom attached to his room. He gave up after a minute, throwing the cotton on the floor and then just shook off the excess water drops like a puppy after a bath. He was trying to ignore the inevitable – the issue revolving around Matthias' volatile emotions. It had been a problem for years, but he hadn't had this much stress thrown at him in one place in a while.

He needed help.

Help they couldn't give.

Help that not even Mia could offer.

The hardest part would be convincing Matthias to accept it.

"We'll figure that out. Right now, he's safe and he's in his room. We'll take turns to make sure he doesn't go off and do anything stupid." Mia had been threatened more times than they could count and Natalie was not making this any easier. "Now, what did you find out there?"

Kenn shot him a boyish smile, bounding into the room and plopping onto his mattress. If the man hadn't been so big, Jan would have thought a child had just entered his sacred space. "So many pretty things." He chortled at his terrible humor, pulling out his phone as Jan took a seat beside him. "Aside from the blood spatter, I found our golden ticket."

"Golden ticket?"

"The weapon."

"*Excuse me?*" Jan stared at Kenn like he had lost his mind. Minutes into searching around the scene, they had received a call from Quinn that Matthias had been marched to the station in handcuffs. There had been few details about the scuffle, Chad freaking out in the background, but Jan had gotten enough before they hurried to the office to rescue the kid. Somehow in the chaos, Kenn had managed to find more information than most detectives found in hours.

Kenn giggled, leaning forward and thrusting his phone into Jan's face. A wrench lay on the ground, covered in crusted crimson pebbles, the absence of blood revealing a handprint at the base of the metal.

Jan didn't even have to ask where the evidence was, knowing full well that Kenn had called one of their contacts to retrieve it. Unfortunately, with everything that was going on, Jan wasn't so sure that piece of evidence would make it to a lab.

"We're on the same page, buddy." Kenn turned his phone off, that grin widening as his eyes flashed with a giddiness that had been dormant for months. They hadn't gotten this much excitement from their cases in a while, and as gruesome as these deaths were, Kenn needed a little bit of chaos in his life to stay sane. They all did. "I called one of my guys. We should have the results in a few hours." Jan blinked a few times, realizing that Kenn's guys weren't from any of the official channels, and while it made sense, any evidence they came up with meant that it couldn't be used in court.

Then again, they were way past using legal channels and following the rules. Following the rules and listening to authority had gotten the town into this mess, finding loopholes and finding which ones to break was going to be the only path forward.

Jan just hoped they didn't break the wrong rule before they could fix it.

SIXTY-EIGHT

MIA

Unlike the pleasurable silence of the drive into the city and the sensual feelings of Nichlas by her side at the medical examiner's office, the ride back was tense, and Mia couldn't help the emotions warring in her head as she tried to fight the one thought that had to be wrong. It *had* to be. Her men couldn't be part of this. It wasn't impossible. She wouldn't let it be possible, even though she knew that's not how crime worked.

Nichlas gave her a few curious glances over the past hour but didn't press her, the moment the car came to a stop, Mia climbed out and raced inside. She wasn't sure what her first move would be, whether it would be to grab her bag and run home to Ma or confront her men or cower in a corner of self-hate like she used to when she realized she had fallen into a trap again.

Any of her plans might have had a chance of working if her other men weren't currently having a pow-wow at one of the tables. She skidded to a halt, sucking in her bottom lip as her entire body reacted to having all four of them in the same room. Nichlas stepped up behind her and then around her so that she could see all of them at the same time, her expression souring as her thoughts continued to haunt her.

"Mia?" She wasn't even sure who had called her name as she drank in their presence, unsure how to catalog what she was seeing. Jan seemed a little on edge, more so than he had this morning, but he was definitely the calmest of the four. Kenn's eyes were nearly midnight, a torrent of emotions running through his expression, his lips pulled tight in contrast with the upbeat detective he usually was. And Matthias, just his presence terrified her at the moment, the darkness wrapping around him, a low growl vibrating in his chest.

They seemed content with her nonanswer, Jan offering new information on the case. "We had some fingerprints run. They came back as classified. Someone with—"

Mia shook her head, unable to separate that one thought from reality. Her bottom lip trembled as she gathered her thoughts, meeting Nichlas' gaze, her confidence flickering. "You ... it's not you, is it?" She took a step back, all four of them rising to their feet, dread flooding their expressions. Slowly, Mia unearthed the green fibers, what was left of her demonstration from Nichlas, and placed it on the table.

She watched each of their expressions, frowning as recognition flickered in three of her men's eyes. They seemed confused about why the piece was sitting in front of them, but not regarding *what* it was. That thought cut at her as she tried to distance herself from the very real possibility that one of them had a hand in these deaths, or at the very least, a connection with the killer.

Either way, Mia needed to hear them say it as she explained where the evidence had come from. "I found something, but it's not accessible to the public, and then you just said the fingerprints are classified? That—"

Nichlas didn't even flinch, as if he had already known where her head was at, but it took the others a moment to follow her thought process. Jan was at her side in a heartbeat, dragging her against his chest and pressing kisses to her forehead as he mumbled through an apology. "Angel, *no*. It's not us. Fucking hell, how long have you thought that?"

He glared at Nichlas, but the guy didn't acknowledge it. Mia refused to fall apart, needing all the facts to make a decision. It couldn't possibly be her men. That was too obvious, and the timeline didn't add up. However, knowing something and believing it were two different things.

"I *know* it's not you. I know that. I just ... there's too many thoughts in my head. Whoever's killing people knows what they're doing. It's also been happening for a long time."

Kenn's expression softened as he approached her as well, stealing her from Jan's embrace. He strung one arm around her waist and placed a finger under her chin to angle it upward, their eyes meeting so that she could see the concern on his face. "What's a long time, sweetheart?"

The warmth of their touch was overriding her panic as she leaned in to take a swig of his musky scent. "Years," she breathed against his chest. He tensed against her, the room dropping a few degrees as they all seemed to move in a step closer. The sheer weight of their presence tugged at her as she removed herself from Kenn's arms, putting distance between them again.

Her gaze frantically moved between the four of them, each of them looking more tortured than they had a few moments ago. She hated that her emotions were so unstable, but she couldn't help it. With everything that had happened and had been happening, she needed all of the information.

It made sense that Jan caught on first, reaching out his hand with a silent invitation. He had been the first to sit her down and truly explain the dynamic, her men's needs, and that it would be a learning process through and through. Timidly, Mia took his hand and let him lead her upstairs into his room, the door closing with a soft click, but in the silence, it was almost deafening.

"I need—"

"I know what you need, angel, but there's a few things that happened while you were gone, and discussing this with all of them present isn't the smartest idea." Mia knew it had something to do with Matthias, but it didn't seem like the right moment to ask. Jan took a deep breath and sat her on the mattress, crouching in front of her much the same way Nichlas had done last night. "Mia, there's a lot of cards in play right now. I can't tell you everything, for your safety and because we're all sworn to a certain code. That being said, those green fibers aren't foreign to us because we all have access to technology like that. Pretty sure Matthias used to use it in tactical, and Kenn and I have pretty good connections with a few labs that test our evidence."

"What about Nichlas?" Mia blurted out.

Jan gave her an uneasy smile. "He's probably come across it, but he wouldn't have known what it was. He's not into investigating evidence like we are, nor is it his job to collect it. He's observant, so if he'd seen it before, he'd know but knowing what it is, is a different story. Were you really worried about this?"

"How could I not be?" Mia huffed, scooting back on the mattress until only her feet were dangling off the edge. She leaned back against the wall, staring at her lap as she tried to sift through her emotions and figure out what she was truly feeling. It wasn't anger. It wasn't even fear at this point. It was just uncertainty. She didn't like not knowing. As she rose to meet Jan's expression again, she realized that there was more. "What is it?"

Jan climbed onto the bed beside her, drawing her into his lap in a way that made her feel protected. It was strange that Jan's touch gave her a sense of comfort that the others didn't. Around Jan, she felt completely bared for him to see, his ability to read her like an open book almost terrifying. "It seems that Natalie's upped her game."

"Meaning?"

He tensed beneath her, his arms tightening around her waist as if she was going to run. She wouldn't, but the way his chest stilled against her had her looking at him, waiting for his response. He gave her one, in the way of a distraction, pressing his lips to hers as he parted them with his tongue. The kiss was slow and sensual, Jan tasting her from the inside out as he took what he wanted.

Mia tore herself away from him before she could forget her train of thought. She shook herself out of the haze, frowning. "Don't distract me. Just tell me. Jan, you're making me worried. What did Natalie do?"

"She has a vendetta out for you and possibly Matthias. We haven't found out why. She accused Matthias of beating her earlier and Kingsley dragged him off to jail." Hackles raised, Mia sat up, pushing away from Jan, her breath coming in quick pants as she tried to wrap her mind around that. "We're not really sure who's pushing what envelope at this point but—"

Something in Jan's eyes told her that the accusation wasn't the whole story, his words trailing off and the air tightening around them. Her request for the truth hadn't made their new relationship any easier to manage. It had just made it more difficult to weather emotions and feelings. With each new piece of information, Mia wondered why they just couldn't catch a break.

She waited patiently for Jan to gather his thoughts, his next words nothing she could have predicted. "Matthias snapped, Mia. It wasn't his fault. They jumped him from behind, but he's on edge. It's not good."

Mia didn't even know how to handle that information, so she did what any normal, healthy adult would do – she shut down.

SIXTY-NINE

NICHLAS

He stared longingly at Jan's closed door for a few more seconds before stepping into Kenn's room to join the impromptu meeting that had been scheduled. They were all on edge, all worried that Mia was going to fall apart from the continued assault of this case on her nerves. It had only been a matter of time before she panicked or shut down, the later one the reason why she was curled up in Jan's bed, clutching the sheets like they'd protect her from the big bad world outside.

He hoped she'd still be there in the morning, but he couldn't fault her if she returned to Quinn's home where she felt safe. Kenn stared at him from a chair by his desk, Jan perched on the edge of the mattress having slipped out of bed a few moments ago.

"So?"

Jan shook his head, "She's not doing well. I told her about Matthias, but she didn't take it well. It's a lot. You forget that we've been doing this for years. She's just a small-town coroner."

Nichlas hadn't forgotten that this type of shit was stuff he dealt with every day. That he had seen things most men passed out from, dealt with pain that people wouldn't wish on their greatest enemy, and had to make choices that would make grown men break down from indecision and guilt. It ate away at his emotions over time, making it harder to understand the fragile heart most people kept with them, a heart that Mia had, even as big as it was.

She had told him that she loved him earlier this morning, a confession while out of the blue, didn't seem hurried. It felt right, and Nichlas wanted to do right by her, despite his orders or his current mission.

Fuck the mission, Mia was more important.

He leaned against the wall by the door, folding his arms across his chest. "What now? The evidence isn't readily available and the fingerprints are classified. Kenn, what do you have?"

Kenn perked up, his shoulders rising just a bit. "Why me?" There was the ghost of that cheeky smile on his lips, but the humor had died out. They were getting too close to a killer they still didn't understand. Matthias hadn't even been able to draw up a profile that made sense.

"Because," Nichlas chuckled, "you're more observant than I am." He wiggled his eyebrows, eluding to the weapon they had found.

"I didn't find ... Well ... " His eyebrows furrowed as he fumbled for the right words.

Jan finished Kenn's thought. "We have a suspicion that we weren't sent here to clean up the issue, just to make it blow over."

The room quieted, the possibility that their higher-ups had a hand in whatever was going on, a rather terrible notion to consider. It wasn't that far-fetched, though. Despite Jan and Kenn's expertise, they hadn't been able to gather more than a few clues, Kingsley doing everything in his power to shut the autopsies down by sending the bodies to the city almost immediately. And Nichlas had been forced to focus on an outside case that had nothing to do with the bodies but had brought more trouble back to the cozy little cafe then his mission warranted.

What should have been a few days and a quick investigation had turned into two weeks of craziness. Craziness that was far from over.

"Our boss is trying to get elected, so he just wants it to go away, and it's weird that they don't want you anywhere near this."

Nichlas couldn't argue with that. He usually had free reign on his missions because of his background, but not in this town. He had a few names in mind, but nothing he could cement before he asked around. "I need to ask Matthias a question," he stated it as if asking for permission, but the other two knew he wasn't, as he slipped out of Kenn's room and down the hall. He knocked once, waiting for a response, but when he didn't receive one, he opened the door to reveal a neatly made bed and no Matthias.

They should have been keeping a better eye on the kid in the wake of recent events because Matthias was in one of two places, and neither of them were any good.

SEVENTY

ANDERS

He tried to shift in the bed, groaning as a wave of pain washed over him and exploded in his head. He reached up to hold his temples as he squirmed on the mattress, remembering the beating he'd dealt with just a few days ago. Everything hurt, and not even the enormous amounts of morphine pumping through his veins had helped get rid of the images.

Another groan slipped from his lips as he tried to reach over to the counter and grab the glass of water waiting for him. His throat felt like he had swallowed chalk for the past several hours, his fingers groping frantically in the dark and coming up empty. Just as soon as he was about to give up, he felt the cool glass being pushed into his grip. He didn't even wait to think about it, chugging every last drop and trying to forget the predicament he was in as he placed the glass back on the table.

A few broken ribs, a left wrist fracture, multiple lesions on both legs, a black eye, bruised jaw, and a dislocated shoulder. The ribs had bruised his lungs and someone had cracked his skull, but he was still alive to tell the tale. No one but that bitch had been to see him and he was just about done playing that stupid game with her.

"You should be dead."

Anders paled at the familiar voice that held none of the warmth he remembered, a body coming into view, deep-purple eyes flashing with a tumultuous anger he hated being on the end of. He scooted farther into the hospital pillows, whining at the assaulting stare. He rapidly pressed his help button, wishing that nurses from every direction would rush in and drag the barista away.

"You should know that's not going to work."

He had always known that Matthias wasn't *just* a barista. Not only did his physique give it away, Anders' knack for drawing in information had given him a not-so-pretty profile of the man standing before him. A dark past didn't even begin to explain Matthias' service or the things he had done before turning to coffee and bagels. Anders' gaze flitted around the room, trying to find a way to escape the inevitable.

"Screaming won't help you either. Seems like they've given you quite a bit of morphine."

His eyes widened as Matthias stepped closer, drawing a seat to the bed so that he could rest his forearms on the mattress. Anders had watched enough TV to know that his life was being threatened in some way, so best not anger the murder machine, especially since he knew that Natalie had sent someone after Matthias and Mia, a someone who still hadn't returned.

"What do you want?" Anders whispered, coughing as the effort scratched his throat.

"A truth for a truth."

Anders hadn't expected that. He had expected more pain and a lot more violence.

"What do you want to know?"

"Everything."

Anders knew he owed it to the guy for everything Natalie had done. He still hated Matthias for taking Mia away, but she would be back at his feet soon enough when she began to see Matthias for the real man that he was.

"Natalie's with bad people," Anders croaked out, resituating a little to get comfortable. It took the pressure off his wrist, but sitting up still hurt like hell. "Wants you dead. Mia, too. Stop finding the killer."

That seemed like news to Matthias, but it also didn't seem to satisfy his need for truth. "Why?" It was a simple word but paired with Matthias' rage, it was a command and a promise, a promise of nightmares yet to come.

"She's…" Anders trailed off, unsure how he wanted to word it or if he wanted to voice it all. Natalie could be right around the corner, although she hadn't visited yesterday. Matthias didn't like the quiet, jumping out of his seat so fast that it crashed to the ground, a thick hand wrapped around Anders' throat. Anders whined, his eyes rolling into the back of his head as he lamely scratched at the fingers cutting off his airflow. "Working with him," he spat out, hoping that it would cause Matthias to let go.

It did, but not without a rough jerk to his head, setting off another round of pain. "Who's *him*?"

"I… I don't know."

"Not good enough," Matthias barked, his eyes glowing again with the need to act out his emotions.

"No more! Please!" Anders whisper-yelled, fiery sensations running along his skin as everything twisted and throbbed. Tears spilled down his cheeks as he silently pleaded with Matthias, telling him that that was all he knew.

"Who beat your wife?"

Anders frowned, shaking his head but unable to speak. Matthias didn't believe that either and leaned in to grab him again, a second force yanking him away before he could do any damage.

Matthias let out a wild growl, silencing instantly when Nichlas pressed him against the wall with enough force to knock a man on his ass. It only momentarily quieted Matthias, the deep purple of his eyes softening back to that amethyst of the barista Anders had first met. Watching the kid snap back was almost as terrifying as the hand that had been around his neck.

"Fucking snap out of this shit. You need to get your fucking emotions in check before we have to send you back!" That seemed like a private conversation, but Anders was in awe of the way that Matthias seemed to shrink a little in size, his head bowing apologetically as Nichlas released him.

Anders tensed at the thought that Matthias was going to charge at him again, but he needn't have worried. Instead, Nichlas did, a different kind of fury in his expression but no less terrifying. A few days ago, Anders had been hiding behind this man and trying to drum up a friendship. He should have never been so stupid to think that Nichlas was on his side.

"You need to be *real* clear on what you say next, or I will set Matthias on you and I'll watch like the sick bastard that I am."

"You *wouldn't*."

Nichlas smiled, a smile that was all teeth and sinister wiles. There was no remorse in his expression, no apologies, no guilt for what he was about to do. These men were dangerous, and Anders couldn't wait to pull Mia away from them. "I *would*. You have no idea how well we can hide a body, but actually, you'd know that, wouldn't you?"

Anders shuddered with the weight of his question. They *knew* he knew about whoever had burst into Mia's lab. Fucking hell, they knew *everything*. It was the first time he was truly seeing Nichlas and understanding that there had been a reason for this mysterious man to cozy up to him. It wasn't just for a job or some feud between brothers. Nichlas was here for him, wasn't he?

Why hadn't he done anything?

As Anders went to ask, he realized he should refrain from it and decided to answer Matthias' last question instead. "No idea. Wasn't me. She was fine yesterday."

Nichlas nodded, a lot less violence in his expression than Matthias – a fact that Anders was grateful for. "Anything else?"

"No?" Anders couldn't think of anything off the top of his head, eyes flitting between the two self-proclaimed killers in his room – well, at least, they had alluded to it. No one would believe him though. Not after an attack that Natalie had so wrongly pinned on Mia and her men. He knew it had been the attackers' intent to kill him, but he was resilient and fought back until a passerby had called Kingsley for backup.

The attackers were from the same group as Mia's intruder, but that wasn't information he wanted to pass on just yet. He needed to do his own research into the woman he had so haphazardly married. If it hadn't been for the pregnancy, Anders wasn't sure he would have ever left Mia's side. She wouldn't be stuck with these dangerous men, and he wouldn't be in this bed, beat to hell.

Nichlas turned back to Matthias, the kid shifting uncomfortably in place. "Now, do you have any last words before we leave?"

Matthias didn't look like he wanted to leave but he grinned and nodded, offering his a few words. "I said truth for truth, and I meant it. That bitch of a woman you traded for Mia." A wry grin spread across his lips, those eyes darkening again. "She's not pregnant."

Anders blinked in disbelief. He had no reason to disbelieve Matthias, but Anders had *seen* Natalie naked, multiple times. He searched his brain for all the moments in the past three months, throwing each one out as he realized that he hadn't actually seen her stomach. He'd seen various parts of her, but never her stomach. As if she was hiding something.

Nichlas and Matthias wore matching smirks at his shocked state, Nichlas having the last word. "Tell your *wife* that she needs to find a new target. She's not playing in the little leagues anymore. It would be a shame if someone got hurt."

Had it been anyone else, Anders would have burst out laughing, not just because the threat was dumb but because it eluded to both of them going after Natalie. Catching their expressions as Nichlas all but pushed Matthias out the door, Anders knew that the "someone" was him. If Natalie tried something else, Anders would pay for it.

He couldn't even focus on that though, because Matthias had just blown apart the one reason he had been blindly walking down this road.

Natalie wasn't pregnant, and while she had lied about a lot of shit, this one had wrangled him into a marriage he hadn't wanted with anyone other than Mia. A fact that still rang true for him. Anders settled into his bed, laying back down as he tried to plan for the immediate future. Natalie had some explaining to do and then Anders was off to court so that he could win back his woman from the dangerous demons that had ensnared her.

SEVENTY-ONE

KENN

With Mia curled up in his lap like a kitten, nose stuck in a book and a mug on the table, Kenn never wanted to move. He shifted slightly under her, her minty shower gel a breath of fresh air. He had been worried she would stay locked up in Jan's room, but while everything was still a bit tense, she seemed content to spend Saturday morning in the cafe.

Matthias hadn't come back last night, and neither had Nichlas, but since there was nothing in the news and Natalie wasn't accusing them of anything at the moment, it was safe to say that Nichlas had wrangled the kid back from acting out. Mostly.

More than likely, Matthias had slipped into Anders' hospital room for answers with every intention of killing the bastard once the impromptu interrogation ended. Nichlas was one of the only ones that could drag him out of those moments, but it didn't mean that Nichlas would have. Hell, they all wanted a piece of Anders after the fucker had dragged Mia all over the place and shattered her heart.

Kenn wasn't sure he'd have a problem if Anders went missing either. He was the scum of the earth, and he deserved every last bruise and broken bone he had suffered. Honestly, he should have suffered more.

Kenn stuffed his head in the crook of Mia's neck, kissing at the curve of her skin, smiling as she shivered beneath his touch. He loved how responsive she was, even if initiating something at the moment wasn't appropriate. She curled in tighter against him, the tension in her shoulders slowly seeping out as the morning unfolded. She hadn't asked where everyone was as she stumbled down the stairs, in search of coffee and comfort.

She hadn't even asked why the cafe was still closed at eight in the morning and she hadn't resisted when Kenn pulled her into his lap while she made her way through breakfast. He did notice, however, how her attention kept darting to the front door as if she was waiting for something – something he soon realized was the presence of her other two men. Mia wasn't inattentive like their other girlfriends. She drew strength from all of them in different ways and she noticed things that the others hadn't – like when one or more of them was gone.

Mia wasn't searching for an explanation, he understood that, but rather the peace that came with knowing they were all safe. After finding out about Matthias and his outburst, she had been more worried about his health than anyone he had hurt, which was in stark contrast with their other relationships. Everyone else had been quick to condemn Matthias or shy away from him. Mia had wanted to run straight to him, but Jan had kept her from leaving his room, no need for her to experience Matthias in that state just yet.

Mia preened once again, eyes glued to the door, her body trembling when the back door opened, one – that by the look of it – Mia hadn't known existed. She twisted around as a very worn-out Nichlas stalked in, a tipsy Matthias trailing after him. The kid stumbled into the wall, grasping at the wallpaper helplessly, groaning at the sheer effort it took to stand. From the concern in Nichlas' expression, calming Matthias down had taken most of the night between drinks and a friendly fight if the bruise forming just above Nichlas' collarbone was any indication.

Their woman threw her book down and raced forward, hands at the ready to embrace one or both of them as she skidded to a stop before Nichlas. There were no questions, just silent acceptance as Nichlas embraced her, arms tightening around her back as he leaned in to kiss her. She melted against him, drinking him in before he released her, all of them wondering what her reaction to Matthias would be.

From here, Kenn could see the kid's tear-stained cheeks as he tried to come to terms with the emotions rolling around inside him. He was at his breaking point, and it would be difficult weathering the path forward as they tried to help him.

It would also be a wrench in the relationship they were starting, Mia standing a few feet from Matthias, frozen in place. She was still trembling, but one look at Nichlas who could see her face told Kenn that there was still hope to be had. Nichlas leaned down to whisper a few words in her ears, Mia turning to look at him with such love and adoration that Kenn nearly melted into the floor.

She had told that bastard she loved him, hadn't she?

The most mysterious of them all, she had fallen in love with him. Kenn couldn't be more conflicted at the moment – he wanted to be happy that this would all work out, but Matthias …

Mia nodded and slowly approached Matthias, her arms pulled tight in front of her until she was close enough to lay a hand on his arm. The kid let out a whimper, dropping to his knees in front of her like he had before, pressing his face into her stomach as he held her tight. She let out a small gasp as she bent to place a soft kiss on his head, the embrace warming Kenn from the inside out.

It almost felt like they were intruding on a special moment, but it was this that they had been missing with the others – the concern, the emotions, the *acceptance* of their demons. Kenn cursed as his cock stirred in his pants, wanting to show Mia just how much he loved her, how much they all loved her, but he'd wait until she was ready.

Matthias pulled back just enough to prop his chin on her stomach, their gazes spearing into each other. Kenn couldn't miss the tortured expression on the kid's face as he spoke. "I can't lose you, Mia. Not now. Not ever. I love you so goddamn much to lose you."

Too soon? Maybe. But in the end, it didn't matter. They all felt the same way about her.

"I love you, too, Matthias," she whispered.

Even from Kenn's seat, he could tell that she was smiling as she leaned down to press her lips to his, hands cupping his cheeks as they melted against each other. Matthias' arms tightened around her waist as he leaned against her, their kiss turning almost desperate as they tried to pull every bit of comfort and love from each other's lips.

This morning had been a pleasant surprise, a step in the right direction. Two of their four, the ones that were usually discarded first, were the ones that Mia had gravitated toward. If she had accepted them, it would only be a matter of time before she turned to himself and Jan.

If she hadn't already.

The kiss deepened, Matthias rising to his feet and pulling Mia with him until her legs were wrapped around his hips, his hands gripping the back of her thighs with the need that they were all feeling. And when Nichlas saddled up behind her, pressing soft kisses to her neck, Kenn knew the morning schedule had been set. He willed his cock to take a hike, tugging at the discomfort between his legs as he watched the three make their way upstairs in a haze of desire and need, leaving himself in the silence of the cafe. Something stirred in the kitchen, Jan making his presence known as the smell of hazelnut and chocolate filled the sexually charged ambiance of the space.

Jan didn't even need to ask as he brought over a full pot of coffee and plopped into a seat opposite of him with a tight smile. They weren't really going to get much work done with what was about to unfold upstairs, but they could try.

SEVENTY-TWO

MIA

Her skin prickled beneath their touches as Matthias laid her gently on his mattress, cradling her head and moving to lay beside her. They hadn't so much as come up for air as Matthias walked up the stairs, Nichlas' dark presence trailing behind and now settled on her other side. His lips attached to her neck again, drawing a needy whine from her throat. She squirmed beneath the attention, heat surging through her body as they tormented her with feather-light touches.

Her hands flew to Matthias' chest as her fingers curled into his shirt, feebly yanking at the material to make it disappear. He grinned against her lips, momentarily disentangling himself to remove his shirt and his pants. Her lips parted at the tent in his boxers, the outline of his cock leaving little to the imagination as it strained against the fabric. Nichlas' attention had moved south, those lips dragging down past her waist, his hands parting her legs until her hips were thrusting upward to chase the connection. He pressed a firm hand on her belly, holding her against the mattress as his lips clamped down on her mound through her panties.

Mia screamed at the sensation as her entire body thrummed with heat. Her fingers dug into the duvet as she shamelessly rode Nichlas' mouth, chasing an orgasm that had her crying out, an explosive warmth coating her skin. Between the two of them, she was going to die today if their devious smiles were anything to go by.

"Sweetheart, we're only going as far as you let us."

She could see in Matthias' eyes that those words were true but she wouldn't need them. She wasn't going to ask them to stop, panting and out of breath as the tingles from her orgasm continued to swell in the pit of her belly. Despite the kinkiness that both of these men boasted, Mia knew that this moment was going to be swallowed in passion and their need for each other rather than dirty talk and foreplay. It was going to be raw and fast and full on.

And Mia was *more* than ready.

She reached for Matthias, guiding him to settle between her legs as Nichlas slipped off the bed and undressed. Mia watched with rapt attention, her tongue darting out to lick her lips as he stepped out of his pants and boxers, his cock bobbing against his stomach, precum smearing against the steel cut of his abs.

Her panties were grabbed and wrapped around a rough fist before the fabric snapped off, Mia letting out a little squeal as a breeze brushed against her sopping entrance. A second later, Matthias' cock was pressed against it, parting those wet lips and pushing forward. A grunt left her lips as she arched against him, still fully clothed, minus her panties, every inch spreading her wider and wider until she couldn't imagine any more fitting inside of her.

When he was fully sheathed, his hips flush against hers, he gave an experimental rock forward and she gasped at the fullness, the way his cock seemed to touch every spot until she could see stars. It was too much and not enough as her gaze drifted back to Nichlas, the man's hand wrapped tightly around his cock as he gave it languid strokes.

"I need—"

Matthias laid a short kiss on her lips, rocking forward once more and then pulling out. "Yeah, you do." She didn't even need to explain – not sure she could – as Matthias flipped her over and pulled her back until she was on all fours. Shocked at the quick change in position, Matthias didn't wait before sinking back into her heat, Mia's eyes wide as he snapped his hips against hers, a crack against her ass causing her to jolt forward, meeting the searing heat of a milky substance coating her lips.

Mia didn't hate it, her pussy clamping down on his cock as he smacked her ass again.

Her lips parted immediately, Nichlas groaning as he slid into her mouth, the weight on her tongue both foreign and absolutely delicious. Her eyes rolled into the back of her head as they filled her from both sides, slowly rocking their hips as she became used to their size. Nichlas' hands dropped to her head, one wrapping in her hair and tugging slightly. "This ok, firecracker?"

Her cheeks warmed, being taken by two of her men but she didn't get the chance to answer as Matthias slapped her ass again, her pussy clenching around his cock like a hungry bitch. She didn't even care. It felt so fucking wonderful as she lost herself to them and she hummed her appreciation around Nichlas' cock.

"She fucking loves it, Nichlas. She's sucking me in, god, baby girl, if you keep doing that—" Matthias thrust in deeper than before, pushing her face forward until Nichlas' cock was at the back of her throat. They stilled, unsure of her comfort but Mia gripped Nichlas' thighs in response, swallowing the cum on her tongue and sucking him in further until he lost himself to the sensation.

Her men were naked as the day they were born, taking her in her dress, *using* her for their pleasure and her own. Nichlas' hands tightened in her hair and Matthias' hands gripped her waist as he rammed into her from behind, one hand dipping lower until two fingers began massaging her clit. She spasmed between them, moaning through another explosive orgasm as they continued to thrust into her mouth and pussy, murmuring sweet words of praise, owning every inch of her skin.

They weren't far behind, Mia's nails digging into Nichlas' thighs so he didn't pull away, his seed spilling down her throat as she drank him in, her nose resting against the lower curve of his abs, his musky scent filling her senses. Matthias grunted from behind her, thrusting through his release, flooding her pussy, the squelching sounds of their movement causing her thighs to shake as her body prepared for more.

Mia fell to the mattress, quivering and stuck in a dreamy concoction of sex and pleasure as the two slipped out of her, cum dripping down her thighs, leaving her empty and waiting. Nichlas bent down to kiss her, tasting himself on her lips as she gave in, the man rolling her over onto her back. She felt Matthias' rolling her dress up her body, every drag of his fingertips against her skin leaving a trail of fire in its wake. By the time they were pulling the dress over her head, she was so worked up, Mia was sure she could come again with their touch alone.

And when each of them latched onto one of her breasts, swirling their tongues around the swell of her skin and sucking on her hardened nipples, Mia arched and screamed again.

SEVENTY-THREE

MIA

Mia rolled over, confused to find the absence of the two men she had fallen asleep between. Pleasant memories from earlier flooded her mind, the pleasurable ache between her legs reminding her that every last bit of it had been real. A smile stretched across her face as she slowly opened her eyes, blinking a few times to adjust to the dim light of the room.

A scrappy note written on bright yellow paper stood at attention on the nightstand, a few words etched in chicken scratch staring at her.

Morning, love. Had some errands to run. Be back for dinner.

A giggle slipped through her lips as she wondered who the atrocious handwriting belonged to, probably Nichlas. She could imagine them climbing out of bed, trying not to wake her up as Nichlas tore off a piece of paper and scribbled a note. Just the little gesture warmed her heart as she slipped out of bed, wondering where her other two men were.

When the sound of running water reached her ears, her smile widened. It was easy to forget how hard it had been to come to this point and all of the problems unfolding in the town when she knew that one of her men was taking a shower just a few feet from her.

Mia's phone buzzed and she scrambled to find it, staring at the voicemail that had popped up. She eagerly opened the message as she waited to hear one of her men's voices on the other side. Instead, the voice was one she wished she never had to hear again.

<<Mia>>

She growled at the phone and almost hung up when she heard Anders' violent cough through the speaker. Against her better judgment, she continued to listen.

<<Baby, please, when I say you have to listen to me. You need to listen to me. Your men, they're dangerous. They came...>>

There was more coughing as Anders struggled to breathe, and while she felt for him and the pain that he had endured, she believed he deserved it. Especially after his own wife had gone after Matthias.

<<They came and threatened me. They're ... they're the ones you need to be careful of. I – I'm coming to get you. To take you from them. They ... it's ... don't trust them.>>

The voicemail broke off into another round of coughing before it ended, Mia fighting the urge to rage out against the man who had made her life a living hell for the past few years. If the communication between her and her men hadn't been so open, she might have believed Anders' lies, that her men were behind everything.

But it was clear that Anders' lies were just that, not to mention his ploy to get her back was a weak one. Even if she left her beautiful men, she would never run back into Anders' arms. She was too strong now. She knew her worth and she wasn't going to degrade herself for mere companionship. Not ever again.

With a deep sigh, Mia slid from the bed and stretched, her cheeks pink as she realized she was only dressed in Matthias' shirt. It barely covered her ass and as she raised her arms over her head, the shirt rode up to her belly button, revealing a whole lot more than she bargained for, the cool air of the room shocking her bare lower half.

"Well isn't that a sight for sore eyes?"

Mia let out an embarrassing squeak as she tugged at the bottom of the shirt, her terrified gaze falling on Jan who had just stepped out of the shower, naked as the day he was born. Water droplets ran off his chiseled form, her eyes traveling south until they hung on the thick member between his thighs. She swallowed, feeling the heat rising to her cheeks as he cleared his throat.

"I–"

"You can stare all you want, angel," he purred, stalking toward her and gathering her up in his arms. Her hands fell to his bare chest as she pushed against him, still a little uneasy about all the attention that was focused on her between four men. Jan pulled her closer with a cheeky smile. She figured out why when she felt his cock thicken against her bare pussy, Jan walking her backward until she was sandwiched between a wall and Jan's very hard body.

He rolled his hips against hers, his cock rubbing against the apex of her thighs as he leaned down to steal a kiss but it wasn't just a peck on the lips. It was a deep, passionate one as he made her body sing with pleasure and desire. He kissed her until her toes curled and she was clutching at his chest for more.

Jan pulled away with a chuckle, placing one last soft kiss on her lips. "Your terms, angel." He said, in reference to the many conversations she had had with him, that all of this was at her speed and on her terms. Despite knowing there were other things she needed to do, Mia leaned forward to continue what Jan had started, but he just shook his head. "As much as I want to, we all have somewhere to be. Tonight though." His voice dropped several octaves. "I want a replay of the first time, but this time you're on *my* lap while they watch."

He disappeared back into the bathroom after grabbing a set of clothes before his words registered in her head.

SEVENTY-FOUR

QUINN

He stared at Chad, the kid who had dragged him into the city to "take a day off" and "blow off steam." The day had spiraled into fucking around Chad's college campus, going so far as sharing a kiss in one of the empty classrooms that Quinn still couldn't get out of his head. He hadn't planned it, although Chad didn't seem surprised by it, and since then, they had been walking through the halls hand in hand, silent but together.

His eyes drifted to where their fingers were intertwined, Chad gripping them a little tighter as they turned a corner, entering the science wing, a place Quinn had inquired about earlier. Chad looked both ways before dragging him into one of the rooms, locking the door behind them. It wasn't until Quinn looked at *what* was in the room that he understood the need for secrecy.

"Kinky," Quinn joked as his eyes fell on one of the lab dummies. As he took a step forward, letting go of Chad's hand, he realized it was in fact *not* a dummy. Go figure.

Chad let out a deep breath, eyes trained forward, no reaction to what room they had stumbled into. "I'm not staying in town, Quinn."

Quinn let out a nervous chuckle, glad that it hadn't been anything more serious. "Neither was I. I grew up there but I was never going to stay there." His eyes roamed the half-naked male, intrigued but also disturbed that out of all the science rooms Chad could have taken him to, it had been this one. His gaze snagged on a certain detail that shouldn't have been possible, Quinn leaning closer for a better look.

"Don't touch them! They're for–"

"I'm not *stupid*, Chad. I just ..." His words trailed off as it became apparent that the "mole" on the dummy's neck was in fact *not* a mole. "It's another one. What is it doing here?" He looked at Chad accusingly, as if the kid could have had anything to do with it.

Chad just shrugged, showing a lot less concern than he should. "Bodies here are donated to science."

"But it's part of an active investigation!" Quinn screamed, eyes peeling to the window to see if anyone had heard him. Strangely enough, no one was even in the hall. He didn't dwell on it as he turned to face Chad, fuming. "Mia never closed any of these reports. This body shouldn't be here."

Quinn surveyed the room, realizing there were a few bodies littered about. He took the time to inspect each one, finding that three other bodies sported the same mark. It couldn't be a coincidence. When he turned to face Chad again, the kid looked guilty as hell.

"What did you do?" Quinn seethed. When he didn't get an answer, he changed his question. "You did something, didn't you? You're not just someone brought in to get Mia out of the office. It was on purpose. Chad, talk to me." He sincerely hoped that it wasn't anything they couldn't fix, but by the looks of it, Chad had fucked up big time.

Chad bit his lower lip, eyes wide as he took a moment to gather his thoughts. "I'm … I work in the medical technologist office across the way, but you knew that. I was told to see why they the cases from Bryxton were still in limbo status and then close them."

"*Without* additional information?" Knowing that there was so much more to this investigation didn't sit well with Quinn. Mia was in danger because of Chad.

"Yeah … I found something weird weeks ago, and I was almost fired when I brought it up."

"What was it?" Quinn demanded. Chad squeaked, taking a step back, but Quinn didn't have time for Chad to be scared. Quinn needed answers. That kiss they shared a little while ago didn't feel so special anymore.

He cleared his throat and shot Quinn a tight smile. "An imprint in one of the victim's arms." He whipped out his phone, scrolling through what seemed like a photo album.

"Why tell me now?" Quinn had an inkling that Chad leading him to this room was not as coincidental as he had been led to believe.

"People are dying, Q. Mia's gotten hurt multiple times. This is absolute madness and not what I signed up for. I don't want this on my conscience."

Quinn barked out a laugh. "It already is, you idiot." He snatched the phone and squinted at the blurry pictures, the outline of a badge imprinted into one of the victim's arms. Whoever the suspect was must have been pretty dumb.

Chad grabbed his phone back. "I just assumed that those guys were part of it. They all have badges. I did some research and … it's definitely an official badge, but I couldn't find out which department it belonged to."

Quinn weathered his expression, trying to keep it neutral so that Chad wouldn't get any ideas. He nodded his thanks and stalked out of the room, making a beeline for transportation back to town. There was only one type of badge that couldn't be looked up like the rest of them.

And there was only one guy he knew who had a badge like that. Quinn wasn't accusing Nichlas of anything, but things weren't adding up, and he needed answers before someone got hurt again.

SEVENTY-FIVE

JAN

Kingsley and his father knew fuck all about whatever was going on in town, both of them revealing that they had been paid to look the other way, and since the town needed the money, they greedily took it. What Jan *hadn't* expected to find out was that they weren't the only ones being paid to shut their trap.

Mia's father had been paid off as well until his conscience had gotten the better of him and he decided to say something. For the past year, Mia's father had brushed off the sheer number of cases rolling through his lab as evidence of where people came to die. The stigma wasn't great, but since he didn't make a big deal about it, the sheriff and the coroner kept mum. The partnership didn't last long when the kills ramped up and Mia started hanging around the lab more often.

Mia's father died in his sleep shortly after, but Jan was pretty sure that was just more bullshit added on top of everything else. It didn't make the situation any better that Mia's father never had an autopsy and he'd been cremated. Even the records surrounding the state of his body at death seemed to have gone missing.

Which is why they were now at Anders' place grilling him for answers, answers he didn't seem to have.

"What the fuck do you mean you don't know?" Kenn growled out, inches away from Anders' bruised face. Anders groaned, scooting farther up the couch, giving up when another jolt of pain shocked his system. Apparently, the hospital had released him into Natalie's care, but she was wherever the fuck she was while Anders suffered on the couch. Personally, Jan thought the couch was too good for him, but they couldn't very well do anything about it without the incident finding its way back to Mia, and she didn't need any more shit on her plate right now.

"I just – I just don't know, okay! Fuck, you guys – the other two already asked me and I said I didn't know either. I told Mia all about you guys and–"

Jan recognized the lethal stare in Kenn's eyes and realized that he had to be the bigger man, dragging Kenn away from the injured fuck on the couch. Barbie boy loved hard but fought harder. Jan never wanted to be on the receiving end of one of Kenn's fists. The kind of damage Kenn inflicted wasn't just physical but mental. Kenn's lips were pulled up over his teeth in a nasty snarl, but he didn't fight the hold on the back of his shirt. Jan gave him a pert nod and released him, Kenn stalking toward the front door for some fresh air.

"I suggest you leave Mia out of this conversation if you would like to survive another day. What Nichlas and Matthias approached you for is their own business. We're here on official duty, as we stated when we walked in and flashed our badges." Jan hated playing the official card but the less-than-legal route meant that any information they gleaned from Anders would be inadmissible in court. "Now, Anders." Jan crouched at the edge of the couch, losing the gentle edge to his voice. He knew what he looked like in that moment, a look he had trained over the years, a look that was meant to induce terror. With the way that Anders had stilled against the cushions, Jan knew it was working. "I need you to tell me what the fuck is going on because we're hearing a whole bunch of different stories, none of which seem to have the entire truth."

Anders just blinked.

"I'm going to take that as a yes. Good. That's good." Jan blew out a deep breath, trying to keep a handle on the anger brewing inside his chest. This man in front of him had beaten their girl and there was nothing he could do about it, yet. "Nichlas told us all about how you met Natalie but I'm sure you know by now that that meeting was manufactured. Tell me, at what point did you realize she was lying to you?"

"About the baby?" he squeaked, struggling to sit up so that Jan was looming over him. It didn't work, Anders sinking back into the cushions.

"No, I mean *everything*. Anders, you're not stupid. You threw Mia around like a goddamn rag doll and then fell into bed with a witch. I just want to know when you figured out that the woman you were married to was more than just a homewrecker." He didn't seem to understand what Jan was saying, a fact that Jan was more than overjoyed to explain. "Natalie has been fucking around with more than just you, Anders. She's got at least three other men wrapped around her pretty little finger."

"*What?*" Jan grinned at Anders' shock as it was the only pain he could deliver at the moment. "Your woman has made her way through the sheriff *and* his father and another unknown contender." The last bit was a stretch, but it made sense. Natalie's bruises weren't fake, and she had to have gotten them from someone. At first, Jan thought that Natalie might have been working with someone else until he realized that she was just another minion in the grand scheme of things. She had probably used her powers of seduction, and they would have worked until her haughty attitude got her in trouble.

Add in the failed accusation she filed against Matthias and it was only a matter of time before her shady dealings began falling apart.

"I ... I knew she wasn't faithful to me. I prayed that baby was mine because it would make it all worth it, but when it wasn't ..."

Jan didn't have time for Anders to feel guilt. "Next question: Who beat your wife?"

"It wasn't me."

Jan growled at him. "That's a given."

"I don't know."

"Like fuck you don't. Anders—"

"Stop threatening me!" Anders screamed, writhing on the cushions. "I get it. You're all really scary and you murder people." Jan bit back a laugh at the son-of-a-bitch lying in front of him. He wasn't such an alpha male, was he? All bark and no bite. "I don't really know the extent of what Natalie does. I just didn't want to be stuffed back in jail, but she's into things that are really dark, and I think they're coming back to haunt her. If you want answers, you have to ask her."

"Oh, I plan to."

Anders let out a deep sigh, the sound rattling through his chest. "I just want everything to go back to normal so I can get Mia back—"

Jan knew better, but at this point, he also didn't care. His fist connected with Anders' cheek, the son-of-a-bitch howling through the pain, whining about how Jan was there in an official capacity, but there was no force behind it. Seeing as how Kingsley was now following *their* orders, Anders didn't have a leg to stand on.

"I told you to keep Mia's name out of your fucking mouth."

"You're a *detective*. An officer of the law!"

"And Mia is the light of my life. If I have to lay down my badge for that woman, I fucking will." Jan didn't wait to hear more of Anders' piss-poor arguments or the fact that he still loved the woman he used to abuse. When he made it outside, Kenn had one of his lopsided grins plastered on his face.

"You'd give up your badge for her?"

Jan hadn't meant to say it but it was the truth. "Wouldn't you?"

"Not even a question."

SEVENTY-SIX

MIA

When Mia finally made it down the stairs, to her surprise, Nichlas and Matthias were sitting at one of the cafe tables, speaking in hushed tones. It still irked her to some extent that the gossip surrounding her had affected Matthias' business, and no amount of explaining that they didn't need the money was going to make her feel better about it. She hesitantly approached them, unsure how to address last night, but she needn't have worried – a fact Mia was slowly becoming used to.

Nichlas drew her onto his lap, placing a soft kiss on the curve of her neck, Matthias retrieving a cup of coffee and a cinnamon bagel for her. She tried to protest all of their smothering and their kisses in between words but to no avail. Mia had even tried to slip off Nichlas' lap to eat her breakfast in peace, but his arms just tightened around her. She gave up fighting, stuffing half the bagel into her mouth, cinnamon exploding on her tongue.

He situated her on his lap as Matthias' and his conversation continued, her legs splayed over his thighs. Mia saw Matthias' amused smile widen across his face at the way Nichlas ever so slowly spread his legs, causing hers to do the same. The cool air of the cafe hit her bare pussy, a whine slipping from her lips, two purple eyes darkening with lust.

Mia scrambled from his lap, Kenn's warning from yesterday ringing through her head.

Listen to me, angel. All he needs is the perfect grip and he'll slide right in, anywhere, any time.

She had work to do, and it was already later than she would have liked. As much as she wanted another round with her men, the pleasant ache between her legs told her that she needed rest. And more coffee. *Way* more coffee. "I need to run to my office. I want to—"

Both men groaned, but she stomped her foot in response, knowing that it was childish. Every moment they had, they needed to be working on the case and while Mia didn't know much, she could at least look over the autopsies one more time to see if something else popped up at her.

"*Fine*, but one of us is coming with you," Matthias replied, giving her no room to argue. At a different time, Mia thought it would be fun to resist his demands if only to see what his reaction would be. However, right now, Mia knew it was for the best. None of them were sure who was out there, but the killer was getting bolder and some of the other players – like Natalie – seemed to have a direct connection with them.

Mia shuffled her ass back upstairs to slip into something more decent than Matthias' shirt, nearly barreling into the man himself on her way back down. "Baby girl, I *know* you're just as wrapped up in this as we are, but you don't have—"

"That's sweet," Mia cut him off, standing up on her tiptoes to press a soft peck to his lips. "But I need to see this through. It's been happening for too long and in my own lab. I just have to know." Matthias nodded, releasing her into Nichlas' company, but not before she caught the haunted look hidden in his expression. Coming from an abusive relationship, Mia knew what an outburst was and that they happened more often during stressful situations. If someone didn't do something soon, Matthias wouldn't be so lucky a second time, the horror of finding him in jail too much to bear.

She turned back to Matthias, the barista throwing her a tight smile as she stepped into his chest. "We'll figure it out, okay?" Mia wasn't even sure where the words were coming from, but she believed them and Matthias needed to hear them. "I'm not going anywhere. They're not going anywhere. But I'm not going to lose you, Matthias."

His name rolled off her tongue as a sob escaped his chest, Matthias crushing his lips to hers, taking the comfort he needed. Mia melted into it, smiling as she realized she wasn't just *dating* these men. This wasn't just a passing thought or something to do in her small town. Somewhere along the way, Mia's mindset had changed, and she loved it.

Matthias slowly released her, that boyish grin returning. The haunted look wasn't gone, but his eyes were several shades lighter. "I love you, Mia."

"I love you, too," Mia mumbled, Nichlas groaning in the background like a sore loser. She twisted around to see him adjusting his cock in his pants, his eyes half-lidded with arousal. "Really?" Nichlas just shrugged, holding a hand out to her so they could walk across the street.

It dawned on her that this was the beginning of the public relationship she had been so terrified to display, but she was done with the hiding. Mia almost laughed at her response to her troubles, threading her fingers with Nichlas' as she made her way to her office. She put in the code, Nichlas' gaze scanning the entrance before giving her the go-ahead to answer. The gesture warmed her heart, especially after what had happened earlier.

"Did you pull the short stick?" Mia jested, Nichlas scowling at that.

"Mia, I actually *like* spending time with you."

"*Babysitting* me," Mia corrected, not that she minded her mysterious fourth's company.

Nichlas didn't respond to that as he began inspecting the security equipment he had set up last week, a deep frown spreading across his face. When muttered curses started streaming through her lips, distracting her from her files, Mia decided to address it.

"Nichlas?" He whipped around, Mia taking a step back, which had been the wrong thing to do. She knew she was dating four lethal men, but that didn't make it easier when expressions like *that* were trained on her. His features softened, but he didn't approach.

"Sorry, I ... the cameras aren't put together correctly. Someone planned for them to fail." Mia didn't like the sound of that. "Take this and those fingerprints? *Shit.*" He raked his hands through his hair, whipping out his cellphone and pressing a number on speed dial. "I need to speak with my handler to see who'd have access to any of this shit. Don't open the door for anyone, Mia." He kissed the top of her head before walking outside and leaning against the outside wall. With his attention peeled for anyone approaching the building, Mia knew she didn't have to worry, returning her focus to the documents on her desk.

SEVENTY-SEVEN

NICHLAS

"What the absolute fuck, Cross?" He could hear Cross swiveling around his chair, the fucker seemingly unperturbed by the current situation. Apparently, in the last few months, due to budget cuts, a third party checked all the equipment. Nichlas called bullshit about the budget cuts, but he had no way to refute it without being an ass to Cross.

"Look, if it's busted, just go talk to Pendant Industries. I'll text you the number." Nichlas opened his mouth to protest, but he didn't get the chance. "You won't need it, though."

"And why the hell not? Cross, stop fucking around and just spit it out."

Something had been off with Cross ever since Nichlas had told him there wasn't any more information to glean from Anders or Natalie.

"Next job is a go. We need you up here immediately."

It was a common enough occurrence that it didn't shock him, but it was the first time Nichlas had someone waiting for him when he returned. Never in a billion years did Nichlas believe there would come a time when he wanted to turn down an assignment, but that day had come.

Unfortunately, disobeying a direct order wasn't in the cards. "Give me fifteen minutes."

"No time." Another thing Nichlas was used to, but today he was wholly unprepared. "Car's pulling up." The call ended, giving Nichlas seconds as a black escape rolled to a screeching stop, inches from him. The door swung up, Nichlas letting out a deep sigh. This was the part he hated, disappearing into the night, unable to tell anyone where he was going or how long he'd be gone.

He dialed Matthias, hung up, and then dialed again before shutting down his phone. It was the only mode of information he could spare as he climbed into the car and closed the door behind him. Matthias would accompany their girl and he'd be able to answer any questions she might have.

"Where to?"

The driver peered at him through the rearview window before shrugging. "My orders were just to take you to the base. My clearance isn't high enough for anything else."

"Figures," Nichlas muttered, leaning back in his seat and closing his eyes. He wanted to break protocol and power his phone back on but that would have everyone in all sorts of danger, not to mention that going to the nearest base would allow him to do some research.

He'd be able to inquire about the green substance Mia had found.

He'd also be able to contact Pendant Industries.

And lastly, he'd be able to search the database for the owner of those classified fingerprints.

Maybe with all of that information, he'd be able to figure out *why* bodies were showing up, or maybe he'd be opening pandora's box.

For now, he just hoped that Matthias had already hauled his ass across the street so that their girl wasn't left alone.

SEVENTY-EIGHT

MIA

She was pleasantly surprised when Jan pulled her out of her office and plopped her into the front seat of his car without much of an explanation nearly ten minutes after Nichlas had left. "Where's Nichlas? I thought—"

Jan's expression hardened for a mere second before relaxing. "He got called in."

"But—"

"It's not ideal, but that's how it works, Mia. He gets called in. He leaves. There's no time to do anything else."

"He couldn't have even said goodbye?"

"Mia." His lips pulled tight as he tried to find a way to explain the situation. It seemed like a difficult topic, one that more often than not shook up the dynamic of their relationships. *This* was what they had been talking about, wasn't it? The moments when they couldn't say anything, the bouts of loneliness, the secrecy …

She let out a sigh, leaning over the console to place a small kiss on Jan's cheek. "I understand. It's just going to take some getting used to. Do you know when he's coming back?" Jan grunted as he put the car in drive and took off down the street. Right, of course, they couldn't reveal that information either. Mia had watched enough TV to know that whatever her men did was a matter of national importance at times and she was not privy to that information.

It bugged her a little, but she was more worried for Nichlas' safety than she was his whereabouts.

"He's *fine*. He goes out and does some recon and then he'll be back. Since you're here, you'll probably find him sliding into your bed in a few days, throwing his hand around your mouth, as he takes you from behind." A cheeky smile split across Jan's face. "If that's what you're into."

Mia's cheeks warmed at the image Jan planted in her head, being woken up by her mysterious fourth as he spooned her backside, carefully but hastily undressing her to take what he needed. Her thighs trembled as she made a conscious decision to sleep in the nude until further notice, a little too excited about being woken up for surprise sex.

"Goddamn, angel. If I had known it was going to get that kind of reaction, I'd have done it sooner."

A squeal left her lips before she could draw it back, Jan letting out a hearty laugh as they drove in silence, the car slowing to a stop twenty minutes later. He parked in a small alleyway, just at the edge of town, Mia leaning forward, confused. She ignored his comment in lieu of the mysterious trip they had just taken. "Where are we?"

"Thought you could use a change of pace, and I could use some company stalking your favorite female villain."

"Villain?" Mia mused, straining to understand the small stretch of street she could see from her seat. Shops and outdoor vendors littered the sidewalk, the chaotic city scene from her trip to the medical examiner's office nowhere to be found. "Jan, I don't understand–"

"Angel, just watch. It seems that the killer's getting sloppy, and so are the people working with him."

Mia opened her mouth to ask another question but thought better about it. Jan was the smart one, the one whose intelligence blew everyone else out of the water, which meant that if he said there was something here – there was something there.

Her expression soured when Natalie emerged from around the corner, her eyes darting from side to side before disappearing into one of the shops. The sound of a camera shutter hit her ears, Mia turning to look at Jan who was snapping pictures of the "villain's" appearance.

"I'm thoroughly confused. I thought she wasn't the killer."

"She's not," Jan said from behind the camera. "Pretty sure she's working with the guy, though. There's no reason for her to have such a vendetta against you and us. Petty girl shit doesn't extend that far." Mia barked out a nervous laugh, still confused. Jan placed the camera back in its bag and threw it in the backseat.

"You brought me out here to take pictures? Did you think this was going to make me feel better?"

Jan sighed, shaking his head as he encouraged Mia to cross over the console and straddle his lap. She hesitated for a moment before giving in, settling across his thighs. His dark eyes threatened to undo her as his hands rested on her hips, fingers digging into her skin with just enough pressure to make her gasp.

"Angel, I knew that if you walked outside and found him gone, you wouldn't know what to think. I knew that you've been abandoned before and that shit wouldn't fly with you, especially since we promised to stay with you and protect you. I also knew if you found out from anyone other than us, it wouldn't be easily forgiven. We're trying to navigate this complicated relationship between us but we rarely get this far. The women stay for the sex, but not for us. Mia, you're not the only one weathering new paths."

She trembled in his hold, still amazed that Jan could always see right through her. She cupped Jan's face in her hands, relishing his five o'clock shadow, which was much softer than she had expected. Words didn't seem to do the moment justice as Mia lowered his lips to his, enjoying his sweet taste. She pressed herself against him, sinking lower into the seat until she felt his erection pressed against her core.

A needy moan slipped through her lips as she gave an experimental rock of her hips, Jan's hands gripping her was it tighter to still her movements.

"I'd want nothing more than to take you apart in my car, Mia, but that's not why I brought you out here." A dark chuckle escaped him as Mia tried to move again.

"Just think of it as practice for tonight," Mia purred, overconfident in this position. These men made her want things, made her want to try new experiences, made her want to step up and step out in *every* aspect of her life. There were a few choice words for her mother that had been sitting in the back of her mind. It was time to set them free. It was time to let *everyone* in town that she was done taking their bullshit. It was time for them to see the version of herself she was meant to be.

Jan dragged her down into another kiss, threading his fingers through her hair as Mia responded the same way, yanking at his thick strands until he involuntarily thrust upward. His tongue pushed into her mouth as his hands wrapped around her back. Seconds later, he was depositing her in the passenger seat, out of breath, and grabbing at the crotch of his pants to release the pressure. "Can't," he breathed out, sounding as wrecked as she felt.

It was a wonder what she could do to these men.

Mia reached over the console again, just to reassure him that it was all right, but he shied away from her touch, lust swirling in his expression. "Better keep those paws to yourself before I take you in the backseat."

Another set of images flooded her mind, her core aching for her to drag him back there. "Would that be so bad?"

"You're insatiable, Mia."

SEVENTY-NINE

JAN

He hurried into the cafe after escorting Mia to one of the tables, telling her that he just needed a minute to confirm one of his suspicions. He had shown Mia the pictures, wondering if she recognized anything strange, but nothing had caught her eye the way it had with him. She idled by one of the front tables, brandishing a sweet but tired smile that didn't quite reach her eyes. Jan hated seeing it, but there wasn't much he could do other than promise her everything would turn out all right.

He stalked to the counter, dropping his reassuring smile and donning a neutral expression to show he meant business. "What's got you all twisted?" Kenn joked, chugging what had to be at least his third mug. He blew a kiss in Mia's direction, catching onto the gravity of the situation. Matthias was scowling at him from behind the counter, holding the coffee pot hostage as Kenn pushed for another cup.

Jan didn't have time for their shenanigans though. He hadn't been entirely truthful with Mia when he had dragged her out to the edge of town for some harmless reconnaissance. While making sure that Mia understood Nichlas' situation was important, that was only a fraction of the reason he had wanted Mia in the car.

Her presence had kept him from doing anything stupid after nearly beating Anders into the cushions of his couch. He was one step away from exploding, Mia the only thing between him and a jail cell. She was the key to all of this, a miracle for them all, but they couldn't keep using her as a crutch. They'd need to deal with their shit eventually, but it wouldn't be today. Tomorrow wasn't looking good either.

Kenn lowered his voice, but in such a small cafe, Mia could still probably hear them. "Jan, spit it out. You look like you're going to murder someone."

"I might," Jan bit out, locking eyes with Matthias. "What'd Nichlas tell you?"

Matthias shook his head. "Just the call. I don't know how long he's scheduled for but that's usual. Why?"

"Does the timing seem odd? It's real convenient that the man who's best at finding clues is now gone. The man who understands all that tech in that building is just unreachable."

Kenn's smile disappeared as he straightened up. "I thought we were done with conspiracy theories. You used to do this shit all the time when Nichlas was called on a mission. Always thought there was some bigger plot."

"Do I look like I'm joking this time?" Kenn opened his mouth to refute him, but Jan held up his camera. "Brought proof." He flicked through a few pictures before landing on the one he needed and shoved it in their faces. "Recognize this bastard?"

Kenn and Matthias leaned in, the latter recognizing him first. "Shit, that's one of Nichlas' guys." Kenn raised an eyebrow and shook his head. "No, not Lt. Fuckface. The other one." Jan wanted to burst out laughing as Matthias said that with a straight face.

While they all came from diverse backgrounds, they still attended gatherings and soirees together, meeting each other's counterparts, superiors, and partners. Lieutenant Fuckface had been one of Nichlas' superiors, one that Matthias had promptly named after the fucker wouldn't leave Matthias alone for "all the great work he had done for his country."

Lieutenant Fuckface then proceeded to try and butter Matthias up to drag him on one of Nichlas' missions, Matthias exiting the soiree not a moment too soon before his explosive anger made an appearance.

To this day, Jan had no idea what the guy's name was, but Fuckface was an accurate enough description.

As for the other individual they had met at Nichlas' soiree, Jan couldn't remember his connection but knew that he worked for the same three letter agencies that Nichlas did.

"Yes, that's him." Jan scrolled through a few more photos, Natalie's blond form moving through the next few images.

"What the fuck are they meeting for?"

Jan shrugged, but he had his theories. He was pretty sure that Nichlas' superiors were in on this goddamn thing, but how they were connected was anyone's best guess. With Kenn and Matthias' expertise though, he was pretty sure they'd figure something out.

"Mia okay?" Matthias inquired, his eyes flashing with worry as he stared at Mia's table, torn between approaching her and receiving Jan's answer.

Jan nodded. "Yeah. She will be when all this shit is over. We're getting close; I can fucking feel it. We're going to be across the street if you need anything." He let out a deep breath as he patted the table twice to signify his departure, stealing Kenn's cup and handing it to Matthias. "Lay off the coffee. I need you at your best, not wired on caffeine." Kenn turned up his nose and just for fun, Jan added, "*Barbie boy.*"

EIGHTY

MIA

The shoes had been chucked into a corner moments after Jan had opened the door and scoured the place for anything out of the ordinary, Mia still hot and bothered from the tongue-curling kisses in the car. It didn't help that Jan kept touching her, little caresses of his hands and lips as he held her in a tight embrace, murmuring the newest bits of information he had gathered from the pictures.

It was strange being aroused while hearing crime statistics, but everything was strange with her men. She tried not to dwell on it.

"I *actually* have work to do," she whispered against his chest, pushing away slightly to meet the wary expression in Jan's eyes. She wasn't surprised to see the emotion, but she didn't like it. Her men were trained, and if they were scared? It didn't bode well for her fragile heart. "I just need to clean a little, and then we can go do all those things you've promised me." Mia tried to smile with as much enthusiasm as she could, but it was tiring keeping a brave face. She just needed it to end.

Jan noticed, placing a soft kiss on her forehead as he released her. "It'll be over soon. I can feel it."

"I hope so," Mia mumbled as her gaze fell on the expanse of the tiled floor, as she decided to focus on organizing to settle her chaotic thoughts. Half an hour later, she had mopped her office and moved to the lab, all under the watchful eye of Jan. He had asked her repeatedly if she wanted help, going so far as trying to steal the mop from her but she waved him off, sat his ass in a seat in the farthest corner, threw him a bottle of water from her desk fridge, and then continued.

He seemed antsy, but there was nothing he could do to quiet her mind. She just needed to process it, and she had been processing things for so long on her own that it was hard to accept the help that Jan was offering. Mia wasn't even sure *how* to accept it, let alone know what help she needed.

Quinn burst inside seconds later, stomping around, his brows furrowed as he fell in step and began restocking the lab as he saw fit, ignoring the two occupants that were already there. He grumbled some sort of greeting, grunting when Mia tried to reach for him. Quinn was one of the most light-hearted kids she had ever known and seeing him like this worried her.

"Quinn, what happened? I thought you went out with Chad." She shot him a small smile.

Unfortunately, she didn't receive the same kind of expression in response. He skidded to a stop, throwing his hands up. "He's a fucking idiot!" Mia watched Jan sit up straight in his chair, but she shook her head to stall his movements. Jan leaned back in his chair, sipping at his water as his eyes stayed trained on her.

"What are you talking about?" Mia stepped closer to Quinn, unsure if he wanted a hug or just an ear to listen.

"Chad's a liar and ... fuck! He came from the medical examiner's office. They've been trying to close all these open Jane and John Doe cases. *That's* why he was here and *that's* why you're men are here, or so he said." She grunted at that statement, no longer believing that her men had any part in the killer's plans, but it was strange Chad believed such a thing. Quinn's shoulders sagged as he leaned against one of the metal slabs, the fight disappearing from his eyes. "He kissed me, Mia. Well, *we* kissed and then I found out that ... How could he do that to me?"

Mia knew what it felt like to be heartbroken and betrayed. She had been through so much worse, but the feeling of someone toying with her feelings? It wasn't a pain she wished on anyone, especially not Quinn. "He had his reasons, Quinn, but that's no excuse. I'm so sorry." Mia tugged him into a hug, rocking him back and forth as he shuddered in her embrace. His next words were muffled against her chest. "Someone much higher on the food chain is trying to sweep all this shit under the rug."

That information tracked based on the tidbits she had picked up from her men and the conversations they had thought had been discreet. She released Quinn and moved over to one of the cameras in the corner of the lab. "Nichlas said that the cameras were busted, like the parts. The insides." She knew fuck all about high-end technology, but she had picked up that much.

Quinn stomped his way over to the camera. "The fuck? That's impossible. The IT guy or whatever checks that before it goes to the agent." Jan chuckled as he moved into the lab, but the sound was dark and unsettling.

"How do you know that, Quinn?"

Quinn whirled around, surprised at Jan's presence, but he managed a shrug, playing off his initial shock. "TV. It's their job to check everything. Nichlas might not know all about it, but the person who hands it to him would. Right?" Jan nodded, folding his arms across his chest. He weathered a cough, slapping a hand on his chest to clear his throat before coughing again.

Mia turned to stare at the device, waving at it as she thought about Matthias watching the screen. It bugged her that the red filming dot that usually showed up wasn't beating like it usually did, a sign that it wasn't doing its job. "The cameras are off," she whispered, eyes widening as she turned to Jan for a response.

Three knocks pounded against the front door in quick succession, Mia and Quinn freezing in spot before she glanced at her watch. Five p.m. Deliveries from the city office always arrived late and even later on the weekends, so it wasn't out of the realm of possibility for it to be that. Unlikely, but probable.

Jan frowned, moving to grab his gun situated in the back of his pants. Mia wondered why it wasn't strapped to his hip, but she didn't have time to question that when Jan stumbled forward a few steps, the gun clattering to the ground.

"Jan!" Mia rushed over to him, her man crumpling to the floor as he scratched at his throat, his face turning beet red, struggling to breathe. Strangled gasps escaped Jan's mouth, his eyes rolling into the back of his head as he flailed about on the tile. Tears streamed down her cheeks as she fumbled for her cellphone to call someone, *anyone* who could squash the nightmare unfolding before her, but she never got that far, the front door opening with a terrifying squeal.

"I wouldn't call anyone if I were you, not unless you want him to *die*."

EIGHTY-ONE

MIA

Phone clutched in one hand, she shuffled Quinn behind her, hearing the scrape of shoes worth more than her salary on the floor of her office. Her eyes darted to Jan's limp form, a sob racketing through her chest. He couldn't be dead. The happy ending she had been looking forward to couldn't have been ruined. She couldn't deal with any more pain.

Deep down though, she was pretty sure happiness had never been in the cards for her, and with that pesky piece of technology, it wouldn't be long before Jan suffocated. That technology expanded when in water, but that bottle had been unopened, and it had been in her fridge for longer than it would have taken for that green stuff to react.

Which meant two things – that bottle had been planted and whatever Jan had drunk was more advanced than the evidence she had found on the bodies.

A lean figure entered, his deep-green eyes penetrating the dark ambiance of her lab as they fell on her.

"I was hoping *you'd* be the one to drink that bottle of water. It's been *days*, and you never once reached for it. Shame about him though, really." The man's eyes darted to Jan for two pitiful seconds before rising back to Mia. "Although I'm pleasantly surprised I have two more specimens here. Two for one? *You shouldn't have*." A greasy smile spread across his lips as he stepped closer, a sense of dread settling in the pit of Mia's stomach. She knew that voice but couldn't place it.

I thought he'd be a little more ... pudgy.

Mia wracked her brain for why she had thought that, trying to remember where she had heard his voice. He was a little heavy set, his tailored suit bulging around the middle, but he didn't match the picture she had formed in his head. She also *still didn't know where she had heard his voice.*

And then it clicked.

Mia opened her mouth to let out her revelation, eyes going wide when the man unearthed a gun and pointed it at her face. The time for screaming was over as she stumbled backward, pushing Quinn farther into the lab. With the cameras off, Matthias and Kenn would have no idea what was happening. Since Jan had been with her, they were under the impression that she was protected.

"*You–*" Even if she had wanted to say something more, she wouldn't have been able to, fear flooding her senses.

He chuckled, stepping into the lab and over Jan's body, gaze zoning in on her bare feet before returning to her face again. "You're a smart girl," he purred. His predatory stalk forward was nothing like the way her men playfully approached her before smothering her in love and affection. The way his footsteps shuffled forward *terrified her*. "I never thought you'd piece it all together so quickly. It's a shame you couldn't be swayed like your old man, though."

Mia frowned. That didn't make any sense. Her father had started uncovering this before he died. She had all his notes and pictures and conclusions he had tried to connect, not that she could focus on that with a gun pointed in her face. There were a billion things she wanted to ask, but only one word slipped through her lips. "*Why?*" A tear rolling down her cheek punctuated the question, the floodgates opening in response.

"Because, my dear." The man's eyes darted to Quinn, his smile widening. "You're all about upholding the law. I was going to let it go, but you just couldn't leave it alone." The gun stopped twirling. "You had to go to the city to *confirm* things. You *shouldn't* have." Mia whimpered, opening her mouth to scream, but nothing came out. A muffled bang rang out through the lab, Quinn howling seconds later as he fell to the ground, holding his leg.

Blood seeped through his fingers as he rolled around the ground, clamping his mouth shut when the man threatened to shoot again. Mia glanced at the cameras, wondering if any of them were working or if she was trapped in this little hellhole to deal with the terror on her own.

"Sweetheart, you know those damn things aren't working. I handed them to Nichlas myself, knowing full well they wouldn't do their job. He came whining to me several times about it, the poor bastard." He let out another laugh, the sound like nails on a chalkboard, his belly rumbling with the vibrations. "Now, keep that pretty little mouth shut. You know I have no qualms about killing people."

Mia did know that, but there was something else she had figured out. While many of the victims fought for their lives, they weren't *beaten*. They weren't shot. They weren't mangled. That gun wasn't going to do more than threaten her. It didn't bring her much comfort, but a little was more than nothing. Her heart broke for Jan, but other than following this man's commands, there wasn't anything else she could do.

Her screams wouldn't reach across the street, and most of the town refused to step inside of her office. Dialing 911 now wouldn't do her any good because they were at least thirty minutes outside of her small town. Mia mentally kicked herself for not saving her men's numbers on speed dial as she fumbled for a new plan.

"Now, *Mia*, be a good girl and have a seat, all right? I have so many plans for you." She complied, finding a seat on the floor beside Quinn, who was still moaning, tears streaming down his cheeks. For a kid who had just been shot, he was a stronger survivor than she could ever hope to be. His hand clutched at her arm and his fingers clamped down on her flesh hard enough to make her squirm.

His eyes had slid shut, his breathing becoming shallower with each breath, and she could tell he was scared. No one should ever have to deal with a situation like this, let alone her nineteen-year-old assistant. This wasn't how she wanted to go out. Mia had so many plans for the new life she had started carving out.

No, he's going to get what's coming to him. I know it. He has to. For what he's done to this town. To my men. To Quinn. To me.

Mia tried to steel herself against the emotions racing through her head as the man crouched down in front of her, that terrifying smile widening. "Ah, yes, you'll do just fine." The last thing she remembered before the gun hit her upside the head was his grubby fingers caressing her cheek, his rough lips pressed to her forehead.

EIGHTY-TWO

MIA

She startled awake, gasping for air, fear racing through her body. She scanned her surroundings, relieved to see Quinn beside her, looking at her wide eyes. There was a bruise forming beneath his eye, and his leg was wrapped in bandages, the horror of the gunshot coming back to haunt her.

But she couldn't find Jan. She also had no idea where she was. They were on some sort of makeshift cots, but they weren't in the town's clinic.

They also weren't in the city's.

A nurse flew in, checking the machines, and began asking her questions a mile a minute, Mia rattling off answers about how she was feeling and what she remembered last. Everything was a bit fuzzy but there was one man she knew she was missing..

Where's Jan?

The nurse tapped her hand, Mia looking up to see that the woman had been trying to get her attention. "Sweetie, are you okay to speak with a detective? You've got a few bruises and a minor concussion but if you're feeling up to it, I'll let him in. If not, I'll let him know to come back in an hour or two."

Mia looked at the door for a moment. "Where's Jan? He was with us and-"

The nurse let out a pitiful sigh, clutching her clipboard to her chest. "I'm sorry, sweetie. I don't know. You can ask the detective. He was the one who brought you in." Mia nodded, an officer pushing his way into the hospital room a few moments later.

Her gaze trailed to the walls, massive thick foggy glass pieces encasing her in this small room. It seemed off for a hospital but Mia was more focused on trying to find out Jan's whereabouts.

The officer dragged a chair to the edge of the bed, giving her a comforting glance before looking at Quinn, a tight smile on his face.

"Where's Jan? Where's—"

"I understand that you're a little disoriented, Mia but I'm here to figure out what happened. I'm Detective Johansson and I was the one who brought you two in."

She frowned, not sure how the detective knew her name. In a small town like hers, carrying around identification wasn't needed. Everyone knew everyone, but this was the first time she had seen this detective. Mia brushed it off, in search of different information. "Where is—"

"Are you asking about the man that was with you?" Mia nodded eagerly, leaning toward the detective. "I'm sorry. He didn't make it. He went into cardiac arrest shortly after being brought to the hospital."

She sat back against the pillows, blinking a few times to keep the tears from spilling down her cheeks. Jan was … dead? That didn't make sense. He was the smartest of her four, the strongest, the one who always saw right through her. Just this morning, he had promised her a repeat of that heated moment in the cafe.

He had dinner planned with all of her men in attendance. He couldn't be dead. Detective Johansson gave her a few minutes to gather herself, placing a gentle hand near hers for comfort.

But she didn't want that.

She wanted Jan.

She wanted her men.

And she wanted some fucking answers.

"Where are we?"

"In a small hospital just off Route 90. We found you three in a small warehouse after an anonymous call to the department."

The intruder to her office didn't seem that inexperienced to have left them alone, but stranger things had happened. Her eyes scanned the room, snagging on the Route 90 logo, the presence of something real softening her nerves.

Still, Jan was gone. And Route 90 was nearly 45 miles south of Brxyton. Things weren't adding up.

The officer scooted a little closer. "Mia, I know that this is tough for you, but I need to know what happened. We have a suspect in custody, but he's not talking."

"How do you know my name?"

His lips curved upwards a little. "Because your phone has been going off the hook. You're a very special woman to some wonderful men, Mia. I'll have you both returned as soon as humanly possible, but I just need help connecting some dots."

Mia took a deep breath, trying to push down her feelings so she could help the detective. She poured every last detail of the bodies in her office as well as the many incidents over the past two weeks. Quinn filled in pieces she missed, Mia watching the officer's face as he jotted down a few notes, though not enough in her opinion.

As she trailed on, her voice wavering between uncertainty and sorrow, she began to realize that the officer seemed a little too interested. In fact, his questions continually pointed toward finding out how much she knew *just so he knew* rather than using it to determine the killer's guilt.

Mia drew back, biting her bottom lip. Something was wrong. She followed his gaze to the cups of water at her bedside and the bits of applesauce and pudding. Quinn had torn one open, a spoonful of white gloop halfway to his mouth when she realized *why* the officer was so forceful with his questions. She smacked it out of Quinn's hands, Quinn opening his mouth to yell at her before he realized.

Quinn didn't know everything about the substance, but he knew enough to trust her and that's all she needed.

"Where are we *really*?"

The officer let out a deep sigh, standing and moving back to the door, waving in whoever was on the other side. Mia wrapped an arm around Quinn's shoulder, pulling him into her chest.

"Hello, Mia. It's so wonderful that you're awake again."

Her heart dropped into her stomach as she stared at the man who had killed Jan, shot Quinn, and dragged her into this place.

"It seems you know *a lot* more than I had hoped you would, which doesn't fit well into my plans. But that's all right."

Mia let her rage from everything that had happened rush at her as she scrambled from the bed and raced toward the man who had caused her so much grief. "You … you fucking piece of shit!" The officer held her back, tears streaming down her face, her head pounding in anguish from having moved so quickly.

The man just laughed at her, reaching out to tussle her hair. "Mia, we're going to get along just fine."

"Just … *why*?"

"It isn't my fault some people couldn't handle it, but I assure you that they were all volunteers."

Quinn shifted on the bed, groaning as he did so. "Highly doubt that," he muttered in between pained breaths.

The man just smiled. "And he speaks. All will be explained to you in due time, not that you'll need it once this is over."

Over?

"Where's—"

"That gorgeous man? I left him lying on the floor, gasping for breath. Not sure how long he can hold his breath, but he's probably dead by now."

A sob left her lips as she fell limp in the officer's hold, her body giving out as she felt herself close down. She wasn't going to get her happy ending, was she?

EIGHTY-THREE

MATTHIAS

He threw another punch at the bag, grunting with the rage swirling in his chest. Everything just kept getting worse. They couldn't find the guy behind all this shit. Anders and Natalie were a mess of epic proportions, and that bitch just kept sticking her nose where it didn't belong. And for what? What was her endgame?

Matthias was fucking done. He wanted out. He wanted them all out, safely tucked in another city, far away from this shit. He also knew that any of them leaving before they found the killer was unlikely. They were all too goddamn good at their jobs to leave loose ends, not to mention that Mia would never get the closure she needed.

"MATTHIAS!"

Matthias froze, slowly turning around to see Kenn staring at him, a worried expression on his face. By the volume of his voice, Matthias realized that Kenn had been calling him for a while. The punching bag was swinging dangerously close to his face, Matthias putting a hand out to stop its momentum. He gave the detective a sheepish smile, dropping his hands to his side. "What?" He tried to weather his voice, but the rage seeped through anyway.

"You're not going to get rid of your anger doing that. Let's go."

"Go where?" Matthias bit out. He didn't want to go anywhere. Unless they were going to find Anders for a little target practice. A wild grin spread across his cheeks seconds before a punch landed in his chest. He stumbled back a few steps, Kenn standing way closer than he had before.

"Stop it. We're not fucking putting anyone in the ground. I made a fresh batch of coffee. Let's go across the street."

"You just want kisses," Matthias teased, but if he were being honest, seeing Mia would do wonders for his mental state. It wasn't fair to her that they all kept using her for their happy moments, but there wasn't much else to do. Kenn didn't argue, heading into the hallway as Matthias followed. "I just need to—"

"Nope. No changing. Maybe if Mia sees that you're breaking down, you'll actually get some help."

It wasn't meant to be a jab, but it still cut deep. Matthias had been avoiding talks about therapy for years. He knew he needed help, but having someone he didn't know run around in his head terrified him. Having Mia see him at his weakest point and again at his most lethal was terrifying in and of itself.

He chose to focus on seeing Mia and her bright expression as they made their way downstairs, his nose turning up when he caught the scent of orange and hazelnut. "What the fuck is that?"

Kenn took a large swig of his cup, expertly handling a to-go cup and two small bags in the other hand. "I like it. The mixture you made last time. It's weird but nice."

"You weren't supposed to *like* it."

"All right, you're a moody little fucker. Let's get you over there so Mia can give you kisses, too."

The cheeky air to his words was still present, but they were masked by the unrest that this case was causing. Matthias just shook his head, grabbing the other two prepared coffees, and made his way across the street, his hackles immediately rising when his gaze laid on the door slightly ajar.

Coffee forgotten as it splattered to the ground, he stormed in, whipping out a piece from the back of his pants that he wasn't supposed to be carrying. While he had a license, Nichlas had told him that carrying a gun wasn't safe with his mental state. It was a fair assessment, one that Matthias had ignored in the past couple of days, refusing to be bested again.

He stomped around the office, fear racing through his body, dread settling in his chest when he saw Jan passed out on the floor. Matthias dropped to his knees, frantically starting CPR as he shifted back into his military training mindset, separating himself from his emotions. He pinched Jan's chin, freezing at the sight of green fibers on his tongue.

"Salt," Matthias croaked out. His eyes scanned the office, falling on a water bottle at the far end of the office. "I need salt." Had Mia not brought that piece of evidence back the other day, he would have never figured it out. But someone had taken their woman, and Jan had drunk water that had this in it. Why it didn't work the same was beyond him, but he hoped and prayed that the remedy hadn't changed.

Kenn ruffled through Mia's drawers, pulling out a handful of little salt packets as he rushed over and fell to his knees on the other side of Jan. They hurriedly ripped them open, pouring them down Jan's throat, hoping and praying that it wasn't too late.

There was no telling how long Jan had been like this, but his lips weren't blue and his body was still warm.

Please. Please. Please.

A lone tear escaped before more followed, cascading down his cheeks. Matthias gripped one of Jan's hands, squeezing for fear of losing one of his best friends, his family. If anything was going to make him rip this small town apart, it was going to be this.

No one took one of his men and got away with it.

No one.

EIGHTY-FOUR

JAN

Beeping and whirring machines sounded around him, pounding in his head, rousing him from his unconsciousness. He blinked a few times, shifting with a groan as pain shot through every limb, burning until his skin felt it was on fire.

"You're awake." Lips were pressed to his forehead, tears coating his skin. But they weren't Mia's. They were Matthias'. Jan reached up to run his fingers through their barista's hair, sighing into the man's hold as he cried. "You're okay," he began mumbling, repeating it every few seconds, but it didn't seem to be for Jan. It was words meant to soothe Matthias' fragile emotional state.

Jan found Kenn on the other side of his bed. *"What is this?"* he mouthed, referring to Matthias' embrace. They all knew the kid was fragile to some extent, but affection between the four of them was rare. Matthias bared his heart for his woman and *only* his woman. This was something new, but now wasn't the time to point it out.

Kenn just shrugged. Jan dropped his hand to the man's shoulder, patting him a few times to get Matthias to release him. His throat felt sore, but they didn't have time to lose. "Where's Mia?" Jan croaked out, hating how the words scratched on the way out.

Kenn let out a deep sigh. "No idea. We were waiting for you to wake up. Thought you could tell us."

Jan opened his mouth again, grimacing when no sound came out. He gestured for something to write on, Kenn handing him his phone.

"I'm not sure who he is. It's the same guy that we met at one of the parties. He works with Nichlas, though. Maybe for Nichlas?"

Matthias leaned over Jan's shoulder, frowning at the words that had been typed out. "Nichlas' handler? The little fat computer guy?"

Jan shook his head, typing again. *"He's not fat. Big, sure. Not fat."* Still, that explained how it was so easy for the killer to continue on under the radar. *"How long have I been here?"*

"Half an hour tops. We're at one of the clinics in town, no need for this to escalate to the city," Kenn offered. Jan nodded, content that they hadn't lost too much time, but internally, he was freaking out. He knew both of the men standing with him were as well, but he was of no use to them like this.

"There's something else, isn't there?" He looked to Kenn, knowing full well that Matthias hadn't left the room for a second.

Kenn shifted uncomfortably, settling into a seat inches from the bed. "Anders succumbed to his wounds." Jan froze, wondering if his uncontrollable anger had dealt the final blow. "It wasn't you. He called me earlier, said he had more information. But he was rushed to the hospital for 'complications,' and now he's in the morgue with a pinprick in his neck."

Silence filtered between them.

Someone was tying up loose ends. When they found out Jan was still alive, the killer would come for him again.

They didn't have time to sit here and figure shit out.

Jan started ripping at the cords, the machines sounding alarms as they were disconnected. Matthias didn't try to stop him, pulling plugs out of the wall to keep from alerting the nurses. Jan wasn't sure the staff wasn't already on their way, but it was a valiant effort. Kenn seemed a little less gung-ho about leaving the place, but Jan didn't care.

Their woman was in the hands of Nichlas' crazy coworker for reasons they didn't understand. A killing ground didn't make sense if the government was involved, because all this shit seemed interconnected.

Jan slipped back into his clothes with Matthias' help. He leaned into the kid's chest for support, gesturing for him to give them a better insight into the killer's profile.

"They're doing experiments."

Matthias didn't offer anything else, not that Jan expected him to. The fact that the kid hadn't torn up some part of the town at this point was a feat in and of itself.

Experiments didn't seem too far-fetched a thing for the government to do, especially not with a substance like the ones being found on all these bodies. It was unfortunate *for the government* that Mia hadn't been so easily bought.

But if Jan didn't figure out where the fuckers were soon, Mia's stubbornness would have been for nothing. There was only one thing to do now, the timing of Nichlas' newest job even more strange after finding out his coworker was heading up this entire thing.

"Nichlas," Jan whispered. "Find him."

EIGHTY-FIVE

MIA

Slowly waking up, voices filtered in around her, several men talking about an experiment that she didn't understand. It wasn't until the word ORCSORB hit her ears that she perked up, never having heard the brand name before but knowing exactly what it referred to. She struggled to sit up, restraints wrapped around her wrists and legs, arms tied behind her back. They had been haphazardly thrown on the paneled floor, Quinn slumped against her lap. He was still breathing, but his breaths were shallow, and Mia feared she didn't have a lot of time before her luck ran out.

The warehouse was sparse except for three strange white rooms at the back, windows instead of walls, bright lights, and whirring machines visible on the other side. Mia wondered if one of those rooms had been the one she had woken up in. It made sense.

Nichlas' coworker had deposited them behind barrels of the green substance – ORCSORB written in a harsh, unforgiving yellow font – out of sight and out of mind, she guessed. She leaned forward, straining to hear the voices, her mind still groggy.

"Why the fuck did you bring her here?"

The man from before let out a bitter laugh. "She's too damn close to it. She's picked up on more than the last sheriff had in three years! Can't have her roaming around spreading information that isn't meant for her."

Someone in a lab coat sighed. "Cross, that's great and all, but people will be looking for her. Why the fuck didn't you just–"

"Don't fucking question me, Harold. Killing her would have brought way more suspicion than taking her. Her father got dumped the same way. It would look weird."

Mia stifled a gasp at that fact. She knew very little about her father's death, her mother refusing to talk about it, but finding out that Cross was the reason made this whole situation worse.

"Really? That fucking agent of yours is going to rip us apart."

"If I hadn't dealt with him first. You really thought I didn't cover my ass? I'm not a fucking amateur. I may not have trained him, but I know what he's capable of. Sent him on the next mission. Per protocol, he can't contact anyone outside of the mission other than me." Cross ended the conversation as he stomped over to Mia, his face lighting up when he realized she was awake.

Cross crouched in front of her, reaching out to run a hand down her cheek in a way that made her squirm. She held still as much as she could, refusing to give the man a reaction. Tears gathered in her eyes as she stared at him, biting her lip to keep from yelling out her frustration. After all, the man before her had killed her father *and* Jan, beaten and shot Quinn, and stolen them for some agenda she still didn't understand.

ORCSORB wasn't supposed to be this massive thing. It was an experimental scientific substance used for altruistic reasons such as helping to rebuild nature, not for killing people.

"You poor little thing. I really am sorry about that, man, but you have to understand that I meant him no harm." That didn't make her feel any better, especially since his words were full of amusement and he was *still touching her face*. "If you had just listened to that piss-poor excuse of a sheriff and we wouldn't be here. But you just had to be the hero. It's a shame."

He stood up, sparing a glance for Quinn, and then shook his head. A whimper slipped from Mia's lips as she shifted beneath his unforgiving stare. "Why are you doing this?" she croaked out.

Cross barked out a laugh, the sound echoing through the warehouse. "I'm not giving you a villain's speech because, frankly, it's beneath me. You stumbled upon information you shouldn't have and you pursued it. I needed you out of the way, but like a cockroach, you just kept coming back." He punctuated his words with a shrug, as if killing and kidnapping were reasonable responses to the issue.

She shrank back against one of the metal tins, unsure of what else to say. Mia knew she was going to die here. There were no other options, and by the look of things, death was going to be painfully slow.

She knew Matthias and Kenn would do their best to find her, but Cross had thrown a wrench in everything her men had tried over the last week. It'd be a miracle if they swooped in before Cross did something that couldn't be undone.

EIGHTY-SIX

MATTHIAS

Jan had protested, saying to leave him behind so he wouldn't slow them down, but Matthias was having none of it. He hadn't been there when they took Mia from him, and he hadn't been there when they attacked Jan. His heart was in pieces, and he wasn't sure where the feelings were coming from, but they had been feelings he'd been avoiding for a while.

Feelings that involved more than just the brotherhood he'd built with these men.

Feelings that would make or break the five of them when things settled and conversations were had.

He tried not to think of it, tried not to dwell on what Mia would do when she found out if she hadn't somehow caught on already.

Shaking himself out of his stupor, he glanced in the rearview mirror, sending a hardened stare to Jan's weary form in the backseat. Minutes after Jan's protest, Matthias had checked him over and then again before hauling him over his shoulder and carting him out of the hospital. Kenn's apologies could be heard echoing through the hall as Matthias dumped the detective in the backseat and climbed in on the driver's side, waiting for Kenn to join them.

Kenn had berated him for his actions, but Matthias was done fucking listening and waiting for everyone to act. He'd reached out to Nichlas, and surprise, he hadn't answered, but Matthias' connections and experience went a long way, long enough to find out that Nichlas was stationed at a base two cities over, preparing to deploy overseas.

If they didn't catch him in the next three hours, Nichlas would be out of reach until god knew when.

And that just couldn't fucking happen.

Speeding through back roads, Matthias dialed every last contact he had to stop Nichlas' departure. In the end, Lieutenant Fuckface had been the last blow, Matthias having to promise a full sit down with the man to discuss future opportunities. It took all of his control not to rage through the phone, but if it was going to bring Nichlas home, he'd do anything. An hour later, the car skidded to a stop, Matthias jumping out to meet a confused Nichlas standing just outside the base. Matthias's thoughts were scattered as he stalked toward the man, the one who'd been by his side every step away, unable to stop the emotions pouring from him.

Without thinking, Matthias grabbed Nichlas' face and crushed his lips against Nichlas'. He pulled back to see the shock in his friend's eyes, grunting at his impulsive thoughts. *Shit.* Matthias had never meant to let any of them know that he thought of them as more than friends, as brothers, as family, but in the last day, he almost lost two of them. For years, he had been grateful to have them by his side. Moments like this were ones that Matthias had avoided like the plague for the very look plastered on Nichlas' face.

Nichlas stood there, his jaw tensing as Matthias waited for the fallout. It didn't come. Although the moment was tense and awkward, Nichlas' hesitation was enough of an answer. Matthias opened his mouth to apologize and explain, but he didn't get that far, Nichlas pulling him back to continue the kiss.

Their lips dueled for dominance as one of Nichlas' hands sat at the front of Matthias' neck, slowly squeezing until Matthias was fighting for air. It was a delicious hold, and the man's lips were everything Matthias had expected them to be *and more*. Their chests brushed together, Matthias groaning as his cock thickened in his pants, pressing against the seam. He'd been fighting these feelings so long that now the door was open, they were spilling out with no way to stop them. Melting into Nichlas' arms was *everything*, and yet the inevitable conversation that would follow was going to be brutal. All too soon, Nichlas pulled away, playfully tugging at Matthias' bottom lip, his eyes dancing, another unexpected development.

"What a welcome, Matty." Nichlas seemed more than enthusiastic about this turn of events, especially with his own erection pressed against Matthias'. "We have a lot to talk about, don't we? We'll get there."

"You–"

Nichlas just shrugged, placing another light kiss on Matthias' lips. "We never talked, and we both suck at feelings." He ran a few fingers down Matthias' cheek as he sported a small smile. "Now, what's this about me being released from the mission on a technicality?"

Matthias tried to shuffle away from Nichlas as Jan and Kenn approached, but Nichlas was having none of it. Apparently, since *that* was now in the open, clingy Nichlas had also made an appearance. Matthias wondered how that would work when they got Mia back, but first, they had to actually get her back. With his hand securely wrapped up in Nichlas', he was sure they'd get to her in time.

Jan and Kenn didn't seem shocked as Kenn relayed the latest details. "Your fucking handler took Mia. Tried to kill our boy over here."

Nichlas glanced at Jan and then Matthias as if he knew what had drawn out Matthias' change of heart. Then his expression darkened. "Cross? Not fucking possible." He whipped out his phone, dialing the fucker, receiving the answering machine. He tried again – same thing.

They all knew the gravity of the situation as a handler was always supposed to be available.

"Cross said a third party had been dealing with all the security equipment. I'm guessing that was all bullshit." Kenn nodded, Nichlas growling out his frustration.

"How the fuck didn't we know?" Jan croaked out.

Nichlas let out a sigh, gesturing for them to get back in the car. "Because he's a nasty fuck that flies under the radar. Let's go find our woman. I'm feeling like murder tonight." His eyes flashed with anger, his hand tightening around Matthias' as the other two returned to the car, Matthias once again about to apologize. Nichlas cut him off though. "No, we're not going to dismiss this. It's out in the open. We're going to address it. The other's feelings are their own and you'll have to accept whatever happens."

"The others?"

"I have *eyes*, Matty. You try to hide, but your face is so fucking expressive. I'm also not stupid to think they aren't part of this." Matthias frowned, wondering how many times they had all seen right through him. Nichlas just laughed. "It wasn't *that* obvious. Now, let's go get Mia."

Matthias froze, wondering what Mia would think of this new development, Nichlas immediately calming his fears.

"She loves you. Loves everything about you, the good and the bad. Seeing you happy makes her happy, and *yes*, that includes this." Nichlas placed one last kiss on the barista's lips, the fight leaving Matthias. "Come on, we have a woman to save and a few heads to bash in. If you're good, I might even let you slit a few throats."

A wild smile spread across Matthias' face as they returned to the car, ready to take on anyone and everyone who had tried to fuck with them.

EIGHTY-SEVEN

MIA

Trying to wriggle out of her restraints was futile, but she kept trying. Someone had placed a tray of food inches from Quinn, the kid rousing from his unconscious and reaching for what looked like a sandwich. She nudged his side, Quinn immediately coming to and shifting into a sitting position. She silently pleaded with him to stay quiet, the boy's face paling from the pain she knew he must be feeling.

Quinn raised an eyebrow, asking her what was going on, but just then one of the scientists started talking again.

"The fucking experiment is over, Cross. We don't have any more funding, and the last batch killed every single participant. We're running out of excuses."

Another scientist entered the conversation. "And participants. There's only so many Jane and John Does you can drop before someone starts asking questions. Fuck, someone *already did*."

Cross didn't look bothered in the slightest. "Harold, we've got nothing? I gave you guys the utmost freedom with the project. It's been nearly a decade and you've *nothing* for me?"

The first scientist – Harold – just sighed. "We have one last batch we didn't test but–"

"Great. Get me two samples." Cross held out his hand, his brows furrowing with anger. Harold hesitated for a moment and then dove into one of the testing rooms before returning with two liquid specimens the size of small glasses. Cross turned to the second scientist. He was much younger than Harold and instead of cowering, the kid smiled. "Is this the new batch? The same one we put in her lab?" Lucas shook his head. "Oh, it's an improved one. Excellent. Lucas, how many successful participants do we need?"

"Two, sir."

Cross grinned before yanking one cup from Harold's hands, undoing the top and shoving it mercilessly down Harold's throat. The scientist gurgled as he fought but ultimately lost, dropping to the ground like a bag of bricks. Lucas held his ground, but there was no mistaking the fear in his eyes. Cross, however, had turned his sights on someone else – Quinn.

Mia tried to keep the man from approaching, but without the use of her hands or feet, there wasn't anything she could do as she watched, yet again, someone fuck with her life. Cross marched over with the second specimen, grinning like a madman before offering it to Quinn.

"No. I'll take it. Just leave him alone!" Mia screamed.

Cross let out a bitter laugh. "No, I don't think I'll do that. You played the nosy bitch, so you get to understand how it feels when everything important is taken from you. Just like you did with me." And then he grabbed Quinn's chin, prying his mouth open in a firm grip before dumping the contents of the second cup into the boy's mouth. Quinn's body trembled as he fought for air, the reaction immediate before slumping back against the metal containers.

His eyes closed and his chest stopped moving, his airways completely blocked. Mia didn't even know how to react as Quinn's limp body.

"How could you?" Tears raced down her cheeks as she sat there helplessly, wondering how much more harm Cross was going to inflict before he just killed her.

Cross stared at her, his grin waning at the unsuccessful experiment. "Science has all these pesky rules. We can't release things until after we've tested them. But we can't test unless we have approval. Lots of gray areas, Mia. Too many hoops."

"Killing people is not a hoop!" she screamed, trying again to wriggle out of her constraints.

He laughed again. "A few for the sake of many? I assure you it is."

Mia thought over all the dead bodies that had ended up at her office. "Those were *people* you killed. People that had families and loved ones! They had lives!" All the confidence her men had helped her build up was spilling over. Cross needed to understand, even if men like him never truly understood. "Those–"

"Mia, *please*, I'm begging you to shut up, all right? You aren't going to make me see 'reason.' This is necessary. Once we have the data, it'll all be worth it. Just you wait."

She was about to protest when a cough exploded out of Quinn's mouth. Mia realized that whatever had been poured down Quinn and Harold's throats hadn't killed them. ORCSORB had been modified to expand and contract on its own, but why, Mia had no clue.

He stared at Quinn's form, his eyes lighting up as he glanced at a terrified Lucas. "It works! We've done it. We need to run a few more tests, but you've done it, young man. You will be thoroughly rewarded."

Lucas nodded timidly, Harold clutching at his neck as he sat up, murder in his eyes. "Sir, we don't have—"

Cross shook his head, standing back up and stretching. "See, that's where you're wrong. I saved the very best for last." He grabbed Mia around the neck, dragging her to her feet as she wriggled in his grip. She had nothing to help her brace against the man's hand as he cut off her air supply, Cross laughing at her feeble attempts to free herself. "You're a spry one, I'll give you that. Let's see if we can't get this show on the road, eh?"

Mia continued to squirm, Cross cursing when his hold slipped and then yelled out in pain when she launched herself forward and chomped down on whatever she came in contact with. Her teeth connected with his arm, the bitter taste of copper flooding her tongue as she held on. Cross grabbed her hair and roughly yanked her off, grunting as blood strickled down his arm.

She knew the punch was coming before she felt it, the blunt force connecting with her cheek and sending her head back onto the concrete floor. Stars blinded her vision as pain flooded her system.

"You fucking bitch! I ought to—"

Lucas raced over, cradling her head. "Stop! If you kill her, there won't be anyone else." That stopped Cross, and Lucas helped her to stand. He undid the bindings on her feet, but she couldn't have run if she tried at this point, sagging against his chest for relief.

"Don't hurt her," Quinn rasped. His eyes were bloodshot as he tried to swallow, but Cross just turned and spit on the poor boy.

"Be glad you're alive. Stay quiet or I might need you again." Then he stalked off toward one of the testing rooms, Mia helplessly hoisted into Lucas' arms as the kid followed his boss. When the door closed behind her, she knew that this would be the last few moments of her life. She just hoped she could bring Cross a little more pain in the process.

EIGHTY-EIGHT

NICHLAS

There were so many things they had to figure out as they spilled back into the cafe, everyone racing to gather information they had stored in their rooms and behind the counter, Matthias sitting oddly at one of the tables, watching the rest of them. Nichlas knew the kid had information stored, but Matthias could also recall all of it at a moment's notice, which was yet another reason why he was so burdened by his past.

He remembered. Every nightmare, every happy moment stolen from him. In perfect detail, just like it was yesterday. Nichlas couldn't imagine what that shit was like.

After gathering his supplies, guns, ammo, and bulletproof vests, plus anything else they might need, Nichlas returned to the table, gathering Matthias against his chest, placing a soft kiss on the top of his head. The barista stiffened before trying to pull away. "You don't have to—"

"*Matthias*," Nichlas said, sitting next to him and angling the kid toward him. "I am not doing this because I have to or because you showed me how you felt. I'm doing this because I want you just as much as you want me. I'm doing this because while I've watched you grow and fight and bleed, I've wanted you so much it hurts, but there was never a good time. There was never a *right* time. But after finding Mia? If we had not approached her, she would have still been dealing with Anders. We probably would have packed up this case without much more than we have. I'd have been off on another mission. There's never a right time, Matthias."

The kid was trembling in his seat, the words just a little too heavy for the moment. Nichlas didn't know how much he had even wanted Matthias until this moment. He just knew he couldn't lose the purple-eyed kid who had the world riding on his shoulders, and somehow that had manifested into feelings and love and desire.

"You can't tell me that you—"

"I can," Nichlas cut him off again. "I can absolutely tell you that." He took a deep breath, wondering if he believed the words he was about to say as he stared into those irises that were always so damn expressive. Nichlas reached forward, cupping Matthias' face in his hands. He drew the kid closer until their noses were brushing before continuing. "That I'm fucking in love with my best friend." Then he closed the distance between them and kissed Matthias like his life depended on it.

Matthias melted against him, the whole world fading away as they kissed, Nichlas' heart hurting with the absence of Mia at their side. He pulled away as his thoughts took a dark turn, Matthias giving him a pert nod when the others walked in. Nichlas noticed that Matthias plastered on a look of indifference as Jan and Kenn took a seat at the table with a stack of papers as if trying not to dwell on the bits of emotions that were spilling out of him.

Nichlas caught Jan's gaze, raising an eyebrow to see if he could understand the detective's thought process. Jan gave him a small smile, easing his worries before Kenn began talking. "I called in a favor when we realized it was Cross." Nichlas nodded. His only real contact had been Cross, but with the guy not answering his phone – obviously – Nichlas had no other contacts within the agency without starting up a whole new connection or contacting his superior directly.

And that took time.

Time they didn't have.

"Tried pinging his phone, but the bastard's at least that smart. However, Natalie isn't." Kenn choked on a laugh. "We all think she's involved, and we all saw the pictures. Well, Nichlas, you haven't. She met up with Cross earlier. Pretty sure she's with him at this point."

The men started toward the front door, Kenn laughing as he shouted an address he'd gotten just before the phone had been turned off. For as smart as Cross was, he was also dumb as shit when it came to the "spy things," a fact that Nichlas was wholeheartedly grateful for at the moment. Had he been in the right mindset, he would have checked everyone's gear, *especially* Natalie's, provided that she was with him.

He jumped into the driver seat, ignoring Kenn's request to drive, the others piling in. The rough shape of their bags and the heavy clunk of metal told him that they hadn't packed light. Nichlas spared Matthias a glance, the kid's tortured expression now swapped out for the desire to kill. His eyes were nearly midnight as he stared forward, waiting for them to arrive at their destination and go after Cross.

Nichlas couldn't say he was just as excited, but he *was* a bit worried about what it would do to Matthias' progress. It had been a minute since Matthias had joined in on any of their missions and for good reason, but there was no way to ask him to back down.

Kenn leaned between the console as Nichlas sped off down the road, address set in the GPS. "Found something else and you're not gonna like it. Apparently, it's some sort of weaponized experiment. No idea what it's for but let's just say it hasn't been very successful."

No shit. Not with the bodies piling up in the coroner's office.

The problem was that Cross now had their woman, and if she became one of those bodies, Nichlas was going to fucking tear the world apart trying to bring her back.

EIGHTY-NINE

MIA

Lucas deposited her on a chair in a small nook, complete with a door and window, with barely any space to move as they prepped the testing room. She hadn't even seen the space from her perch by the metal tins, but it was evident now that they were prepping for her end. Mia fought the tears, trying to be strong, trying to stay put together. Quinn was trembling, his breathing shallow.

He wasn't looking so hot either, between the gunshot and nearly suffocating with the newest version of ORCSORB.

"I don't know why you're keeping on that brave face. You're not getting out of here." Mia turned to see the last person she would have expected – the blond-headed bimbo – waltzing into the testing room, tapping on the glass like she owned the place. Mia had her suspicions, especially when she had gone with Jan earlier to see Natalie's shady dealings, but working so closely with Cross? It was a bit of a shock.

Mia struggled to gather enough strength to stand up, knowing it was futile to run. Her hands tied behind her back made standing nearly impossible, but she managed. Still, against Natalie, she wanted to prove until the end that she was strong. "What are you doing here?"

Natalie let out a bitter laugh, leaning to the right. It gave Mia a moment to focus on the bruises littering the left side of her face and shoulder. "I sell information, but apparently I'm not worth as much as I want to be." Mia had no doubt Cross was responsible for the bruises.

"You don't have to do this." It was a feeble attempt, but an attempt, nonetheless.

"I value my life, so I have to." Natalie took a step away from the glass, glancing back to check on the preparations. They seemed close to ready. "For the record, I never wanted Anders." Those words were supposed to hurt, and two weeks ago, they would have. Not anymore.

"Glad you took him," Mia spat, trying to show just how much she had grown with those four men standing at her back. "I wouldn't have seen who he truly was if you hadn't."

"He's dead anyways. Too many loose ends, and Cross likes to be in control. Look, don't fight them. If the experiment is successful, you'll live another day. If not …"

Mia wanted to be horrified, but she knew the outcome was inevitable. "I'll end up outside of my town, won't I?"

"But this time there won't be anyone to investigate," Natalie said.

Mia held back the whimper stuck in her throat as Natalie disappeared into the warehouse, leaving her alone with her thoughts. Blowing out a deep breath, Mia leaned against the glass and said one last prayer.

NINETY

MIA

She knew fighting wouldn't get her anywhere, but she wasn't going to go without doing everything in her power to let Cross know she wasn't going to just give in. Mia realized that this was what had happened with the bodies she had examined. They had fought till their dying breath against Cross' evil scientific experiment.

He laughed at her pitiful attempt to bite him again, moving out of her reach. "Don't be such a bitch. This isn't going to hurt."

Fear had fled her, only the need to survive left as she gnashed at Harold when he tried to come closer. Lucas strapped her arm down on the other side, while she weakly used her other arm to whack him in the face. He stumbled back, groaning and holding his eye.

Deep down, Mia knew that her men were on their way. They *had* to be. "You don't have to—"

Harold chuckled as he finally caught Mia's arm and strapped it down. Lucas grinned as he rounded the table and began attaching nodes to her forehead. "You don't get it. We have a vision. Well, Cross has a vision, and we get to be part of it." Harold didn't seem to share the same sentiment, as he had nearly died from Cross' antics. Why he was still helping was beyond Mia's comprehension.

Cross patted her shoulder, drawing her attention back to him. Strapped down to a table gave her an uncomfortable view of the three men, at their mercy. "Your father knew the rules, but then he grew a conscience. It really isn't my fault. Everyone was a willing participant, but sometimes things just didn't pan out."

"Bullshit," Mia blurted out.

He took a deep breath, his eyes darkening at her insolence. "Look here, *sweetheart*. You're not special. You're not going to keep me from doing this. My own husband was part of this damn experiment." Cross paused for a moment, and Mia remembered the killer caressing a body and taking it. *Oh.*

He was pure evil, plain and simple.

"Now, open that pretty little mouth of yours or I'll drag that boy you're helplessly trying to protect in here and start on him," Cross said.

Mia felt the tears spilling from her eyes but nodded slowly. *They're going to come.*

Lucas gripped her chin and pried her mouth open, wiggling a small brown item above her before placing it on her tongue. For a brief moment, the taste of chocolate coated her tongue and then it exploded, filling her airways and blocking her nose. She thrashed around on the cot, trying to dislodge the foreign substance and failing as it filled every available space.

Mia strained for air, whining, her legs kicking at the air for relief. Her heart beat erratically as it worked in overdrive, her lungs constricting until pure pain shot through her system. Her eyes slid shut as darkness crowded her vision, the inability to breathe too much. Just seconds before she lost her breath, the substance receded, Mia coughing violently as she gulped for air, vainly trying to find relief.

Cross stood beside her laughing. "This is fantastic! Trial – what is this? Trial number 372 is a success. Again. We need two successful trials, right Lucas?"

Terrified, Mia turned to look at the kid as he nodded, slowly. "Yes, but … if … she needs to rest. If she hasn't started breathing properly again, this one will suffocate her. I–" Mia coughed again as if to prove a point, but Cross looked unperturbed as he held out his hand.

"Give it to me, Lucas."

The kid hesitated, and Cross reached out and grabbed the kid by the neck. "Don't fucking test me. If she dies, she dies. I can always find another participant, Lucas. Your throat's looking positively *unused*."

Mia lay still, watching the exchange above her, trying to suck in as much air as she could. She knew scientists like him, well … not *like* him, but she had met overeager people who didn't know when to stop. Cross was just like them. There wasn't an end to the project. He was going to repeat this damn experiment until he had enough evidence.

But for what?

What the fuck was ORCSORB actually for?

Lucas handed over another piece of the newest version, scrambling back when Cross released him. "Excellent. Mia, open up like a good little girl." Tears clouded her vision as her body shook with the horror of going through that feeling again, Cross shoving the piece into her mouth. This time when it exploded in her mouth, she didn't fight against it, even as her toes curled and hands clenched from the pain of blocking her airways.

Cross' expression darkened, almost as if he was disappointed that she wasn't writhing around. His hand curled around her neck and squeezed, Mia screaming through the pain. A sinister smile spread across his face as his grip tightened.

He enjoyed the pain he inflicted, the sick bastard.

Mia knew that death would not come easy, but she wished it would.

It'd been what felt like hours, although she was fairly sure it hadn't even been thirty minutes. Her throat was sore, and she weakly fought her restraints. They'd moved from solids to liquids, giving her mere moments in between to catch her breath with each trial. She tried to scream or reason with them, her voice hoarse, but that only made Cross laugh harder.

She was going to die from lack of air, her face strained with the mere effort of trying to stay alive, and it was pure hell. She didn't wish this shit on anyone, but she had learned a few things while she had been near death.

ORCSORB wasn't *just* a government experiment. It was a weapon, a torture device. Cross and his people had been experimenting on regular people with a device meant for terrorists, and they saw nothing wrong with it. Cross stood off to the side, his wild gleeful smile making her sick, especially when he wrangled Natalie back into the room before groping her and kissing her for no other reason than he could.

From the corner of her eye, Mia could see that Natalie wasn't as into it as she proclaimed to be, wincing from the unhealed bruises along her left side.

Mia felt used as her head lolled to the side, Cross' terrifying laughter bouncing along the walls, but she could barely focus, her eyes falling closed, her body giving up. Her breath came in pants as she struggled to stay conscious, but she couldn't hold on any longer.

Cross just chuckled. "Get the goddamn smelling salts. I want to go again."

NINETY-ONE

KENN

Checking the last of his guns, he shoved it into the holster and then looked up to see Nichlas and Matthias grinning about the destruction they were about to cause. He stared at Matthias for a little longer, wondering what had prompted the kid to bare his bleeding heart to them.

Sure, the heat of the moment, with all of the stress over the past two weeks might have been the reason. But it could have also just been building. Unlike the others, Kenn's love language was touch, but he was also hyper-observant when it came to emotions. They were his jam. Jan understood people. Nichlas was clingy as fuck and Matthias was the charmer. But Kenn? With his honest-to-god need to make everyone smile, he was also the one who picked up the most.

Like the lingering looks Matthias gave them when they left on their missions or returned to work. The brief touches after a long night, and the way he just needed a little more grounding. The extra care he gave as he tried to make sure they were all taken care of.

Kenn wasn't stupid, but he also wasn't going to read into something that wasn't there. He wasn't sure how he felt about Matthias, definitely not as full-on as Nichlas, but that relationship hadn't really been a surprise. If things hadn't exploded, it would only have been a matter of time before they gravitated together.

What he hadn't expected was the reaction to Jan or himself. And the longer he stared, the more he realized he didn't mind the change within their group. Jan shuffled at his side, tapping him on the arm to signal that they were ready to go.

Nichlas turned to look at all of them, his eyes a shade of midnight Kenn hadn't seen before. It was a testament to how these men could easily turn off their emotions to get the job done. "I spoke with my superior, Thane Watts. He's given us thirty minutes. We go in, get Mia and Quinn, and get it. We have no backup, no one to call, *nothing*." Kenn could only think of the action movies that required soldiers to go dark for one last mission.

Each of them grunted their approval, Kenn looking out the window at the warehouse at the end of the path. There wasn't any security, which just provided more proof that Cross wasn't expecting anyone to find him out here. The strangest part was the fact that this "abandoned" facility was barely forty-five minutes outside of Mia's little town.

It didn't matter though, they were going to drop a few bodies, and then Mia would be back in their arms before they knew it.

"Casualties?" Kenn hated to ask but it was important. He didn't want these next thirty minutes coming to bite them in the ass just after they began their new life.

Nichlas snorted, shaking his head. "For the next thirty minutes, Thane's decided he'll look the other way. Don't go overboard."

"Well, shit," Kenn started as he threw the door open, "You must have pulled a shit ton of favors for this."

Nichlas nodded. "You have no idea."

Kenn marched into the building, using his training to bring the door down and start firing. No one was ready for the onslaught of gunfire, Kenn and the others easily trampling through personnel without resistance.

Screams could be heard echoing through the warehouse as Kenn marched through, eyes peeled for anything that could point to where their woman was. When the others signaled toward one of the glass rooms, Kenn's heart dropped into his stomach. Mia sprawled on a hospital table, her head lolled to the side, Cross leaning over her with rapt attention.

Those walls had to be soundproof.

Kenn wanted to be selfish, but he knew Mia would be saved. He grit his teeth together as he raced to the other side of the warehouse, picking a limp Quinn up into his arms. The kid mumbled against his chest as Kenn waded through terrified employees, giving them little attention as he returned to the car.

That shit had been much easier than he had planned, and he hated it. Hated how easy it had been to take Mia and how easy it had been to get her back once they knew where she was, because now she had suffered through so much. He wasn't sure what their future held for them or how difficult it'd be to navigate with all these new pieces.

But he was sure of two things: Soon Mia would be back in their arms and Cross would be dead. But first, Matthias and Nichlas would make him wish he had never existed.

NINETY-TWO

MATTHIAS

Red was the color he saw as he ripped the door off the handle, barging into the testing room and picking up the first thing his hands fell on. A small tin stand was chucked across the room, one of the occupants yelping in pain as he clattered to the floor with metal on top of him.

A wild grin split his face as he rushed at the next occupant, unable to see the terror on his face but knowing that it was there by the trembles of his body. Matthias thought about chucking this body, too, but he needed blood. He needed their head. He needed them to understand everything he was feeling. Everything he had felt when they had stolen his woman. When they had tried to kill Jan. When they had thought shipping Nichlas off would keep them from protecting their family.

His hands moved to cup the body's face as he chuckled, the sound deep and terrifying before twisting, *hard*. A loud snap erupted into the room, the body falling limp and crumbling to the floor.

Matthias straightened up, rolling his shoulders back as he stared ahead, looking for more victims to enact his rage on, eyes locking with the blond-haired bitch who had tried to get him locked up. Her squeals were music to his ears as he marched forward.

"Stop! I was just doing–"

But he couldn't hear her. He didn't want to either. Mia's demons were meant to die, and Natalie was one of those. That bitch would roast in hell, and so would he, but when he arrived, he was going to be her worst nightmare all over again.

His hand swiped one of the tools from a nearby table, clutching at the cool metal between his fingers. Natalie squealed again and tried to take off, but Matthias was faster and his hand shot out and caught hold of her hair, yanking her back against a wall. He crowded her space, his smile widening even further, that little tool feeling quite comfortable in his hands. Had it been anyone else wielding the scalpel, they would have done minimal damage, but Matthias was lethal with *anything* he chose as a weapon.

"You made her suffer. Now it's your turn." Matthias couldn't have stopped if he wanted to as the scalpel scrapped against the woman's cheek, Natalie howling to be released. "Feel her pain." He growled, dragging the sharp edge down until it connected with her chest. "My pain." The edge sunk into her flesh, blood trickling from the open wound. "Their pain." He continued south, Natalie yelling and fighting against him, but a grip on her neck, cutting off her air supply, gave her little room to move.

"You're a psychopath! Get off of me!" She kicked forward, pain shooting through his leg, but Matthias didn't budge. This was needed. He needed to let the bitch understand who she had been messing with, which is why he pulled the scalpel out and started a new line from her shoulder down to her stomach. Blood splattered across his face, the excitement of watching Natalie sagging against the wall heightening his adrenaline. He made another line. And another. Until she was just a mass of artwork, Matthias losing his mind to the darkness.

NINETY-THREE

NICHLAS

His eyes first landed on their woman sprawled on the table, then on Cross, who was leaning over her one moment and then pointing a gun at his face the next. He seemed shocked to see Nichlas standing there, his hand shaking a little.

Cross had always been on desk duty because of his nerves, and now Nichlas understood why. Shaking in the heat of the battle? Laughable.

The man's eyes darted outside, fear flooding his expression as he realized what had taken place already. Kenn worked quickly when he needed to. Jan skirted around Nichlas, Cross' eyes widening even further.

"You're supposed to be fucking dead. Wait … it worked?" Even on his death bed, the fucker was more interested in his experiment than the lives he had ruined, that he was currently ruining. Nichlas had worked with the man for years, but he fucking hated that this was the man that had been sitting behind that desk.

It hurt that Nichlas had never gotten even an inkling of what Cross was capable of.

Nichlas watched as Jan gathered Mia's body up in his arms, his eyes searching for any signs of life, a tight smile on his lips as he found her heartbeat. He granted Nichlas a pert nod before slipping past him, leaving Nichlas to face Cross.

In the background, Nichlas saw Matthias ripping Natalie apart, and while *that* would have to be dealt with, Nichlas had his own demons to face. Cross' smile had disappeared, gun still shaking as Nichlas closed the distance between them and ripped the gun from his hand.

"If you aren't going to shoot me," Nichlas seethed, "then don't point a fucking gun at my head." The man was shorter than him and hadn't had half the training Nichlas had, making it way too easy for Nichlas to wrangle him onto the same cot that Mia had been moments ago. He had planned to rip the guy apart, but his new plan was so, *so* much better.

"You don't understand!" Cross pleaded, still worried about his experiment. "I have to—"

Nichlas landed a punch in the fucker's face and then two more for good luck, smiling as blood sprayed onto his face. Cross cried out at the pain, heightening Nichlas' desire to make the fucker truly hurt, the way Mia had.

He had seen Mia's face when Jan carried her out. It had been bruised and beaten to hell, her throat swollen, her skin flushed. If the physical horrors of what she had experienced didn't scar her, the mental ones would.

And Cross was going to pay for every last one of those.

"You're supposed to be hours from here." Cross tried to fight against Nichlas' hold, but it was worthless, Nichlas strapping the guy to the table with expertise. Years of training had made him a ruthless machine, years of training Cross could only dream of.

"You're stupid to think you could have won. Thane's on the way, *Cross*." The man shrieked, struggling against the restraints like a little bitch, but Nichlas was having too much fun watching the man who had nearly ruined his happy ending scream for help. Did that make him a bad person? Probably. He didn't care.

The moment Nichlas had called Thane and debriefed him on the situation, his boss gave him a thirty minute window to retrieve his woman. Nichlas hadn't expected the permission but he wasn't going to waste it. Whatever happened at this warehouse in the remaining fifteen minutes would be off the record, and while Nichlas knew he should leave the fucker alive for questioning, he also believed Cross had lost that right.

Lost the right to breathe the same air as Mia.

Grinning, he looked up to see Matthias still driving a scalpel into a fileted carcass. His boy had lost his mind, trying to dole out every last bit of justice he could.

Nichlas chucked a tool across the room, his purple-eyed barista whipping around to meet his gaze. Blood covered his front, liquid dripping down his face, his eyes violently dark with unspoken promises.

Bringing him back was going to be nearly impossible this time, but right now, making Cross suffer was more important.

"Matty, I need one of those jars by you. Be a doll and bring it." Back at the cafe, Matthias would have fought him over the nicknames, but the kid swiped a few of the jars and stalked forward, plopping them onto Cross' lap. The man kicked, trying to ward off the inevitable as Nichlas patted Matthias' cheek lovingly. "You did good, Matty. Now I need you to use that pesky little shower over there." Matthias stared at Cross, ignoring the command, the guy pissing his pants at the bloodied sight.

"I—"

Nichlas just shook his head, knowing that if Matthias waltzed outside like that, they'd catch all the wrong attention, not to mention what would happen if Mia saw his bloodied clothes. "I'm serious. Mia would be proud." Of that, he wasn't sure, but they were words Matthias needed to hear right now. "*Shower.*" Matthias stalked over to the pulley system and reached upward to release the emergency water, looking like a drowned rat when a cascade of water fell, scarlet mixing with it on the floor and washing away the sins of the last few minutes. It wouldn't be perfect, but it'd be enough.

Satisfied, Nichlas turned back to Cross.

Science wasn't his forte, but he absolutely knew what he *wasn't* supposed to do with the substances. He didn't even know what he was looking at as he picked up one of the jars and swirled it around. The nearly clear liquid didn't look like anything special. With a shrug, he pried open one container, Cross stiffening.

"What are you going to do? Wait! You're not supposed to mix those! They're different strains ... that's years' worth of work!" He continued to ramble as Nichlas dumped them into a nearby bin, his eyes trained on the crazy concoction he was making. Fumes rose from the mixture, Nichlas stepping back slightly when he lifted it and walked it back to Cross. The man screamed for help again, but that only gave Nichlas the opening he needed as he began pouring it down the man's throat.

Cross sputtered and wriggled on the bed, trying to yell through his death sentence, but the sounds were soon changed to mere vibrations of his vocal cords as he struggled to breathe. His hands and feet curled as his lungs fought for air, that pesky green substance expanding and filling his airways until it was bulging out of his mouth and crawling upward like ectoplasm in the air.

Nichlas stared in awe as Cross' throat expanded with the substance, the man's eyes doing the same until Nichlas was sure they'd pop out of the man's head. A dark chuckle sounded behind him – from Matthias – when Cross' throat turned red, veins bursting within. Bones shattered and bent outward, poking through the flesh until scarlet spurts escaped into the room.

One last cry later, Cross was dead on the very table where he had taken so many lives. Nichlas stared at the horrific sight a moment longer before joining Matthias outside and moving toward the car. He wanted to believe that the worst part was over, but that was just wishful thinking, he realized when he caught sight of their woman curled up in Jan's arms, the man rocking her back to sleep to escape her nightmares.

NINETY-FOUR

MIA

Mia awoke suddenly and started scratching at her neck, mouth open as she silently screamed for air. Her voice failed her as beeps and machines whirred around her, fear overwhelming her senses as she scrambled about the bed. Tears streamed down her face as she panicked, waiting for the inevitable moment when Cross strolled back in to try yet another test.

He hadn't let up the entire time, growing increasingly more ruthless with each experiment, laughing as each one succeeded. Lucas had tried giving her breaks, but not even his soft demeanor could make the pain any better. She couldn't breathe anymore, her lungs giving up on her, her eyes sliding closed as she succumbed to the trials. And still, Cross hadn't stopped. She'd wake up from unconsciousness, unable to breathe before passing out again. And *still*, Cross continued.

Mia noticed her arms were free and she rolled over, using the last bit of strength to claim her freedom. She wanted to let everyone know she hadn't gone without a fight. She wanted Cross to know that she was a stubborn woman to the end. He might have taken her father and Jan from her, but he would not take her will to live.

Two strong arms caught her just as she tumbled out of bed, Mia weakly beating against the hard chest until she was sobbing for help.

A quiet voice tried to calm her, a familiar hardness to his tone, with none of the usual power behind it. "Just me, Mia. You're safe now. It'll be all right. We're here."

Jan?

She stilled in the man's arms, leaning her head back just enough to see her man standing before her alive and well. Mia blinked several times, unsure of the reality she was staring at. Cross had told her that he was dead, that he had taken from her the happy ending she had been looking forward to.

But here he was, staring at her with those beautiful dark eyes, seeing straight into her soul. Mia reached up to cup his face, her fingers delicately running across his cheeks.

He's here.

Jan gave her a small smile, his arms wrapping around her waist as he pulled her closer and dipped his head to kiss her. Their lips met in a passionate embrace, tears flowing down her cheeks as Mia realized that her man was actually here. She tightened her grip as if he were going to leave her, letting him dominate the kiss until he was basically leaning her over the bed she had woken up in.

Another wave of panic washed over her, and she pushed away from him, fighting for air, Jan releasing her in a state of confusion. Mia grabbed at her neck, unable to separate the feeling of the kiss from the one of being suffocated. It was too new. Too raw.

Her other men stumbled in, as well as a nurse who chided her for climbing out of bed. Mia wasn't ready for the bombardment of people filing into her room and she cringed against the mattress, opening her mouth to scream again and yet … there was no sound.

More tears streamed down her cheeks as she trembled, her nurse recognizing the signs and shoving her men out of the room. They tried to fight her on it, but she was firm. She returned to the bed and helped Mia back into it.

"Sweetheart, I've only heard snippets of what happened, but you've been through one hell of an ordeal. Your brothers seem quite protective of you." She gave Mia a small smile as she began checking machines. "I'm Patty, and I've been looking after you."

Mia frowned at the term "brothers," but she couldn't quite refute it without her voice. Looking around, she didn't see any of the machines from Cross' lab. She wanted to feel relieved, but her heart was still racing even though she fucking hated reacting like that. Her men were probably kicking themselves for terrifying her, but she couldn't help her reaction. Once again, she was the one ruining things. "Now, your throat's going to be a bit sore for a while. We've got some great options for therapy and some home exercises you can do to stretch your vocal cords, whichever you prefer. You've got some light bruising and a mild concussion, but other than that, you're doing great."

Patty's eyes didn't seem sincere, but her words were soft, which was a strange combination considering her profession. Mia struggled a little against the blood pressure cuff that Patty wrapped around her arm, her breathing ramping again.

"Count with me to ten, Mia. Then it's off. One, two, three, that's good, keep counting. Ten! All done." The cuff was undone and Mia shifted away from the nurse. She wished her men were back in the room now, because Patty was making her uncomfortable. Mia wasn't even sure why. "Get some rest. I'll keep your brothers outside, all right?"

Mia tried to grunt, her hands fisting at her sides as she tried to find a way to let Patty know that they weren't her brothers.

The nurse sauntered over to the door, yelling at the men crowding around the entrance before looking back at Mia. "They're really insistent. You want them?"

Mia nodded as hard as she could despite the hounding pain in her head.

"All right, boys. Slowly. She's been through a lot." Mia smiled at the growl that sent Patty scurrying out of the room, Jan and Nichlas timidly reentering, a mixture of relief and worry plastered on their faces. Her eyes peeled to the door, waiting for the other two, but Jan closed it behind them.

Nichlas approached her slowly, cautiously, eyes glued to hers. "Matthias … needs a moment to calm down. Fuck, Mia." He gathered her up in his arms, trying hard not to smother her. She gripped his shirt for comfort, making sure she had a pocket of air to breathe. "I thought we were going to lose you."

Jan patted Nichlas' back and he released her, both of them finding seats by her bed. They each laid hands on her legs, Nichlas taking a moment to observe her before giving her a more thorough explanation. "We're at a federal base. My superior—" Mia's eyes grew wide again, but he just shook her head. "Cross is dead. You're safe here. My superior is one of the ones who helped us get you out."

She knew they weren't telling her everything because they weren't trying to overwhelm her, which she was glad. Still, there were so many things she needed to know. Now that she wasn't freaking out every five seconds, Mia needed one thing – Quinn.

"Quinn's in surgery, but he's fine."

Mia nodded, gaze trailing to Jan, needing him beside her again. He was *alive*. She reached for him and he complied, leaning over the side of the bed, but it wasn't enough. Weakly, she tugged at his shirt until he understood, climbing onto the mattress and shifting her into his lap as she curled up against his chest.

Her men were alive. They were here, with her. And Cross was dead.

She hoped he suffered.

NINETY-FIVE

KENN

Nichlas had slipped out of Mia's room at some point, telling them that she needed to rest and that bombarding her, even as relieved as they were that she was alive, was only going to set them back further. Nichlas nodded to Matthias, who was stuffed in the hallway corner, his knees pulled tight against his chest, head tucked in his lap. For such a big guy, he looked positively small in that position, a position he'd been holding for the past thirty minutes.

When Nichlas and Matthias had returned to the car, the kid looking like a drowned rat, a crazy look in his eyes, Kenn knew that they had a whole bunch of issues they were going to have to pick apart soon. The nightmares Mia had suffered would be bad enough, but Matthias had let out his demons – for good reason – it was just, putting them *away* was going to be difficult.

Nichlas hadn't described anything that had happened in that room, but Kenn could guess. It was the main reason they had all agreed Matthias wasn't going anywhere near Mia until he had taken a few showers *and* calmed the hell down. Kenn didn't believe he'd hurt Mia, but scaring her was another matter entirely.

"How long has he been like that?" Nichlas jabbed over at the corner.

Kenn sighed, his shoulders dropping at the pitiful sight. As he stared, he realized that Matthias was crying. "For a while. It's bad, Nichlas. *Really* bad." Nichlas nodded. His expression was haunted, telling Kenn that Nichlas had been the one to end it. Whatever Matthias had done, Kenn wasn't sure he wanted to know, and yet that pesky curiosity got in the way. "What happened in there?"

"Cross is dead, and Matthias made Natalie pay for every piece of shit she tried to pull." He grit his teeth together, gaze narrowing. "It's not enough. It won't ever be enough. I trusted that guy!" Nichlas swiveled around and threw a punch at the wall, crying out as his knuckles hit plaster. Kenn knew the man had to be hurting more than the rest of them. They had almost lost their woman, but Nichlas had lost a man he had partnered with for years.

Kenn knew Nichlas was blaming himself for something he couldn't have possibly figured out. There hadn't been any signs, and Nichlas had been taught to follow his orders without pushing back. Kenn spared Matthias a glance, but the kid hadn't even looked up.

Jan exited the room a few moments later, shaking his head when they looked at him for an update. "She's asleep now, but it's going to be tough." His eyes drifted to Matthias, his look sobering as he did something out of character and approached the kid. Jan said nothing as he slipped onto the floor beside him and drew Matthias closer. The kid gave him some resistance and then folded, clutching at Jan's shirt, weeping into the man's chest. It hadn't been what Jan had ultimately been going for, but the man just placed a soft kiss on Matthias' forehead while stroking his hair to calm him down.

Kenn raised an eyebrow in question, but Jan didn't answer it.

"What now?" Jan whispered, holding Matthias even tighter as the kid relaxed into the embrace, the tremble softening. It was strange watching them together and yet just a little too perfect. But that's what they needed right now.

Nichlas leaned back against the wall. "They want me in for questioning. No, not like that. Just to explain everything that happened in town, explain Cross' involvement. Shit, it's gonna look like I disappeared again."

Kenn could see the conflict in the man's eyes, especially because he knew how those interrogations went. They were always drawn out, as every piece of evidence was compiled and investigated. A case like this could take months to figure out, and Nichlas would be wrapped up the entire time, away from their woman while she was trying to heal. It wasn't ideal in the slightest, but they had to put it to rest now. Letting it fester wouldn't do anyone any good.

"How long?" Jan stared at Nichlas for an answer.

"I should have left already. I just needed to see her awake." He pushed off the wall, looking over at Matthias, before making his way over to him and pressing a soft kiss to the kid's head and then headed down the hall. It helped they were already on base, but Nichlas was the only one with clearance to be wandering around freely. Kenn worried about Nichlas' emotional mindset almost as much as Matthias', but there wasn't anything he could do at this point.

Kenn strolled over to the other two and slid down on the other side of Matthias, placing a firm hand on his thigh, letting the kid know he had support. His phone vibrated in his pocket and he pulled it out, letting out a bitter laugh when he saw Detective Hanson's name scroll across the screen.

"Yeah?"

"Kenn? Thank god. I heard about everything and I'm—"

Kenn burst out laughing, cutting his boss off, and shook his head. "Yeah, no. I'll be handing in my resignation the next chance I get." He wasn't going to hear his boss out. He wasn't going to listen to excuses or anything else that the man had to say. It was obvious that Cross' dealings went way up the chain and everyone had been paid off to look the other way. Kenn wasn't going to work for someone like that. His boss sputtered on the other side of the phone, but Kenn wasn't done. "I speak for both of us." Jan nodded wholeheartedly.

"But you're my best operatives."

"And you're dishonorable as shit." Kenn ended the call, shifting slightly, wondering what the hell they were going to do now. He'd been a detective for as long as he could remember. It was one of the only things he had been good at. Sure, his boss could give them glowing recommendations, but Kenn wasn't sure he wanted to step into another role, answering to someone who could be just as dishonest.

Not to mention that they had an entirely new dynamic to think about.

His eyes drifted to Matthias, who had sat up, his expression devoid of any emotion, his gaze locked on Mia's door. Kenn knew the kid wanted to see her. He also knew that neither one of them were ready for that confrontation.

His mind lingered on Matthias' unspoken confessions, the idea that there could be something more to them. When Matthias turned to look at him, the faintest smile on his lips, something bloomed in Kenn's chest – a spark of hope, something resembling the happiness they had before this nightmare started, and at that moment, Kenn knew.

He knew.

That something more was possible. That something *more* was what Kenn wanted.

Unfortunately, getting past all the goddamn hurdles was going to be a bitch.

NINETY-SIX

MIA

Being able to sit up in bed was a welcome surprise, Patty propping her up before leaving her to her own devices. The silence was unbearable as she sat there, waiting for something to happen, staring at the door, hoping and praying that one of her men would step through. Between a host of doctors and even a psychiatrist who had attempted to prod into how she was feeling using yes or no answers, her men hadn't entered. When lunch rolled around, Mia perked up, gesturing to the men parked outside the door.

The nurse just frowned. "Your brothers? I was told not to let them in. That it's too much."

Mia ignored the onset of a headache as she shook her head frantically. She smacked away the lone tear that had escaped, wanting the company so fucking badly so that she didn't have to sit alone with her thoughts. They were killing her at this point. Cross' face had been permanently burned into her retinas, and she needed something else to focus on that wasn't suffocation or the terror she had experienced.

Knowing that Quinn had exited surgery and was now safely back at home with Ma was helping a little. But not enough.

"Please," she whined hoarsely.

The nurse didn't seem convinced but placed the tray of food by her bedside and slowly opened the door. "You need *anything* and you just press that red button, all right?" Mia nodded, leaning forward, waiting to see those familiar faces, a smile cracking between her cheeks when Kenn filed in, followed by Jan and Matthias.

"Ma'am, we're not her brothers." Mia had been waiting for this moment, settling back against her pillows as Kenn added. "We're her boyfriends."

"All of you?" The nurse squealed. "Mia … I …" The nurse looked to Mia to confirm, grunting when Mia just smiled wider. "That's … strange. I'll be just down the hall. Red button, Mia." Then the nurse was gone, leaving Mia with three of her men. She looked to the door, silently asking where Nichlas was.

"He needed to wrap up some loose ends. He'll be back."

She noticed that none of them had approached. A frown replaced her smile the longer she stared at them, Matthias refusing to meet her gaze. Slowly, she slipped from the bed, testing her legs. They all rushed toward her but halted when she cringed against the mattress. This was going to be a chore, dating men with such powerful auras after the nightmare she had just been through, but she could do this.

One wobbly step at a time, Mia made her way to Matthias, reaching up to grab his face so their eyes met. She hadn't been prepared to see the absence of the charming barista she had first met a few weeks ago.

Everything hurt, pain flooding her system, but she knew they both needed this moment. She tapped his cheek softly, Matthias melting into the touch in a way that seemed so unlike him. Her heart broke for him, unsure of what her men had gone through when she had been away.

Had this been a few weeks ago, she would not have understood their emotions, their desire to see that she was okay. She wouldn't have known what to do with their love, their protection, or their possessive auras. Seeing Matthias so lost would have terrified her, because having someone love her so much like that? It didn't make sense.

It still didn't. That their love was so strong and yet so new.

"Matthias," Mia whispered, slipping her other hand to the other side of his face. "Come back." Her legs were about to give out, but she needed her purple-eyed barista back. It wasn't going to be a permanent fix, she knew that much. Jan had explained to her that the only path forward was therapy that Matthias refused to get. She stumbled against his chest, the movement making his eyes flash with worry.

His arms wrapped around her, a semblance of the man he used to be staring back at her.

"Here. With me," Mia croaked out. She'd regret talking later, as Patty had told her to rest her vocal cords, but seeing Matthias respond was *everything*. Matthias let out a little cry as he pressed his forehead against hers, gathering her up against his chest just as her legs gave out.

Two more hands, firm and comforting, landed on her shoulders, enveloping her in a cocoon of warmth that she had been missing. She closed her eyes as she rested there, her breath evening out until sleep began to overwhelm her, Jan giggling as her body sagged. The deep sound was foreign but lightened the mood as he picked her up and transported her back into the bed.

"Did he suffer?" she asked, knowing there were so many more important things to hear about, but that was the only thing she wanted to know. Mia grabbed Matthias' hand to ground him, the kid shuffling a little closer as Kenn nodded, giving her a soft smile.

That's all she needed right now. And when Nichlas returned, she would be complete.

NINETY-SEVEN

NICHLAS

It had been nonstop questioning for the past six hours, everyone wondering how they had missed Cross' involvement in such a dark experiment. His boss, Thane Watts, had told him in so many words to keep his involvement in the warehouse on the down low, only revealing that he had found out *where* Cross was but hadn't engaged.

Nichlas stared down at the ick on his clothes that was beginning to make his skin crawl. He hadn't even showered since the whole ordeal, let alone taken a nap, and his body was starting to rebel against him. He was eager to get back to Mia and the others, especially since he couldn't so much as contact them while he was on base. He had, however, received word from one of the nurses that Mia had been given the green light to return home in a day or two. He had also heard whispers that weren't so nice regarding her "boyfriends" and the fact that she was a selfish bitch.

He had heard worse over the years, but he hadn't loved anyone like Mia. It hurt a little more this time around.

"Nichlas, we could use you." Thane waved him over. Nichlas grunted and pushed out of the chair he had parked himself in, wondering when they were at least going to let him take a breather. He had been placed in one of the conference rooms – one of the many reasons Nichlas knew he wasn't in trouble.

"You need me to run through the events or–"

Thane cut him off. "No. I need you to pretend you weren't even there. Nichlas, what I'm about to tell you is highly classified information." Nichlas frowned, unsure if he wanted to take on another mission right now. He wanted to return home. He wanted out. He wanted a *break*.

Fuck it. Fuck all of it.

It was as if Thane could see right through him. "Son, I need you to listen to me."

"I can do that," Nichlas responded, although he knew it was never *just* listening.

Thane sighed, his expression darkening. "Cross was into some dark things. He had his hands in a few pots we weren't even aware existed." Nichlas knew that much. Cross had blindsided everyone. He had been that wonderfully dorky kid who sat behind a desk. Only a few hours ago did Nichlas find out how truly evil the guy was, going so far as to sacrifice his own wife for a torture device that hadn't even been approved. "Those pots, Nichlas, we have to find them."

Nichlas reined in his anger, biting back the remarks he wanted to spew. He was done with the shady shit that kept coming their way. He was done running off in the middle of the night, not knowing when he would return. It had never really bothered him before, but now? He was just *tired*. "Respectfully, whatever you're about to ask me, I'd like to decline."

"Respectfully, I'd like to ask you to reconsider."

"And why's that?"

Thane unearthed a small folder and slid it to him. "Look through this and then come find me when you've made your decision. I know you want to return to your family, but regardless of what you choose, I will make sure they are well taken care of. I've also got a new handler for you."

"I don't–"

"You know the rules, Nichlas. Active agents require a handler. Don't fight me on this. Just read through the file and then come talk to me." Nichlas opened his mouth to protest, to let Thane know that he didn't need some file to make a decision, but his boss wasn't one to beat around the bush. He nodded and returned to his chair, pulling out the few documents shoved inside. A flutter of pictures fell in his lap, Nichlas frowning at the discovery.

His face was in a few of them, as was Matthias', but he couldn't understand why. It had been a while since they had been on active duty, and he had no idea why these memories would have changed his mind. If Thane was threatening him …

"Shit."

In the background, Nichlas could just make out a barrel with the word: ORCSORB written on it in military print. Cross' little experiment hadn't just come out of the blue. It had been years in the making, and it had involved Matthias, no less. Another set of pictures were from the town they had just spent the last few weeks in, unassuming pictures of everyday life – until Nichlas noticed a glaring similarity between his active-duty days and Mia's home.

He ruffled through the papers, reading through reports that had been in Cross' possession. He didn't understand half of the formulas, but there was something else, something worrisome that had him frantically searching for more information.

Nichlas stormed into Thane's office, shaking the files at his boss. "What the fuck is this shit?" On any other day, he would have been yelled at for speaking to his boss like that. It was a good thing it wasn't just any other day.

"Have you made a decision?"

"Who the fuck is this?"

Thane leaned back in his chair and grinned, but it didn't quite reach his eyes. "That's what we would like to know. No one remembers who he is. No one really remembers seeing him. Seeing the way you just came in here, you don't remember him either. He's quite good at falling beneath the radar and yet, we don't know why. We do, however, believe he's involved."

Nichlas' face drained of color as his fists clenched, those papers crinkling, the sound deafening in the silence. "It says Stage One, Thane. *Stage One.* Tell me that—"

Thane nodded. "We have reason to believe that there are more stages. That man is a clue, amongst other things."

"And you know I'll take it because he knows who I am."

"You always did want to protect your family, but I'm giving you a choice. If you don't want in, I'll have you set up under protective detail and—"

Nichlas shook his head, knowing full well that there was no way they'd agree to include Mia in witness protection with them. She wasn't permanent in their group unless someone proposed to her, and it was much too soon. "I'll do it."

"Great, let's go meet your handler, shall we?"

"Can I at least check in with—"

"Your phone's still on, right? You've got until I retrieve your new handler to check on your family, and then we begin. I won't bullshit you and tell you that this is going to be quick, but I will let you in on a little secret. Something that hasn't been signed off on but I'm fully prepared to stand behind."

Nichlas blinked a few times, unsure he was ready for whatever Thane had to say. "That sounds suspicious as hell."

"Your … team, for lack of a better word, was highly effective in neutralizing the threat from Stage One. If your team is interested, I would be glad to have them around for this next mission."

He didn't even know what to say to that. Thane was offering him a chance to pick his own team, to bring in Jan and Kenn's expertise and Matthias' profiling skills. If they agreed, it would be the first time they had ever truly worked together with agency backing, no less. It would be a wonderfully lethal group that would be nearly unstoppable.

It was almost too enticing to resist.

"I thought you'd like that idea. You'll be home by the end of the week. Discuss it with them then. I'll give you some time to figure things out. We'll go from there. Now, call your boys and that sweet little girl. I've heard she's a fighter."

"Yeah, she is." Nichlas cracked a small smile as he whipped out his phone and called Kenn for an update. Hearing that this shit wasn't over made things a bit worse but knowing that he could return home by week's end was something he was looking forward to.

NINETY-EIGHT

MIA

It had been a long three days in the hospital as her injuries healed, but she was more than happy to leave when Thursday morning rolled around. Her voice came back slowly, as well as her comfort level around her men, but she was still jumpy when they got too loud or crowded around her bed. Even those long, tongue-curling kisses Mia loved so much were still a no-go, as memories of being suffocated by ORCSORB plagued her mind.

The nightmares hadn't gone anywhere either, although every time she woke, Matthias or Jan had been holding her, rocking her back to sleep. Kenn had been in and out of the room, making calls, checking up on her, and yelling at her nurse whenever Mia didn't have something.

Quinn was thriving back at home with Ma, constantly texting Mia for updates and sending her funny memes to alleviate the somber mood. The doctors said it'd be a while before he could walk normally again, but the kid was in high spirits and would be moving to Colorado in the fall for college. All in all, it could have gone worse.

Now that she had been discharged, the only thing she still needed was Nichlas.

She leaned forward and peeked out the car window to see the cafe that had brought her so much joy last week. It's where she had found her forever and yet, this place no longer felt like home. The car door swung open and Jan slid an arm around her waist, hoisting her off the seat before placing her firmly on the ground.

Her body trembled as she remembered the last time she had been here and the horrors she had been through, stepping into Jan's chest for comfort. The town seemed emptier than usual, no passersby wandering to see her panicked reaction. It didn't make her feel better, as memories of what had happened in her lab attacked her thoughts.

Jan lying there, suffocating.
Helpless to save Quinn or her man.
So scared.
Terrified.
In pain.

She didn't even notice when she came to that she was sitting on one of the booths inside of the cafe, Matthias kneeling before her, encouraging her to take deep breaths. His eyes were dark with worry, his hands on her knees as he applied just enough pressure to bring her back to the present. Mia looked around to see Jan and Kenn staring at her with the same expression, her breathing erratic as she choked on a sob.

"You're safe here, Mia. He can't hurt you anymore."

Matthias was right, but words didn't get rid of the memories. Being in his arms made things better, though, as she leaned down to press a quick kiss on his lips. Matthias took that as a win and gathered her up in his arms and set her in his lap as he stole her seat. She curled up against his chest, relishing the safety of his embrace. It wouldn't help her sleep, but it helped her remember she wasn't alone.

For so long – between her mother, Anders, Natalie, Kingsley, and the rest of the town – she had been the outcast. The one no one liked. The girl who played with dead people. And now, she was the focal point of a relationship between four gorgeously intimidating men who would do anything to save her. To have her. To love her.

Her thoughts drifted to the days she had spent in the hospital and the shift in their relationship. No one had come outright and said anything, but she had noticed both Jan and Kenn doling out little kisses and touches to Matthias when they thought she was asleep. She hadn't noticed before but realized how beautiful it was to watch Matthias open up in a way that seemed to heal his tortured heart.

Mia decided to ask about it later when nightmares weren't torturing her every time she fell asleep and was a little more rested.

"Mia, let's get you upstairs. You need to rest." Kenn stepped toward her, but she just shook her head. Sleeping was the last thing she wanted to do even if her entire body felt weak. Her throat wasn't as sore anymore, but her words still came out a little scratchy if she didn't drink enough water.

She shifted slightly, her gaze falling on her office across the street. She could just barely make out the front door through the cafe's windows, a shiver running down her spine.

Jan immediately noticed from his perch against the counter. "Angel, we don't have to stay here." Mia frowned and threw him a confused glare that he immediately responded to. "We came for a job. It's over now."

Kenn rounded the counter, obviously looking for coffee. He seemed to find it by the giggle that slipped from his lips before he turned around to face Mia. "Where would we even go? We have too many lethal skills to just get a job at McDonald's." That brought a smile to Mia's face, but she could see the seriousness in their expressions. They weren't joking about picking up and leaving, and it was almost a kick to the gut that they were even thinking about it.

Jan nodded, pulling up a chair beside her. "Kenn is missing his little property in a little city called Blossom, near the coast. What is it, like 100 miles south of here? Matthias can open a shop anywhere, and I was offered a professorship in Kenn's city a few months ago. It'd be a good change of pace since we won't be working as detectives anymore."

Kenn nodded. "Sounds good to me. I haven't been back there in like five years."

Mia tensed in Matthias' lap, looking between the three of them. They really were going to leave, weren't they? She should have known her happy ending wasn't going to last. "You'd … you'd leave?" She slowly crawled off Matthias' lap, straightening her clothes and making her way to the counter.

Matthias followed her, placing a gentle hand on the small of her back as Jan approached the counter as well. Kenn grabbed the coffee pot and snatched two cups from the drying rack. "Mia, what's stopping us? We all have skills and connections outside of the agencies we've worked for. Nichlas still has his missions, but he can be stationed anywhere. Mia, how's that sound?" Once again, she looked at all of them, tears streaming down her cheeks. She didn't know how to answer until Kenn added, "Mia, we're not leaving *you*."

The other two burst out laughing at her bewilderment, Jan kissing the top of her head as he passed her one of the fresh cups of coffee from Kenn. "Silly girl, we can stay here if you want. Just thought you might want some different scenery. But Mia, we're going where *you* go, not the other way around. Kenn's place is large enough for all of us until we figure things out." She clutched the coffee in her hand, the absence of a nightmare the only thing that told her she wasn't dreaming. Mia nodded slowly, watching their faces light up. "Great, it's decided."

Mia stared at Jan, shocked. "Now?"

"Unless you'd like to wait?"

She shared another glance with all of them before sipping her coffee again. There wasn't anything tying her to the town anymore. Sure, she'd be leaving behind her father's legacy, but knowing what had taken place there, Mia didn't want any part of it. Maybe it was time to be a little reckless and leave town. She had a bit of savings, and spending time with her men seemed like a great idea, one that was getting better by the minute. "No, no. I don't want to wait. Is Nichlas coming with us?"

They collectively nodded, her cheeks warming as images of all four of her men and herself sharing one house, far away from the horrors of the past two weeks.

Matthias drew her back against his chest as she stared down at her coffee, the mingled hazelnut and chocolate aroma not settling the lingering fears she still had. "I just ... I feel selfish. You guys are all doing this for me and–"

She heard Kenn bite out a laugh in between gulps, noticing for the first time the dark bags beneath his eyes. Jan's, too, for that matter. Kenn grabbed the pot and poured himself another cup, Matthias scowling from behind her. It didn't deter him. "You can't think like that. You're our world." We love you and want a future with you, *wherever* that takes us. And as our girlfriend, you are allowed to be selfish. We *want* you to be. Because you are ours and we are yours."

Mia looked between Jan and Kenn, wondering if this was the time to bring up the burning question. They'd have to discuss it eventually and for some reason, it felt like they were keeping it from her because they weren't sure how she was going to react. She gave them a small smile as she placed her cup on the counter.

"But you're also his." She gestured to Matthias, her barista tensing behind her. The other two fell silent. "Why didn't you just tell me?"

"Didn't know how to," Matthias whispered. "Didn't know if you would leave. "Mia swiveled around, reaching up to hold his face in her hands. "I love that you feel comfortable enough with them to be yourself. I just ..." She squashed those pesky thoughts that were trying to tell her she wasn't allowed to be selfish. "I just don't want you to stop loving me."

Matthias gave her one of his famously boyish grins, gently wrapping his arms around her. "Not even an option." And then he kissed her, releasing her before that annoying panic could bubble up in her chest.

NINETY-NINE

JAN

She was safe, but it would be a long road to full recovery. They all had come too fucking close to losing each other. His first priority was making sure Mia was safe and healthy, that she knew they wanted her for more than her body or her ability to calm Matthias when he was going off the rails.

Despite resisting multiple times, they had finally gotten Mia to rest, but not before she told them that she didn't want to return to her office or her house. Jan wholeheartedly agreed that the less stress they could impose on her, the better, and both of those locations were full of triggers.

He was going to make sure she knew just how precious she was to all of them, how much they loved her, and how much they wanted to spend the rest of their lives with her.

Rest of our lives?

He shouldn't have been surprised that that's where his thoughts had been straying recently, especially with all of the fantasies that had been running through his head of her walking barefoot through their house, pregnant with their child, and positively radiant. It didn't help that some of those fantasies included waking up to a naked Matthias in his bed, their beautiful pregnant woman on the *other* side of Matthias.

After they had all agreed to pack up and move in together, those images had only grown bolder in the last few hours until Jan had to slip away and take care of his needs in a lengthy cold shower.

It hadn't helped though, after gorging themselves on Chinese food and now splayed on the couches, resting after a full day of cleaning up the shop they were leaving behind. Mia had spent most of her time with Kenn, both of them showing up moments before dinner looking freshly washed, Mia clad only in one of Kenn's large shirts.

He looked like a kid in a candy shop with the way he kept staring at her, her long legs resting out in front of her, a tempting little treat that Jan wanted to partake in. Unfortunately, he was torn, Matthias' arm curled around Jan's stomach, his fingers drawing little circles on his hip just beneath the shirt. Jan tried to keep from shifting, but his cock was growing hard from the connection even though they had never gone further than kissing.

Jan tore his eyes from the TV and to Matthias, whose eyes were half-lidded with disinterest, his fingers slowly moving to grip Jan's waist, a movement that had Jan biting back a groan as more heat jumped down to his cock. He felt like a high school boy as he grew hard, the little smirk appearing on Matthias' face telling Jan that none of this was innocent. He tried to shift without alerting Mia and Kenn next to them, but Mia's eyes snapped over to him at the same time Matthias decided to place his lips on Jan's neck.

She gasped, both Matthias and Jan freezing at the sound. She had told them she was okay with it, but saying it and seeing it were two wildly different things. Jan leaned forward, ready to apologize when Kenn didn't even wait before slipping two fingers between their girl's thighs. Kenn's attention was trained on Mia, watching for discomfort before dragging his digits through her folds. "Keep going, Matthias. She's fucking soaked."

Matthias gladly accepted the challenge as his lips reattached to Jan's throat, his grip tightening on Jan's hip until Jan involuntarily thrust forward. Jan watched with rapt attention as Kenn gently slid to the floor and spread Mia's thighs, still watching her expression. "Sweetheart, I'm going to eat you out while you watch our boys over there. How's that sound?" This was a much bigger step than Jan had thought they'd take so soon but it felt right. He waited with bated breath as Mia nodded, her eyes glittering with excitement. "There's my girl," Kenn purred before stuffing his face in the apex of her thighs, Mia screaming at the pleasurable sensation. Her fingers dove into his hair, her thighs squeezing around his shoulders as he lapped up the juices coating her core.

Jan took Mia's little moans of approval, turning to Matthias with a crooked smile. "Stop thinking so much." Mia was all for it and he had been dreaming about how Matthias would feel wrapped around him for days. He had all the permission he'd ever need. Drawing Matthias closer, he smashed his lips to their beautiful barista's, dragging the kid's hand to cup his bulge. Jan rocked into the new grip, wondering why they hadn't started this sooner.

Matthias' slim fingers squeezed his cock, growing bolder as he shoved his hand down Jan's pants instead and unearthed it to the world, Mia's resulting whine making him even harder as Matthias' hand stroked him.

"Watch our girl," Matthias whispered, seconds before Mia screamed through her release beside them. Jan watched Mia's eyes slide close, her breathing erratic as Kenn pulled away, his face glistening with her orgasm. Her whole body was trembling, heat licking up Jan's spine as Matthias' strokes became faster and more deliberate until Jan was thrusting into Matthias' hand, searching for his own release.

The barista's thumb moved over his slit, precum coating Matthias' fingers until he was stroking Jan with his own lubricant. He grit his teeth together as he ran a hand around Matthias' neck, squeezing hard which only had the barista grunting, his eyes darkening with desire. An image of fucking Matthias into the mattress while grabbing his neck came out of nowhere, Jan fighting the urge to explode. He wanted just a few more minutes of this, a few more minutes of ecstasy.

That wasn't in the cards though as Mia's whimpers started up again, both of them looking over to see that Kenn had pulled her off the couch and stuffed her with his cock. Mia was no longer watching, propped up on her knees, holding onto the edge of the cushions for dear life as Kenn fucked her into oblivion, but what Jan hadn't been ready for was the dark look in Kenn's eyes as the detective stared at Matthias.

Matthias grinned and then dipped his head forward before swallowing Jan's cock whole, Jan groaning at the sensational pleasure of the barista's tongue and warm mouth on his flesh. "I'm … shit … I'm gonna cum." Jan squeezed Matthias' neck to warn him, but it spurred the kid on, his tongue moving faster along his length. When Matthias reached down and cupped Jan's balls, Jan lost it, his release spilling down the kid's throat in hot, heavy streams.

Kenn came at the same time, filling their girl up as she flopped to the carpet, a sweet, freshly fucked smile on her face. Jan threw his head back against the couch as Matthias released his cock, grinning like he had won the lottery.

He knew that the road ahead was going to be a tough one – between Mia trying to avoid her nightmares and Matthias needing more help than they could offer – but Jan was all in. And hell, if there were more nights ahead like this one, he was absolutely looking forward to them.

Jan stuffed himself back into his pants as Kenn helped Mia back up onto the couch, their girl immediately curling into Jan's side. Matthias sat awkwardly on the other side, sharing a glance between the two of them and it took a moment for Jan to realize the issue.

They always kissed Mia after eating her out and they hadn't shied away when she had done the same for them. But Matthias was new territory. Jan didn't even know how to approach the subject, but he didn't have to, Kenn roughly grabbing Matthias and kissing him like he owned him. "I've been curious." Jan knew for a fact that Kenn didn't have feelings like that for him, but that one gesture helped lighten the mood.

Which it did when Mia started squirming again.

Jan just chuckled. "Looks like our girl is ready for another round." She grinned and nodded, moving toward one of their bedrooms, waiting for them to follow her. He could get used to this.

100

KENN

The night had delved into madness, each of them thoroughly spent before they had disappeared for showers. Matthias had stayed with Mia, Jan and Kenn slipping back into the room so that they could all sleep together. She needed it. Matthias needed it. And hell, if Kenn was honest with himself, he needed the added comfort of his family there with him.

It was the first time it had ever truly felt like a family with a woman in the mix. Their previous women had always just been a passing thought. But Mia felt like more than that. He couldn't imagine a day without her, let alone what the fuck they had been doing before they met her.

But they couldn't stay in bed forever, as much as Kenn wanted to, knowing that they needed to hand in their resignation as soon as possible. The plan had been to leave on Saturday, giving them only Friday to tie up loose ends. Telling Kingsley to fuck off had been easy enough as well as gathering Mia's clothes from her mother's house. Her mother hadn't even blinked when they knocked on her door and told her that Mia wasn't going to see her again.

Kenn wanted to ask how much Mia's mother knew about Mia's father, but that seemed like it would be in poor taste. With Jan pushing him to just grab what they could and avoid the house's occupant, Kenn kept his mouth shut and packed the car.

Reassuring Mia that their connections could pull in a job, Mia relaxed even further, seeming a little happier about leaving everything behind. They had even given her the task of visiting Quinn for the day, something sweet and easy. Granted, giving Matthias an easy day had also been on the agenda. Kenn had noticed him getting antsier and less sure of himself, the shiftiness in his eyes telling Kenn that the kid was losing his grip on his sanity. He needed help. Help they couldn't give him. Kenn hoped and prayed that Matthias would stop being so fucking stubborn and reach out before things got worse.

The hardest part was when they arrived at their main office, an office they hadn't stepped foot in in months. They hadn't had to, all of their jobs taking them across the country. This would be the last time they went inside and it was a bittersweet feeling. Kenn loved his work but it had taken a toll on their relationships and their mindsets. It was time to let go.

The fact that Jan was here with him made it easier.

Crushing the resignation in his hand, Kenn took one last deep breath and marched into the building, Jan on his heels. They passed through security easily enough, nodding to a few employees they recognized, and entered their boss' office uninvited.

For a moment, he just waved to the seats across from his desk until he realized they weren't going to sit.

"What – ah – what a surprise!" Detective Hanson's eyes dropped to the paper in Kenn's hand. "You can't be serious!" Kenn placed the paper on Hanson's desk and nodded, biting his lip to keep from saying anything that would shred the last bit of dignity the man had. "This won't solve anything, Kenn. You're my best detectives! Where will you even go with skill sets like yours? The FBI won't take you. And no one else will either."

Kenn knew that. He knew there weren't many options for trained soldiers that had lethal knowledge like they did. He also knew that staying in his current profession wasn't healthy, not with a shady boss like Hanson.

"You think you guys are so important, but you haven't stopped anything!" Hanson reached across the table and shredded the resignation. Kenn frowned, realizing that their boss knew a lot more than he had originally alluded to. "You've caught a rat. One measly little rat. But you haven't caught the true vermin, the leader. You've accomplished *nothing*."

Kenn took a step back, desperately trying to rein in his anger. He had never had a problem holding back because he had never been the one with anger issues. The problem was that he trusted too easily, and when that trust was broken? He saw red. Like now.

Jan caught on, yanking Kenn backward and pushing him toward the entrance. "You knew about *everything*, didn't you?" Jan spat; his hand firmly placed on Kenn's chest to keep him from charging. "Anything to help you get that council seat. You're a crooked fuck, and I hope something really helps you see that one day. As for us, catching one rat is better than none." With that, Jan pushed Kenn outside, both of them unloading their government-appointed badges and guns at the main desk, avoiding the sputtering excuses falling from Hanson's mouth as he followed them.

It wasn't following protocol, but Kenn hoped it was a big enough statement that they wouldn't be called back in. They shuffled back into the car, Kenn tearing down the road to get back to their family. Jan's expression was just as dark and bothered as his, the man taking a deep breath before bringing up the conversation they had been avoiding for a while.

Kenn kept his eyes focused on the road, hands tightening on the wheels. "It works. Mia's fine with it. Nichlas is fine with it and … do you love Matthias?" he blurted out, instantly hating the question.

Jan didn't hesitate, though. "It's too soon to tell, but that's definitely where it's headed. He's more than just family, but I'm not ready to say those words yet. You?"

"Seems stupid to say it out loud, but I think I've always kind of liked him. Those purple eyes were always so intense, but it just never really crossed my mind that way until Matthias opened up like that. Now that it's an option though? I want him, too, and fuck – now I know Mia feels. It does feel selfish to want both of them and yet … I need it."

The words hung in the silence, but it was no longer tense. It was comfortable as they sped home, the inner workings of their new family opening new doors. They weren't going to be bogged down by a corrupt boss. Matthias and Mia were safe. They were going to have the support they needed. And when Nichlas returned? Their little family would be complete.

101

MIA

Matthias had been abnormally jumpy all morning, his eyes shifting around, his hands constantly finding her shoulders or her arm to hold onto. He had said about three words since they had left the house, but Jan had said that Matthias was on edge, that he just needed a little comfort. Unfortunately, that didn't make Mia feel better as they walked to Ma's house for her final goodbye.

She nearly jumped into Ma's open arms as she was let into the house, tears streaming down her face at the warm welcome. Mia wished she could have done the same to her own mother. Mia scrambled over to the couch seconds later, checking out Quinn's leg, the kid slapping at her hands and reaching forward for his own hug.

It was wonderful to see that Quinn hadn't been as traumatized by the accident as she had. It was even funnier to hear him talk about Chad and how Chad had tried contacting him after everything that had happened. That had brought up another conversation that pointed to her four men, Mia revealing that she had actually come through to say goodbye.

Quinn hadn't even blinked an eye at that, and neither had Ma, both of them telling her that she needed to go where she was happiest. Once again, it reminded her of all the support she *hadn't* had since her father died.

Giving them one last round of hugs, she grabbed Matthias' hand and led him back to the cafe, fighting the urge to ask him if he was okay. While she was still dealing with her nightmares and regaining her confidence, Matthias had fallen apart. All those pieces he had put together so expertly to hide his pain were cracking and crumbling.

He hid it well, but there were times she had seen through it. Sometimes, Matthias just looked lost. Other times he seemed seconds away from a panic attack. Other times, he seemed perfectly fine except for the overwhelming need to be in contact with one of them.

Matthias made his way upstairs when they made it back, the sounds of pounded leather hitting her ears moments later. Mia sighed, hanging her head low as she shrugged off her coat and followed in his footsteps. He couldn't fight his anger out anymore. It hadn't worked then. It wouldn't work now. She couldn't even be his remedy. He needed to talk to someone. Someone that could help him fight the demons he was trying so hard to hide.

A sob left her as she found Matthias beating one of the boxing bags in their makeshift gym, his knuckles already bloodied from the force he was using. His eyes were black with anger, his body trembling from the overwhelming emotions he refused to face. Her heart shattered as every punch landed just a little harder than the last. Mia knew she wasn't the right person for the job, but she couldn't watch him tear himself apart any longer. Slowly making her way to the bag, making sure she was in his sight, Mia grabbed his attention. His punches faltered, his gaze turning to her and then back to the bag as he warred with his emotions.

"Matthias, what's wrong?" He grunted, shaking his head, but Mia knew what hurt looked like. She had been through an abusive relationship of her own, and she knew when someone was hurting. Taking a deep breath, Mia stepped forward again, shivering from the power radiating off her charming barista. She placed a timid hand on his chest, the man tensing up at her touch. "Let's go cool off." She drew her confidence from deep inside her, knowing that she was on the verge of her own panic attack. If Matthias threw a fit in the next five minutes, Mia wasn't sure how she was going to handle it.

They both needed to heal, but at this moment, Matthias needed her help.

He didn't fight her as she led him into the bathroom, slowly shedding him of his clothes, watching him tremble. She guided him under the heated spray after stripping as well, placing soft kisses down his chest, trying to soften his resolve. Mia knew that she was in dangerous territory, that she was going to scare the shit out of herself but she didn't have any other weapons. Jan and Kenn weren't supposed to be gone long, but it was long enough and she couldn't watch Matthias fall apart anymore.

Her kisses continued south, her lips gracing the base of his shaft, Matthias' hands running through her hair, fingers tangling in the wet mess. "Mia," he breathed. It was the first of many tender touches as he responded to her attentions, her kisses becoming firmer down his length until she swallowed just the tip. He melted against the shower wall, releasing a groan so deep and guttural that it ran down her spine and straight to her core.

"There's so many. So many demons, Mia," he mumbled. From this angle, Mia could see the tears making their way down his cheeks as she ran her tongue over his rapidly hardening length. Her hands wrapped around his thighs, Mia taking deep breaths to steady her racing heart. She had been working up to this for days, telling herself that it was *her* men and not Cross and his evil plans on her tongue.

With the steam swarming her like a warm blanket, Mia relaxed, waiting for Matthias to meet her gaze. She let his cock slip from her mouth, "Do you trust me?" Matthias took a moment and then nodded. "Then use me. Stop thinking. It's just us. You and me. Use me."

This was a temporary solution, but Mia couldn't think of any better way to show Matthias that she fully and completely trusted him. She wanted to give him something she hadn't even offered to the others yet. She wasn't just doing this for him, but also for herself. She wanted to forget. She wanted to move on. Matthias guided her back to his cock, slipping his throbbing length back onto her tongue and when he thrust forward, Mia for the first time in several days felt truly free. These were *her* men. And nothing, not even someone like Cross could take them from her.

MIA

She awoke to Matthias curled around her back. It was dark outside, most of the day gone after she had given herself to him and he had carried her to bed shortly after. They slept like babies, holding each other through their nightmares until only pleasant memories remained.

She slipped out of bed and headed down the stairs at the sound of voices. Jan and Kenn had probably been back for hours but left them to sleep, which she was grateful for. She didn't expect to see the cafe bare of her men's personal touches, most of their belongings packed away and stored by the door.

Even two boxes from her office were neatly placed by the duffle bags, as well as several boxes she recognized from her house. Hushed conversation continued as she made her way into the cafe, a smile spreading across her face as she recognized the third voice. Mia raced across the open space, jumping into Nichlas' arms, planting short little kisses on his lips. He grabbed her ass and lifted her, taking advantage of her lack of clothes.

"A little underdressed, aren't we?"

She ignored his question and the others' laughter as she continued to press little kisses on his lips. "You're back?"

He chuckled at her antics and nodded. "Just needed to see my girl." He squeezed her ass, making her gasp as she pulled away with a playful frown.

"You're coming though, right? To Blossom?" Mia searched his eyes for any doubts. She really needed them all to be together but she also knew what kind of men she had started a relationship with.

"Wouldn't dream of being anywhere else, firecracker. They gave me an hour break and I might have pulled some strings." He nodded out to the car parked by the entrance, Mia's expression falling as he put her back on the ground, placing one last kiss on her head. His attention focused on their newest arrival, Matthias prodding down the steps, scratching his bare chest, his hair in complete disarray, his eyes red from fighting his demons all night. Their eyes locked for a minute before Nichlas stared down at her.

She just giggled. "I already know."

Kenn came around behind her, wrapping his arms around her waist. "She also finds it incredibly hot. Now, go kiss our boy. Looks like he needs something other than coffee to wake up."

"Our?" Nichlas questioned before making his way over to Matthias with one more nod of encouragement from Mia. He grabbed their barista and kissed him with every bit of passion and desire Mia wished she could endure right now. Instead, she pleasantly watched Nichlas tongue fuck Matthias, Nichlas' hands dropping down to Matthias' ass and pressing them together. The barista melted into the kiss, his hands fisting into Nichlas' shirt, guttural moans filling the air.

If that wasn't hot, she didn't know what was.

"Didn't you have to go somewhere?" Mia whined, shifting in Kenn's arms, all of her men breaking out in laughter. Nichlas laid one last kiss on Matthias' lips before nodding. Matthias followed Nichlas to the door, his eyes shifting again. It was amazing to see how in tune her men were as they waited for him to voice his thoughts rather than brush him off.

"I ... the first step is acknowledgment." His gaze dropped to Mia and she beamed up at him, clasping her hands together. She couldn't be happier at this moment. "I ... I need help. I can't deal with these demons on my own anymore."

Nichlas threaded his fingers through Matthias' and brought it to his lips, placing a delicate kiss on the barista's knuckles. "You'll let us help?" Matthias nodded. "Then that's all I can ask for."

The tender moment lasted for a few short moments before Nichlas disappeared into the car, leaving her with the other three. Matthias seemed a bit brighter this evening than he had that morning which warmed her heart, but there was still a long road ahead.

"What now?" Mia asked just as her stomach rumbled. Her men shared a chuckle, Jan answering her question.

"Pack the car and get on the road. We've got a bit of a drive ahead of us." He pulled her from Kenn's arms, pressing a short kiss to her lips that had her already wanting more. "But first, I have a certain dinner date that I was promised a little while ago that I never got a chance to do." Mia blushed when she remembered what that entailed. "And I can work within your limits, Angel. But it's up to you."

Mia's cheeks turned a deeper shade of red, the memory of Matthias' cock stuffed down her throat from earlier that morning. She had had a moment of panic but it passed once she remembered who she was with. "I want to do it." Her words came out breathier than she had hoped, her desire bleeding through as Jan turned her around to face her men.

Her nipples hardened through her shirt, Jan and Matthias' expressions darkening with the lust she was so familiar with. Jan leaned down; his growing bulge pressed against her bare ass. "Angel, who gets your mouth?"

Her thighs trembled, her pussy aching for Jan to fill it. "Uh … Matthias." She wanted to feel him again.

Kenn groaned playfully, palming his cock through his pants. "I have to watch? Fuck!"

Mia tilted her head to the side, "Does it help if I say I love you?"

His eyes grew wide as the words seemed to short-circuit his brain, his eyes flashing a brilliant green. "Please tell me I can kiss you, sweetheart." Mia nodded enthusiastically as he smushed her against Jan's chest and tongue fucked her the same way Nichlas had just done to Matthias. She lightly tapped his shoulder, panic rising in her chest. Kenn released her immediately, mumbling a sorry, but she waved it off.

Jan kissed the back of her neck, scraping his teeth along the sensitive skin, his hands moving south and then back up to grab her bare waist beneath her shirt. "Where's mine?" She arched forward at his touch, slapping away at his hands with a giggle.

"I'm sitting on your dick." Mia lost her smile for a moment, wondering where those words had come from but grabbed her confidence back when they all burst out laughing. "But yes, I love you, too." She twisted around for a kiss from him too before being shuffled farther into the cafe to partake in the date she had promised him.

Amidst all the chaos, Mia thoroughly enjoyed moments like this. Mia caught her cheeks burning, but this time from smiling too much, a problem she never thought she'd have. This was her future, her everything, her *forever*.

Her gaze darted to the front door, silently counting down the minutes until her mysterious fourth returned.

I love you, too, Nichlas.

EPILOGUE

MIA
One Week Later – Saturday Evening

K enn had told them all about his quaint little dwelling tucked in the small city of Blossom by the water. He had lied. He lived in a mansion, which Mia soon found out had been in the family for nearly a hundred years. The property was well kept by paid staff that Kenn was more than familiar with to the point that she realized that they had probably been his true family growing up.

Mia tried to bring up his childhood a few times, but Kenn expertly skirted the conversation either with sex or by shoving the mysterious folder that had shown up on their doorstep a few days ago from Sheriff Kingsley. She refused to open it, even if the guys had told her time and time again that it was left over from her father's time as the town's coroner.

Over the past week, her men had used every chance they could to touch her. Matthias and Nichlas were hardcore flirting at this point and Mia kept finding Jan wrapped around Matthias, whispering in his ear while they watched old movies on TLC. Kenn was a lot more subtle with his moments but it was almost like he didn't understand where he fit in rather than he didn't want to be there. It was an interesting dynamic, but Mia couldn't think of anywhere else she wanted to be.

They had been wildly attentive to her, while also trying not to overwhelm her, Nichlas not leaving her side since he had shown up earlier that morning. Now, full after dinner, snuggled into the cushions with Nichlas draped over her on one of Kenn's luxurious couches, Mia began thinking of what the future held for them. Jan had accepted the professorship at the local college, Matthias had begun setting up his new café, working on much of the equipment himself – and although Mia knew he was good with his hands – she had no idea he had a tinkering for metal, and Kenn had been working through the city doing odd jobs, settling back into the city he had grown up in.

With her throat healed, there had been a *lot* more of that, especially when she was trying to prove that her nightmares weren't a problem, which occasionally resulted in a panic attack or two. Even with the tiring aspect of trying something new – Jan had encouraged her to return to school – it hadn't helped her weary self sleep any better, and with the prospect of starting therapy on the horizon, Mia avoided all talk about the nightmare from a week ago as best she could.

Worse still, Matthias' reaction to therapy on Tuesday had been less than favorable. He had stalked into the house like someone had just kidnapped her all over again, refusing to speak to anyone. When he found out that his prescription made him tired enough to pass out, he flushed them – Mia only discovering that tidbit after he broke down yesterday. His doctor had already written him a new one, reiterating that another instance would require a little more "hands-on" help.

It had been a rough go of it, but they were slowly settling in, and Mia hoped that the calming feeling starting to wash over her new life would remain. Hearing Kenn and Matthias bicker about coffee flavors in the kitchen while Nichlas was settled between her legs, his arms wound around her waist and head on her chest was helping.

The front door squealed as it opened, Mia twisting around to see Jan step inside. She slipped out from under Nichlas, to which he grunted, and joined Jan in the foyer, peppering kisses all over his face. He bent her backward and kissed her back, thoroughly and passionately before releasing her. "God, could you not answer the door like that? What if anyone sees this?"

Mia couldn't help the giggle that bubbled up from her throat, staring down at the shirt that barely covered anything below her waist. That was another change she had been wholly excited to adopt – her confidence. Her men loved everything about her. They loved her smile, her enthusiasm, and they loved the way she embraced her body – whether it was bundled up in a billion blankets or walking naked through the halls to distract them from their work.

Mostly though, she felt comfortable in their shirts, surrounded by their scents. Maybe it was crazy, but Mia didn't care. She loved them and they loved her. That's all that mattered.

Jan guided her to the kitchen, Nichlas stumbling in after them. Mia let Jan pull her back against his chest as he leaned against the counter, the coffee discussion ceasing as Nichlas stood behind Matthias and reciprocated Jan's action, Matthias immediately melting into the embrace. They looked so fucking good together that it was scary.

Kenn wiggled his eyebrows at the pair as he snatched a mug off the counter and took a sip, Matthias looking wholly defeated. They all had their issues, but Kenn avoided them with copious amounts of caffeine. Drinking this late at night meant that he wouldn't be sleeping either. Mia made a note to speak with him about it, but there was something else weighing on her heart first.

"Nichlas, why do I feel like you're going to tell us that you're leaving?"

He shifted uncomfortably, resting his chin on Matthias' shoulder with a deep breath. "I'm not going anywhere, but he told me that … shit – Mia, I don't think–"

Mia shook her head, rolling her shoulders back to show her confidence in the situation. "Just tell me. Cross is dead and he can't hurt me." All of her men smiled at her, reminding her that it had been a little while since she had been herself.

Nichlas released Matthias, running his hands through his hair, his eyes growing dark with the information he was holding back. "My superior told me that Cross was just part of Stage One." Mia swallowed the panic rising in her chest. She wasn't going to freak out right now. She was going to stay strong and freak out later, because that was a completely healthy thing to do.

"That's what our boss meant? Shit." Kenn reached for the coffee pot but was stopped by Matthias' lethal glare.

Mia looked to Nichlas for an explanation. He had said he wasn't leaving, but there was another mission. It wasn't lost on her that he had told her way more information than it seemed he was supposed to. "He gave me a choice – he wants me on it, but I told him I wasn't ready to leave again. There's … we're connected somehow, so I don't want to leave you all vulnerable."

That was it, wasn't it? This perfect little life they had started to carve out for themselves wasn't supposed to last. "You can't just leave?"

Nichlas shook his head. "If we were to go into witness protection, I couldn't bring you, Mia. I can only bring family and those with high enough security clearances." Doubt began to chip away at her confidence, but he squashed that quickly as Jan's arms tightened around her waist and a kiss was pressed to the top of her head. "Mia, you *are* family even if they don't see it that way, which is why I want to do this."

Jan interjected, "What's the catch?"

"He's offered me a choice in choosing my own team."

Silence met Nichlas' words, Jan tensing behind me. "You don't mean—"

"I do. He told me that my last team was positively lethal and that he wouldn't have any other team he'd rather stand behind." Nichlas' gaze moved to Mia, a warm smile on his lips. "*The whole team.*"

"Me?" she squeaked.

Again, Nichlas nodded. "You were quite pivotal in finding ORCSORB, sweetheart. Yes, you, too. There's a lot of paperwork and documentation you'll have to go through, but yes, Mia. If you want to." Mia could see the subtle plea in his expression, hidden by concern for her mental well-being. It was sweet, but she needed the extra distraction. Besides, if any of the other bastards out there were doing anything like Cross, she wanted them gone. Dead. Unalived.

"I want all of the people like Cross to die horrid painful deaths just like the ones they're inflicting on others."

Nichlas approached her, cupping her cheeks and pressing a firm kiss on her lips before letting go. "That's my girl."

Mia took a deep breath and leaned away, still hating the fact that there were times when she couldn't indulge the way she wanted to. "Where to?"

"Funny you should ask. It's in a little city called Blossom."

She froze, wondering if Nichlas was playing a joke on her. Seeing as the other three weren't trying to hide their laughter, she guessed it wasn't. "We're in Blossom." Mia also realized that their lack of shock meant that they all had already known some part of Nichlas' news.

"Yes, we don't have to go anywhere."

Mia sucked her bottom lip in between her teeth, leaning around to catch Matthias' attention. "Will you still make me coffee?"

"Do you even have to ask, baby girl?" His purple eyes flashed with the charm she remembered from a few weeks ago, his dimple making a rare appearance.

Mia then nodded, Nichlas bursting out laughing. "Shit, that was your only condition? Should have thrown that in earlier." His cheeky smile soon turned deviant; his gaze full of desire. "Now, firecracker, I heard a few days ago that there were a few fantasies you were positively drooling over."

Her cheeks reddened as she squirmed in Jan's hold. The professor had revealed some very private information about combinations between her men and which ones turned her on more. After one too many bottles of wine, Jan had coaxed her into spilling some of her naughtier fantasies, which now had been told to the entire group if the growing bulges between her men's legs were anything to go by.

"I've been drooling over some of those myself, Mia." Mia shifted again, her body flush with heat as she felt Jan's cock press against her ass. His hands moved to grip her waist, grinding her down so that she felt the full hardened length. Nichlas stepped closer until she was caged in between them and pressed two fingers beneath her chin before raising them so their eyes met. "My favorite one was where you watch me fuck Matthias into the mattress while Jan and Kenn stuffed you full, how's that sound?"

A whimper was her only response, Kenn taking the opportunity to steal her and throw her over his shoulder like a caveman. "I'm on board for that shit." A large hand smacked her ass, Mia yelping at what she thought would have been more painful than pleasurable. It was quite the other way around, her pussy clenching at nothingness, her thighs rubbing together for relief. "Looks like our girlfriend likes that. Race y'all to the bedroom."

Kenn took off down the hall, Mia left with a nice view of his ass as well as Nichlas gripping Matthias through his pants, the two sucking face like horny teenagers. This was the beginning of her forever and Mia was more than ready to embark on her new journey.

END

Be ready for Book two of
The Passion Series in 2023